D0260695

THE
GLANVILLE
WOMEN

Also by Dulcie Gray

Crime

MURDER ON THE STAIRS
MURDER IN MELBOURNE
BABY FACE
EPITAPH FOR A DEAD ACTOR
MURDER ON A SATURDAY
MURDER IN MIND
THE DEVIL WORE SCARLET
NO QUARTER FOR A STAR
THE MURDER OF LOVE
DIED IN THE RED
MURDER ON HONEYMOON
FOR RICHER FOR RICHER
DEADLY LAMPSHADE
UNDERSTUDY TO MURDER
DEAD GIVE AWAY
RIDE ON A TIGER
DARK CALYPSO

Short Stories

STAGE DOOR FRIGHT

For Children

DEATH IN DENIMS

General Non-Fiction

BUTTERFLIES ON MY MIND
(winner of the Times Educational Supplement
Senior Information Award 1978)

THE GLANVILLE WOMEN

Dulcie Gray

Michael Joseph
LONDON

To Michael

First published in Great Britain by Michael Joseph Ltd
44 Bedford Square, London WC1
1982

© Dulcie Gray 1982

All Rights Reserved. No part of this publication may be
reproduced, stored in a retrieval system, or
transmitted in any form or by any means, electronic,
mechanical, photocopying, recording or otherwise,
without the prior permission of the Copyright owner

ISBN 0 7181 2164 3

Typeset by Alacrity Phototypesetters, Banwell Castle,
Weston-super-Mare
Printed in Great Britain by Hollen Street Press, Slough,
and bound by Hunter & Foulis, Edinburgh

CONTENTS

PROLOGUE

Dear Geoffrey

I have finished the book at last. It has taken a long time and you have been very patient: I shall be most interested to hear what you think.

As a piece of writing it is important to me because it has been cathartic. I had been feeling for some time, in spite of my success as a writer, that my personal life had been a failure — and was blaming everyone but myself. At last I decided to have a look at myself, to see why I had failed. This made me want to examine my roots; not in search of alibis or excuses, but of self-knowledge.

I decided that, just as my mother had probably had the most influence on me, so her mother was likely to have had the most influence on her; so I researched back as far as my grandmother's marriage. The enclosed manuscript is the story of my grandmother, my mother and me — in fictional form, as I have no wish to write either biographies of my family or an autobiography.

Since my grandmother is long since dead and Mother, as you know, died just over a year ago, the only two people likely to be affected by this are my son, 'Harry', and my long-time lover, 'Tom'. 'Harry' will understand why I have written as I have: it may even help him. He has a serene and happy temperament (I wish to God I had!) and will withstand all the inherent shocks, probably assimilating them cheerfully and becoming more mature in the process. 'Tom' will have to fend for himself. He always left me unaided in times of stress so I have no feelings of remorse . . . nor of revenge either, in case that thought had crossed your mind! Anyway, both of them were forewarned.

For myself, writing this book has brought me two great rewards. It drew me closer to my mother in her last years (since naturally it was she who supplied me with most of my information) and it has indeed greatly increased my self-knowledge. Perhaps my wisdom, too? I hope so. What I know is that finding out about my family has helped me to realise that I was not after all in isolation in my behaviour — and when one is unhappy, the feeling of isolation is agony.

In their different ways, 'Kate', 'Bess' and 'Laura' were all searching for emotional fulfilment, and only Bess came near to finding it. One of the great difficulties ... and the Lord knows there are many ... about being in love (and by being in love I mean hooked imaginatively as well as physically) is that the person we seek and immediately recognise as the love object must be someone with whom we can act out the most profound desires and fantasies resulting from our early maladjustments. But whatever the motivations and excuses, the mature adult cannot escape his moral duty to choose what to make of his life.

A psychiatrist once told me that the lack of a secure and affectionate relationship with at least one person, whether blood relation or substitute, seems to be a significant cause of emotional disorder in adulthood. Am I therefore saying that falling in love is an instinctive defence against such maladjustment? Perhaps. He made a further point — which applies to me — that a child thus emotionally deprived has a tendency ever afterwards to seek immediate gratification at any cost and experiences difficulty in sustaining close relationships. I am sure now that this is why, at over forty years of age and in spite of having a good brain, I have to admit that I have never felt fulfilled, either as a woman or as a creative writer.

You will learn from 'Laura's' story that in my early years I instinctively preferred women to men. At Oxford I was an ardent feminist. I wonder if I might have felt a truer sense of achievement if I had carried on fighting for women's rights? But I didn't. I fell in love with 'Tom', who would only tolerate a doormat. And the choice to remain with him for so long was entirely mine.

Incidentally, I believe that strong-minded women, however 'feminist', do tend to look for the sheik-type lover — and it doesn't work. Most women in fact look for strength in men, and we mistake success, experience, wealth or selfishness for it. Feminists are particularly outraged when they discover how few strong men there are and protest vehemently at being forced to accept a subsidiary role to the weak and ineffectual. I sympathise: women have an appallingly unfair deal in society. But I do think that the rôle-playing I was talking about earlier should be understood by us all, rather sooner in our lives, so that we can be fully aware what we are doing when we enter into important sexual relationships.

A sense of awe went out with the eclipse of candlelight. Our modern diet of half-digested science, technology and an urban-orientated life which precludes a sense of kinship with nature, has played havoc with our need, acknowledged or not, of a faith by which to steer ourselves. I for one have certainly felt a loss in the ensuing vacuum, and the pattern of heredity comforts me some-what. It is because of this that I have written as I have.

Don't be alarmed, dear Geoffrey. This is not just an excuse to bare my soul, nor an exercise in metaphysics. It is the story of three middle-class women from one family, with normal physical appet-ites and a fair amount of intelligence; and of how, in the widely differing circumstances of their lives, and of their times, they tried to find themselves. As such, I hope you may find it of interest.

Thank you, my dear, for everything. Without your friendship — and indeed, without my long association with 'Tom' — I might, who knows, have had an even more pronounced lack of emotional maturity!

Bless you.

Marion ('Laura') Foster

Part One

KATE

CHAPTER ONE

On a blazing hot Saturday morning in mid-July, in the year 1910, Kate Glanville was married to Edward Marchmont at St Mary Abbott's Church in Kensington. King Edward VII had died in May but public mourning had ended a month later, so the ceremony was attended by royalty, the nobility and millionaires, as well as everyone who was anyone in the theatrical world, in all their finery. Crowds had been lining the flagstoned pavements since dawn and police, both on foot and mounted, were everywhere.

Kate was the daughter of Madge and Harry Glanville, two of the most famous actors of their day; they were out to show the world that the wedding of their daughter was a social event of some consequence.

Kate had refused her parents the grandeur of St George's, Hanover Square: she wished to please Edward's mother and father who, somewhat surprisingly, wanted their son to be married in the church in which their own uneasy union had been blessed some thirty-one years before. Besides, her relations with Madge and Harry at this time were at a low ebb. But the Glanvilles were determined not to let that spoil the occasion: a bishop had agreed to perform the ceremony; there were three hundred guests; the church was filled to overflowing with yellow and white roses and there were four pages and eight bridesmaids, also dressed in white and yellow.

Until almost the last moment, carriages were still rattling noisily down the dirty wooden-block streets. For the most part the more aristocratic guests travelled in closed carriages. Society favourites, actors and actresses and those who wished to be seen came in open landaus, delighting the crowds who, near to the church door, were close to rioting in the general euphoria.

A little late, bowing to right and left to acknowledge the homage of the multitudes, came Kate and her father.

Kate was sitting bolt upright, clutching her bridal bouquet, tense with nerves. Harry was enjoying himself and he patted

Kate's hand proudly. She drew it away sharply and stared out of the window.

Harry sighed. He loved his daughter, had loved her from the day she was born, but there was no denying that she had been something of a handful over the last few years. He recognised that the fault was his own but that had made her no easier to handle. Here she was, one of the great beauties of London, in a position to marry almost anyone she wanted, throwing herself away on a dull nobody of a lawyer whom he could swear she didn't even love, and planning to spend the rest of her life in Malaya, at the other end of the world.

Kate Glanville was tall and slim, with her mother's huge grey eyes and delicate nose. Both she and her mother had exquisite complexions but, whereas Madge was considered handsome, everyone agreed that Kate was the real beauty.

Harry himself was small and dapper, with bright blue eyes and an infectious sense of humour. Half the women he met fell in love with him and the devil of it was that he couldn't resist them. He and Madge were a good theatrical partnership, indeed a famous one; but now that their early tempestuous physical love was over they had found themselves domestically incompatible, for Madge had suffered from his many infidelities and could no longer respond to his sexual demands. She was a fine business woman and it was she who managed their careers; Harry naturally appreciated this but he also found it unfeminine. He was the type of man who enjoyed silly clinging women, women who would look up to him and adore him. Madge knew him for exactly what he was and behaved accordingly. She was instinctively careful with money, while Harry spent prodigally and gambled into the bargain. Only on stage or when they were entertaining did they still have much in common. And yet, each was fundamentally devoted to the other.

Both of them came from theatrical stock (Harry's parents had been well known on the touring circuit) and there was never any question for either of them that they should look for another career. In those days it was the expected thing that a successful theatrical couple should found a theatrical dynasty. Madge's mother was a Norwegian beauty, who had made all her success in London. Her father had also wanted to be an actor but soon realised that he had little talent and contented himself with managing his wife's career. Finally he had bought a theatre for her; he ran it for many years and retired a rich man. Madge and

Harry were equally successful, both in London and on their many tours together.

Until the day which destroyed his relationship with his daughter, life had been almost ideal for Harry. Madge had more or less reconciled herself to his infidelities (there was no question of a divorce, which would have been both social and theatrical suicide), so within reason he could do as he liked; and with his little daughter Kate, the apple of his eye, growing lovelier every day, he was a very happy man. Then he had met Phyllis Bainbridge, a young and ambitious actress, and his affair with her was more serious than the others. Madge sensed it at once. Phyllis was not content with clandestine meetings in dressing rooms and second-rate hotels, or the discreet anterooms provided by the more opulent and accommodating restaurants. She liked 'proper beds', as she called it, and she preferred either her home or his.

On this particular day, young Kate was out shopping with a friend of her mother's while Madge was away. It had seemed quite safe for Harry to smuggle Phyllis into the house for their 'tuck up', as she called it. It was spring; Phyllis was his ideal bedfellow, laughing, teasing, adoring and pouting by turns; and Harry was enjoying himself. Outside it was cold; colder than Kate had anticipated. When tea at the fashionable Berkeley Hotel was suggested — a great excitement for a fifteen-year-old — Kate decided to return home for one of her mother's fur coats. She dashed into the bedroom to fetch it . . . and discovered Harry with Phyllis. Phyllis was bundled unceremoniously out of the house and explanations and rows had followed; but Kate took the shock very badly and things were never the same again. She had idolised her father. Now she despised him. She had loved her mother and had been outraged on her behalf. But when she had told Madge about it on her return, she refused to listen.

'If I can put up with your father's philandering without making a fuss, so can you,' she said sharply.

'You mean he has done this before?' asked Kate, horrified.

'Times without number,' replied Madge.

'How beastly! How absolutely beastly!' flared Kate. 'And I had thought him the most wonderful of men!'

'Men are men,' said Madge, 'and idols have feet of clay, as you must have heard.'

Totally disillusioned, Kate not only turned from them both but against the theatre, too. She had already appeared with them

successfully in a couple of plays and they had set their hearts on her
following them on the stage to carry on the Glanville name and
tradition. Now she scorned the idea, insisting that she would prefer
to become a painter. Reluctantly they had agreed to let her go to
the Slade, hoping against hope that she might one day return to
them. To their dismay, the assistant head of the school, the great
Henry Tonks, had told them that she had a genuine gift as a
painter and might become a really good artist one day.

Now she had turned away even from that and was determined
on this ridiculous marriage. They had done everything in their
power to dissuade her but she had been adamant. Perhaps even at
this eleventh hour Harry could prevent the catastrophe? He and
Madge would look exceedingly foolish if the wedding were cancel-
led at this stage — and Kate's refusal would create a social scandal
— but would it not be worth it if her self-inflicted, and surely
unhappy, exile could be averted?

Harry cleared his throat anxiously. 'All right, darling?'

'Yes, thank you,' she replied primly.

He saw how pale she was and couldn't bring himself to speak
harshly to her. 'No regrets?'

'None.'

'You are sure you really love Edward?'

'I have agreed to marry him.'

'That is not what I asked.'

She pursed her lips but didn't answer.

'It's not too late, even now, to change your mind, darling,'
urged Harry. 'Your mother and I would understand.'

'I have agreed to marry him,' repeated Kate.

'But to live so far from home, Kate!' exclaimed Harry. 'We shall
be so lonely without you!'

'Malaya sounds exciting, and it's where Edward has a job.'

'And Edward?'

'Edward?'

'Yes. Do you find him exciting?' asked Harry.

'Edward is a good man,' said Kate vehemently. 'I have no
doubts that he will make me a good husband. I need not fear that I
shall find *him* in bed with a mistress, nor shall I have to explain to
my child that men are untrustworthy creatures who don't care
how much they hurt their families so long as they have their
pleasure.'

'But good heavens, I'm not the only unfaithful man in

London!' retorted Harry, exasperated. 'All men are the same!'

'I doubt it,' said Kate. 'Edward is not.'

'You'll never forgive me?' asked Harry. 'Never forget?'

'Never. You were like a god to me, and you failed.'

'All men fail to be gods,' replied Harry.

'Please don't let's quarrel, Papa,' said Kate. 'We have so little time left together. In a few minutes I shall be married to Edward, then we shall leave for our honeymoon, and after that we shall be out East for three whole years. Don't let's quarrel now.'

'Three whole years...' echoed Harry.

'Yes.'

'Won't you miss England?'

'Perhaps.'

'Your mother and me?'

Her jaw hardened. 'Perhaps.'

'London?'

'I may.'

'The theatre?'

'No.'

'What is wrong with the theatre, for God's sake? What has the theatre ever done to you?'

'It encouraged you to have those women of yours!' said Kate.

'Nonsense,' replied Harry. 'I would have been just the same in business. I am weak and vain and I love a pretty face. Besides, the theatre is the rightful home of the Glanvilles.'

'Not this one.'

Harry sighed again and gave up the struggle. The crowds were waving wildly, shouting their good wishes, Kate and Harry turned again to wave.

Kate had never looked better. A Grecian filet bound her luxuriant hair and over it was a soft tulle veil. Her wedding gown was in white satin, encrusted with pearls and silver stitching. Bands of embroidery inset with pearls ornamented the low-cut bodice and edged the elbow-length sleeves. Her satin skirt was cut closely to her figure and her train was in cloth of silver, covered in silver net and tulle. She wore long white gloves and carried a bouquet of white and yellow roses.

Henry, in a black frock coat with silk lapels, a high poke collar, an Ascot four-in-hand tie and a pearl stick pin, was looking very handsome and the crowd adored him.

'Well, darling, I can only pray for your happiness,' he said sadly.

'You have chosen your life in defiance of our wishes, but we both hope that you will never regret that you didn't take our advice.'

'Thank you I know you both wish me well and I wish *you* well, too.'

They reached the church in silence.

Head held high, Kate walked up the aisle on Harry's arm to admiring murmurs from the congregation. When she reached Edward's side they exchanged nervous, reassuring smiles. She felt calmer immediately. Edward had that effect on her; it was one of the reasons she was marrying him. He was unlike any of the other men she knew. Her artist friends and the men she knew in the theatre were attractive, and often exciting; but they reminded her too much of her father. Edward was the epitome of steady common sense. He was gentle and kind and, even if he was a little dull, she could sense the real goodness of his nature. He was tall and thin and in his own way good-looking, and was nearly always rather serious, which gave his sudden smile unusual radiance. She knew that she wasn't in love with him, but so far (and she was now twenty-three) no other man had stirred her emotionally — although for a brief time the controversial young painter, Augustus John, who had been a student at the Slade some years previously and was now making his reputation, had made her heart beat faster.

She turned her head to look for her mother, and smiled. Madge tried to smile back but her eyes were full of tears and her mouth was trembling. Iron-willed, dictatorial Madge was openly crying! This shocked Kate profoundly; for a few moments she could hardly attend to the service. She had thought too little of Madge's emotions and too much of her own these last years, and all of a sudden felt agonisingly guilty. After all, Madge and Harry had been good to her! They had been loving, generous parents and she, with no thoughts of gratitude, had hurt them both. Harry had just suggested that even now it was not too late to refuse Edward; he had even hinted clearly that he would be delighted if she did.

Yet if she did, what could follow? All the women in her circle were destined for marriage — even at the Slade, where the intoxicating ideas of the feminists were taking root, and where idealism and independence in life as well as art had become the rallying cry for both men and women. Only a few girls, the freaks and the cranks, felt that becoming a wife was too great a price to pay for companionship and position. And Kate was no crank. Self-willed she may have been in many ways but she was deeply conservative. If marriage was inevitable then Edward was surely the best possible choice. He would allow her freedom. He offered her a new and quite different kind of life, and he would remain kind and steady and loving until the end; of that she was sure.

When the moment came, although the word 'obey' disturbed her, she said 'I do' very clearly.

CHAPTER TWO

The reception was held in the enormous drawing room of the Glanville house off the Earl's Court Road, a very fashionable part of London as far as the theatre of that time was concerned. Kate, Edward, Madge, Harry and Edward's parents, Mr Marchmont (an insurance broker) and his wife, Martha, stood in the receiving line to greet the guests. Here again, as in the church, white and yellow roses were everywhere. Edward, seeing them, whispered, 'Yellow roses, Kate. They stand for friendship. I like that as an omen, don't you?'

Kate was touched. She realised that she knew far too little about the man with whom she would be spending the rest of her life and, as so often in the short time she had known him, his unexpected sensitivity delighted her.

'Yes, Edward, indeed I do,' she replied with feeling.

Madge and Harry were in their element at the reception. In spite of their heartbreak at Kate's defection, they could see that the wedding had turned out to be a splendid social occasion, and they loved splendid social occasions. This one had the added advantage of demonstrating their social success to their theatre friends and their standing in the theatre to the social big-wigs, who were now pouring into the house. First came the Royals: the Duke of Connaught, with his ramrod military bearing; the Earl of Athlone; and the enchanting Princess Alice, who, to their great excitement, kissed both Madge and Kate as they rose from their curtsies. Among the many representatives of high society were the Headforts, he another distinguished military figure, she the ravishing Rosie Boote, only recently retired from the Gaiety Theatre to marry him. Then came cohorts of theatre folk, interspersed with Marchmont friends and relations.

Kate was acutely aware that Edward was even more out of his depth with her friends than she was with his. She had been accustomed to stage celebrities all her life and relished their ebullience, their humour, their quick generosity of spirit and their intelligence. She knew, however, that there was a less rosy side to the medal and that for many people, including Edward, this was the predominant image of actors — larger than life, jealous, ridiculously vain and socially unreliable. For Kate, though, it was the positive qualities that counted: in her eyes, 'the profession' made a colourful statement in a world where so much was trivial and grey. That she had turned her back on them deliberately made her see them more clearly, and she savoured them with a lingering regret. Yet she was certain that her decision to marry Edward was right. It was a bid to escape into an entirely unknown world — a prospect which filled her with excitement and apprehension in equal measure . . .

Ellen Terry, probably the most beloved actress of the day, was standing in front of her now. Happy tears were in her blue eyes.

'Have a wonderful life, Kate darling,' she said, kissing her warmly. 'Live! Live every minute of life, as I have. It's the only way!'

At sixty she was still lovely, with her red-gold hair, faded only a little, cascading carelessly from beneath a huge green hat. She was accompanied by her two illegitimate children — the bumptious young Gordon Craig, now making a name for himself as a scene designer, and her possessive, eager, clever daughter, Edy, whose short-lived romance some years earlier she had put down so savagely that Edy had turned away from men altogether.

How extraordinary, thought Kate, that Ellen was accepted so completely in a straitlaced society, when from adolescence onwards she had lived just as she had felt inclined! Edward greeted her warily but Mrs Marchmont, the very soul of rectitude, looked flushed and flattered by the prospect of meeting her. Her pink hat awry, she bobbed and chattered and laughed too often. By contrast her husband's sardonic features rarely lightened and his clothes hung inelegantly upon his bowed shoulders and skeletal frame; but even he straightened his tie for Ellen.

After Ellen, as though following in her train, came Ellaline Terris, tiny and blonde, with the imperishable prettiness that would last her for over a hundred years, and, beside her, her husband, Seymour Hicks, small, amusing and arrogant; Mrs Patrick Campbell, dark and glamorous, with an unidentified young man in tow — perhaps to counteract the persistent rumour of a liaison between herself and Bernard Shaw, who was also there with his green-eyed wife Charlotte; Ben Webster, the tall, relaxed and charming matinée idol, escorting his energetic and forceful little wife May Whitty — both great friends of Madge and Harry; Julia Neilson, the statuesque blonde wife of Fred Terry ('the most unfaithful husband in London'); and then the new young stars of the day — Owen Nares, Gerald du Maurier, the Dare sisters and the Vanbrugh sisters. Bringing up the rear came Tonks and Kate's fellow students from the Slade.

Above the hubbub presently came the voice of the toastmaster announcing that the cake was ready to be cut. The best man, a school-friend of Edward's, read out the telegrams and cables inaudibly and made a dim and inaudible little speech, including the statutory funny story which everyone would have known if they could have heard it. The Bishop pontificated. Harry was mercifully both witty and audible. Then Kate and Edward stepped forward to cut the cake.

As Edward's hand covered hers on the knife, Kate looked up laughing to respond to someone's friendly banter — and across the room caught sight of a pale red-headed young man who was staring at her intently. She had a sense of shock, almost of familiarity, although she had never seen him before. He was extremely attractive, and he nodded to her in what seemed to be recognition. There was no mistaking the admiration in his eyes, nor indeed the current of sympathy which passed between them.

'Who is that over there?' she asked Edward.

'Who? Where?' returned Edward.

'The young man by the right-hand window, looking at us.'

'Everyone is looking at us!' laughed Edward.

'He raised his glass to us,' insisted Kate.

'Oh, him!' exclaimed Edward. 'That's Patrick de Moulins. We were at school together. He's awfully bright. You'd like him.'

'I wondered if he was your guest or mine,' she said lightly. 'I seem to recognise his face.'

'Perhaps you've met him somewhere,' replied Edward absently.

'Perhaps I have.' She was ashamed of herself, both for her lie and for her interest at such a moment, and turned away so that she couldn't see Patrick any more. Almost immediately her mother suggested that it was time to change into her going-away dress; Kate left the room with relief, dismayed by the impact the young man had made.

In the charming bedroom she had known all her life, her tearful little maid, Alice, helped her into her new lavender-silk suit and matching hat — a huge beribboned affair with lavender veil and masses of pink silk roses. But as she took up her new grey gloves and the small fur muff that her mother had given her, Kate felt a sudden wave of panic. What was she doing, leaving her beloved home for good, under such circumstances? She knew she wasn't in love with Edward. Was she really only marrying him so that she would have a faithful husband, as unlike her father as she could imagine?

She wandered over to the window, and stared out at the garden below. It was very pretty, and kept in trim with passionate care by Harry and the gardener. She could see the swing her father had made for her as a present for her fifth birthday, and the hammock in which she had rested so happily only yesterday. Had she after all made an appalling mistake? Would Harry and Madge keep well and successful while she was away? Had she the right to abandon them in such a manner? And what about the attraction she had just felt for Patrick de Moulins? For those few seconds he had seemed to be of great importance to her. She had had a physical feeling for him, which she had never experienced before. Could that have been love at first sight? Was there such a thing?

How silly! She would be leaving England within the month, and she would probably never see him again!

But she would like to see him again.

Madge swept into the room. 'Come along my darling child,' she said. 'It's time you were off.' Her voice broke. 'Be happy, my baby, won't you? Don't forget how much we love you. Write to us often, and one day please grow up enough to forgive your father. He deserves it.' She hugged her daughter to her fiercely. 'You look so beautiful, Kate, and we both love you so much.'

'I know, I know,' answered Kate, 'and I love you Mama, too. You have been the most wonderful parents, both of you, and I'll never forget it, I promise. I have been headstrong and silly, and I realise it now, but thank you darling for all that you've done. I'll miss you with all my heart.' She clung to her mother for a moment, then kissed Alice who was making no effort to hide her tears, and went with her mother down the stairs.

Edward was waiting for her outside the front door. He looked nervous as he helped her into the decorated crimson carriage. Confetti was thrown, and rose petals, and a boot had been tied to the back. The horses were decked with white ribbons and white roses, and to the sound of cheers, applause and laughter they headed for Paddington Station and the train for Cornwall.

In spite of the Slade, and the progressive views of the students, Kate knew very little about sex. Like other Victorian mothers, Madge had found such matters almost impossible to discuss, and Kate's rows over Harry's infidelities had created a further barrier. At the Slade, although the girls were far from prudish, ('Life class' used nude models), the lack of any safe contraception had made all but the most emotional or foolhardy stay clear of affairs. The scandal of illegitimacy was so extreme that it was not unknown for parents to turn their daughters away from home if unwanted children were born; so sex was still a loaded subject. Kate was therefore ill-equipped for marriage, as were so many of her contemporaries, and when she had pressed her mother on the subject, determined to find out what to expect, Madge, anxious, embarrassed and unhelpful, had merely murmured, 'Some people like it, darling, and some don't. So much depends on how the husband treats his wife on the first night. If he is kind and gentle and experienced, it can be wonderful, but I have heard stories from my friends which have horrified me, and have turned them away from any pleasure in marriage for the rest of their lives.'

'But why?' asked Kate.

'You'll be all right, darling. I'm sure Edward will be patient and kind,' Madge said evasively.

Kate was worried. She could't go to her father for a more explicit discussion, as he would have been shocked; and she had no married friends whom she knew well enough to question on such a subject. In the event she was pleasantly surprised by the wedding night.

Edward was indeed gentle and kind. He was also patient and loving. But he was almost as inexperienced as Kate, and his love-making evoked no answering passion in her: she was not repelled, but she was not remotely aroused. On the other hand, the more time she spent with him on the honeymoon, the more she liked her husband. He was in his own dry way an amusing companion. He talked to her about his job as though she was an equal, which she enjoyed, and described his life in Malaya vividly and with affection. He also had a passion for ornithology which kept him happily occupied when she wished to be away from him from time to time, to sketch or walk or even to gossip with the fishermen in the harbour.

Polperro had been Edward's choice, and a good one. The village, set steeply on a hillside with cobblestones leading down to the jetty and the sea, was satisfactory to her painter's eye: the houses were old and pretty, clustered engagingly along the narrow pavements. There were donkeys to take them up and down the streets, and wealthy friends of Edward's who lived at the top of the hill lent them horses to ride. The weather was good, the hotel comfortable; and if the physical side of the marriage was unexciting, Kate had had no expectations of anything better, and so for the moment was content.

When the honeymoon was over, they returned briefly to London. The tropical clothes which Kate had already bought for the long voyage to Malaya were packed by Alice. Two of the trunks were marked 'Wanted on Voyage'; the rest were to be consigned to the ship's hold.

Madge and Harry came down in the train to Tilbury to see them off. Despite her natural excitement, Kate found the parting with her parents very painful. Away from their glossy West End background they suddenly looked frail and vulnerable, and she longed to be able to take them with her. For Edward's sake she tried to hide her feelings but, when the great ship began to draw away from the quay, she burst into tears; and as England itself faded from sight she was desolate. Her only consolation was that she would be away from her in-laws too, and with them she knew she had nothing whatever in common.

The voyage was quite unlike anything she had imagined, in spite of what Edward had told her. This was perhaps because, being an exceptionally bad sailor, he always went to his cabin at the first hint of bad weather and so had seen little. By contrast Kate took to the sea immediately, even finding rough weather exhilarating.

Male passengers far outnumbered the women, and life on board was extremely social. Deck coits, table-tennis, sports days and fancy-dress dances followed each other in quick succession, organised by the indefatigable ship's purser. Kate was fascinated by a set of people quite outside her previous experience; and not surprisingly she was an object of great fascination to them. Many of the men fell a little in love with her — such shipboard romances were almost de rigueur in those days — but she was no flirt and gave them no encouragement. The women, on the other hand, though impressed that she was the daughter of Madge and Harry

Glanville, were shocked by her stage connections and scandalised that she had been an art student. For good measure they were also jealous of her beauty.

The ship was completely full, its cargo including great quantities of livestock which were killed freshly for the various enormous meals eaten in the first-class dining room: a four-course breakfast, a six-course luncheon and a seven-course dinner. There was also a large tea, served from four until five o'clock. The second-class passengers ate only slightly less well and fresh supplies of animals, poultry, vegetables and fruit were taken on board at every port.

At Gibraltar, Edward although exhausted after a bout of sea-sickness in the Bay of Biscay, struggled up to show her the baboons whose survival is superstitiously linked with a continued British presence on the Rock. At Marseilles he took her to visit the Château D'If, where the Count of Monte Cristo was supposed to have been imprisoned. At Port Said, the 'gully-gully men' (Egyptian conjurors in red fezes and soiled white cotton robes) came on board to make pathetic little day-old chicks appear out of what seemed to be thin air and performed brilliant sleights-of-hand with scruffy half-starved rabbits and coloured paper streamers. Snake charmers, playing high-pitched tuneless dirges to swaying cobras, also invaded the ship; and ashore Edward bought himself a new solar topee from Simon Arszt, as did the young men who were going out East for the first time. Kate and Edward lunched at the Grand Hotel, and here Kate saw punkahs for the first time: strips of cloth attached to the ceiling by ropes, which could be pulled backwards and forward to make a cool breeze. She was told that the *punkah wallahs* (the men or little boys who controlled them) worked such long hours to a rhythm so monotonous that they would often fall asleep with the ropes attached to their toes, while still performing their duty.

As they steamed down the Suez Canal, escorted by a busy little pilot boat, Kate saw her first of many dramatically brilliant tropical sunrises. The Eastern sky turned yellow, intensifying in one spot which deepened rapidly into a vivid carmine, spread itself quickly over a vast area in enormous bands of threatening colour, paled to pink and faded. Suddenly the sun, hot already and blazing yellow, wheeled above the horizon in a flood of flashing glory and sailed magnificently into an azure sky.

At Aden next day, tiny little Arab boys dived over the steep sides of the ship into the sea to collect the pennies and sixpences thrown for them by the passengers, catching the money in their mouths well below the surface of the water with astonishing dexterity. But it was in Ceylon that Kate's love affair with the East began.

To Edward's amusement she bought a very large ebony elephant from the sellers who came on board. 'Just like any tripper,' he teased. He was in high spirits, and Kate was delighted that she was making him happy. From what he had told her about his life he had been a lonely little boy, the only son of elderly parents who were both poor and proud; his education on a scholarship to a minor public school had also set him apart, as most of the boys came from well-to-do families and were snobs into the bargain. As a young man, making his way in a strange country, he had been shy and found it hard to make friends; but with Kate at his side he seemed to be at ease with himself and with others. He too loved the East and was impatient to show her the port of Colombo.

Just before they disembarked, news came through that the ship would be staying in port for two or three days. There had been an outbreak of smallpox among the Lascar crew and everything would have to be disinfected while the sick were taken ashore and replacements found. Kate had often pitied the condition of the Lascars, who were small and bow-legged and emaciated, wearing dirty loin cloths and working at all hours of the day and night. She was worried by the apparent indifference to their plight shown by most of her fellow passengers, but the ship's doctor wanted no amateur help, so reluctantly she joined the others ashore. After wandering round Colombo and its bazaars, she and Edward took ponies and, with friends they had made on board, went up into the hills at Kandy to spend a night in the cool.

It all seemed like a life on a new and more exciting planet. Kate wrote home regularly, and sometimes felt homesick, but Edward's constant solicitude for her welfare touched her deeply, and she realised clearly how fortunate she was to have married so unselfish and affectionate a man. If occasionally his lack of passion, his slow precision of speech and his entirely predictable approach got on her nerves, she felt at the moment that it was a small price to pay. Once or twice, though — and it astonished and unsettled her — she had a vivid picture in her mind of Patrick de Moulins, and wondered with a curious sense of urgency how these new experiences would have seemed if they had been shared with him.

At last they reached Singapore where, to Kate's surprise, the

head of the Singapore branch of Edward's legal firm, with his wife
and several of Edward's friends, turned up to greet their arrival.
Edward, she discovered, was popular in Malaya. In spite of his
shyness, he was thought of as a thoroughly decent up-and-coming
young fellow, of exactly the right type and outlook. Honest,
courteous, and bright in the office, he was also — scarcely less
important in the eyes of some — much in demand as a medium-
paced bowler with a safe pair of hands. He was a fair golfer, not so
good as to be unpopular, and could hold his own without difficulty
in the drinking sessions that followed these activities.

They stayed in Singapore for five days, to accustom Kate to the
heat and humidity of the climate in which she was to live. The
place charmed her. She took to the Malays at once, finding their
manners and self-respect, as well as their love of life and laughter,
much to her liking. She thought Malay women the loveliest in the
Eastern world, and found their clothes even prettier than those of
the Chinese or the Indians — although their habit of chewing betel
nut, which stained their mouths and blackened their teeth, saddened her.

Wherever she looked she was enchanted. In dazzling sunshine,
in a city brilliant with flowering shrubs and trees, the comfortable
wooden bungalows and great white government buildings of the
British rubbed shoulders with a tumbling confusion of multicoloured Indian and Chinese shops, little native huts on stilts
and roadside food stalls. Rickshaws drawn by Chinese runners
crowded the streets, and all around them was the intense blue
sea, which turned phosphorescent at night. It caught her heart —
as indeed did 'up-country' Malaya later — and kept her in thrall
for the rest of her life.

With Edward's friends she went to the races, had drinks, dined
at Raffles and danced the night away. She swam in the pool at the
exclusive Tanglin Club and, when Edward's boss, Mr Braddell,
and his wife Ena entertained them, she liked them both. Because
she was Kate Glanville, she and Edward were also bidden to dine
in the regal splendour of Government House: here, on her best
behaviour, she scored a distinct success. She noticed compas-
sionately that most of the women's dresses were dated, and that the
women were intensely eager to talk about the latest London
fashions and plays.

When the time was up, Edward and Kate took the night train to
Kuala Lumpur; for travelling in the heat of the day would have

been intolerable. Without seeing them, she passed through oil-palm estates and great tracts of jungle, and crossed broad yellow sluggish rivers. The dinner they were given, attended by Indian waiters in scarlet and white uniform, was a curry of a high standard; and the lace-covered bunks were comfortable to sleep on. At Kuala Lumpur Station their head boy, Amin, had come to meet them, with the head 'syce' in charge of the horses, to take them to their home on the outskirts of the city. It was a fair-sized building in white stucco, with four shallow steps leading to an imposing front door and a wide verandah all around. Although Chinese-built, it stood well off the ground in the Malay manner, and half an acre of garden surrounded it.

The staff — eight in all, and all Malays or Javanese — were on the steps to greet them; when the greetings were over, Amin and the Malay Ayah (who would be Kate's personal maid) showed Kate round the house. She pleased them by asking to see the kitchen and staff quarters straight away. Everything everywhere was spotlessly clean and the main house gleamed with polish. There were bowls of flowers on every available table.

To Edward's embarrassment, but the delight of all the staff, Kate threw her arms round his neck: 'Thank you for bringing me here, dear Edward,' she said. 'I'm sure that I will be very happy. Please thank everyone for such a lovely welcome.'

The servants giggled with pleasure, and Edward mumbled, 'My dear, it is only to be expected that things should be in order!'

'Nevertheless, please tell all of them how delighted I am with all that they have done.' And Edward did so, in his fluent Malay.

Life settled down to a routine and for several months Kate was content. Since the days were so hot, she and Edward were woken at six-fifteen, just after dawn. This was almost Kate's favourite time in the day. They had fruit and China tea together, and Edward would discuss the cases on which he was working. In Malaya legal practitioners were not divided into barristers and solicitors, so, although a solicitor, Edward was frequently on his feet in court, representing his clients in both civil and criminal cases. As few of the European lawyers spoke anything but English and Malay, Chinese and Indian interpreters were hired to assist their respective communities and the courts. It was well known, though difficult to prove, that they were often heavily bribed; and it was a constant anxiety to Edward that miscarriages of justice resulted.

He loved, too, to tell Kate the history of his adopted country, and she loved to listen. She had always thought of the Empire as having been won by conquest, so she was amazed to learn that the British connection in Malaya had been almost haphazard.

From the establishment of East India Company trading posts in Penang and Port Wellesley in the eighteenth century and the founding of Singapore (thanks to the genius of Stamford Raffles) and Malacca in the 1820s, there had followed a gradual development of spheres of influence — 'more by invitation than annexation,' said Edward — in the larger native states: their populations saw the advantage of living under the security of the British rule of law rather than the ruthless and often cruel law of the jungle (enlivened by pirates and Siamese marauders) to which they had been accustomed. From this unlikely material there had evolved a government in Singapore, with important outposts in Kuala Lumpur and Penang, in which the Chinese (the majority), the Malays, the Indians and the British lived together with a remarkable degree of tolerance, if not enthusiasm, for each other's cultures. Here the Malay Sultans kept their State, but the British Royal Family was everyone's Royal Family. And since it had come about through enlightened self-interest on everyone's part, it seemed to work.

After Edward had dressed, a full Edwardian breakfast was served at eight-thirty, which they also ate together — Edward usually rather hurriedly. Then he left for the office by rickshaw and Kate either sewed or read until lunchtime. Lunch was formally served at one o'clock but, unless Edward was in, Kate ate frugally. She found that she was unable to manage the enormous meals that the other women consumed in the middle of the day. Like them, however, she then had a rest until tea-time, when she either played mixed badminton in her own or in someone else's garden, or played tennis at the Lake Club. The routine could be varied by Mah-Jong parties for the women in the morning; nearly everyone gave curry tiffins for Sunday lunch; and there were often little dinner parties and bridge parties in the evenings. There were also many flirtations and minor scandals. The ratio of men to women was at least ten to one and, as any form of miscegenation or 'going native' was taboo, white women were in great demand.

Kate was both a social success — her guests were as carefully chosen as her menus — and a source of some disapproval. This was not on moral grounds, for she never indulged in the flirtations or the opportunities for intrigue which so freely offered themselves;

but she had, thanks to her theatrical upbringing, a natural frankness with men which shocked the women; and her beauty was a constant temptation to envy. She was becoming bored, however, with her idle life; and the unconventional side of her, which she had tried to suppress for Edward's sake, began very gradually to take over. The other women would send their servants to do the household shopping, or travel in their carriages if they wanted to buy things for themselves: Kate now formed the habit of riding to the shops on Matty, the game little polo pony which Edward had bought her. She also started painting again, not only socially acceptable flower pictures, but vivid portraits of her native servants and sketches of the countryside. She could be seen along the roadsides on the outskirts of a kampong, or even of KL itself, sitting at her easel under a parasol in the full heat of the day.

One evening, when she had gone to watch the men play polo on the race course and one of the players failed to turn up, Kate was asked, almost as a joke, to take his place on Matty — and not only did so but played quite well for a beginner. She aroused further disapproval by taking lessons in Malay and Chinese and, to Edward's dismay, took to wearing a novel type of hat which offended the other women but suited her well. Disliking both the topees and the enormous veiled creations which were the usual feminine wear, she designed large, pale, very lightweight men's felt hats, which she had specially made for her. Edward remonstrated that she would only make herself unpopular if she failed so signally to conform; she was concerned for his sake, but replied that these hats were the most practical wear for her sketching expeditions. When Edward said that these too were causing comment, she said firmly, 'I must do something, Edward dear, or I shall go mad! The women in my family all work as hard as the men, and I've been brought up to be active. It's bred in me.'

But in spite of these differences they had good times together. They often rode along the jungle paths to picnic up in the hills on a Sunday, and started quite a fashion. The women who joined them were looked on as fast, since they bathed with the men in the jungle pools — an attitude which Kate considered laughable in view of the morals of most of their critics. She loved best the pools near waterfalls, which were not so leech-infested: and one of her great joys was to climb up to the ledge behind the fall and watch the water pouring down from above, smooth, green and steady, and as solid as a wall.

Edward's passion for birds was fully satisfied here. He became absorbed for hours on end, watching toucans and hornbills, bantam fowl and peacocks and, at night, listening for the ravishing Argus pheasant. Both of them were happy in these wild surroundings.

The jungle had come as a complete surprise to Kate. She had certainly envisaged great forests, but had never expected such profusion. Vast trees, some of them supported at their base by trunks wider than thirty men standing abreast, carried other trees on their top branches, also of considerable size. From all of them, it seemed, cylindrical strands descended — up to six inches wide and often a hundred-and-fifty feet or more in length — then plunged into the earth below, as stout as ship's masts. Beneath these giants flourished coconut palms, nipah palms (from which the betel nuts were collected), great tree-ferns, bamboos and vivid flowering trees; and under them again, lesser ferns and ground orchids and aromatic shrubs. Rattan crept along the ground or climbed the tree branches, knotting them all together with strands hundreds of feet in length, while monkey cups, insect-eating pitcher plants and multicoloured flowers made a dense carpet. At the very tops of the tallest trees, flowers seldom seen blazed at the blue sky, and liana cascaded from branch to branch bearing huge clusters of orange blossoms which illuminated everything they enveloped. The animals which inhabited the jungle kept out of sight during the day, so there was little danger. Only a King Cobra or a panther would attack unprovoked, or a man-eating tiger, ill and hungry and too slow on its feet to catch its animal prey; although in the swamps and the broad tumbling rivers there were always crocodiles watching for anything foolish enough to come within their reach.

England's countryside was tame beside such plenitude, and Kate preferred her new home. To Edward's sorrow, however, she did not become pregnant. He was still besottedly in love with her, and a child would have made his joy complete. Kate wanted children too, but not just yet. She knew how much they would restrict her, even with ayahs to take charge — and she cherished her freedom. Besides, she was enjoying herself. If she sometimes realised that there was more to life than having a good friend for a husband and having a good time, without much mental stimulus, she was aware of it with only a limited regret.

By the time they went to England on leave she would have described herself as happy with the life she had chosen.

CHAPTER THREE

England in 1913 was a very different place indeed from Malaya. There were rumours of war, which had not yet troubled the East; and, although it was April by the time they were home, the weather was still cold and the skies were grey. To Kate's disappointment, Edward had arranged that they should visit his own parents, near Colchester in Essex, before going on to the Glanvilles. Since his mother had been ill, Kate sympathised — but she was miserable not to be able to see Madge and Harry at once. She had not realised how much she had been missing them, and was overwhelmed now to be so near, yet unable to see them.

The visit to the Marchmonts was a difficult one for all of them; to Kate they epitomised the lack of colour which now depressed her so much in England. In their narrow undemonstrative way, both Mr and Mrs Marchmont adored their only son and they resented Kate as an interloper. Any girl who had married Edward would have aroused their jealousy; but Kate's quick sense of humour, her brusque manner, her now slightly outdated clothes (and the mannish felt hats which she had chosen to wear in England as well as Malaya) made her seem almost a foreigner to them — and therefore embarrassing, and even frightening. They could't see the beauty which they had heard was so universally admired and, since they were unable to disguise their dislike of her, she in turn found it hard to have any affection for them.

Edward on the other hand was delighted to be with them. In spite of his lonely childhood, he had always enjoyed his home; the house and garden and the surrounding countryside brought back only happy memories. Since he was only gregarious when there was no alternative, as in Malaya, the lack of an interesting social life didn't worry him; also he liked feeling cool for a change. He didn't mind the bad food or his mother's rigid sense of propriety, since he expected them; his father's dourness and bad manners also left him unmoved because he knew his father loved him. He was naturally aware, though, that Kate and his family didn't get on, and he found himself defending her vehemently.

'Leave her alone!' he said. 'She suits me, and we're happy. It isn't Kate's fault any more than mine that we have no children. She wants them as much as I do, so please don't make her miserable.' But on this subject he wasn't at all sure of his ground. Like his parents, he wondered just how much she did want children, and this made him feel disloyal.

At the Glanvilles', the boot was on the other foot. Here it was Kate who felt contented and he who was the outsider. Madge and Harry were determined to make the most of their time with their daughter, and unconsciously they wanted to show her how much she was missing by going out of their lives. They were acting together in a great success at the Princess Theatre and had taken a cottage in Sussex, where at weekends they still entertained their famous friends. Edward had nothing in common with any of them. He found Madge intimidating and Harry slightly shocking, although he admired his talent. The fashionable women and the elegant, often affected, young men who surrounded the Glanvilles seemed to him unattractive, and they considered him a prig. Nothing in his previous experience had fitted him for their company and, although he was slightly in awe of their fame, he had a positive contempt for them. His contempt didn't include Ellen Terry, who managed to charm him as she charmed almost everyone who ever came into contact with her (with the obvious exception of Henry Irving's estranged widow, who blamed her entirely for the breakup of her marriage); but he positively hated the beautiful manners and caustic wit of Bernard Shaw, who was never allowed to meet Ellen Terry at the Glanvilles', and whom he considered a dangerous charlatan. He found May Whitty's tireless social conscience discomforting: her espousal of the feminist cause and the suffragette movement was to him ridiculous and embarrassing, and he could't understand how her handsome husband, Ben Webster, condoned it.

Kate's Slade friends alarmed him even more. He disliked clever women who paraded their cleverness and he found the bohemian (and often dirty) young men decadent and unsettling. He believed that their work, which was much too advanced for him to understand, was a positive threat to his ideal of England. Kate's 'eccentric side', as he called it, had never appealed to him, and the stories with which these friends regaled him — of her riding to school in knickerbockers on a man's second-hand bicycle, with her hair down to her waist — quite horrified him. That she had been attracted to Augustus John, who was already renowned as a womaniser, came as an added shock.

Oddly enough, this reaction of his didn't upset Kate at all. In fact it actually drew her closer to Edward. She had made her choice and was touched that so conventional a man should love her in spite of traits which were anathema to him. To her this only proved the strength of his feelings; she could see that he was doing his best to please her circle in spite of his misgivings, and his failure touched her. Having settled for his kind of life in Malaya, Kate could understand his point of view. She was touched, too, that he agreed to accompany her to the opulent dinner parties and balls to which they were invited by the Glanville's 'society' friends, and delighted when he joined her sprees to buy fashionable clothes in Bond Street — gifts from her parents, who wanted to show off their lovely, cherished daughter. For the moment Kate was entirely happy to be home revelling in the stimulating intellectual con-versation of her friends and family and living for a while in London, which was still considered the most important city in the world. The persistent rumours of war naturally troubled her, as they troubled everyone she knew; but, being young, she was an optimist, and inclined to believe that nothing would come of them. Surely not even the Germans would challenge the might of the British Empire? And besides, the Kaiser and the King were first cousins.

All the same, when the time came to return to Malaya, she was desperately worried at leaving her family at such a time of crisis. If the worst happened, a war might actually be fought on English soil, and then what might happen to her parents and her friends? Madge and Harry bade them an emotional goodbye; and Madge reiterated how much they looked forward to having grandchildren.

Back in Malaya, in spite of the sunshine and colour, with the routine of their home life closing in on her again, Kate found herself restless. She eagerly resumed her painting and her language classes and was delighted to see her household again; but the first of their social occasions, the St Andrews's ball (to be held at the 'Spotted Dog', as the Selangor Club in Kuala Lumpur was affectionately called), seemed to her now to be very small beer.

It was to be a fancy-dress affair, which appealed to Edward because he wouldn't have to wear a stiff collar and boiled shirt in the stifling heat. They were to go in a party of fourteen, Edward as

Robin Hood and Kate as Maid Marion — another cool and easy
costume. Kate's dress suited her, but she slightly scandalised the
other women with a dramatic décolletage, and a skirt which
showed her ankles. The whole party had dinner at the Marchmont
house before going on to the dance, and Kate felt suddenly at the
top of her form. With her long blonde hair hanging almost to her
waist, she looked like a girl... the girl who went to the Slade,
thought Edward uneasily.

The ball at the 'Spotted Dog' was to be a 'programme dance', as
most of the largest dances of the time then were. The women never
enjoyed them as much as the men, since each dance was numbered
and reservations were deemed inviolable. Often the least attractive
men were the first in the field, but they were accepted because any
partner was preferable to being a wallflower. Even so, the ladies'
cloakrooms tended to be full throughout the evening of unescorted
women pretending to adjust their hair and clothes rather than sit
alone at their tables.

After leaving her wrap, Kate glanced at herself in the cloakroom
looking-glass and for once was satisfied with what she saw. She
really did look her best tonight! She had no idea why she felt such a
sense of excitement and pleasure but indeed she was almost
euphoric. Edward danced well and she always found dancing with
him a pleasure; but she was certain to have to partner several
uninteresting men, and in fact already booked dances she would
not particularly enjoy — so why was she suddenly so happy?

She savoured this moment alone, lingering reflectively in front
of the mirror. Briefly, she thought of her family back home and
wondered what they would be doing. Lunching, perhaps, with
other actors? With the Websters, with Ellen, with some of their
grander friends? How far away they were... And what did the
future hold for her here, in Malaya? Would having children
perhaps make life seem less trivial? Was she after all a maternal
type? Or would her life consist, until Edward's retirement, of small
social occasions like this one: with Edward, perhaps, becoming
more and more successful and, for herself, in this beautiful but
strange country, a comfortable but stultifying routine broken only
by trips to Singapore, Penang or into her beloved jungle — and of
course leave, to a homeland which would become progressively
more strange to her as Malaya became familiar? She had been so
certain that something worthwhile awaited her here! But perhaps
life would offer only second best — perhaps all lives offer only

second best: Madge in love with Harry, and having to put up with his infidelities... Edward loving Kate, who wasn't in love with him... Kate herself liking Edward but being always unsatisfied. Even Ellen Terry, with all her talent and courage, and with London and indeed the whole country at her feet, was eating her heart out for Godwin, the father of her children, who was content to live an uninteresting country life in East Anglia rather than commit himself to a partnership whose responsibilities he was unable to face...

Edward meanwhile was waiting impatiently by the bar. All the other women in the party were already at the table, so what on earth was keeping Kate? He was just about to go in search of her when he felt a friendly blow on the black and turned to find Patrick de Moulins, standing at his side.

'Good God!' he exclaimed enthusiastically. 'What the devil are you doing here?'

'I've got a job on the Sungei Pahang Rubber Estate at Pekan,' said Patrick. 'I came out just after you'd left for England. I'm here in KL on a few days' leave.'

'Are you with a party tonight?'

'No.'

'Then why not join us? We'd love it.'

Patrick hesitated. 'I don't want to gate-crash,' he said.

'My dear fellow, you're not gate-crashing! You're as welcome as the day! Why didn't you let us know you were coming out here?'

Patrick grinned. 'I'm not very good at writing letters.'

He was tanned and looked extremely fit. He had filled out in the three years since Edward had seen him. He carried himself well, and he was more self-assured.

'Malaya seems to suit you,' said Edward. 'How do you like it?'

Before Patrick had time to answer, Kate came towards them. At the sight of Patrick she stopped dead, the colour rushing into her cheeks. She hoped fervently that Edward hadn't noticed, and realised wryly that her heart was pounding.

Patrick was equally shaken. He had thought of Kate from time to time, as a very attractive woman; but he had forgotten until now just how strongly she had affected him. He stared at her in astonishment and Kate felt again the vivid current of sympathy between them.

Edward was laughing happily. 'Look who's here, darling!' he

said. 'Do you remember him at our wedding? This is Patrick de Moulins, one of my best friends at school.'

Kate and Patrick shook hands, and to Kate's dismay the physical shock was so great that she found it difficult to speak.

Patrick managed to murmur, 'How do you do?' and Edward rushed on: 'Great news! He's got a job out here, so we'll be seeing quite a bit of him, and tonight I've asked him to join us at our table!'

'You don't mind?' asked Patrick, searching her face.

'Of course not,' she murmured faintly.

As they walked to their table, both Patrick and Kate tried to assess their feelings. Patrick enjoyed women as a distraction and had had many affairs, but none had meant much to him: between adventures he was a man's man, with a horror of entanglements. Kate was totally inexperienced emotionally. They were both, therefore, wary of the sudden mutual attraction. During the introductions at the table, Kate saw how eagerly the other women reacted to Patrick's charms. Although this reinforced her wish to be on guard, it did nothing to lessen the attraction.

As convention demanded, Patrick asked each of the women for a dance. When he came to Kate, however, his request was urgent. 'Give me all the dances you can.'

'I've only three left,' said Kate. 'But people will talk if we dance too often.'

'Nonsense,' said Patrick. 'I'm a stranger here. Your friends will realise that I don't know anyone except you.'

'You don't know me,' protested Kate.

'I shall,' said Patrick firmly, as he escorted her to the dance floor. He was surprised at his own gallantry, especially since he wished to be cautious as she was Edward's wife; but he spoke almost in spite of himself.

He danced well. In his arms Kate felt she had come home. They didn't bother to talk at first: it was enough to be together. Kate knew that people were watching them, but for the moment she didn't care. She was always being watched and discussed (she knew that too) and sometimes, for Edward's sake, she was sorry. Was it the theatre in her blood that made her so different from the others or was it just that, coming from such a famous acting family, she would always be a target for gossip? Even when she had tried hard to conform she hadn't fitted in out here. Perhaps Patrick would be the same: he had an ease of manner, and a sense of style — and he was catnip to women. Perhaps he even looked for trouble. He, like herself, was an outsider.

Kate's next partner was Kenneth Henderson, a colleague of Edward's who was with another party. He was conceited and overbearing, with a loud laugh but little sense of humour. Kate disliked him but, since he was important to Edward professionally, tried not to show it. At this moment he was already slightly drunk, which didn't please her.

'Who's the boyfriend?' he asked, as he and Kate reached the dance floor.

'Boyfriend?' she said coldly. 'I don't know what you mean.'

'The red-haired fellow who's just joined you.'

'Patrick de Moulins — a schoolfriend of Edward's,' said Kate. 'He works with Sungei Pahang Rubber.'

'My wife considers he's a good looker,' said Henderson. 'Do you agree?'

'I haven't thought about it,' replied Kate.

'Oh, come now, Mrs Marchmont!' said Henderson boisterously. 'You can't fool me! Being an actress and all that, I'd say you knew a good deal about men.'

'Which is why I chose Edward,' replied Kate firmly. She was having difficulty concealing her anger.

'Oh, yes. Quite, and all that,' said Henderson. 'I say! Jolly good!' and he gave her an encouraging squeeze.

'Edward is a very remarkable man, Mr Henderson,' said Kate seriously. 'In my opinion there isn't another man here who could hold a candle to him.'

Henderson looked at her in amazement. 'Good Heavens!' he exclaimed. 'I didn't mean to be rude, don't you know, but you must admit that you and Edward aren't quite the same kind of people. At least that's what my wife and I think.'

'The same as who?' asked Kate, innocently.

'The same as each other.'

'If you mean that Edward is too good for me,' said Kate, 'then I thoroughly agree with you.'

'My dear Mrs Marchmont! You surprise me!' Henderson was again amazed. 'I wouldn't have put you down as a milk-and-water miss at all.'

'Wouldn't you?' asked Kate. 'Why not?'

'For one thing, you're a raving beauty.'

'Thank you. And for another?'

'Well everyone knows that you do pretty well what you like, don't they?'

'Do they?'

'Well, of course. You paint and play polo and wear what you like. Look at you tonight! And why not, I say? If it came to the point where you wanted your way and your husband wanted his, I'd back you every time — aren't I right?'

'Would you?'

He didn't seem to notice that her voice was now icy.

'Come on now!' he said. 'You know it! You're the most emancipated woman I know. All the other women here envy you. You should hear my wife on the subject! They don't know how you get away with it! To tell you the truth, you rather shock them.'

'Why should I?' she asked disdainfully. 'I try to harm no-one. I love my husband, and what's more I don't cheat on him, which is more than can be said for most of my critics.' Henderson frowned, but she went on, 'And I don't gossip either, which most of them do!' She was trying to control her temper now. 'And you?' she demanded. 'Do I shock you?'

He laughed again, and his grip round her waist tightened. 'As a matter of fact, you do,' he said. 'But with looks like yours it's rather exciting, my dear.' He was sweating a little, and he leered at her provocatively.

Because he was senior to Edward in the firm, Kate was determined not to quarrel with him; but she didn't want to dance with him any longer either. She disengaged herself and said calmly, 'I wonder if you would take me back to my table, Mr Henderson? I have rather a headache this evening.'

'Yes, I thought you must be out of sorts,' he agreed heartily, 'the way you were talking about Edward! It didn't sound like the real Mrs Marchmont to me.'

'Oh, it was the real Mrs Marchmont, all right,' replied Kate. 'I meant every word. I am only sorry to have given you any other impression.'

'I must tell my wife,' said Henderson. 'It will surprise her no end.'

'Please do,' said Kate. 'She could do with a few surprises.'

He drew away from her. 'What does that mean?' he asked belligerently.

'It means that she, like yourself, seems to have been under a misapprehension about me, and I would be grateful if you would dispel it.'

'Forgive me,' he said. 'I see that my wife is alone at our table.'

'And I see that Edward's friend is alone at ours.'

Henderson sat her down in her chair, bowed stiffly and left her, and Patrick came round the table to join her. He had seen at once that she was upset, and asked sympathetically, 'Are you all right? Has that man been bothering you?'

'Mr Henderson is a colleague of Edward's for whom I have singularly little liking,' said Kate emphatically.

'At a snap judgement I'd say I admire your taste,' smiled Patrick. 'The man looks a bore, and a bounder.'

Kate laughed. 'He is,' she said, 'but Edward doesn't see it. He has such a charming disposition!'

'Yes, indeed,' said Patrick. 'He's the dearest fellow in the world. Let's finish this dance,' he continued. 'It's a pity to waste such a good tune.'

'I think we'd better sit it out,' said Kate. 'I made the excuse of a headache to Mr Henderson, and my recovery would appear a bit sudden, don't you think?'

'Whatever you say,' said Patrick.

She smiled, and they sat together in a companionable silence which Patrick was the first to break.

'Do you like it out here?'

'Yes, I do. I adore the country and its people and the climate, and I love the outdoor life. But...'

'But?'

'You may not like what I'm about to say,' said Kate.

'I'm sure I shall,' he answered. 'I shall always like what you have to say.' He looked at her very directly. 'So, go on.'

'Do you make all your judgements so quickly?' she teased.

'In your case I made them at once,' he said, and she heard in his voice a fierce sincerity. He was silent for a moment, then continued: 'You said "but". But what?'

'But what we Europeans have done, in such wild and natural surroundings is to recreate suburbia — with all the usual suburban values, but with a level of affluence which seems to make the idle women here care for nothing but trivialities!' said Kate strongly. 'I've just been accused of stepping out of line because I paint, and wear what I want to wear! Have you ever heard anything so ridiculous? In their eyes a painter or an actress is half way to being a loose woman. So Edward is to be pitied for having married me! And yet — and everyone knows it — nearly all the married women here have affairs. Surely to try to create something beautiful instead, or contribute in some way to one's surroundings, can't be a bad thing?'

'Excellent, I should have thought,' agreed Patrick warmly. 'But the contrasts you speak of — and I've noticed them too — even happen in the same person. Up in Pahang I've met a number of these really exceptional young men, thrust very early into positions of immense responsibility, on their own miles away from anywhere — and certainly from suburbia — ruling areas the size of Wales and doing it conscientiously and successfully. Yet none that I've met seems to have developed a real curiosity about the country they are ruling, in terms of the races that live there, or their history, their beliefs and aspirations. Mention the word politics, or indeed religion, to them and they become embarrassed and even resentful. And yet both should be crucial to their job.'

'Are you a religious man?' asked Kate, surprised.

'Not in the sense of a "good Christian",' said Patrick. 'But the subject of religion, and indeed of comparative religions, interests me very much. What a conversation for a dance!' he added with a laugh.

She laughed too. 'I like it,' she said, then changed the subject. 'When do you go back to Pahang?'

'Too soon for my taste, I'm afraid. The estate is six miles up river from Pekan, which as you know is a one-horse town, so any intellectual activity has to be self-stimulated. But I quite enjoy the life. However, I shall be moving down to KL very soon, and I'm looking forward to it, especially now that you and Edward are back.'

She tried to hide her pleasure. 'Good. I'm glad,' she said, calmly.

'And I shall be sending for my motor car from England soon, though God knows how I'll use it on the dirt tracks in Sungei Pahang!'

'Your motor car?' echoed Kate, astounded. 'Surely a motor car is very expensive to bring out here?'

'You mean, on my salary?' he asked, slightly mockingly.

She flushed. 'Well, yes.'

'I have a bit of money of my own,' replied Patrick.

'Then why on earth did you come out here as a planter?' Kate asked, surprised.

'I got a little bored with England, and decided to see the world. The East sounded attractive and then I chanced upon this job, so I took it. Besides, for the moment I am not very popular at home.' He smiled sardonically.

'May I ask why not?'

'I'll tell you one day,' he said. 'Not now, if you don't mind.'

'Of course.'

There was another short silence between them. Kate thought how strange it was that Patrick and Edward should have been such friends: they seemed so unlike each other in every way.

'I've heard so much about you,' said Patrick at last. 'Now that I've met you, I feel that we have a lot in common.'

'I'm glad,' said Kate. 'Edward will be pleased if you and I can be friends too.'

'You see,' said Patrick, 'we're both rebels in a way. Only you seem to have rebelled from what most people would have considered freedom — whereas I've done it more conventionally, from the constraints of class! The trouble with rebelling, though,' he said wryly, 'is that deep down we are marked by the very thing we have rebelled against. So we create a conflict within ourselves.'

'You mean we turn ourselves into two different sorts of people?' asked Kate.

'Two at least! People are seldom anything but complex,' replied Patrick.

Kate considered this, then decided to lighten the conversation. 'You said you'd heard a lot about me,' she said. 'I hope not all of it was to my detriment?'

'I heard that you were very beautiful, and very independent,' said Patrick.

'And I hope you heard that I was not a flirt,' said Kate forcefully. 'My last partner thought differently and I had to put him wise.'

'Point taken,' grinned Patrick.

Instinctively they both turned to look for Edward on the dance floor. His partner, a dark-haired woman called Nancy Banks, was gazing into his face adoringly, and Edward was looking at her with an expression half pleased and half embarrassed.

Patrick and Kate shared a moment of almost guilty amusement, then Patrick said gently, 'I try not to listen to malicious gossip, or indeed gossip of any kind, but I was interested to hear about my friend's wife.'

'I understand.'

'And if the women do gossip, one can hardly blame them.' He added enthusiastically, 'You're from a different world. Half their husbands are in love with you, I'm told.'

'I'm sure that's not true!' exclaimed Kate.

'I'm sure it is,' contradicted Patrick. 'And I can tell you this: if you weren't Edward's wife, I'd be in love with you myself.'

'But I am Edward's wife,' she murmured.

'Yes,' he agreed quietly. 'My friend is a very lucky man.'

CHAPTER FOUR

Kate did not see Patrick again for several months, but he was seldom out of her thoughts. In her mind's eye, she constantly saw his amused blue eyes, thick red hair, broad shoulders, and the lazy walk — and she went over their conversations again and again, memorising every inflection and examining them in detail.

He had said they were both rebels — rebels of a different kind, perhaps, yet with much in common. She wondered just how much? If he were rebelling from a straitlaced world and she from an emancipated one (as far as she understood him), where did that leave the two of them? She knew without the shadow of a doubt that she had fallen in love with him, and was astonished at the intensity of her feelings and the speed with which they had developed.

She discussed Patrick with Edward, who was only too pleased to talk about him.

'What was he like at school, Edward?'

'Who, my dear?'

'Mr de Moulins,' said Kate.

'Terribly bright,' answered Edward. 'Almost too clever for some people's tastes, except that he was good at games too. He was a real swell, you know, titled family and all that, but he had no *side*, and he was very funny. Made us all laugh a good deal.'

'He sounds a paragon.'

'Well not quite.'

'Why not?'

'He was a complicated sort of chap,' said Edward. 'One moment he'd be hail-fellow-well-met, and the next he'd retreat inside himself, for days on end. He was always getting into hot water with the authorities, too. If he hadn't come of such a good family, there were times when he might have been expelled.'

'For what?'

'Breaking bounds. Going up to London. Bad debts. All sorts of things.'

'That doesn't sound much like a paragon,' laughed Kate. 'I wonder what made him do it?'

'Oh ... boredom, I should think. He was always restless and easily bored,' said Edward. 'But he's generous, and kind to anyone in trouble, and he's a good companion.'

Kate brooded over what Edward had said, and tried to relate it to her own impression of him. There was one thing she wanted to know, above all. 'Mr de Moulins said that he was not popular at home at the moment, Edward,' she said. 'What did he mean by that, do you know?'

'I'm sure it wasn't really his fault,' replied Edward warmly, 'though I'm afraid it doesn't sound very good. His family objected very strongly, I'm told.'

'To what?'

'Well, there was an awful fuss about a girl — the daughter of close family friends,' said Edward. 'Patrick got engaged to her when he was no more than a boy but, when the time for the wedding came near, he jilted her.'

'Oh! ... Why?'

'Said he couldn't go through with it. Refused point blank. Both his own family and the girl's took it very hard.'

'Surely it was better not to marry if he wasn't in love with her?' said Kate. Yet that's what I did to Edward, she thought, with sudden guilt. She looked at Edward and saw, with gratitude, that the thought had not occurred to him.

'Perhaps it was indeed better,' he said equably. 'Anyway, his family were only too pleased to get him a job out here.'

'The black sheep...' murmured Kate.

'Patrick is a good fellow,' said Edward defensively. 'Don't get the wrong idea.'

'I won't,' said Kate and, in truth, none of what Edward had told her had set her against Patrick. On the contrary, she liked the sound of him more and more.

Strangely enough, in spite of Patrick's absence, she was content. She knew with a fatalistic certainty that the meeting on St Andrew's night wouldn't be the last. He would find a way to see her again — not only because he was Edward's friend and was moving to KL, but because her attraction for him was as strong as his for her.

Yet despite this, and despite Edward's praise of Patrick, one thing worried her. Could she like him? She had heard disquieting rumours of his conduct in Sungei Pahang. It was said that he was having an affair with the wife of the District Officer, and also that he had a Chinese mistress in one of the kampongs near by. By chance, Edward had remarked idly once that Patrick reminded him a little of Harry Glanville; and the last thing she wished was to further a relationship with a man like her father! She must find out the truth from Patrick himself. But even if she did, and he confessed to his affairs, could she control the passion she already felt for him? It was important to her that she should admire and like a man she loved.

One of Edward's chief attractions for her, and one that other people never understood, was the friendship she felt for her husband. She realised that friendship between a man and woman was rare, but she also realised that a physical love, however profound, which didn't include this quality would fail to bring her happiness.

One day, when she was lunching at home alone, a note was delivered from Patrick, to say that he had been transferred to Klang, not far from Kuala Lumpur, and looked forward to entertaining Edward and Kate the following weekend, if they were free: from dinner on Friday until after Sunday luncheon.

'Now you can really get to know him!' exclaimed Edward on his return that evening. 'I know you'll like him!'

'You really care that I should, don't you?' asked Kate gently.

'Certainly!' replied Edward. 'It may sound absurd, but he was a kind of hero to me at school. He was older by two years, and no end of a big shot, but he was against bullying and he helped some of us smaller boys a lot. There was a great deal of bullying, you see, and if you weren't one of the brawny, spoiling-for-a-fight kind of boys, you could have a difficult time. Patrick came to the rescue of quite a few of us, and I, for one, have always been grateful.'

Kate dressed very carefully for the dinner party, and Edward praised her lavishly. 'You look even more lovely than usual, Kate,' he said fondly. 'What a lucky chap I am!'

Kate felt guilty again. She knew she was dressing to attract Patrick, and Edward's blind generosity made her ashamed. Yet she couldn't suppress an intense longing to see Patrick, and a determination to be at her best for him.

His bungalow was a surprise to her. Through fear that flying ants would destroy all good furniture, most of the British community had settled for rattan tables and chairs, which could be easily replaced. Few of her friends had books, since these might be eaten by silver fish, and fewer still had pictures on the walls. Patrick, however, had furnished his home with Chinese ebony furniture and Chinese glass pictures. He had also risked bringing out quite a library from England, and had used Chinese and Malay silks for his cushions. Since he was only a junior on the estate, his bungalow was a small one; but he had made use of all the verandah space by extending his mosquito netting to the rails, and had laid Chinese silk rugs on the floors. In this way he had produced an atmosphere of luxury, almost of opulence, which was very rare at that time.

He met his guests at the door, wearing a Malay baju and sarong. (The baju was of white silk with loose three-quarter-length sleeves and a stand-up collar, open at the throat; the sarong, worn over white trousers, was iridescent with gold thread.) They suited him well.

The dinner party was a success. Patrick had seated Kate on his right, but he was careful not to devote too much attention to her. His neighbour on his left (a Mrs Juniper) was openly admiring, and Kate found herself anxiously listening to see if Patrick was enjoying such flattery. Half way through the dinner he turned to her and said, 'I can't tell you how glad I am to have come to KL, Mrs Marchmont!'

'You didn't enjoy your one-horse town, then?' she laughed.

'It had its compensations,' he replied solemnly (and she immediately remembered the rumours of his affairs), 'but I am glad to be somewhere a little more civilised.'

'Edward is delighted that you have come to live so near,' she said.

'And you?' There was intensity in his question.

'Naturally I am delighted, too,' she replied.

'Naturally.' He smiled, and seemed to relax. 'I hope I can make you comfortable during your stay,' he went on. 'This place isn't exactly a palace, but I have done my best.'

'I can see you have,' answered Kate. 'And the flowers in our room were a charming thought. Not many men would have remembered that women like such touches.'

'You should have flowers wherever you walk,' said Patrick ardently. 'Armfuls of them.'

The woman on his left overheard this. 'I'm sure Mrs Marchmont is very used to flowers,' she said maliciously, 'since her parents are so famous. Actors, you know. Bouquets of all sorts must mean nothing to her.'

Patrick flashed a sudden intent look at Kate before turning to his neighbour. 'All women should have armfuls of flowers on every occasion, whether they are famous or not,' he said amiably. 'Don't you agree?'

'You must tell that to my husband,' said the woman, but she was visibly mollified.

After dinner, when the women were on their own, Mrs Juniper said to Kate, 'What a delightful young man my dear, and I do believe you have made a conquest! He is so attractive, don't you agree? I declare, my head spins when he looks at me with those blue eyes of his, and I noticed the way he looked at you. He positively dotes.'

'Nonsense!' exclaimed Kate, both alarmed and delighted. 'He wants to make a favourable impression on me because he and Edward were such friends at school.'

'Really? And is it true that he is related to the aristocracy?' demanded Mrs Juniper.

'So I believe.'

'How exciting! And how flattering for you that he wishes to take so much trouble over you!'

Kate was determined to put a stop to such insinuations. 'Mrs Juniper,' she said firmly, 'if you persist in talking to me like this, I shall begin to think you have fallen for his charms yourself. As for me, this is only the second time I have met him, and though my husband likes him very much and I agree with you that he *has* charm, I haven't had time to make anything but a superficial judgement. If you must know,' she went on mischievously, 'I thought he admired *you*! Perhaps he is the kind of man who actually enjoys the company of women, and that is why we find him charming.'

Mrs Juniper dropped her voice. 'We are not alone, I understand,' she said conspiratorially.

'I beg your pardon?'

'Have you not heard that there are scandals about him?'

'If you and I listened to scandal, Mrs Juniper, we should doubt the integrity of a great many of our friends,' retorted Kate.

Mrs Juniper, about whom there had been a great many scandals in her day, shot an anxious glance at Kate and hastily agreed.

The weekend passed very happily for Kate. Apart from his

physical attractions, Patrick's social ease and sophistication made her feel more at home with him than with anyone else in her circle; and, though he was not an intellectual, she found his conversation positive and stimulating.

Edward, too, was happy. Although realising that there was an affinity between Kate and Patrick, he had no idea of its strength and was delighted that the two of them seemed to enjoy one another's company. Although Kate and Patrick had little time alone together, they had enough for Kate to realise that her feelings for him were deepening not diminishing, and she was sure that for Patrick it was the same.

On the Sunday evening, when she and Edward were about to leave and Edward was supervising the arrangement of the luggage in the carriage, Patrick took her aside. 'I shall miss you, Kate.'

'We have loved being with you,' she replied.

'When shall we meet again?' he asked.

'When you and Edward arrange it,' she answered lightly.

'Only then?'

'I don't understand.'

'I think you do.'

'Then perhaps I don't wish to.'

'Please!' he exclaimed. 'You must know how I feel about you.'

'Edward is your friend, and my husband,' said Kate warmly.

'Kate, the feeling we have for each other is important!' exclaimed Patrick. 'We mustn't deny it or we shall regret it for the rest of our lives!'

'Do you say that to all your women?' asked Kate defensively.

Patrick was genuinely hurt. 'That was unkind!' he said. 'I swear to you, my affairs have meant little to me. You already mean a great deal.'

'Now, perhaps,' said Kate. 'But if I deceived Edward, would you feel the same?'

'We must have the strength to live the important things in life, whatever the outcome!' retorted Patrick passionately. 'Otherwise we waste ourselves.'

'You talk of strength,' said Kate, 'because at the moment, your emotions are strong. But to surrender to them in such a case as this isn't strength, but weakness.'

'Surrender?' he asked quickly, and she saw the flash of hope in his eyes.

'An affair must always seem important at the beginning, I

suppose,' said Kate, 'but by the end it may only have destroyed the love that caused it.'

'An affair?' he asked.

'Isn't that what you are talking about?'

'Do you love me, Kate?'

'Do you love me?'

'I have never yet felt for any woman what I feel for you now,' said Patrick quietly. 'I knew you were the woman I was looking for the moment I saw you at your wedding! It was because of you, I think, that I threw over my childhood sweetheart and quarrelled with my family.'

'Really? Is that true?'

'It's true.'

She was silent for a moment. 'And you really haven't experienced such emotions before?'

'*No*, I'm trying to tell you. No! No! No! Nothing like this. Ever.'

'I wish I could believe you.'

'You can.'

'And those other women?'

'I'm no monk, and they were willing.'

'Then, if I allowed you to persuade me, this . . . this affair, if we had one . . . wouldn't be simply one more in a long list?'

'Certainly not! You are unique, Kate. How often must I tell you?'

'If Edward were to find out, it would break his heart.'

Patrick said slowly, 'Why did you marry him?'

'Because he's the nicest man I know.'

'A good answer, Kate.'

'Besides, my father had affairs and made my mother and me very unhappy, and I knew by instinct that Edward would be loyal.'

'And the little woman he was dancing with at the St Andrew's Ball?' asked Patrick drily.

'She flatters him outrageously and, being a man, he likes it,' said Kate. 'But you are Edward's friend. You must know him better than to think he could be disloyal.'

Patrick nodded. 'You're right. He would have to have changed out of all recognition. You've no idea what an odd little chap he was at school, Kate! Weedy and shy, and a swot. You know he went there as a scholar? He wasn't bad at games, though, which helped him, and he was the pluckiest loser you can imagine!'

'Pluckiest loser?'

'Yes. You couldn't help but admire the little fellow.' He smiled. 'They'd gather round him, those great bullies, and they'd taunt him, provoking him to a fight, and when at last they'd roused him, he'd let fly. Of course he hadn't a chance, but he gave a good account of himself, for all that.'

'You helped him a great deal, I understand.'

'I did what I could, but he'd have won through in the end. He is that sort of a chap.'

'He admires you, too.'

'I know. That's one of his troubles,' said Patrick solemnly. 'He hasn't a high enough opinion of himself, and has too high an opinion of others.'

'That's true,' said Kate, and liked Patrick more for having discerned it.

'So what are we to do, Kate, since we only met after you had married Edward?'

'Do? Nothing. What can we do? We mustn't allow ourselves to love each other, that's all.'

'But we do.'

'I don't know you well enough to risk so much,' said Kate. 'We should have to know each other well before we allowed our feelings so much sway.'

Oddly Patrick seemed pleased. 'You are kind and true, Kate,' he said. 'A nice woman, and a puritan at heart, as I am.'

'You a puritan! With mistresses?' asked Kate.

'Yes, Kate, a puritan — as you'll understand one day.'

'Yet you wish me to be untrue to Edward!' exclaimed Kate.

'How can I help it? The sight of you sends my senses reeling, and the sound of your voice makes me tremble like a foolish schoolboy. When you are near me, even in public, I have to force myself not to take you in my arms. You are magic to me, Kate Marchmont, and there are times when I wish I had never met you!'

Impulsively he took a step towards her, but over her shoulder he saw Edward returning so continued loudly, 'Then one day you and Edward will invite me to your house?'

'Of course we will!' exclaimed Edward enthusiastically. 'Won't we, Kate? The sooner the better!'

'Certainly, Edward, if you wish.'

'I do, my dear. I do. Consider it done!' He turned back to Patrick. 'Any time that suits you, will suit us!'

'I will write to you,' Kate said sedately, but to her surprise she had a sinking of the heart as she spoke. Was it a premonition of unhappiness, she wondered, or just that she knew almost for certain now that one day she would be deceiving Edward, who trusted her to implicitly and loved her so well?

'I shall look forward to hearing from you,' answered Patrick, seriously.

'Capital!' replied Edward, and on the way home he sighed happily: 'There! I knew you'd like him Kate! And he likes you too. He said so! So everything has turned out well.' He patted her hand. 'Hasn't it?'

Kate felt tears coming into her eyes. 'If you say so, Edward, dear,' she answered quietly. 'Perhaps it has.'

CHAPTER FIVE

Patrick and the Marchmonts met frequently from now on and Kate discovered that he was almost as easy to talk to as Edward. She was puzzled by his personality, which was certainly complex; but the magnetism he held for her never slackened for a moment. Indeed, to be near him yet unable to touch him was, for her, a violent mixture of happiness and frustration.

To her surprise he went frequently to the theatre when he was in England, and was very knowledgeable on the subject. He had often watched and admired her parents, but he preferred the experiments going on at the Royal Court, where Granville Barker and Bernard Shaw had initiated their 'new wave'. He was fascinated by Kate's stories of Shaw, for whom he had a great respect. Again to her surprise, taking into account his wealthy background, he was somewhat to the left of Liberalism. He was worried that he had come to Malaya at what might well be a time of crisis, but had resolved to return home if war was declared. He was certain that a war with Germany was inevitable.

'Surely you are being too pessimistic,' protested Kate. There were certainly rumours when we were in England, but only rumours.'

'The Germans are power hungry, don't you see?' replied Patrick. 'They are also very powerful, and spoiling for a fight. They created their High Seas Fleet ten years ago and now they want to prove that it's the finest in the world.'

'But to declare war!'

'They know that until the Royal Navy is destroyed they can't take over from us as a world power,' said Patrick.

'But King Edward was called the Peacemaker!' exclaimed Kate. 'Didn't he see the way the wind was blowing?'

'Of course, but he had politicians with varied views in his Cabinets. That's what democracy is all about.' He grinned cheerfully. 'The strange thing is that we look back on his reign as a golden time, a time of opulence and stability. It's odd that he made such a powerful personal mark when, in fact, the nation in his last years was full of internal conflict. The coal and railway strikes six years ago, for instance. I sympathised with both, I might say.'

'My parents didn't,' said Kate. 'They considered them the work of agitators.'

'And the threat of civil war in Ireland?' demanded Patrick.

'My parents and their friends were worried about that, certainly.'

'And the conflict between the Lords and the Commons? And the talk of revolution in England?'

'There would never be a revolution in England,' exclaimed Kate. 'It's unthinkable!'

'Not at all,' retorted Patrick. 'Old values are changing fast, Kate. As for war with Germany, we came very close to that with the Agadir incident two years ago. It was a timely warning to Churchill and Asquith that we should renew our defences. Now, with Russian encouragement, Italy has declared war on Turkey. Serbia, Bulgaria and Greece have joined in, and they've driven the Turks back as far as Constantinople. Germany is not best pleased, as you can imagine. The Middle East could easily be the cradle of a new world war.'

Kate was a good listener. European politics had not previously been within her range. At home, although the Suffragette Movement was discussed with passion, Socialism often debated and the Irish Question regarded as of immense importance, Europe, and in particular Germany, were seldom 'on the agenda'. Continental squabbles had seemed irrelevant to that 'progress' which was an article of faith in her parents' artistic circle. The circle was nothing if not insular. What Patrick had to say, therefore, was new to her.

Edward was astonished that Kate should take such an active interest in Patrick's political discussions. He himself had been careful not to 'bore' her with such things.

Although she listened, Kate was unconvinced, particularly by Patrick's prophecies of revolution. Her family, like most of the middle class at that time, were Conservative. They loved to argue about a changing future, and Kate herself had had heady visions of a classless and freer society, especially when she was at the Slade; but she had had no real desire to change the status quo, least of all if violence were to be involved.

Change of any kind was alien to Kate's nature; and she could see now that the effect on her personal life of an affair with Patrick would be revolutionary change. The arguments against it were many and strong. It would mean a betrayal of Edward and of her principles of loyalty; not to mention an end to the serenity she felt in his company. As she had told Patrick, finding her father with his mistress all those years ago had scarred her for ever; however strongly she was attracted now, she recoiled from the prospect of being her father's daughter in that respect. The independence of spirit on which she prided herself — her dress, her polo playing, her social ease with the opposite sex, and no doubt many other 'unfeminine traits' discussed over the Mah Jong tables of KL — had always been there for all to see. There had been nothing underhand, nothing of which she was ashamed. All this was true and valid, and she knew it; but working against it now was something stronger ... her love for Patrick, and her longing to be sexually aroused by him.

Yet again, although Edward was even more of a Tory than she was herself, and deeply conventional, with an almost absurdly narrow pride in the Empire, England and St George, he was tolerant of Kate, and respected her views, even if he didn't always agree with them. He would have preferred her to conform, and indeed had told her so; but he never forced her to be other than herself, and would be prepared to defend her to the death against outside criticism.

Patrick, though ostensibly much broader minded, was less lenient to women's aspirations to be free. If she grew closer to him, he would demand that she restrict herself to his conception of correct behaviour. He might believe in more political freedom for the masses, but those masses would be male. Women were an adjunct to the male community, not people in their own right. Also, he had a streak of callousness which Edward had not. He cared, and quite deeply, for the workers on his rubber estate; he was involved in a project to better their children's schools; he visited them in their houses, and interested himself in improved hygiene for them. But when a man-eating tiger appeared on the plantation and killed the last of a file of tappers every time it needed food, he laughed at the men's stupidity in walking single-file. 'The fools,' he said. 'They never remember to walk together, so it serves them right!'

Kate was shocked. Yet analyse him as she might, physically she was totally obsessed. When he was away from her she longed for him ceaselessly. When he was near, every sense seemed alive and she was filled with an unreasoning joy. When his eyes blazed his passion for her, when they were alone, she had to will herself not to walk into his arms; and when he touched her, she felt faint and breathless. Her head ridiculed these feelings, but her heart seemed satisfied that it had found its home. Days and hours passed in a daze of unreal glory.

Patrick too found Kate a puzzle. She was quite unlike any woman who had attracted him before. Her beauty never ceased to move him, her intelligence and high spirits entertained him, her obvious love for him touched him; but to his mind she was too outspoken, too wilful, too unfeminine to be the perfect companion. Her naiveté, her innocence (and even ignorance) of the world, never ceased to surprise him, and her background, though he found it interesting, was not one from which he would have chosen a wife for the great house which one day he would inherit. He had talked with her about her trauma with her father and felt little sympathy. Surely in an actress such a reaction was exaggerated? The Glanvilles had, to be sure, brought her up in a carefully enclosed world, so that she might one day take the place in society which they could never quite attain — but then she had been an art student! Was it possible that she had really retained her innocence at the Slade? Art students were noted for their licentiousness, men and women alike! Had she really been unscathed? That she was unawakened sexually seemed certain. It was very strange. Yet how wonderful it would be to awaken her! Patrick divined the passion of her nature; he knew her to be sensual and, like her, desired her constantly.

As the war clouds gathered over Europe, Patrick was one of the first to join the Malay States Volunteers. Edward soon followed, so the three of them were thrown into even greater proximity and the two men had now even more in common.

In February 1914, Edward and Kate were on one of their regular visits to Patrick. By this time the friendship between the three of them was so well known that it raised no further comment. On this particular Saturday, Edward received an hysterical telephone call from a woman whose husband (a good client of his) had died very suddenly, in suspicious circumstances. Edward decided characteristically that it was his duty to go and comfort her and insisted that Kate and Patrick continue with the morning ride, as planned. On their return for lunch, they found a message from him, to say that he would be detained until the following day.

After the meal was over and the servants had retired to their quarters, Kate went to her room for the afternoon siesta — and there Patrick came to her. In silence he undressed and lay down beside her, drawing her quickly to him. All hesitation swept away on a tide of uncontrollable emotion, she responded with passion.

Patrick's love-making was tender, expert and experienced; as he had guessed, Kate had inherited her father's sensual nature and was now at last fulfilled. Her abandon and generosity enchanted him; she had no false coyness, no feminine wiles; she was straight-forward and adoring, and a brilliant pupil. They made love all afternoon. When at last they lay quiet together, all passion for the moment spent, she whispered to him, bemused with happiness, 'Oh Patrick, I do love you. Say that you love me, too.'

'Hush!' Patrick replied gently. 'Hush, my darling. Don't talk. Lie still.' And when ever they made love thereafter and she wanted him to say how much he loved her, he always answered, 'Hush, my darling. Never talk at such a time. Lie still.'

At dinner Kate was radiant. The afternoon had brought her all that she had ever dreamed of and she was touchingly grateful. The whole world seemed now to revolve around Patrick and her love for him. Nothing and no-one else mattered. From now until death, she was his woman. Patrick, too, was moved; as far as he was able, he also was genuinely in love. But, with Patrick, his head would always rule his heart; just as, for Kate, her heart would always be the more important.

They were careful not to show what they felt in front of the servants, but, when bedtime came and Patrick once again came to her room, Kate gave herself to him as ecstatically as before. He left her just before dawn. And it was fortunate that he did, because Edward returned soon afterwards, tired out by the hysteria of his bereaved client, and by the long interviews he had conducted on her behalf with the police. He slept in late and, by the time he had recovered, Kate was able to behave towards him almost normally.

During the next few weeks Edward was ordered to go to Singapore, where Head Office needed him, and from there to an important case in Penang. He was doing well these days and was considered one of the firm's brightest luminaries. While he was away, Kate and Patrick made love almost every day and Kate was totally content — her sense of guilt forgotten in the strength of her obsession. Edward's final homecoming was difficult for both of them, not only because the exercise of caution did not suit their nature, but because Edward's delight at being back made him reluctant to let Kate out of his sight.

It was during this time that Kate began to realise the significance of the disparities between Patrick's outlook and her own. Her life had been transformed by the affair, but Patrick had no intention of changing his ways in any single respect. He regarded himself as being bound to no-one and by no-one, and, if he found another woman attractive, he declined to believe that it was any business of Kate's. He wasn't married to her, he said; and, even if he were, he would make love to any woman he wished, whenever he wished. Kate suffered tortures of jealousy.

Paradoxically, Patrick disliked doublecrossing Edward even more than Kate did. He knew that it was he, not Kate, who had started the affair, and this made him feel guilty; and his firm belief that physical love could not last, and so was less important than a good friendship, made him value his love for Kate less than he might otherwise have done.

Kate, believing that her feeling for Patrick was the most important thing that had ever happened to her, wanted to make the most of every moment; more than anything, she wanted Patrick to be faithful to her, so that the affair should not be 'cheapened'.

Patrick found this ridiculous. 'An affair is simply an affair,' he said. 'It doesn't help Edward if we decide to call it important. We are doing wrong, and we know it.'

This curious dichotomy in Patrick's nature, which was at once puritanical (as he had warned her) and recklessly sensual, shocked her. For his part, the singlemindedness of her passion, which had so fascinated him at first, now began very slightly to irritate him. His mind was still filled with forebodings about war with Germany. He found it almost incredible that Kate seemed unaffected by anything at all outside their love for one another.

At one point, as near to voicing criticism as he was able in these early days, he said wryly, 'You were made for love, my darling.'

Kate sensed his disapproval and responded tartly, 'And lucky for both of us that I was, Patrick! Neither you nor Edward like me to paint: with you, at least I can employ my only other talent.' Patrick heard the bitterness in her tone and made no answer, since it was true that he didn't admire her paintings, thinking them too strong and too coarse for a woman's work.

Sometimes, restlessly, Kate would say, 'You never mention the word "love", Patrick, and you never say you would like to marry me.'

'How can I break up the marriage of my best friend?' he would retort. And, when she looked at him sharply, he would add, 'He still loves you.'

'I like him,' said Kate. 'You know I do. With all my heart. But I love you.'

Since the physical side of their affair was so good and necessary to them both at this time, they did their best to ignore the fact that they had little else in common. For Kate, her ardent sexual nature now satisfied (which was a joy she had never imagined), this didn't matter too much. For Patrick, it mattered more. He was a selfish man, who all his life had been spoiled by women — and indeed by the knowledge that one day he would come into a great inheritance. Poor Kate was in love for the first and only time in her life; Patrick was not. By the time he learned the strength of his feeling for her, it would be far too late.

Edward meanwhile sensed clearly that Kate was drawing away from him, and was deeply distressed. Being the kind of man he was, it would never have crossed his mind that his adored wife and best friend were lovers. He decided that she needed a holiday, and suggested that she should go away for a week or so. 'I can't come with you,' he said, 'but you should go somewhere a little less humid for a while, darling. This damned climate can get one down. Why not go with friends to Penang Hill?'

Excitedly Kate reported this to Patrick. 'We could go together!' she urged. 'Wouldn't it be wonderful?'

Patrick refused. 'You can imagine the gossip,' he replied. 'I wouldn't dream of it.'

'We would make up a party!'

'People would still gossip.'

'People here gossip even if there's nothing to gossip about,' replied Kate unhappily. 'I heard plenty of gossip about you in Pekan!'

'We have no right to make Edward seem foolish,' retorted Patrick. 'Edward is my friend.'

For a moment Kate nearly struck him. Eventually she told Edward that she had decided not to go on holiday, since it was not the heat but the political situation in Britain that was making her edgy and distressed.

It was now early July, and the news had reached them of the

murder of Archduke Franz-Ferdinand of Austria, in Sarajevo on 28th June. Anxiously Patrick explained to Kate how this might involve all the great continental powers, Russia and France on one side, Germany and Austria-Hungary on the other; if that happened, he said, Britain would surely get drawn into the conflict. It all seemed a bit alarmist and far-fetched in Kuala Lumpur in early July 1914, but on the 24th Austria sent an arrogant ultimatum to Serbia — and Serbia's conciliatory reply was rejected. Austrian armies began to move into the Balkans and against Italy; Austria's ally, Germany, prepared for hostilities against France and Russia. On 3rd August, German armies moved into France and Belgium: Britain, having guaranteed Belgian neutrality, responded swiftly.

The next day, Winston Churchill, First Lord of the Admiralty, sent the following telegram to HM Ships and Establishments: 'COMMENCE HOSTILITIES AGAINST GERMANY.'

The Great War had begun.

CHAPTER SIX

Patrick and Edward now spent most weekends training with the Volunteers. All over Malaya the British newspapers (though long out of date by the time they arrived) were anxiously read from cover to cover. Important items were relayed by cable and such news was up-to-date, but details remained vague; the situation was analysed and re-analysed by the whole country.

For the first year Malaya seemed little affected by the war. In 1915, however, there were two unpleasant incidents. In Singapore, the Indian troops in the Garrison mutinied; but order was restored by the Royal Navy (aided by French and Russian Marines) and the Japanese. Then in Kuala Lumpur, the Malay Police suddenly rioted, and this insurrection, although also easily put down, was a shock to the whole white community. The Malay Police Force, smartly dressed in the little velvet caps which the Malays called Sonkoos and in white 'tutup' (meaning shut or high-necked) jackets, bright blue sarongs and white drill trousers, were thought to be wholeheartedly loyal to the British crown. They were well disciplined and very intelligent, and it had been assumed that they had volunteered to be policemen because of their loyalty to Britain. It had also been accepted as an article of faith by the white community that all the Asian races had not only agreed to British rule, but were positively proud of it. The riot showed this not to have been true as far as all Asiatics were concerned, and a feeling of unease was widespread. No-one doubted that the Royal Navy could defend Eastern waters if need arose, but the willingness of the native population to help in a struggle inland could no longer be taken for granted.

Both Patrick and Edward were frustrated at being out East and unable to help their country's war effort more directly; for a time Patrick seriously contemplated leaving for Home. He was persuaded, however, that should the war spread to the East — or, as seemed more likely, if the internal security situation deteriorated — his presence would be needed. So, reluctantly, he stayed.

His affair with Kate had weathered all storms so far, and indeed at this time he came to depend on her a good deal. She was always there to listen sympathetically to his worries, to soothe and comfort him. She always seemed to understand his moods and her love never faltered.

For Kate, letters from England were a lifeline: she too was frustrated at not being back home. For the first time, she deeply regretted leaving the active working life of her parents and friends. She was forced to live their lives at second hand, and everything her mother wrote described events and occasions which she wished to share.

Edward's mother wrote complaining of the 'inconvenience' of war. With Edward out East and her husband far too old to be called up, and having no other relatives, she had no-one to become particularly anxious about. In Colchester where they lived, although like everyone else they were bound to be a little affected, they didn't appear to be in any danger. But it *was* inconvenient. She knitted for 'the boys' and had coffee mornings to raise money for various good causes, and Mr Marchmont made himself available for suitable para-military duties should the need arise. Food was sparser and domestic help more difficult to keep (since young women were volunteering for all sorts of 'unsuitable' and unlikely jobs). Otherwise their way of life stayed much the same, but Mrs Marchmont felt it to be 'grimmer' and 'more tiring'.

At the Glanville household, matters were very different. Madge's great friend, May Whitty, had thrown herself heart and soul into the war effort, and Madge followed suit. They had been friends since the 1890s, and May was always the leader.

The Whittys lived at 31 Bedford Street, Covent Garden, in a pretty top-floor flat which could only be reached by walking up eighty-four stairs. They had a housekeeper called Frances (who kept enormous cats), a cook and two maids and also a small fox-terrier called Tuff. Though May was often in pain (she suffered greatly from migraines), and Ben, one of the most popular West End actors of the day, was nearly always in work, this didn't stop them from creating a 'salon' of gifted and interesting actors and writers, of which Madge and Harry were regular members.

At first the little dinners for twelve or fourteen were fairly formal; though not lavish by the standards of the time, a typical menu would include soup, fillets of sole with mushroom sauce, kidneys on toast, hot ham with port-wine sauce, corn fritters and new potatoes, lemon soufflé and coffee. Soon, however, the circle grew to such an extent that the suppers became less formal and more frequent, and friends would drift in nearly every evening for cold meat and salad, fruit, cheese, beer, wine and whisky. Among the regular visitors were the beautiful young actress Ethel Barrymore, with Winston Churchill in constant attendance; Henry Esmond the playwright and actor, with his wife Eva Moore; Anthony Hope, author of *The Prisoner of Zenda*; and Granville Barker, whose work Patrick so admired, and whose avant-garde productions at the Royal Court had changed the face of British theatre.

In the summer, most of the gang would go down to the river at Cookham, Marlow, Henley or Maidenhead, and naturally Madge and Harry went too. The Glanvilles were never in the theatrical or social vanguard, as the Websters were; May was quite happy to discuss venereal disease and to question the sanctity of marriage (though her own was so happy), which shocked Madge — but the two women loved cycling and punting and the tuppenny tube, and May's ardent feminism, which had left Madge cold before the war, now came to be of importance to her as well.

It happened like this. May Whitty's first foray into activities other than acting had come in 1892 with a meeting, which Madge too attended, of the Theatrical Ladies' Guild. This organisation was set up to help those in need in the profession (not only actresses but wardrobe mistresses and stage-hands, too). It took care of children, paid doctor's bills, and provided blankets and coal in the winter and spectacles and dentures at all seasons. To Madge's initial dismay, May had then been attracted to the Women's Suffrage Movement, not least because she had heard that, in the eyes of the law, women were legally bracketed with 'children, criminals and lunatics'. Here she had the support of Edith Craig (Ellen Terry's daughter) and her friend (Miss) Christopher St John, who lived in the flat under hers in Bedford Street. To her shame ('I'm a coward,' she said), May was never a militant, but she marched in procession and went to meetings. Eventually she joined, and soon became Chairman of, the Actresses' Franchise League. Its original function was to hold meetings, write and distribute propaganda for the suffragette cause, organise mass demonstrations and deputations and produce and perform propaganda shows. Its shows were written, acted, directed, stage-managed and publicised by women. But now, under May Whitty's influence, it became the first of the suffrage organisations to put its talents and experience to wartime use. It was this that attracted Madge.

Madge lost no time in relating her adventures to Kate. She had all her life been an enthusiastic and 'chatty' letter-writer, who never came to see the telephone as an adequate substitute. Her urgent need to communicate was further stimulated by the war and by her beloved daughter being half a world away. Although vivid and amusing, her letters were sometimes difficult to decipher: her handwriting was large and generous, and she was a great underliner, but in a patriotic attempt to economise she had adopted the practice of turning the notepaper sideways when she had filled it up, and writing across what was already there. One such letter, dated 20 November 1914, read as follows:

My own dearest Kate,

Oh what a treat! Your darling letter with its birthday wishes arrived this morning, on the *very day*! *Wasn't* that clever of you?! How *did* you manage it? I told Papa it was my favourite present, and he didn't mind a *scrap*, though he had given me a *beautiful* necklace of seed pearls which I *wish* I could show you. Yes darling we are *both well*, as I hope you and Edward are.

Now my dear for my *great* news. I have joined the Actresses Franchise League!!! May (Whitty) insisted and I felt I couldn't refuse, though I'm afraid your father is less than pleased! Oh *dear*!! It doesn't of course mean that your old mother has become a suffragette and is expected to chain herself to railings!! May has managed to transform the League into a *patriotic* organisation which she intends shall show the men that *we women* are as indispensable to victory as *they* are, and shame them *that* way into giving us the Vote. Isn't that a perfectly *splendid* idea?

We are working on a scheme to replace men with *women* in office work, in hospitals and factories, as cab drivers and on the land. I am turning my sitting-room here into an *office*, and if Papa doesn't like it — and I'm afraid he *doesn't* poor dear — well, he'll just have to spend even *more* time at the Garrick Club!

Eva and Decima Moore have started another *splendid* thing which I have joined called the Women's Emergency Fund, to help the *poor* refugees from Belgium and to find worthwhile occupations for our young actresses, dancers, wardrobe mistresses etc., who have been thrown out of work. Among other things they are being trained to make *toys*. Almost all the toys in the shops before the war were made by the *Germans*! Would you credit it?

You cannot imagine darling how splendidly the women are answering the many and different calls made on them. As you know I haven't always seen eye to eye with May, much as I love her, but *now* I *know* she is *right*. Whatever else comes out of this war, women will *never again* accept that their place must *only* be in the home. And what better people to teach them this than we *actresses* who have *known* it *all the time*!!

My darling I must stop now or I shall miss the mail. Papa joins me in sending you *all our love*. Please God the war will *soon* be over and we shall see you again — this is the prayer of

Your Ever Loving
Mama

In other letters Madge described how, after much heart-searching among the original members, the League had been rechristened the British Women's Hospital (thereby winning many new recruits, not only from the theatre) and how it had set about raising money to turn the Star and Garter Hotel at Richmond into a home for permanently disabled ex-service men; also how her own pet scheme, the Nation's Fund for Nurses, was becoming so successful that it looked like becoming 'a central organisation for the training and welfare of that much-put-upon profession'.

The early letters faithfully reflected the general euphoria of the first months of the war — the cheering, singing, flag-waving crowds, all over England but especially in London, massing in front of Buckingham Palace to show their loyalty. Madge declared that everyone knew that Britain was certain to win in the end, as she had always won in the past. The only worry was that, because of the fear of air raids, the theatres had been closed — which made Harry very restless and frustrated, as his current play had been a great hit. Never mind, the war would be over by Christmas, she said — as, indeed, did everyone she knew. Meanwhile Harry was filling in time with a large map of the Western Front, moving little coloured flags to represent the opposing armies. For many weeks the movement was all in one direction, until the Germans were eventually held at the very gates of Paris. Total disaster had been narrowly averted, but it was now clear that the war would *not* be over by Christmas. As the mood of the nation changed, the letters became obsessed with the terrible casualties in the trenches, the shell-shock and gas attacks, and with the shattered boys who returned to British hospitals, or on leave. Most of the Glanvilles' friends had relatives who had died, or were maimed for life, and the war was dragging on and on. When would it ever end?

And here *she* was, thought Kate — in Malaya, doing nothing!

But even had she been allowed to do something, what was there to do out here? The war hadn't touched Malaya. She hated domesticity and gardening, and there were plenty of servants for such things, which anyway couldn't possibly assist the war effort. Her painting, to which she resorted more and more, was of no use to the world at large — and of no interest, either, to the two most important men in her life. It was no help to send food parcels, or do mending, sewing or knitting for anyone at Home from out here. She might fervently agree that a woman's place needn't necessarily be in the home, but under these circumstances there was nowhere else *to* go! What could she *do*?

One day, when Edward was on active service up north in Kelantan, Patrick arrived for dinner and found her reduced to tears by her frustration. He was shocked by this unusual sight.

'Whatever's the matter, Kate?' he asked.

'Nothing,' she said. 'I was just being silly.'

'Edward should be all right,' said Patrick soothingly, misunderstanding the cause of her distress.

'Yes.'

'Are you worried about him?'

'I'm worried about either of you, if you go towards danger,' said Kate.

'It isn't like you to cry,' said Patrick.

'Not in public. No.'

'Do you consider me "public"?'

'In this respect, I suppose I do.'

'I'm sorry.' He sounded hurt. 'I didn't know you worried about Edward?'

'No. I imagine not.'

Patrick was astonished. 'Have I done anything to upset you, Kate?' he asked.

'No,' she said. 'Nothing different from usual.' She found herself impatient with him and wanted to provoke him to a better understanding of her.

'What do you mean?' he asked.

'You have always made it perfectly plain that you think I don't consider Edward's happiness enough,' said Kate sourly, 'and that you yourself consider it far beyond my own happiness. I resent it.' He considered this in silence, and Kate went on. 'What's more, you make it obvious that you only worry about possible gossip about our affair when you think it might hurt Edward or you, but not when it might hurt me.'

After a moment he said, 'You mean that you and I should be chaperoned tonight, for instance?'

This took her by surprise, but she answered firmly, 'If we don't want to cause gossip, yes.'

'No-one will know.'

'There is always a risk.'

Patrick nodded thoughtfully. 'Yes, you're right, Kate. I have been insensitive. I agree, and I'm sorry.'

'Thank you,' she answered quietly. Immediately she was touched.

'Why have you never told me before?' asked Patrick.

'I had no idea that you would care.'

'Come now, Kate. That's not fair!'

'It's the truth.'

'That sounds as if you don't like me very much,' he said.

'I love you physically,' said Kate. 'That's what you always say to me, when I ask if you love me. I'm beginning to understand what you mean.'

Again he considered her remark with care. 'Have I hurt you very much then, Kate?'

'Sometimes.'

'Is that why you were crying? Because I have been insensitive?'

'No, as a matter of fact it was not about you or Edward that I was crying. Like both of you, I *hate* being here in Malaya while the war rages in Europe! I'm homesick! I long to be Home with other women of my age — nursing, or driving an ambulance, or even working in a factory — not leading this empty, useless, frivolous life.'

'Being a wife is not a frivolous matter,' said Patrick sententiously.

Kate looked at him in complete amazement, then laughed without amusement.

'You find that funny?'

'Coming from you, very funny! Anyway,' she continued, 'one can't exactly describe the domesticity out here as burdensome, can one? Especially as Edward and I have no children!'

'Would Edward have liked children?'

'There you go again,' said Kate softly. 'Always the implied criticism! We both would, as it so happens. It simply hasn't occurred.'

'I beg your pardon.'

'And the fault is not necessarily mine.'

Patrick changed the subject. 'I'm sorry you are feeling homesick,' he said. 'I can understand your wanting to do something in this war. We all do. All I am saying is that as Edward's wife your first duty is to him.'

Kate laughed. 'And my second to you? You two are my war work are you?'

'I'm afraid I don't find that at all amusing.'

'Neither do I, Patrick. You've sometimes said that I have the brain of a man...'

'That's true,' replied Patrick.

'...yet the idea that I should use it, and *work* like a man upsets you. Why?'

'It's unfeminine.'

Kate laughed again. 'How like my father you are, sometimes!' she exclaimed. 'Unfeminine! You fear it as a threat to your masculinity. When we first met,you called yourself a rebel...'

'In many ways I am one.'

'...and unconventional!'

'At least my standards are not "suburban", as you call it. I live honestly.'

'If that means selfishly, I agree.'

'It means that I don't say one thing and do another!' retorted Patrick hotly.

'You would deny me the satisfaction of doing the same,' said Kate.

'You are married.'

'By all accounts it was expected that you should have been married too,' said Kate.

'I don't understand you at all this evening, my dear.' Patrick was white with anger. 'I'm sorry you feel sad, but you seem to be taking it out on me.'

'And, goodness knows, a diet of total flattery would suit you better!'

'Bitterness doesn't suit you Kate. You have never discouraged my wish to love you.'

'No, indeed I haven't!' agreed Kate. 'My love for you has been the only profound emotion I have felt since childhood. So it's hardly surprising, is it, that I should become a little sour when my lover shows no comparable depth of feeling? I believe you're embarrassed that I care so much! You'd be more at home with a woman as superficial as yourself. Wouldn't you, Patrick?'

'I like women to be gentle and natural and loving,' said Patrick.

'For "natural", substitute "feminine",' murmured Kate acidly.

'Very well, feminine,' said Patrick. 'And if that means to you superficial, then you're right. I like my women to be superficial.'

'Perhaps we're all superficial in the end,' sighed Kate. 'All except the great contributors — great scientists, artists, writers, philosophers and religious leaders. And what a waste! I always used to think that life should be lived to the hilt. Ellen Terry told me on my wedding day never to be afraid to live, yet for most of us it's so difficult to achieve! Don't you mind about not living fully? Don't you think all of us should be encouraged to live life fully and truly? Every single one of us? Men and women alike?'

'I don't know,' said Patrick. 'I enjoy my life. I suppose I tend to accept things more than you.'

'You have had so much more given to you than most people.' said Kate.

'I haven't thought about life in those terms,' said Patrick.

'And yet you care so idealistically about so much else in the world!' exclaimed Kate.

'I agree that life is short and should be used to some purpose,' replied Patrick. 'But whether women would be happier if their interests ranged outside the home is another matter. I gather that *is* what you're saying?' He suddenly sounded distantly polite.

'What we might lose, if we became freer from the home, is our disastrous need for total satisfaction in love,' said Kate bitterly. 'Marriage is a trap, because the life the man leads entirely conditions the one the woman will lead with him! But perhaps free love is even worse because, with our passionate need for fulfilment, we might all allow ourselves to become attached to entirely unsuitable men. I don't know ... but heaven knows, I care!'

'You married Edward, who is a good man and gives you the best life he can: and I am your lover, and you have often told me that I am satisfactory,' said Patrick forcefully.

He still sounded stiff and disapproving, and Kate, realising his displeasure, retorted, 'I sometimes wonder if your social ideals are a substitute for love of a closer, warmer kind!'

'Now you are being unkind!'

'And we're quarrelling!' exclaimed Kate. 'And life is certainly too short for that!'

She went over to him impulsively, and kissed him.

Patrick sighed fondly. 'There are times when I don't understand you, Kate my love,' he said, 'but luckily there's more to our affair than that!'

This made Kate laugh, and they were happy and at ease again.

The conversation then turned to more practical channels, and Patrick stayed at the Marchmont house for the ten days that Edward was away.

Years afterwards, Kate was glad that they had had this particular spell of time together. Patrick treated her gently, and with a consideration for her feelings which he hadn't shown before; and she in turn was able to show him that she ran her house with extreme efficiency. She saw to it that he was excellently fed, and they lived for the time at their disposal like husband and wife, though ostensibly they slept in different rooms. She had the satisfaction of knowing that few other women in Malaya could have provided the material comforts so attractively, or indeed the sexual delights, and because of the quarrel she too was gentler and more considerate.

During this time alone together, Patrick told her about his early life and she felt that a new and perhaps friendlier phase of their relationship had begun.

Like Edward, Patrick was an only child. He was the poor relation (though not in any sense poverty stricken) of a very wealthy family. He had been sent to the same school as Edward because his parents didn't wish to afford Eton, and was despised by his cousins on this account. His mother, who was connected to many of England's greatest families, was very pretty but frivolous and cold-hearted, and had no time for children. Patrick had always adored her but he never felt close to her. Now she was chronically ill with an undiagnosed complaint, and Patrick, al-though he could have been of no use to her, would have liked to have been able to see her more often. Malaya seemed very far away from her, as well as from the war.

His father was a rascal. Amusing, attractive, idle and a spendthrift, he drifted through life, borrowing money and doing no work at all.

Julia Lavingham, the girl there had been all the fuss about, was the daughter of great friends of all the family. Julia and he had met as children, and it was because it had been so completely taken for granted by everyone that they would marry that Patrick had suddenly felt trapped.

He and Kate spoke of the great house he would inherit one day, and it was evident that Patrick was in love with it.

'It's an odd thing,' he said. 'For the last few generations the house has gone from uncle to nephew every time. Never father to son! It's a wonderful place, and I'm a very lucky man.'

'I long to see it,' said Kate.

'Yes.'

Patrick didn't press the point, but Kate didn't notice.

'Won't the fact that you came here in some disgrace affect your chance of inheritance?' she asked.

'No. Not unless I really blot my copybook, like going to gaol or something!'

They talked about the war endlessly; they talked about Kate's home and family, about the theatre and the Slade. They didn't talk about her relationship with Edward, however, nor ever again did Patrick imply that he pitied her husband.

It was the last opportunity they had to spend any length of time together. From then on, Edward was at home.

CHAPTER SEVEN

The war in Europe dragged on but nothing further happened to shatter the calm in Malaya. Tin and rubber, the two economic mainstays of the country, were in tremendous demand. The country became even richer. More schools were being built and they were well run; so were the railways. Hospitals were efficient and roads were enormously improved. Although the casualty lists in Europe grew longer and longer, Edward, Kate and Patrick, having become inured to their own situation, lived relatively normal lives. Even the emotions, tensions and evasions affecting two of the trio had come to seem normal to them.

All of them still wished to be in England — Edward and Patrick to fight, and Kate to help in the war effort in any way she could — but since there was no hope, they made the best of what they had.

Meanwhile Kate's passion for Malaya was growing ever stronger. She was eternally fascinated by the hot sun, by the great variety of the costumes, the flowers, the food and the scents, and by the national customs and pageantry — the Chinese weddings, the even more colourful and joyful Chinese funerals (the Chinese view being that if you are going on to happiness when you die, death is cheerful not sad), the great dragon parades of the Chinese New Year; Taipoosum, the Indian religious festival, where spectacular parades included men who threw themselves into trances and put nails through the flesh of their bodies, their hands and their noses without feeling pain; the firewalkers in the Batu Caves, who walked on blazing coals and strips of molten metal, and again knew no pain; the Malay 'wrongings' (their word for dancing); Javanese puppet plays; the Tamil Dramas which lasted two days, and the Chinese Operas which lasted anything up to a week. Even the jungle was being opened up, and Fraser's Hill was becoming accessible on horseback.

'The Hill' was sixty-three miles from Kuala Lumpur. At night it was very still, the silence sometimes suddenly broken by weird sounds: the almost human 'coo-ee' of the Argus pheasant, the call of the orang-utangs, noises like steam whistles from large monkeys, and isolated yells, growls, plungings and slitherings — the sounds of pursuit and capture. Day broke in a heavy mist which disappeared at sunrise. Immediately, the jungle became a riot of sound. Cicada beetles clattered, insects of every description chirped, screeched and buzzed. Birds whooped, yelled hoarsely, and screamed. Monkeys called, quarrelled, chattered and crashed the branches as they swung from tree to tree; the wah-wahs hooted as troops of them, accompanied by their females, gyrated and leapt in the morning sun; and magnificent butterflies of all colours and sizes flittered through the glades. Kate and Edward went there as often as they could.

Back in the plains, elephants were still used to help with felling and moving timber; and sultans would ride out on them in bejewelled howdahs on their gala days. Kate loved it all.

For Patrick it was rather different. Such spontaneous deep attachment was out of the question. He quite enjoyed Malaya as a country but his whole being was directed to the time when he would inherit Mallerby. Everything that happened to him until then was of secondary importance.

One day, out of the blue, Edward was sent for again to Head Office in Singapore. He came back with exciting news: they had offered him the chance to buy the Kuala Lumpur branch as an independent firm which would carry his own name. Excitedly he discussed the situation with Kate. It would mean getting a loan from the bank: was she willing to keep her expenses down for a time? Kate was as enthusiastic as he was and, in due course, the firm of 'Marchmont' was established.

A few weeks later, Kate realised that she was pregnant.

'Are you glad?' Patrick asked when she broke the news to him.

'Of course,' she said. 'Aren't you?'

'Yes, of course.'

Kate smiled happily.

'You do sleep with Edward?' enquired Patrick.

Kate looked at him sharply. 'Yes!' she said. 'Why? We are, after all, still married.'

'Then the baby could just as well be his,' said Patrick.

'Yes,' said Kate. 'But it could also be yours.'

'Edward has always wanted a child,' said Patrick. 'He has often told me so.'

'I have always wanted one, too,' said Kate.

'He must never know if it isn't his.'

'Of course not.'

'I'm glad you feel that.'

There was an awkward pause.

'Aren't you pleased that there is a possibility of the child being yours?' Kate said slowly.

'No,' said Patrick. 'It may be very risky.'

'In what way?'

'We may be found out at last.'

'Is that all that matters to you?'

'It has its importance.'

Kate was deeply hurt. 'How little our affair must have meant to you!' she exclaimed bitterly. 'I thought you would be proud and happy!'

'Rather premature for that,' he replied drily. 'We'll have to see who it looks like first!'

'You are right,' said Kate. 'How silly and sentimental of me to have wished that all those hours we have spent together should have been worthwhile for both of us! After all, a loose woman can't expect *love*. Only sex. And sex is far easier than love. It is narcissistic, it massages the vanity. And it involves no obligations.'

'You know I don't like it when you get bitter, Kate,' said Patrick.

'Or honest,' added Kate drily.

'Or honest. If honesty means wishing that the child was mine.'

'It also means I wish I'd never met you,' flared Kate.

'Oh come on, Kate. We've had wonderful times together,' said Patrick pacifically.

'Why not?' retorted Kate. 'I'm a good lover. I am also clean, so there's no danger of disease for you. And I don't cost you money.'

Now even Patrick was outraged. 'I don't know whether I can ever forgive you for what you have just said!' he flared.

'Yet I'm supposed to forgive you for what you have just said to me!'

'It is not quite the same thing,' replied Patrick.

'No wonder Mother and her greatest friends are feminists!' exclaimed Kate. 'One day women will refuse to be treated like second-class citizens, and I don't blame them!'

'They will lose a great deal,' said Patrick. 'They don't realise how much!'

'The lazy ones and the ones who use their femininity to gain money and position, may be. But in my view, the others stand to gain more than they will lose!' said Kate. 'It isn't only love I've learned through knowing you, Patrick.'

Patrick looked at his watch. 'You will forgive me if I go now?' he asked coldly. 'I have an appointment.'

'I feel sure you have,' agreed Kate.

When he had gone, Kate broke down and wept. This time she had probably gone too far, but she believed that the relief of speaking absolutely truthfully for once was worth it. She also saw that, in spite of being central to two men's lifes, she was very much alone.

Kate saw very little of Patrick during the next few months; and when she did, she realised he had changed towards her. There was nothing she could pin down in his behaviour but instinctively she knew that he had drawn away. For the moment, however, nothing mattered except that she was carrying the child.

She didn't feel well. The heat, which she had so enjoyed until now, seemed suddenly intolerably foreign to her. So did the constant blue of the sky, the continuous flowering of the trees and the raucous calls of the tropical birds; and yet, when the rainy season came, with thunderstorms darkening the skies for an hour or two as regularly as clockwork at the same time every afternoon, she felt just as ill, just as homesick. Lightning lit up the lowering clouds. Rain marched relentlessly across the forests and towards the city, in a great restless roar. Birds and insects fell silent and she had blinding headaches.

Patrick's absence began to fret and disturb her and Edward's delight made her guilty. She wept over her mother's letters, with their loving and excited messages from herself and Harry; and Ayah's solicitude gave her no comfort.

The months dragged by and when at last the time came the pregnancy was a hard one.

Kate's baby daughter was born in August and Edward was as proud a father as there had ever been. The baby had grey eyes like her mother's, and vestigial traces of red hair which he found enchanting. Kate realised at once that the child was Patrick's. She breast-fed her, but felt frail and tired for several months. Patrick had shown no sign of appreciating his paternity and seldom enquired how Kate or the child was doing.

'Strange...' mused Edward, puzzled by his friend's attitude. 'I suppose that he doesn't realise how we feel about having a child, Kate, being a bachelor!'

'As long as you are happy, then I am,' said Kate, feeling guilty and sorry for him.

'I'm happy,' said Edward. 'Never been happier in my life.'

CHAPTER EIGHT

To Kate's astonishment, Edward seemed to suspect nothing. He seemed not at all surprised that the child had red hair, even though neither his nor Kate's family had ever had a red-head between them. It was Edward who suggested that Patrick should be her godfather, and Patrick reluctantly agreed. The baby was christened Elizabeth Katherine, and called Bess in honour of Elizabeth the First, who was a heroine of Kate's. She was large and placid and showed early signs of above average intelligence.

Edward insisted on seeing his 'daughter' every morning before he went to the office and immediately on his return home in the evenings, when, with a drink in his hand, he would watch her being bathed by the second ayah. Second ayah — called 'Ayah Ketchil' (meaning little ayah) — was a pretty young Malay girl, niece of 'First Ayah', who was Kate's own personal maid. The little Malay girl adored Bess and Bess happily responded.

Only one thing worried Kate in these early days. Although nothing was said in her presence, both the Ayahs and indeed the entire staff quite clearly regarded Patrick as the father. But still Edward seemed to notice nothing. Kate was relieved but ashamed by Edward's acceptance of his paternity, and even despised him for being so trusting, and so blind. In time, she recovered from the difficult childbirth and to her surprise and pleasure found that she had a much stronger maternal instinct than she had expected. She hoped that when he had adjusted to the situation, Patrick would return to her with his love strengthened; but nothing of the sort happened, and once she was well again he made it quite clear that the affair was over.

'How unfair!' she exclaimed. 'Bess was certainly as much your fault as mine!'

'A child needs a settled home,' said Patrick crisply. 'We must think of the child, Kate.'

'What about me?' demanded Kate. 'Surely the child's happiness depends on the mother's?'

'It depends on its mother's *love*,' replied Patrick, coldly.

At last Kate came to realise that Patrick did indeed mean that the affair was over. She tried to reason with him but he would have none of it. They quarrelled, bitterly and often; and, since a reconciliation could no longer be celebrated with love-making, their relationship became openly hostile.

In her despair, Kate began to drink too much. It was a deliberate act of self-destruction. Edward, believing her drinking to be the result of her illness, was gentle with her but also horrified. 'You've a baby to think of Kate!' he protested. 'She needs you. You don't want to hurt her, do you?'

'No, I don't want to hurt her.'

'Then don't drink, darling,' he implored.

'I can't help it.'

'We must see a doctor.'

'No!' Kate was violent. 'Leave me! Let me recover in my own way.'

Patrick made no secret of his disgust. 'If there's one thing I cannot bear, it's a drunken woman, Kate,' he said. 'For God's sake, pull yourself together!' But she took no notice.

Things came to a head at a party about eighteen months later, at the Marchmonts' home. Kate, who was openly flirting with an all-too-willing young planter, lurched over to Patrick with the young man in tow.

'Hullo, Patrick,' she said, and her speech was slurred, 'I don't think I remember your having said good evening to your hostess.'

'You seemed to be otherwise occupied when I arrived,' said Patrick, glancing distastefully at the planter.

'Indeed?' asked Kate. 'Is that meant to be an excuse for your very bad manners?'

'I made my salutations to Edward,' said Patrick. 'And when you had had time for me, I would have made them to you.'

'Johnnie,' said Kate, smiling sweetly at her escort, 'run away now, will you? I think Mr de Moulins needs a talking to, don't you? I'll see you later, my dear.'

'Is that a promise?' asked Johnnie, eagerly.

'It's a promise,' said Kate. She gave him a lingering look, for Patrick's benefit as much as Johnnie's, and blew him a kiss. The young man left them, happily.

'The first time I ever met you, Kate, you told me that you weren't a flirt,' said Patrick warmly. 'It was one of the things that

attracted me to you! You seem to have come a long way since
then.'

'Haven't we all?' retorted Kate.

'I wish you wouldn't drink, Kate! You'll wreck yourself and you
know I hate it!'

'May I ask what my drinking has to do with you?' demanded
Kate coldly.

'I'm still fond of you,' said Patrick.

'Are you?' Her heart lurched, in spite of herself.

'Of course! But when you behave like this you make me
ashamed of you. As for leading that young man on, in public in
your husband's own house, it's despicable! *You* should be
ashamed, too.'

He was jealous though neither realised it; and Kate was deeply
hurt.

'Damn you, Patrick! Damn you for being a callous, pompous
prig! Whose fault is it that I have become what I am?'

'Women who swear bore me,' said Patrick, furiously, and he
began moving away.

Driven beyond self control, Kate tried to throw her drink in his
face, but the tumbler slipped from her grasp and hit the wall. It
broke and a flying splinter caught Patrick above his right eye,
cutting the eyebrow. Very deliberately, he took out his handkerchief, and pressed it against his forehead.

'And I abhor self pity, too!' he added contemptuously, then
turned on his heel and left her.

Edward was welcoming late arrivals and hadn't seen the
incident. But Nancy Banks had. She was still fruitlessly pursuing
Edward and lost no time in telling him that there had been a
quarrel, though she had not been near enough to hear what was
said. Edward appeared to dismiss her story but was in fact very
upset. Ironically he made the correct assumption that the
cause was Kate's drinking and that Patrick shared his distress
at it.

Edward had a few weeks' leave owing and decided there and
then to take Kate and Bess away. First they went for ten days to
Port Dickson where Kate, who loved swimming, began to feel
restored, and Bess, in the care of Ayah Ketchil, was enraptured by
her introduction to the seaside. Next they went to stay with friends
in Singapore, where the social life was as usual very hectic. Then,
leaving Bess and 'little Ayah' behind, they sailed for Japan. Japan

had signed a peace treaty with Britain in 1912 and was a popular spot for local holidays: on the whole the trip was a success. As usual Kate revelled in life on board ship; and she found in Japan another country that she would be in love with all her days. Also, Patrick's jibe about self-pity had had its shock effect and she was enough of a fighter to determine to pull herself together. But the central cause of her unhappiness remained.

They returned home nonetheless in better spirits and Kate, who had been as alarmed as Patrick and Edward by her behaviour at the party, had almost managed to stop drinking.

Soon afterwards, the war ended.

When Bess reached her third birthday she began taking part in the daily ritual of the other children of her own age in the white community. She went every weekday morning with Ayah Ketchil to the 'padang' in front of the 'Spotted Dog', to play. The padang was a large open space on which the ayahs and Chinese amahs congregated with their charges — except at weekends, when cricket was played. Bess loved this morning excursion by rickshaw. They went from the Ampang Road where they lived, past the ornate biscuit-pink Federal buildings (and the large bust of Edward the Seventh on its plinth, for which Bess conceived such a passion that she insisted on kissing it each day), and from there on to the huge lawn where, bonnetted or hatted, the children raced or toddled to their heart's content while their nurses gossipped until it was time to return home for 'tiffin'. After the meal Bess would have her daily siesta (regarded as essential for all children and white women in Malaya), followed by play-time either in her own garden or in the gardens of friends.

She already had unusual good looks. Her bright red hair was bobbed and worn with a fringe; it was straight and shiny and looked like a little cap. She had enormous grey eyes in a pale round face, and the Glanville women's straight little nose. Already, too, she had a strong will and well knew how to get her own way. Though remarkably content on her own, she was adaptable and accommodating with other children. With Ayah Ketchil she used charm, and could twist her round her little finger; with grown ups, she had found that clowning produced the best results. She had a fiery temper but seldom lost it. Kate saw the kind of child she was and, though she was enchanted and nearly as proud of her as Edward, was worried at her precocity.

Edward was due for his English leave the year following; the question of Bess's schooling would then become urgent. If they didn't leave her in England this time they would have to wait until she was eight or nine before they had another opportunity, and though four was an early age to be left alone to start her education so far from home, eight or nine was considered too late. The hot and humid climate of Malaya was thought unhealthy for European children; besides which, Kate was anxious to remove Bess from Edward's sight before her growing resemblance to Patrick became too obvious.

Even at this early stage, Edward and Kate were very much against a theatrical career for Bess. After much deliberation it was settled that she should go to a small exclusive private kindergarten in Berkshire, where the headmistress, Miss Wells, was a friend of Edward's parents, and where several other small children from various outposts of empire were also boarding.

The three of them set sail in the summer of 1921. The voyage took a month and Edward, who was still a bad traveller, took to his bunk quite often; but Kate and Bess weathered it well. In fact Bess, though so young, became almost a heroine among the children after routing the ship's bully-boy, who had pinched her. She flew at him with such ferocity that she blackened his eye and when his mother complained to Kate the other mothers all sided with her, so the bullying stopped. Kate was proud of Bess, but astonished and not a little worried by the strength of the reaction in one so very young. Edward when he heard of it was, quite simply, delighted.

Once in England there were visits to both sets of grandparents for inspection.

Kate's reunion with Madge and Harry was rapturous. The seven years of separation had changed them all quite considerably and the Glanvilles had now moved to a beautiful new home on Richmond Hill.

Madge, slower moving now and very statuesque, was busier than ever these days, serving on committees as well as being almost constantly in work. Her hair was greying and there were the inevitable signs of age around her eyes and throat, but her personality had lost none of its assurance. Harry, who had developed a small paunch, was as merry and witty as ever but had become involved with the woman who was to remain his mistress until the end of his life — Violet Tremayne, a dark and soulful young actress with little sense of humour.

Both Madge and Harry took to Bess at once and, despite the

edict that the child was not to be allowed to go on the stage, Madge guiltily gave her a cardboard toy theatre with little puppets to play with. To Kate's consternation this immediately became her favourite toy. Madge was dismayed by the change she saw in Kate. She noticed a marked loss of confidence and self-respect. She dressed carelessly and had become withdrawn and silent. Sometimes, thought Madge, she looked downright unhappy.

Madge determined to put matters right. One afternoon when, at her instigation, Harry had taken Edward to his club for lunch, she tackled Kate on the subject.

'My darling,' she asked gently. 'Is anything worrying you? If it is, I should so love to try and help!'

'I don't understand, Mama,' said Kate, smiling.

'I think you do,' replied Madge. 'You seem so unsure of yourself, and there is such a sad expression in your eyes sometimes. What has happened? I'm still your mother, darling. Won't you talk to me about it?'

'I don't think talking will help anything,' said Kate, 'But it's sweet of you to want to try. I'm sorry, though, that I look sad. I am so happy to be here with you!'

'You also seem a little nervy, darling, and — forgive me — you seem not to care about your looks.'

'Looks!' exclaimed Kate. 'What do they matter?'

'More than you would think,' said Madge. 'If you let yourself go, you'll find that some of your friends will go, too.'

'Then they aren't friends!'

'Maybe not. But they might be entertaining enough as companions, who could take you out of yourself...' Kate looked surprised. '...and sometimes we need that.'

'Yes, indeed we do!' agreed Kate fervently.

'So tell me what's worrying you. You are our only child, and you know how we both love you.'

'I do,' said Kate, 'and it makes all the difference to my life, I assure you.'

'Then tell me, Kate.'

'There's noting to tell.'

'Is it Edward?'

'Oh no!'

'You're happy with him?'

'He's still the nicest man I know.'

'And you don't regret making a life in Malaya?'

'No . . .' said Kate slowly. 'I don't. Even though it means being
so far away from you.'

'You've no idea how much we miss you!'

'And I you, Mama . . . Mama?'

'Yes, darling?'

'May I ask you something equally personal?'

'Of course.'

'You won't be angry with me?'

'Certainly not!'

'You must know about Violet Tremayne?'

'Naturally. I would have to be very blind not to.'

'You don't mind?'

'Of course I do.'

'Then couldn't you send her packing? She's so cheap, and so
silly, and so unworthy of Papa!'

'She gives him a feeling of youth that he needs very badly,' said
Madge.

'But what about you?'

'I learned to live with Papa's whims long ago.' Madge smiled.
'We're back to our old quarrel, Kate!'

Kate laughed. 'I know,' she said, 'but I'm grown up now and it
seems unlike you to be so passive!'

'Kate,' said Madge seriously. 'Please try and understand me.
I'm not passive. I'm what I call a "positive accepter". I've been a
very lucky woman. I married the man I was in love with, and still
love — and not every woman does that.' She looked at Kate
shrewdly. 'I have been doubly blessed in also having work that I
love. But in a full and rewarding life there is bound to be disappointment and frustration and pain. And for that one needs
courage — no less important in peacetime than in war, Kate,
though of a very different kind!'

'Yes,' Kate was thoughtful.

'Does what I've said help you at all with your problems?' asked
Madge.

Again Kate laughed. 'If you mean, is Edward the unfaithful
type, no he isn't.' She took a breath, then spoke in a great rush. 'But
I was silly enough to fall in love with another man, Mama, and the
finish of the business has left me depressed. That's all.'

'There's no question of divorce?' asked Madge.

'None at all.'

'Poor darling! Have courage, my baby,' said Madge softly.

Kate was touched by the old pet name and kissed her mother warmly. 'Perhaps you and Papa could come out to Malaya one day and see us there?' she said wistfully. 'It's a wonderful country! You'd both love it!'

'We're gluttons for work, and our work is here, darling,' replied Madge. 'Though if you were ever in need, one of us would be with you in a flash, I promise.'

'I'm sure you would,' said Kate, and she was much comforted.

The visit to the Marchmonts, however, was as uncomfortable as always for Kate, and as happy for Edward. Mrs Marchmont took great exception to Bess's red hair and Mr Marchmont gloomed in the background. They seemed to regard red hair as a kind of insult; they also thought that Bess was spoilt. But they were pleased to have a grandchild. With uncharacteristic thoughtfulness Mrs Marchmont, discovering how keenly the little girl felt the cold in England, kindly gave her four pairs of flannel bedsocks, decorated with coloured bows — even though it was summer.

Three weeks into the autumn term, Bess was taken to St Mark's, Bendleford. She had been given dispensation to come late, so that she could stay as long as possible with her parents before they returned to Malaya. She was dressed for the occasion in white fur from head to foot, and in her right hand she clutched her silver knife and fork — a present from 'Uncle' Patrick. She had a round white fur hat, a white fur coat and a white fur muff slung round her neck on a cord. Her long grey gaiters were buttoned from ankle to knee, and she wore scarlet shoes and scarlet mittens. She seemed utterly composed and showed no sign of stress at the imminent, and perhaps traumatic, change which school and the departure of her parents might bring. Edward's grief at the prospect of parting with her had been so great that it had been decided that he should stay in London in case he broke down and made things worse for her; so Kate had made the journey to Bendleford alone with her daughter.

In the horse-drawn cab which took them from the station to the school, she looked lovingly at the strange little girl she had produced. Bess wore no expression on her face at all. Kate was often baffled by this inscrutability, which it seemed impossible to penetrate. The child's self-possession seemed almost adult and, though she was certainly an affectionate little creature, it was hard to tell her immediate feelings. Was it perhaps a spin-off from being born in the East? At this moment, for example, Kate had no idea if

Bess was excited or frightened, glad or unhappy at the prospect of being left alone among strangers; but she knew her for a sturdily independent child who had plenty of courage, so the odds were that she would settle down without too much trouble in her new surroundings.

The cab stopped in the High Street. Bess was lifted out of the vehicle by the cab-man and she and Kate stood side by side on the steps in front of the school front door, Bess with her hands hidden in the big fur muff.

It was dusk. The lamplighter with his long pole was opening the glass casements of the street lamps one by one, pulling the shorter of the two chains hanging from the lamp inside and igniting the gas. He went methodically down the road, watched impassively by the little girl. Kate began to cry.

'Here we are, darling,' she said tearfully. 'Don't be too unhappy, will you? Daddy and I will write to you often and often, and we'll come back and see you as soon as we can.' She found a handkerchief in her handbag and blew her nose.

Bess looked at her solemnly. 'Don't cry, Mummy,' she said. 'Bessie won't cry.'

The door was opened by a maid in a black uniform with a starched white cap and apron who gasped when she saw Bess.

'Well, would you ever!' she exclaimed. Then laughed, 'What a funny little mite it is, to be sure! This way, Madam, Miss Wells is expecting you.' And she led them to the drawing room, where the headmistress was waiting for them.

Miss Wells was tall and dark and about thirty-five years of age. She was a plain woman, but her face was kind. She wore her long black hair with a centre parting, in plaited 'earphones' over her ears, and her brown eyes were large and rather fine. She and Bess seemed to take to each other at once. They all talked together for a while in front of a blazing log fire. Then Bess — who, despite her outward calm, was scared and miserable — asked to go to the lavatory, where Miss Wells, astounded by the complexity of her clothes, had the greatest difficulty in getting her ready. The three of them then made a tour of the school.

It was a charming little place. All the rooms were furnished with small-scale wheel-back chairs, oak tables and dressers, pretty little desks, French pottery and reproduction Old Master paintings. There was a pleasant garden and a large playground.

Relieved that she was leaving Bess in comfortable and pretty surroundings, Kate agreed to stay for tea, and it was not until well after dark that she rose to leave. She hugged and kissed Bess while the tears poured down her face unchecked. Bess, hand in hand with Miss Wells, gravely waved her off in the station cab.

Bess was then introduced to the other children, which she found overwhelming. She had supper, which consisted of a slice of brown bread and butter and dripping, white bread and butter and jam, and a glass of milk. Bess hated the milk, which she was peremptorily told to drink, but loved the dripping, which she had never tasted before.

Bed time followed. Miss Fraser, the under matron, bathed Bess efficiently but none too gently, then tucked her into her bed in the room she was to share with four other children.

'Now go to sleep, Bess,' she said. 'We want no nonsense here, you know. These silly clothes of yours will be packed away for the holidays... though perhaps you could use this purple velvet thing for dancing classes... but tomorrow you will be fitted for your school uniform like everyone else. Fur coats indeed! It's almost immoral!'

She bent down to kiss her. She had a small dark moustache which tickled Bess, who made a slight face. Miss Fraser saw it, and straightened up angrily. 'Good night,' she said. 'No talking mind, or you'll get a smack.' And she left the room.

Meanwhile Kate travelled back to London by train, feeling utterly bereft. Edward met her at Paddington Station.

'Well?' he asked eagerly. 'Will she be all right, Kate?'

'I think so,' she said unhappily.

'Oh dear, we're going to be so lonely!' said Edward drearily, hooking his arm through Kate's.

Kate did her best to smile. 'From now on,' she said, 'you and I will be out on our own, Edward.'

Part Two

BESS

CHAPTER ONE

In spite of her bad start with Miss Fraser, Bess settled down well. There were sixteen other boarders and twenty-two day children at this time, their ages ranging from four to eleven, but most of the boys left for their prep schools at eight. Nearly all the boarders had parents living abroad, so were in the same position as Bess.

In time she almost forgot to be homesick. Kate sent her expensive and exotic presents — a tiny and elaborate Chinese village made of porcelain; cardboard Chinese figures dressed in silk, with painted paper faces and real hair and moustaches; a doll in a clockwork ostrich-cart, and plenty of picture postcards with the news from Malaya — but nothing soft or cuddly. They were strange toys, but different from everyone else's, and Bess treasured them with a ferocious pride. Uncle Patrick on the other hand sent her more childish presents: two beautifully dressed china dolls, with eyes that opened and shut; a black fur cat with glass eyes, whose head unscrewed and whose body was filled with sweets; and a 'Dismal Desmond', which was a toy Dalmatian made of felt.

Kate had already taught her the alphabet and a few very easy sums, so she was ahead of her contemporaries who were still moulding plasticine when first she joined them; and as she grew older she enjoyed her lessons enormously. She was clever and highly talented artistically, although rather unexpectedly tone-deaf. Since she was also naturally athletic she was popular with the other children, but not the staff. Her sometimes ungovernable temper, her untidiness and her dogged wish for independence made her at times difficult to control. She suffered unconsciously from claustrophobia; and from the very first, when the staff were at dinner and the rest of the children had gone to sleep, she would get out of bed and slip through the cloakrooms into the garden. There she would walk about for a little under the night sky, to feel free and alone. It was for her a lifeline to sanity, and luckily she was never caught. In all other respects she seemed to assimilate the extreme institutionalism of her life with remarkable ease.

At Christmas, as had been arranged, she spent a week alternately with her Glanville and Marchmont grandparents. The rest of the holidays were spent with the other children whose parents were still abroad, at the staff houses of other boarding schools. Sometimes they went to Bexhill, sometimes to Newbury, sometimes to Dorset. One of the staff always accompanied them, and the children still wore their school uniforms, even on Sundays. She hated the holidays when Miss Fraser was in charge but otherwise found them tolerable. During the few days at Christmas, however, she was allowed to wear 'mufti' sweaters and skirts and for evenings her two dancing frocks, and this in itself was a treat.

She made two lifelong friends at the school. One was Deirdre Baker, whose father was on the staff of the London Zoo, and the other was the grandson of an Oxford bookseller, whose father was in the Indian Civil Service and whose mother was a permanent invalid. The boy's name was Gerald Masters. He was fair-haired, highly strung and (with a lisp) very talkative, but he had a sense of humour which exactly complemented Bess's own. Deirdre was the same age as Bess and already had an indefinable air of chic. She managed to wear her school uniform as though it were fashionable, and her mouse-brown hair, worn short with a fringe, was completely of the period. She had merry brown eyes and an infectious laugh. Gerald was a year younger.

Bess's visits to the Bakers were among the highlights of her childhood. Deirdre's father was a handsome, jolly man, with Deirdre's brown eyes and a passion for practical jokes. He took Bess and Deirdre round the zoo on Sundays, where they watched the zoo doctor, Dr Vevers, treating the sick animals. Bess was allowed to hold the baby chimpanzees in her arms, which she adored, and handle the snakes, which she liked a good deal less — although, to her surprise, the snakes (whose body heat adapted to the surrounding temperature) were not cold and slimy but dry and lukewarm. Sometimes Mr Baker would tell her to shut her eyes to receive a present, and it might be anything from a lizard down her back to a superb ice-cream, or a baby frog put into her hand.

The Bakers took Bess to the first theatres she ever visited, usually to a pantomime if she was staying with them in the remainder of a Christmas holiday, or to Peter Pan. In the summer they took her to Derry and Tom's roof garden to have cream teas or ices, and in spring to the Regent's Park horse show on Easter Mondays. She heard the bell of the muffin man, whose muffins they nearly always bought. She saw the flower sellers around the statue of Eros in Piccadilly Circus, occasionally had a ride in a hansom cab, and was allowed to welcome the milkman in the morning, in his horse-drawn milk cart.

She didn't enjoy staying with the Marchmonts. They were kind, but snobbish and puritannical. They made it very plain that their son could have done a great deal better for himself than to marry Kate, the daughter of a couple of actors; and they had no idea at all of how to entertain a child, now that Mrs Marchmont's days of motherhood were over. The dark, gloomy house in Sussex to which they had moved since Mr Marchmont's retirement had been built only recently, but it was small and ugly and seemed to exclude all happiness and humour. Sundays were not only days of rest, but days when almost everything enjoyable was forbidden. Bess was expected to attend matins with both of them, she and Mrs Marchmont went to afternoon Sunday school (Mrs Marchmont with the air of a martyr) and prayers and bible reading took place before breakfast and in the evening. All toys except books were forbidden. The luncheons were always the same, and the smell of overcooked cabbage on their return from church always sickened Bess. Roast beef done to a cinder, with the dreaded cabbage and boiled potatoes, were invariably followed by dried apricots and rice pudding; and the beef reappeared in various guises for most of the rest of the week.

The Marchmonts had a small back garden where Bess was meant to play by herself all day, unless it was raining or snowing; and the books she read were carefully vetted. They still audibly disapproved of her red hair — though with no reason, as they had no idea that she wasn't their grandchild — and they made it plain that having her to stay was a duty rather than a pleasure.

On the whole, staying with the Glanvilles was far more fun. It was not a happy household as Harry now made no pretence about preferring Violet Tremayne to his wife, but he and Madge were both attractive people, with an aura of fame about them which Bess found exciting. She loved them both, although the atmosphere in the house on the rare occasions when there were no callers was acutely depressing — especially as she didn't understand the reason for the gloom. She could never completely get through to their affections since they had never really forgiven Kate for her marriage to Edward, nor for her defection from the theatre; but at least they were tolerant. They still found it incredible that Kate didn't want Bess to become an actress; and since they were still actively working, and still both at the top of their profession, this inhibited them from sharing their lives with Bess as they would have wished. Nevertheless their home on the top of Richmond Hill, with its view of the river, was large and comfortable and beautifully and richly furnished, and the friends who called constantly were not only distinguished but entertaining.

May Whitty and her husband Ben Webster were still regulars, and Madge was able to show Bess with pride the Star and Garter Home for disabled ex-servicemen which she and May had helped to found, which was now nearing completion at the gates of Richmond Park. Surprisingly, Bess's favourite among the regular visitors was Bernard Shaw, of whose radical views the Glanvilles, unlike the Websters, had always disapproved. He always came with his wife, Charlotte. Now at the height of his success as a playwright, and in his late sixties, with hair, beard and moustache nearly white, he still wore a fawn Norfolk jacket and knicker-bockers — the costume which was virtually his uniform. His love of exercise and long walks was as insatiable as ever, and his pale shrewd blue eyes were undimmed. Bess thought he had the best manners of anyone she knew. He treated her with great respect and never talked down to her, unlike most of the grown-ups. Oddly, he showed little real sense of humour, but, more satisfying for Bess, he had a robust sense of fun and loved pranks and larks like a low comedian.

Another constant visitor with a sense of fun was Gerald du Maurier. His bent for practical jokes infuriated Madge when he indulged it on stage. But she loved him as a man, admired his naturalistic acting — which at first had been the only way he could act, but was now a highly polished technique — and shared his contempt for 'ham'. Sometimes he would bring the fair-haired Gladys Cooper, who was so exquisitely beautiful that Bess used to follow her everywhere, simply to watch her. This didn't disconcert Gladys at all. Capable, imperious, lithe and elegant, she queened it wherever she went.

But Bess's stay with the Glanvilles was never for more than a few days, after which she would be sent back to join the other children whose parents were abroad, while the exciting life she only half wanted to share went on at Richmond.

For all of her train journeys she was put in charge of the guard, who, for a small tip, invariably looked after her with cheerful solicitude. If she had to travel across London, she was escorted by a (usually) dim little woman from the Universal Aunts.

During one holiday at Richmond, there was a great deal of talk about the two theatre unions, the Actors' Association and the Stage Guild. The Actors' Association, founded in 1891, had become a Trade Union in 1918, nine years after the demise of the Actors' Union, which had been too politically militant for most actors. The new union was to make the same mistake and alienate many of the most influential members of the profession. Inevitably they decided to break away; and so the Stage Guild was formed, modelled on the craft guilds of the Middle Ages. Dame (as she now was) May Whitty was characteristically in the thick of the battle between the two unions, and once again Madge supported her. The house, as Harry constantly complained, became as crowded and uncomfortable as a mainline station. For the first time Bess heard them quarrel, and it frightened her.

'I shall give up helping May when you give up seeing Violet,' said Madge furiously one day.

'What the devil has Violet got to do with the unions?' shouted Harry in reply.

'She has disrupted ours,' snapped Madge, 'so naturally I'm interested in forming others.'

'I want a wife, and a home!' yelled Harry.

'And I want a husband,' retorted Madge.

Later in the evening, Bess saw her hurrying to her room in tears.

Back at school, Bess was more or less cocooned from reality, but the outside world did impinge from time to time. The Wimbledon tennis championships with Suzanne Lenglen and Helen Wills Moody was a yearly excitement. So, too, was the Oxford and Cambridge boat race, though few of the children had fathers who had been at either university: they simply chose the side they wanted to win by their preference for dark blue (the Oxford colours) or light blue (for Cambridge). There was much talk of an invention which would 'make telephone conversations visual' (through the black 'daffodil' telephone) and the wonders of flying were excitedly discussed. Politics was embodied entirely in the form of Major Glyn, who won the local seat for the Conservatives every time, as his father had before him. The wireless was introduced dramatically into the school as a gift from the vicar. Spindle-legged, sonorous of voice, unctuous in manner, and with greying hairs sprouting generously from his nose and ears, he was ardently courting Miss Wells, to the children's great delight. The nine-day General Strike of 1926 was seen briefly by the staff as marking the end of civilisation, and Miss Fraser acquired much reflected glory when her brother volunteered to drive the branch-line train from Bendleford to the junction for London, even though at the first attempt he set off without the carriages.

Bess was now eight, and the clowning which had stood her in good stead with adults when she was a little girl had become a part of her character. One day, when she was playing at Weddings (a favourite game at the little school) and for the first time ever had been chosen as the bride, Miss Fraser interrupted the game looking very serious indeed.

'Bess,' she said, 'get changed into your Sunday best at once and go up to Miss Wells. Your mother and father have come to see you.'

CHAPTER TWO

Slowly, and with beating heart, Bess entered Miss Wells' room. In four years she had nearly forgotten what her mother and father looked like; she had longed for them daily but her imagination, influenced by meeting the parents of the other children, had almost completely taken over from her memory.

They were standing by the fireplace talking to Miss Wells and turned sharply when they heard her. Both were taller than she had expected. Edward seemed very thin and had a slight stoop. He had a kind, rather weak face and his hair had receded. His skin was bronzed and his nose was long and bony, but his voice was gentle as he greeted her. He held out his arms to her almost sobbing with happiness, and tears were standing in his eyes. Kate was dressed in the height of fashion, except that she had not yet cut her long golden hair and wore it in a shining plait around her head. She ran forward to take the child from her husband, hugging her and showering her with kisses. Miss Wells looked on, smiling and nodding sentimentally.

Bess was startled by her mother's beauty, but it made her shy. A lump of pride came into her throat that his lovely vision was her own mother. Yet the two of them seemed to her strangers — un-English, and unlike anyone with whom she had yet come into contact. She kissed them stiffly, and waited to be told what to do next.

This seemed to disconcert them and it was left for Miss Wells, smiling brightly and a little uncertainly, to announce that she was giving Bess the day off, so that her mother and father could take her for lunch at the 'George'. Lunch at the 'George' was deemed a great treat, and Bess cheered up considerably.

Over the meal, Kate and Edward considered their daughter with some attention.

Edward, being a simple soul, saw quite simply the daughter he loved. Miss Wells had given a good account of her and he was proud that she was clever. That she didn't get on too well with those in authority, did not trouble him: he felt that this was their fault, and their loss. Bess was pretty and polite, and his own little girl, and as such, she was perfection.

Kate's reaction was very different. Bess still reminded her sharply of Patrick and the unhappiness that his memory always caused her nearly overwhelmed her at this moment. Many of Bess's mannerisms were Patrick's and when the child smiled her sudden smile Kate found the likeness nearly unbearable.

It was arranged during the lunch that Bess would spend six weeks of the coming summer holidays with her parents, at a cottage they had decided to rent in South Devon, near Exeter. She wouldn't see them again until the end of term, as they were first to stay with both sets of grandparents and then to go to Paris for a few days, for Kate to buy herself some new clothes. Bess was wildly excited at the prospect of a holiday with them, but a little apprehensive. Conversation at the table was alarmingly stilted, for Kate and Edward were unused to children and Bess could not conquer her sense of awe.

After lunch the three of them went for a walk by the Thames. They then headed for Bendleford's best toy shop, where Bess was given a fox-cub hand-glove puppet, some paints and a small pottery house whose roof took off. (Her mother had also brought her a long, beautifully beaded snake from Kuala Lumpur and a little ebony elephant from Colombo.) After this they returned her to school.

For Bess and Edward the meeting, though bewildering, had been exciting and full of promise for the future. For Kate, bewilderment predominated.

The intervening years had been extremely unhappy ones for her. Patrick was still living near Kuala Lumpur so she and Edward were forced to see a good deal of him socially. Edward still liked him very much and was always wanting to entertain him, which was a severe strain for Kate since Patrick now invariably held her at a distance; sometimes almost mockingly. He had made no move to see her from the moment that Bess left. He never allowed himself to be alone in her company if he could help it and, when they did meet, he refused point-blank to make any reference to their affair, though he always asked after Bess. He also refused to come to the telephone if, in her despair, she rang him. She could never bring herself to realise that, to Patrick, the birth of a child had seemed the ultimate act of disloyalty to his friend Edward; and from then on he had wished to see no more of her without Bess. He had numerous well-publicised affairs, yet showed no sign of settling down to a marriage.

Kate hadn't known that such unhappiness was possible. She had inherited her father's sensual nature and with Edward had no outlet for it. She was still desperately in love with Patrick (as she had by no means a frivolous nature) and it was an agony to her to realise that his feeling for her was over.

At times she had felt that her mind would give under the strain. She went for long solitary afternoon walks in the Lake Club Gardens with tears pouring down her face, talking aloud to herself, and praying to the God in whom she had no belief. She spent days in bed (only getting up an hour before Edward's return from the office), crying her eyes out or reliving, in a kind of obsessive horror, the affair which had meant so much to her. But with enormous self-discipline she had managed to keep her feelings hidden from everyone except her devoted ayah. Edward was very worried that she might be unwell because she was so uncharacteristically subdued. He sent her to the doctor who gave her a clean bill of health, and a tonic to take three times a day.

Only once had she nearly confided her troubles to someone, but afterwards she was eternally grateful for the instinct which had stopped her; having spent a few days on holiday with friends at Bukit Fraser, she had returned to find that the 'best friend' in whom she had wanted to confide had been making a play for Edward and had done her utmost to usurp Kate's place.

She had given up playing polo, which was a relief to Edward. She also entertained less, and tried hard to cultivate a more domesticated outlook — although with a more than adequate staff this was hardly necessary and, what's more, she found it boring. She had always enjoyed men's company; now she trusted almost no-one. She took up painting again in earnest and this was her only solace.

Fashion had caught up with her style and she began making a considerable success. She had many commissions to paint people's children, and her landscapes were considered very fine. She turned the part of the verandah near her bedroom into a studio and could once again be seen painting under a large parasol by the roadside in one of her special hats. This was now thought of as 'chic' and 'amusing': Edward bathed proudly in reflected glory.

The Marchmont finances were at their peak during this period.

Kate was less extravagant and Edward had had to take a partner, who not only paid a handsome sum for the partnership but brought in a lot of business. Besides this, Edward had been elected recently by the 'coloured races' to represent them, as an 'unofficial member', on the Federal Council, which advised the Chief Secretary, the highest British Official in the Federated Malay States. As such, he became a sort of unpaid MP, and he found this work greatly to his liking. He brought in an anti-rabies bill, which freed the country from a serious scourge, and had become well known for his philanthropy and a much respected member of the community. At heart, however, he was a family man; in spite of his success, his only desires were to see his little daughter again — and to have more children.

Even if this hope was to be denied, Edward was at least seeing Bess again. With his obvious joy in her company, which affected Kate as well, the Devon holiday was a great success.

As for Bess, having parents of her own at last gave her deep satisfaction. Going for drives in the brand new car, for example, was a great excitement. She seldom had anyone of her own age to play with but knew how to spend time happily on her own since she was used to such holidays with her grandparents. The cottage, which was thatched and had a big and beautiful garden, enchanted her. The lighting was by oil-lamps, there was no telephone and the lavatory was a two-seater in a hut in the garden. It was called an EC ('earth closet') and smelt perpetually of Fuller's Earth — a white powder used as a disinfectant. It was a glorious hot summer, with very little rain. Bess revelled in the surrounding beechwoods and the masses of wild flowers on the steep banks beside the roads. Best of all she loved Sooty, the dog which the cottage owners had left to be looked after while they were away: a four-year-old black labrador with the nature of an angel and the appetite of a horse.

By the time her parents left again for Malaya, Bess had established a friendly working relationship with her mother and a loving, but calmer, relationship with Edward. During the following term, she heard that Uncle Patrick was to come on leave. After her bi-annual visit to Harry and Madge, he was to have her to stay with him for two weeks in London.

CHAPTER THREE

At school Bess now found herself very popular. Her famous theatrical grandparents had never really struck the other children as interesting, but a glamorous mother and father with a brand new motor car had elevated her into the position of a 'personality'. During the holidays she had been given a 'bingle' (an especially short and modern kind of shingle haircut) and it suited her. So, with Deirdre and Gerald as constant and loyal escorts, she became a sort of cult.

She hadn't realised how much having no visible parents had depersonalised her in the eyes of her fellow pupils. Even Miss Wells' attitude now subtly changed. Bess recognised the change and became more self-confident. She had never felt particularly lonely before, though she had sometimes found it hard to be giving no-one but herself pleasure when she won prizes for work, or came top in her class, or won dancing competitions against children from rival schools; but now she had parents to please. Above all, she had a flesh-and-blood father to love. She had been bowled over by Kate's beauty, but it was in Edward that she had recognised a genuine warmth of affection.

Bess had always been unduly sensitive about her looks. Partly because she genuinely had no vanity, and partly because of her semi-orphan status, she had never been allowed to believe that she was pretty. The cry of, 'Bess, behave yourself. Remember dear, if you can't be pretty, be good,' had haunted her for years and had undermined any belief that her appearance could please. Now she was learning better. The game of 'weddings' had always been very important to her, because she felt it was a test of her attractiveness: after years as a bridesmaid and a kind of court jester she was now constantly chosen as the bride, and it gave her an absurd amount of pleasure.

Her favourite book, *Misunderstood*, together with her animal toys, had been almost a self-contained family to her. Now she had less need of them.

The years at boarding school had already marked her. When she was being good, she was more than ordinarily docile and her passionate need for independence and escape had become a carefully guarded secret. Even close relationships could now induce claustrophobia, so that, as soon as she felt too strongly about anyone or anything, she switched off her emotions and became a dispassionate observer. In her isolation it had been her world of fantasy that had been most real to her; but the reappearance of her parents was forcing her to adjust yet again, and she was enjoying it.

Her friend Deirdre, on the other hand, was very unhappy, because her own parents were on the point of divorce.

'But what will happen to you if your father leaves your mother?' asked Bess. 'Where will you live?'

'I don't know,' said Deirdre sadly. 'They just don't seem to want me just at present.'

'I wish you could come and stay with me,' said Gerald wistfully. 'There's tons of room.' And he wrote to his grandfather, with whom he lived while his parents were in India, suggesting it. For good measure, he asked if Bess could stay too. 'She has to spend nearly all her hols at school,' he wrote, 'and we're all great friends.'

He received no reply.

'It's not like Grandfather not to answer,' he protested. 'He sometimes doesn't like things, but he always says so.'

'Never mind,' soothed Deirdre. 'You'll be seeing him soon, and then you can discuss it.'

'But he usually writes every week, and I haven't heard a single word!' replied Gerald, worried. 'I wonder if he's all right? Do you think I can have hurt his feelings?'

'You never know with grown-ups,' said Bess seriously. 'Their feelings are different from ours.'

'It would have been so absolutely ripping,' said Gerald. 'I'm always alone there.'

'So am I, at home,' said Deirdre, 'with Mummy and Daddy having rows all the time.'

'Is the other lady pretty?' asked Bess.

'No, and I hate her,' replied Deirdre. 'She's got miles of fluffy brown hair and huge sticking-out teeth and she keeps flashing her great big blue eyes at Daddy, which makes me sick. Mummy just stares at them both, not saying anything, and it's horrible. Poor Mummy! I'm so sorry for her!'

Eventually it transpired that Gerald's grandfather had been ill in hospital, which was why he had not written. Although he was well again, it was now too late to change plans for these Christmas holidays, so Gerald and Deirdre went home as usual and Bess went to Madge and Harry.

Harry was looking ill. He was acting in a comedy called *Don't Darling*, which was a great success, and he himself was the rage of London. To Madge's intense relief there was no part for Violet in it, but he still spent a good deal of time with her. He had a very high colour in his cheeks which stood out against the yellowish pallor of the rest of his face; he became short of breath very quickly and was stouter than ever. Madge was extremely worried about him.

Although Bess had been kept away from Violet as much as possible, and the fiction maintained that all was well with the Glanvilles, she had seen her grandfather's mistress once or twice by this time and was well aware of her position. Once again she marvelled at the mysterious ways of men. Her grandmother was a magnificent looking woman, who wore her years lightly. She was kind and clever and, if not blessed with a sense of humour, was nonetheless lively and interesting. She was still beautiful and, although plumper than when she was young, had a great air of authority. She dressed exquisitely — and, like her daughter Kate, extravagantly — and in Bess's view she was worth twenty of Violet. But Violet was young, or at least a good deal younger, which seemed to cancel out the fact that she was silly and predatory and even more humourless than Madge. True, she had dark flashing eyes, a splendid figure and black curly hair; but simply because she was young, it seemed, Harry loved her.

It was arranged that Bess should see her grandfather in his play. 'He's excellent in the part and it's time you saw both of us in action,' said Madge. 'If you enjoy it you can come and see me in mine. I'm doing an Oscar Wilde in two months' time, and I have a very good part.'

Bess had never been to a straight play before as the Glanvilles had had no wish to lure her towards the theatre if Kate was against it. She was very excited at the prospect.

When the great day arrived, Bentwood, the chauffeur, drove them in style to the Globe Theatre, where Harry had already performed the matinée. Bess was tremendously impressed by the way everyone treated her grandmother. She could almost have been royalty. The box-office staff were introduced to Bess and were obviously delighted, because she was Madge's grand-daughter; then the theatre manager led the two of them to their box, and arranged that drinks should be brought to them in the interval. The usherettes all wished Madge good evening, and she was given her programme free. Her entrance into the box created great excitement in the theatre. People nodded, stood up, nudged each other, pointed her out to one another and smiled and smiled. It was almost, Bess thought, as if they owned her, and were glad to know that she would be seeing the show with them. By the time the house lights dimmed, and the great red velvet curtains parted, Bess felt a rising excitement. Her grandfather received an entrance round, and once again, as she had when reunited with her parents, Bess felt privileged to belong to the family. Watching the tubby, graceful little man weaving such amusing magic for such an appreciative audience, she suddenly saw Harry in a new light. After the show, when they found a small eager crowd already outside his dressing room, her heart beat heavily with pride.

Inside the room, Harry was already holding court. Madge immediately looked round for Violet, but there was no sign of her.

They had reached the dressing room via the pass door and then along the side of the stage itself, where the smell of 'size' (with which the scenery had been treated) was very strong. Here in the dressing room, it was the heavy smell of grease paint that dominated. For the first time, Bess felt a small stirring of desire for a theatrical life — not for the glamour, for she had seen plenty of that in the Glanville home without wishing for more, but for the theatre itself.

When all the visitors had left, Harry took Madge and Bess to supper across the road at the Trocadero, which was then in its heyday. They created a stir as they entered and again Bess saw with what deference her grandparents were treated. She was allowed a glass of champagne, which made her feel giddy but happy, and both Harry and Madge put themselves out to charm her.

How sad! thought Bess. They seem to have so much, and they are unhappy — and the Bakers have so much too, in a different way, and they are unhappy as well — and it's always because of another woman! If another woman comes into my life, I'll kill her!

Perhaps because the evening was such a successful one, indeed one that she would remember all her life long, Bess felt a rapport with her grandparents at last. She sensed their belated approval, and they began making plans to see her more often.

'A week every two years is absurd,' said Madge. 'We'll meet many more times than that from now on, won't we Harry?'

'Rather!' agreed Harry enthusiastically. 'Let's meet three times a year at least.'

Two days later, these plans were shattered.

CHAPTER FOUR

It was three days before Christmas. The huge Christmas tree in the drawing room at Richmond had already been decorated with a fairy doll at the top carrying a wand with a star on it. Coloured balls of thin glass were everywhere. Gold and silver tinsel, clip-on enamel birds in brilliant colours with spun-glass tails, coloured candles and dozens of parcels in brightly coloured paper had been placed all over and around the tree, which stood in one corner of the room.

Bess and Madge had had an early dinner together and were now sitting in front of the blazing log fire, reading. The telephone bell rang, and Effie, who doubled as both Madge's theatrical dresser and the housekeeper in Richmond, answered it. After a moment or two, she came into the room looking scared. 'It's a call for you, Miss Vane,' she said to Madge, whom she always called by her stage name. 'It's from the theatre.'

Madge hurried out. Presently she came back looking as scared as Effie. 'Grandfather was taken ill on stage,' she said. 'They're bringing him back at once. Go to bed, darling. The doctor is coming in half an hour.'

'Can't I do anything?' asked Bess anxiously.

'No, thank you, darling. Run along now. There's a good girl.' Madge kissed her goodnight, and Bess went slowly upstairs to her room.

She heard the preparations for Harry's return. Doors opened and shut all over the house. There were murmured voices, and hurried footsteps. She undressed, shivering a little with nerves, and got into bed. She lay listening to the voices and the footsteps, unable to sleep. Was Grandfather very ill? Was he in pain? Was he very *old*? Bess didn't know (all grown-ups seemed old). Would she be sent away before Christmas — and, if so, where would she go? Perhaps Uncle Patrick would come to the rescue... She heard a car arrive and ran to the window. She could see the doctor by the light of the porch over the front door. He hastened into the house and she heard the front door slam. Bess stayed, watching, by the window.

Another car arrived. The Rolls. Bentwood got out and opened the back door of the car. He dived in and came out almost lifting her grandfather, then, slinging him over his shoulder, went into the house. Seeing her grandfather handled with such lack of dignity gave Bess a shock. Had he died already? She stared into the darkness straining to understand what was going on, and shaking, now, with cold.

At last Effie came in to see her. She still wore the scared look, but was obviously trying to seem calm. 'Now, dearie,' she said briskly, 'what do you think you're doing, staying up at this time of night? Must get your beauty sleep, you know. Grandfather is in bed, and the Doctor and Miss Vane are with him.'

'Is he very ill, Effie?'

'Yes, dearie.' There was a catch in her voice.

'He won't die, will he Effie?'

'What ever makes you say a thing like that?' asked Effie, pretending to scold her, but sounding far from convincing. 'You go to sleep, Miss.' She plumped up the pillows, smoothed the top sheet, tucked the little girl up gently and kissed her forehead. 'Good night now,' she said, and left the room.

In the morning, when Bess woke, the house was unnaturally silent. She bathed and dressed hurriedly, then went downstairs to the dining room for breakfast. Only Rosie the parlourmaid was in the room, with red-rimmed eyes and sniffing into a handkerchief.

'Have you heard how Grandfather is, Rosie?' asked Bess.

'Madam says to have your breakfast, Miss, and then to wait in your room until you are called,' replied Rosie.

'But is he all right, Rosie?'

Rosie sobbed. 'Miss Vane says to wait until you are called.'

The house suddenly seemed to come alive again. The telephone rang several times and was promptly answered. Back in her room, Bess sat at the window, looking out over the circular drive. It was a steel-grey day, and the famous view of the river looked dim and forbidding. A few flakes of snow were drifting halfheartedly down but melting at once as they hit the window panes or reached the ground. At the gates one or two people had gathered to look in at the house, stamping their feet against the cold and blowing on their hands. Even from here she could see their breath, writhing like smoke as they talked.

The doctor's car had arrived again and as he got out this time Bess caught a glimpse of his face under his big black felt hat. He looked self-important but very grave. He carried a black Gladstone bag and wore a black coat with a velvet collar, on which the snow also melted.

Bess looked away from him to the gaily wrapped presents she had brought for her grandparents. What ought she to do with them if Grandfather died? . . . Death! Death happened to other families. Not to hers, or to her friends. Death happened to rabbits when the dogs killed them, or to pigs when they were taken away to market; even to hens who had their necks wrung. One minute the creatures were themselves, the next they were nothing at all — a kind of rubbish. Like the robin the cat had killed at the Marchmonts' last year. One moment a dear, bouncing, bright-eyed little bird; the next, a limp, rather horrible little nothing of bones and feathers. Would Grandfather be a nothing?

But he wasn't, and for years afterwards Bess had nightmares about it.

Effie came to her. She, too, had been crying. 'Miss Vane says to come with me and see your Grandfather, Miss Bess,' she said. 'She says not to be frightened and to hold my hand.'

'Is he dead, Effie?'

'Yes, dearie. It don't seem possible, somehow, but he is.'

They went down the long corridor to his bedroom and Effie knocked on the door. Madge called out, 'Come in,' and Effie said quietly, 'Now remember, as Miss Vane said, don't be frightened, dearie. They always look different when they are dead.'

Bess and Effie went into the room together, Bess clutching Effie's hand tightly. Madge was sitting in a chair beside the bed, dressed in black. Bess gasped at her beauty. Black suited her. Her eyes, bright with unshed tears, looked huge; the piles of white hair and the pallor of her skin contrasted magnificently with the sombre clothes. She turned to Bess and nodded wordlessly, tearing fiercely at a small white lace-edged handkerchief. The doctor was standing beside her looking at his big gold hunter watch and puffing out his red cheeks.

In the centre of the enormous four-poster bed lay Harry. His mane of grey hair had been carefully combed and there was a ruffle of white lace at his throat; the bed clothes were drawn up high above his shoulders so that only the collar of his blue silk pyjamas showed. He looked peaceful, and at once years younger and years older than Bess remembered him. She hardly recognised him. His nose was like a beak in his waxen face. His cheeks had caved in and his eyes had sunk in his head.

Madge struggled for speech. Finally she whispered, 'You may say goodbye to him, Bess. You won't see him again.'

Bess looked at her, bewildered. 'She means to kiss him, dearie,' said Effie, under her breath. 'That's how you say goodbye!'

Bess leaned forward — and was repelled instantly by the smell of death. Harry's forehead was ice cold, and she could hardly repress a shudder.

'He left us in the early hours,' said Madge. 'Another heart attack. The doctor says he would have gone quickly and felt very little pain.'

'I'm glad,' said Bess, and Madge gave her a small appreciative smile.

'You may go now,' she said, 'and I'll come and see you in the drawing room, later.'

'Yes, Gran.'

Bess began walking quickly out of the room, but at the door she turned and looked back.

The whole scene looked unreal to her. The vast and gloomy room, with its dark wallpaper and heavy blue-silk curtains was like a sombre Victorian conversation-piece: life-sized portraits in ornate frames, quantities of tables and chairs, knick-knacks and silver-framed photographs, a monumental mahogany wardrobe, two matching chests-of-drawers, the wash-hand-stand with the big blue china basin and ewer, and the outsize four-poster bed with its blue canopy and crimson coverlet. Grouped round the small lifeless body of her grandfather were the attendant figures of Madge and the doctor, with Effie waiting hesitantly beside them. They were like people caught meaninglessly in a quite different period of time. Bess gave one last brief glance at her grandfather, with his marbled, sculptured face and hurried, sobbing, from the room.

In the drawing room, later, she apologised for her tears, but Madge seemed to have been touched by them. 'I understand, my dear,' she said softly. 'We all cry sometimes, and I know how fond of him you were.'

Was I? thought Bess. I suppose I was. I don't know, really. I hardly knew him. And am I fond of Grandmother? I don't know that, either, and perhaps that's wicked.

Madge's voice broke in on her thoughts. 'I have rung Mr de Moulins,' she said. 'He'll be here very soon. You'll spend Christmas with him instead of with us ... with me,' she corrected herself. 'Rosie has packed your things, and you'll find our Christmas presents in a basket.'

'Thank you, Grandmother. I have some for you, too.'

'Yes. I know. Rosie has given them to me. Thank you, Bess. Your grandfather's funeral will be on Friday, and Mr de Moulins will return with you for that and you'll have lunch here afterwards, before going back with him. He has been very helpful, and I am most grateful to him for his concern.'

But when Uncle Patrick arrived and Madge saw the two of them side by side, she caught her breath and her eyes widened in surprise. Then, with a kind of contempt she said, 'How very like your god-daughter you are, Mr de Moulins.'

'Phew!' said Patrick when he had settled Bess under the white fur rug in the chauffeur-driven car he had hired to take her into London. 'She's quite a tartar, isn't she?'

'What's a tartar?' asked Bess.

'A Gorgon. A terror. A tough old dame,' said Patrick.

Bess was shocked. 'She's my grandmother,' she said.

'That's right,' he said. 'She is. I beg your pardon.'

'Family,' added Bess.

'And famous,' said Patrick.

'I don't think that matters so much, do you?' said Bess. 'The main thing is to have a family.'

'Yes, I suppose that's true,' said Patrick. 'You've seen yours this year, haven't you?'

'I'll say!' Bess's eyes shone with pleasure. 'It was wonderful having them home! You've no idea how wonderful, after so much school!'

'You like your school, don't you?'

'Very much, but it's not like family. Daddy is so kind. He loves me very much, you know.'

'And your mother?' Patrick's voice was sharp.

'Oh, she's beautiful. The most beautiful person I've ever seen.'

'Doesn't she love you very much?'

'Oh, yes! Of course she does! They're both terrific.'

'And how about your Uncle Patrick?'

'He's terrific, too,' laughed Bess happily.

'And family. I'm a godfather and an uncle. That's twice family.'

'Only a friendly uncle, not real family,' said Bess seriously, and Patrick gave her a wry smile.

He cross-questioned her closely about her life, then said, 'Well, it all seems satisfactory, darling, except for the holidays. That right?'

'Yes,' said Bess. 'That's right, but it can't really be helped, can it?'

'I rather think it can,' said Patrick. 'These chums of yours, Deirdre and Gerald... you say that you'd like to be together, but because he's been ill it's unlikely that Gerald's grandfather can take you and Deirdre — that it?' Bess nodded. 'Well, why don't I try to find a holiday home where you could all three go in the holidays?'

'Would you, Uncle Patrick? Would you really? That would be marvellous. So marvellous, it'd be like a dream. Would Mummy mind?'

'Why should she?'

'Perhaps she thinks she's doing her best for me,' said Bess, anxiously.

'I'm sure she does, but she'll understand when I explain.'

'I told you you were terrific,' said Bess excitedly, 'and you are. Thank you, darling darling Uncle.' She hugged him and kissed him. 'Where are we going?' she asked.

'To my brother's flat,' he replied. 'We shan't, I suppose, be able to go to many theatres or parties until your grandfather's funeral, but after it we might as well go on the town, don't you think?'

'Go on the town?'

'Have fun.'

'We'll have fun!' exclaimed Bess happily. 'It will be terrific being with you!'

Bess loved the flat, and her little bedroom, which was filled with Italian-Primitive pictures and beautiful furniture. Uncle Patrick bought her a dark blue coat and hat for the funeral and a black arm band, and a beautiful green silk dress for the parties afterwards.

He didn't attend the funeral and Bess could see that her grandmother was pleased by this, which saddened her.

The funeral was an immense and impressive affair. Royalty was represented and the theatrical world was there in force.

It was a beautiful winter's day, with a pale sun shining out of an ice-blue sky. The cortège started from the house. Bentwood, looking solemn and unhappy, was driving the Rolls, with Mrs Glanville sitting bolt upright on the back seat. Bess sat beside her, while Effie, her eyes brimming with tears, sat on a tip-up seat facing them. Masses of expensive flowers were strewn on the coffin, and all over the enormous decorated hearse. Huge coloured cartwheels of wreaths were stacked against the glass and on the roof. Behind the Rolls came sixteen other mourning cars filled with close friends and the more obscure members of the family, and the traffic was held up behind them as far as the eye could see. The little church at Petersham was so crowded that hundreds of people had to wait outside, and the roads for miles around were thronged. It was evident that Harry's death had affected the entire country. Black cars and thousands and thousands of black-clad people made an extraordinary sight in the narrow twisting lanes.

By the graveside, Madge took her grand-daughter's hand. Bess could feel it trembling, although her grandmother was not crying. Her grip tightened so fiercely, though, when she saw Violet Tremayne (who had purple flowers on her hat and at her throat), that Bess nearly cried out.

After the burial was over, her grandmother had invited a hundred people (though not Violet Tremayne) back to a buffet luncheon, and throughout it she remained calm and lovely and tearless. Bess had never admired anyone so much.

At three o'clock Uncle Patrick came to collect her, and Madge gave Bess a very affectionate kiss. 'Good bye for the moment, Bess,' she said. 'I should like you to stay here for a few days every holiday if you would care for that.'

'Oh, yes, Grandma, I should love it!' exclaimed Bess.

Madge smiled for the first time that day. 'I'm glad,' she said softly. 'Thank you.'

The rest of that holiday was what Bess described, to Patrick's amusement, as 'one huge round of gaiety'. Patrick gave a party for her with a conjuror, which was a great success, and invited Deirdre and the Bakers. When it was all over he took her in the big hired car back to Bendleford. He had a long talk with Miss Wells, the Bakers and Gerald's grandfather, and then, as promised, managed to find a holiday home for the children to be together.

When he went back to Malaya, he was a firm favourite with everyone except Madge.

CHAPTER FIVE

The holiday home was in Surrey. It was run by a Colonel and Mrs Blundell-Jones, who were trying in this way to keep up the big house which had been in their family for generations. They were a snobbish pair, and both rather stupid. She was big and fair, with a loud hectoring voice and shapeless legs. He had been in the army in the war, had a military-type moustache and still called himself Colonel. He had an eye for the girls; sometimes when he got drunk he pinched their behinds, and he was given to demanding furtive kisses. They had a son Edward, known as Teddy, who was weedy and wore glasses and told tales to his mother about the other children. But the house was beautiful and the garden and estate enormous, so Bess, Deirdre and Gerald found it a paradise.

Bess and Deirdre were ten by this time, and Gerald was nine. Although there were several other children there, their friendship was so complete and their tastes so identical that they were immune from any interests or activities outside their world. Mrs Blundell-Jones found this disconcerting and 'unnatural', and she wrote to all their parents in turn, but received no answer from any of them.

They were given bicycles. There was a tennis court to play on and a croquet lawn, and a village sweet shop where they could buy acid drops for tuppence and sherbet in small triangular paper bags for a halfpenny. There was a gramophone in their playroom, with the latest tunes from shows like *Hit the Deck*, and, most exciting of all, a theatre nearby which they were allowed to visit twice each holiday. There was also a cinema. Quite good touring companies came to the theatre and they saw such London successes as *The Ghost Train*, and once even the great George Robey with his trademark of bowler hat and huge corked eyebrows. At the cinema they saw *The Three Monketeers* (acted entirely by monkeys), Joan Bennett in the silent version of *Doctor Fu Manchu*, Charlie Chaplin, Buster Keaton and Laurel and Hardy; and, on one never-to-be-forgotten day, they saw history in the making — the first talking picture, *The Singing Fool*, with Al Jolson.

During the summer months Gerald and Deirdre caught butter-flies for their collections, but Bess hated this. In the spring they found bird's eggs, and taught Bess how to blow them; and in some winters they went skating on the lake.

On and off, the three of them stayed at the Grange for four years, during which they only became separated in term-time. Bess left Bendleford to go to a school called Fossetts in Dorset, Deirdre to Downe House at Newbury, and Gerald to Eton.

Miss Wells herself drove Bess to Fossetts, in her grey bull-nosed Morris Oxford two-seater. Bess's brown, wooden-bound cabin-trunk, with her initials on it in black, was strapped to the luggage rack at the back with ropes, and on the dicky seat was a picnic lunch and some raw potatoes to wipe the water off the windscreen if it rained, which it did. During the first part of the journey though, when it was hot, the little car over-heated several times, and cold water from a watering can had to be poured into the bonnet.

Saying goodbye to Miss Wells was an agony to Bess. As the headmistress, she had been too remote to be a surrogate mother; but, since Bendleford had been far more truly Bess's home than anywhere else, Miss Wells had been — and lovingly — the one unchanging and dependable adult in her life.

At Fossetts, Bess discovered that the teaching at Bendleford had been very good, and that she was far ahead of the others of her own age. This gave her a contempt for the school and a habit of breaking bounds almost daily, which, though she was often pun-ished for it, she continued to do whenever the urge took her. She now began to show a talent for acting, and was given all the leading parts whether male or female in the school plays; she also became a voracious reader. Fortunately the library at Fossetts was well stocked.

Her parents had a winter leave during this period and Bess spent the first Christmas with them that she could remember.

As soon as they landed they had naturally visited Madge, whom they found marvellously composed. Kate by contrast was highly emotional. She was far removed now in experience and outlook from the young girl who had surprised her father with his mistress of the moment. The shock of that had changed her life, driving her out of the theatre, out of England and into her marriage with

Edward, with all that had followed; but even if that was always to be remembered, and always regretted, she now understood from her affair with Patrick how strong and insistent was the sexuality she had inherited from Harry. She felt closer to him now than she had since childhood, and accordingly missed him desperately. Madge, her understanding sharpened by her encounter with Patrick, watched with sympathy her daughter's emotion but wisely said nothing.

From Richmond, Kate and Edward went to the Marchmonts and then out to Davos in Switzerland, to a very grand hotel where Bess joined them for her holidays. She didn't enjoy it much. Her parents seemed to love the social life, while she found the hotel intimidating and her days on the ski slopes lonely. She disliked the evenings, too. Kate arranged for a hairdresser to visit Bess's room twice a week to tong-wave her hair, which she hated; and she had to stay up most nights attending the hotel dances. She danced well, and particularly enjoyed dancing with Edward; but the hotel professional persisted in partnering her, and the two of them made a great success with their exhibition dances, which she found excruciatingly embarrassing.

Bess saw Uncle Patrick twice — both times in London. These holidays she liked considerably more, even though her affection for Edward was now the strongest feeling in her life. She felt sorry for Edward for no reason that she could fathom, which in turn made her feel protective; and she found his gentleness and constant thoughtfulness very touching. For Uncle Patrick she felt admiration mixed with love, but with her instinct for remaining aloof from people and events she found him a shade too possessive for her liking.

Of world events she remained in almost total ignorance. Neither at the Grange, nor at Fossetts did she ever see a newspaper; so the Hunger Marches, the rising unemployment, the dole queues and the other symptoms of the Great Depression — even the rubber slump in Malaya — were hardly noticed by her in the isolation ward of her world. In Malaya, as in America, people were committing suicide when their finances collapsed; but she didn't know it, nor did she know that Kate and Edward had lost their life savings in rubber and that her life in England was coming to a close.

Her habit of removing herself from feeling, from excitement and even from novelty, had been a conscious choice and by now the habit was ingrained. Being only intermittently in a close family circle had made her realise early in her life that one is only a heroine to oneself — except, she supposed, to a husband or lover — and that emotions controlled are less likely to hurt.

By the time she was fourteen she had a remarkably mature figure and was well on the way to being a beauty. She had been aware for some time that Colonel Blundell-Jones had had his eye on her, and one day he managed to catch her on her own. After a brief attempt to pinch her bottom, he forced a kiss on her lips. She struggled furiously, but was still in his arms when the door flew open to reveal his wife.

She was shaking with rage and told Bess to come up to her bedroom at once. She almost ran up the stairs, and slammed the door behind them before shouting, 'Don't you ever dare to try to kiss my husband again, Bess Marchmont, or you'll be out of this house the next day!'

'But I didn't!' exclaimed Bess outraged. 'He kissed me!'

'Be quiet!' yelled Mrs Blundell-Jones. 'I saw you with my own eyes! Have your pains begun?'

'My pains?' Bess was utterly bewildered.

'The pains that show that you are growing up,' replied Mrs Blundell-Jones, impatiently.

'I don't understand,' said Bess.

'Has no-one told you?' demanded Mrs Blundell-Jones, amazed.

'No.'

'Well once a month for the rest of your fertile life you'll get pains and various other unpleasant symptoms,' said Mrs Blundell-Jones grimly.

'What is a fertile life?' asked Bess.

'The time in which you can have babies.'

'But how do I have babies?'

'Have you never been told the facts of life?'

'No. What are they?'

'You're a big girl not to know.'

'Well, I don't.'

'You have babies by getting too excited with men,' said Mrs Blundell-Jones, 'so take care that you don't do it again.'

Bess found the whole converstion incomprehensible, and went to Deirdre for an explanation. Deirdre roared with laughter. 'Good Lord, Bess!' she said. 'But you've always said you *aren't* "young and innocent"!'

'Yes, but I didn't know what it meant! I still don't.'

'If you say you're "not young and innocent" it means that you know the facts of life, so naturally I thought you did!'

'Oh,' said Bess. 'Well, for goodness sake tell me them.'

So Deirdre explained kindly and sensibly, but Bess was extremely shaken by the whole incident.

A few days later, she was back again in Mrs Blundell-Jones' bedroom. Once again she had been sent for. Remembering the previous conversation, Bess wondered how excited Mrs Blundell-Jones had had to get before producing weedy Teddy. Not very, she decided.

'I have just had a letter from your Grandfather Marchmont,' said Mrs Blundell-Jones impressively. 'Mrs Marchmont has passed over. It is very sad but it was all very peaceful. It happened in her sleep, and she evidently had no pain.'

'Passed over?' echoed Bess.

'She has died,' said Mrs Blundell-Jones, trying not to show irritation.

'I see,' said Bess. She remained impassive, and a long silence ensued which seemed to embarrass Mrs Blundell-Jones. 'Well?' she snapped. 'Aren't you sad that she is dead?'

Realising what was expected of her, Bess said hurriedly, 'Of course I am. Very sad. I didn't think you'd want to see it, that's all.'

'And you'll write to your grandfather at once won't you? He'll be very unhappy.'

A vision of her tight-lipped, sour, balding grandfather with his three missing teeth and the blue veins standing out on his crimsoning nose came vividly before her. Bess couldn't imagine him being terribly unhappy at his wife's death. Relieved, more probably, she thought, but she said obediently, 'Yes, I'll write.'

'That's a good girl. You may lie down if you want to,' said Mrs Blundell-Jones.

'Lie down?'

'For a rest. With a book.'

'For a rest?'

Mrs Blundell-Jones became really angry now. Surely it was unnatural for a child to take the news of a death so calmly? Especially the death of a relative? She had been looking forward to the drama of comforting her in her bereavement and felt thoroughly frustrated. 'I only thought you might be suffering just a little from the shock of such bad news, my dear,' she said icily. 'I see I needn't have worried. If you would like me to help you with your letter to your grandfather, you have only to say. That will do, now. You may go.'

But four days later she had yet further news to impart.

She was holding a letter in her hand when Bess went into the room, and looked excited and even a little malicious — a combination which Bess viewed with suspicion.

'Ah, my dear,' she said, as soon as she saw Bess. 'I have had a letter from your mother. Not good news, I'm afraid.'

'Oh?' said Bess, and her mouth went dry with fright.

'You've heard of the Depression in America, I suppose?'

'I don't think so,' said Bess.

'Well, there is one,' said Mrs Blundell-Jones drily, 'just as there is terrible unemployment here.'

'Yes?'

'Yes.'

'What has that got to do with Mummy?' asked Bess, anxiously.

'It has reached Malaya,' said Mrs Blundell-Jones.

'You mean Father has lost his job?'

'No, no!' Mrs Blundell-Jones felt her temper rising again, as it always did when she had a serious conversation with Bess. 'But your parents have lost a great deal of money, and they can't afford to keep you in England, so they will arrange for you to go to them out there soon. Rubber!'

'Rubber?' Mrs Blundell-Jones' way of talking never failed to take Bess by surprise.

'That's how they lost it.'

'They lost rubber?'

'You know perfectly well what I mean, Bess. They have lost their money by investing in rubber, because now there is a world-wide rubber slump.'

'Poor Father!'

'What about your mother?'

'Well, of course — but it will be Father who has to try and work for us all.'

Mrs Blundell-Jones paused to digest this, then she went on, 'Next term is to be your last at school.'

Bess was delighted but tried not to show it.

'After that you will visit your grandparents — this letter of course was before your mother heard of the death of Mrs Marchmont. Then you will be put in the charge of someone responsible, and go out to Malaya.'

'So this will be my last holiday at the Grange?'

'Yes.'

'How extraordinary!'

'Is that all you have to say?'

'I'm a bit bowled over,' said Bess apologetically. 'I can't quite take it all in.'

'No. I did tell you I had bad news.'

'Yes. May I lie down and rest?'

Mrs Blundell-Jones looked at her suspiciously. 'If you want to,' she said.

'Thank you,' said Bess, and she went out of the room.

She ran at once to find Deirdre and Gerald. 'So you'll be leaving us?' asked Deirdre, half-envious that Bess would be embarking on a grown-up kind of life so soon, but also dismayed that their days at the Grange together were to be over. Gerald's exaggerated despair was almost laughable. 'You can't go!' he said. 'You simply can't!'

'But Gerald,' said Bess comfortingly, 'it isn't as though we'll never see each other again!'

'How do you know it isn't?' demanded Gerald furiously.

'Because we're friends,' said Bess. 'Friends don't lose touch.'

'Malaya is millions and millions of miles away,' said Gerald. 'We can't possibly see you out there.'

'I'll come back, of course.'

'How do you know you will?'

'Because I will. That's how,' said Bess.

Gerald refused to be comforted.

'I'll write,' said Bess.

'Promise?'

'Of course I will.'

In the event, however, they all wrote to each other a few times and then the correspondence lapsed.

Bess's last term at school was outwardly normal. She was top as usual, in class and in her exams, and she won the tennis tournament and the diving competition. But to the irritation of the staff and her rivals, her mind was clearly on none of it. She was caught up day and night in an almost physical hunger of anticipation for what the end of term would bring.

Before she left England she visited Grandfather Marchmont, who didn't seem in the least distressed at his wife's death and had already installed an excellent housekeeper, who looked after him very comfortably. He gave Bess many messages of love for Edward, for whom he obviously had a sincere affection. He also gave her the largest present of money she had ever received: five pounds.

Old Madge Glanville bought Bess several very pretty dresses and three pairs of shoes. She also sent messages of love, but this time to Kate.

To Bess, she whispered, 'Never forget, darling, that your Granny loves you. She may not show it very much, but she does, and while she lives, you always have a friend.'

'Thank you, Gran,' said Bess. 'I love you, too.'

CHAPTER SIX

Bess set sail for Malaya under the wing of Lady Calthrop, the wife of an eminent judge in Johore Bahru.

Lady Calthrop was an eccentric and a martinet, but fortunately for Bess she was not a good sailor, so Bess had a great deal of time to herself. She quickly made friends with a pretty blonde girl of eighteen who was also going out to join her parents, on a rubber estate not far from Kuala Lumpur.

Bunty was the belle of the ship and always surrounded by a bevy of admirers, but she was genuinely fond of Bess and, despite the age discrepancy, saw to it that Bess was included in the fun. If Lady Calthrop happened to be confined to her cabin when they reached port, then Bunty took Bess ashore with her party; and on board she always had someone to swim or to play deck games with. Bess even collected a beau for herself — a charming boy of eighteen called Tim Hudson, who was joining the Malay States Police Force. He occasionally squired her to the ship's dances, much to Lady Calthrop's disapproval; and he kissed her once or twice under the stars, which Bess enjoyed though without becoming dangerously 'excited'.

Lady Calthrop considered herself a very great lady; indeed in Malaya, she was treated as one. But her snobbery on board ship, her affectation and the way she expected everyone to do her bidding, however inconvenient or unreasonable, made her universally unpopular. Worst of all, and excruciatingly embarrassing for Bess, was her habit of attending the dances, choosing a young man whom she considered either suitable or a good dancer, and insisting that he not only spend the rest of the evening with her, but should continuously dance her favourite dance, the waltz, no matter what music the band was playing. At Port Said, where the 'gully-gully men' still came on board with their juggling acts, their swaying cobras and their silverware, she took Bess to Simon Arszt, where her father had bought his solar topee so many years before. After an excellent lunch at the Grand Hotel she insisted on her afternoon siesta. The siesta lasted so long that she and Bess had very little time to regain the ship and in their excitement embarked on the sister ship which was homeward bound. By the time they eventually reached their own, they were late for her sailing time — a particularly serious matter in the Canal — and were sternly reprimanded by the captain.

The voyage still took a month, and as they headed steadily East into the Indian Ocean, where the flying fish leapt beside them in the blue water and the great yellow sun became hotter and hotter in an increasingly humid atmosphere, Bess felt a sense of peace and homecoming — a homecoming directed not so much towards her parents as towards the land where she had been born.

Kate and Edward met her in Penang, accompanied by their head boy, Amin, who had been in Edward's service since he had settled in Kuala Lumpur, and whose greying hairs did nothing to diminish his habitual dignity and good looks. The four of them returned by train to Kuala Lumpur, Kate explaining that although Edward was now very badly off he was still a man of considerable consequence, and that Bess had a position to live up to.

The new house in KL, to which they had moved before the slump, was situated on the race-course, where, in the early days of her marriage, Kate had so scandalised the other wives by playing polo with the men. It was in fact a large bungalow of black wood, with two raised wings. At the back was the kitchen which opened on to a courtyard, around which were the servants' quarters. To Bess's amazement there were even more servants. Amin's young wife was now to be Bess's ayah. First Ayah, an old woman now by Malay standards, was still looking after Kate, though her husband was on a pilgrimage to Mecca, to become a holy man, or Hadji. The second boy, Ali, was unmarried; but the syce (or chauffeur) lived in with his wife, as did the cook and his wife, the two kebuns (gardeners) and their wives and the lowly 'tukan ayer'.

Kate and Edward occupied the left-hand wing of the house and Bess the right. The bedrooms and bathrooms were surrounded by a wide wooden verandah. The beds were covered with mosquito nets at night, and the chiks or roller blinds on the verandah served as sun blinds during the day, and for privacy after dark. In the centre of each room was a large electric fan, with great rotating metal blades which looked like oars suspended from the ceiling.

The bathrooms had no running water and were small concrete

structures with simply a hole in the floor for waste water, a huge
stone jar (called a 'tong') which was kept permanently full of cold
water, and a tin bath which was filled with hot water on request
from the kitchen and brought in by the tukan ayer. On very hot
days, snakes would sometimes find their way up through the hole
in the floor, in search of somewhere cool.

The centre of the house was used as an enormous drawing-room
on three levels, on to which the front door immediately opened;
and up one step at the back was the large dining-room, famous for
Kate's special Sunday curry-tiffins — luncheons to which invitations were eagerly sought.

The decor reflected Kate's own taste, though strongly influenced
by Patrick's; and, in spite of the functional rattan furniture with its
obligatory holes in the arms of the sofas and chairs to take the
drinking glasses, she had managed to achieve the semblance of an
English country house. She had eighteenth-century prints on the
walls and some good pieces of china scattered here and there.
There were even two bookcases filled with books, braving the
depradations of the silver fish (which ate their determined way
even through the covers) and the cockroaches, which were
squashed daily on the dark wooden floors, leaving a sweet musty
smell, or were 'flitted' from a pump, which seemed only to stun
rather than kill them. But, as in all the other houses, there were
little bright-eyed transparent lizards called chik-chaks running
over the walls, which detracted somewhat from the English atmosphere. They ate flies, dropped their tails when alarmed, and
made the tut-tutting noise which had given them their name.

Kate was quickly disconcerted by her daughter's apparent
maturity. Men still outnumbered women by ten to one amongst
the expatriates and, with young men queuing to date Bess, Kate
was understandably anxious at so much attention being paid to
one so young. Then, too, though she loved Bess, she was unused to
sharing her home with anyone but Edward, and unused to coming
second in his affections. What was worse, Patrick frequently
telephoned. Kate had seen very little of him lately, and though she
was still unable completely to forget him, his absence had made life
tolerable. Now he was back in their lives again.

She decided on action.

She persuaded Edward that, despite the financial stringency,
Bess must resume some form of schooling. It was finally decided,
much to the horror of the British community, that she should be

sent as a day girl to the otherwise all-Asiatic school of St Mary's, in Kuala Lumpur.

Bess rebelled. For the first time since she had gone out East she lost control of her violent temper, which shocked Edward deeply. She tried to explain to him that she had been enjoying her home, after so many years without one, and that her new-found freedom from routine was very precious. She told him that she loved the tennis parties, the dances, the badminton, the swimming, golf at the Lake Club and the light-hearted flirtations. This last admission was a mistake, and Edward became as adamant as Kate that she should go back to school; at least until she had passed her school certificate, which would enable her to take some sort of a job if money matters became even worse.

Strangely enough, Bess enjoyed this particular school very much. She had become adept at mixing with other children after such a long training; and at St Mary's, as a bonus, there was the fascination of the varied lifestyles of her new friends, whose parents were most hospitable. She now felt that she was a part of this country, as she hadn't before; and she found the friendliness and kindness of her fellow pupils especially rewarding, as she realised she must seem so alien to them.

The Chinese homes interested her most, with their rigid hierarchies of first wife, children, concubines and servants. The houses were all built according to the principles of 'geomancy', a mysterious science which dictated whether a plot of land was suitable for a building, and if so precisely where, and facing which direction, it should be built. Dire evils were predicted by the geomancers—often astrologers or soothsayers—if their advice was disregarded. It never was. (And today, even in great commercial centres like Singapore and Hong Kong, their writ still runs.)

One house in particular delighted Bess. It was an enormous turreted mansion of many courtyards, bright with green tiles and blue ornamentation. At the far end of the room through which one entered from the street was an ever-open door — the symbol of welcome. The rooms all had high ceilings and there were carved ebony chairs, with marble seats and backs, ranged against the walls. Above them hung scrolled pictures and on the ebony tables there were fine pieces of jade and porcelain. Huge lamps lit these rooms at night. Sir Chan Koo, the owner, had been knighted for his philanthropy two years before, and in the almost empty principal reception room was a lifesize and atrociously painted portrait of him dressed in top hat, white tie and tails and wearing the insignia of the KBE. He spoke perfect English (as did his daughter, who was Bess's friend at St Mary's) and seemed to enjoy entertaining his young guest. His wife by contrast spoke only Cantonese. She was fat and jolly, though kept very much in the background in the Chinese tradition. When she appeared she wore exquisitely embroidered silks and satins, gold and diamond earrings, huge gold bracelets, diamond necklaces and jade brooches; she had gold-capped teeth, and her feet, which were bound in the old style, and looked like tiny hooves, were shod in the smallest embroidered slippers Bess had ever seen. The youngest boy-children were nearly always dressed in woollen tam o'shanters and brightly coloured cotton smocks, which stopped just above their genitals. The older children usually dressed in European clothes.

The homes of her Indian friends (who gave her strong curries to eat and played British card-games like rummy and poker) were usually over their shops, with surplus goods overflowing into all the rooms. The Indians, who loved to be more British than the British, spoke excellent English with what Bess thought of as a Welsh accent and often boasted that their fathers and brothers were 'failed BA's'.

Her Malay friends mostly came from the small village kampongs outside KL. These kampongs were usually in clearings in the jungle, or by the rivers or the sea; for Malays disliked towns and loved the simple abundance of their countryside, where fruit fell from the trees, coconuts gave milk and the sea yielded fish. The kampongs were scattered among the trees in a perpetual twilight, and the houses stood fairly far apart. They were built of planed wood or plaited palm leaves, with steep high roofs and deep eaves, and rested on wooden 'gridiron' platforms supported on posts from five to ten feet high. The poorer houses had ladders and the richer ones a flight of steps. Mats were laid over the gridirons, which not only provided ventilation but enabled rubbish to be thrown down on to the fires, which were lit in the evenings to keep away mosquitoes. Often a trained baboon was kept by the house-owner to climb the palms and throw down the coconuts. The richer houses were more ornate, with wood carvings under the eaves, carrying verses from the Koran; but no ornament which had a likeness to anything living in 'heaven or earth' was permitted.

Bess spent a year at St Mary's. When she had to leave after passing her exam, she was sorry to go.

Life at home now took a turn for the worse, although socially the pressure was greater than ever. Bess was nearly seventeen and the few Englishmen around, starved of female company in a country and society which still disapproved of miscegenation, booked her up for months ahead to the three great dances of the year: the St Andrew's Ball for the Scots, the St George's Ball for the English and the St Patrick's for the Irish, all of which were celebrated at the 'Spotted Dog'. Bess loved it all but her enjoyment was clouded by the financial anxieties which were now driving Kate and Edward apart.

Kate had become tired of attempting to reduce expenditure. 'I'm earning a good deal now from my painting,' she said, 'unlike the Nancy Bankses of this world.' Yet even the painting was a frustration to her. Although indeed it was helping financially, it wasn't enough to set them on their feet again. Worse, though she was now famous in Malaya as a painter, the lack of other artists by whom to judge her own standards or with whom to discuss her work, the lack of art galleries where she might look at other pictures, and the lack of a broader, more discriminating, public was shaking her confidence in herself—which was unsteady enough at the best of times. She knew that if she had believed in her heart that painting was her vocation, she would never have married Edward. Tonks's admiration, though it had flattered her, hadn't convinced her that she had real talent.

There was also the problem of Patrick. Sending Bess to school achieved her object, of stopping Patrick from telephoning her; but when the calls stopped she discovered that the brief revival of contact since Bess's return had reawakened her longing for him. She took her frustration and misery out on Edward.

For his part, Edward, worried and ashamed at not being able to maintain their previous standard of living, was becoming short-tempered and intolerant of her.

Bess tried hard to understand, but the storms of tears, the reconciliations which never really reconciled her parents, her mother's flaming tempers, her father's bitter tongue, the eternal music on the gramophone in the evenings, which reflected their changing moods (usually culminating in 'The Ride of The Valkyries' for the worst of the rows, and always to the accompaniment of the whirring ceiling fans) — all this gradually turned her away from them both, and at last she decided to leave home.

She asked if she might try to get a job, saying that it was

worrying her that she was a financial burden to them at such a time.

Kate was all for it, but Edward was appalled.

'Don't leave me, Bessie darling,' he said. 'I don't think I could stand it here without you! Besides, you ought to find a nice young man and settle down.'

'She's not yet seventeen!' scoffed Kate. And to Bess she said, 'For God's sake be careful when you do marry, Bess. Never forget that you marry the man's life as well as him! Why not get a part-time job in KL?'

Now it was Bess's turn to take action. She had made one good friend in KL whom Kate didn't like — Rachel Fields, who ran the town public library. In Kate's eyes, Rachel wore too much make-up and had too loud a voice, but Bess found her warm-hearted and amusing. Bess realised that her own contemporaries couldn't help her — since the girls were all rigidly supervised by their mothers and naturally she couldn't throw herself on the mercy of any of her swains — but Rachel was older, and married, and if she were willing to house her for a time, Bess might be able to find the kind of job she was looking for.

Together they decided that, when the Marchmonts were celebrating Armistice Day at the Cenotaph, Bess should take advantage of the couple of hours which could be guaranteed not to be interrupted. She could then pack her bags and walk out. Once she had left her parents' roof, she and Rachel believed that the Marchmonts would come round to Bess's way of thinking and, since it would indeed relieve their financial burden, allow her to go her own way to find the kind of job and life she wanted. The plan worked.

To Bess's relief, she found a job surprisingly quickly.

A new school, St Margaret's, had been opened on Bukit Fraser (which had now been developed as a holiday resort), to accommodate European children whose parents didn't want to part with them young. The climate up 'the Hill', as it was called, was very different from that in the plains: it was more like the South of France. The head-mistress, Mrs McLaughlan, needed a new assistant as she had quarrelled with her first one, and engaged Bess unseen, and in spite of her age, on the strength of her school certificate. (Few white girls were looking for jobs; they were all on the marriage market.) Bess was told to report in three weeks' time. The salary was almost non-existent — like Bess's qualifications —

but it meant a roof over her head, her keep and a job to which her parents couldn't object. There were thirty boarders at the time of her arrival, and one day-child whose mother ran the holiday bungalows for the big European companies such as Guthries, Harrison Crossfields and Sime Darby.

The school was housed in a very long white-washed bungalow with a dark red corrugated iron roof, set on the topmost peak of the Hill. It was surrounded by a garden, beyond which on all sides was dense jungle. Bess had to use jungle paths to reach the Club or the golf course, or visit friends, and she grew to love the area almost as much as her mother did; but curiously enough she found the tall jungle trees claustrophobic.

Although she was in an institution again, Bess was now independent of all authority except Mrs McLaughlan's, and Mrs McLaughlan was wise enough to exercise it sparingly. Bess and Mrs McLaughlan hit it off from the start and Bess spent the next two years very happily, learning how to teach, and how to grow up. Her social life was as intense as in Kuala Lumpur: at that time, Fraser's Hill was the only hill station in the FMS (the Federated Malay States) and it was full, all the year round, with people whose only idea was to have a good time. The work load at the school, however, was punishing; the children ranged from four to fifteen years of age and varied as widely in accomplishment and potential. Bess took the little ones, and Mrs McLaughlan the rest, for every subject they learned; and she often found herself studying half the night in order to present the subjects as she felt they ought to be taught. She had one half day free each week as did Mrs McLaughlan but when she wasn't studying at night there was always a dinner invitation, and on Saturdays there was a dance at the Club.

Bess became extremely fond of Mrs McLaughlan, who was an enormous woman with a heavy Scots accent. She had the shoulders of a man and an ugly lined face (not improved by several large warts) — but she had a splendid sense of humour, and a heart of gold. She had been happily married to her childhood sweetheart, a doctor, who had died in Malaya three years previously, leaving her penniless and heartbroken; she had courage and initiative, and her idea of running the school had paid off handsomely. She was strict and prudish, and had the devil's own temper, but she was kind to Bess, who for the first time in her life felt completely at home.

CHAPTER SEVEN

For eighteen months of her time on the Hill, Bess was content. She soon made it up with her parents, who came up twice a year on their holidays and seemed delighted that she was so happy.

Relations between Kate and Edward were still strained but the shock of Bess's departure had forced them into some sort of compromise; for the first time since she had fallen in love with Patrick, Kate had no wish to leave her husband.

Edward had grown thin to the point of emaciation. The bones of his already bony face seemed to protrude from his skin, his pale blue eyes were watery and his clothes hung off him in folds. Kate, too, looked thin and peaked. Her fading blonde hair was salted with grey and there were deep lines from her nose to her chin, but she still wore her clothes with distinction and still had immense attraction.

Now at last, luck seemed to favour them financially again.

Edward had been offered a lucrative partnership in Singapore. Although he was reluctant to give up his own firm in KL, the combination of increased security and decreased responsibility, together with the large sum of money he had been offered for the good will of Marchmont and Slade, had made acceptance inevitable. Besides which, Kate was delighted at the prospect. They had been offered a great deal for the house in KL and had found a satisfactory and far cheaper house in Singapore, so they were full of plans for the future.

During their short holidays on the Hill, Bess saw them as often as she could. She felt that it was the least she could do under the circumstances.

She grew closer to her mother for the first time. Although sensing her underlying bitterness, Bess found Kate a marvellous companion and raconteur and loved hearing about the theatre and the Glanville household, and about Kate's childhood. Her mother's stories of her time at the Slade fascinated her, and above all she was delighted by Kate's sense of humour — something she hadn't suspected in her mother until now. Kate, too, seemed surprised at a new-found happiness. 'It's because we're going to Singapore!' she said. 'I didn't realise how much I had grown to hate KL. I really hate it, Bess.'

But if Kate was on the upgrade, Edward seemed lost and almost broken, and Bess's heart ached for him. She tried to make him understand that, even though she had left home, she loved him more than anyone she knew. He was pathetically grateful. They took long walks together in the jungle, when he would talk eagerly to her for hours. He was a keen botanist and taught her the names of many of the plants; but birds were still his passion and on these he was now an acknowledged authority.

'It's a funny thing,' he said one day as they sat by a jungle waterfall. 'I get astonished sometimes at what my life has been about, Bessie. You've no idea, darling, what fun it all was in the beginning. I know you didn't like my parents much, but they were very good to me and I had a very happy childhood. I was clever and everyone predicted a great future for me. It was my own wish to come to Malaya, and it's a country I've never ceased to like. I was head over heels in love with your mother when I married her . . . and when we had you, everything seemed perfect. We had a good deal of money at one time. Then, like everyone else of our age, we lost it in the rubber slump. But that shouldn't have mattered all that much, because money isn't everything. Besides, by bringing you home we still managed to keep up a good deal of state, didn't we? And now everything is right as rain again, and the future is fine. But what I want to know is, what is life all about? What the hell are we doing here? What have I really achieved after a lifetime of hard work? I thought I did a good deal for the Federal Council — but did I? If I turned up there now, I doubt if they'd even know who I was. My firm will do splendidly without me, and even your mother is almost a stranger, though I'm sure the fault is mine. I'm not blaming her, you understand. As for you — the light of my life — you have left us for freedom, even before I have got to know you. That again is not a fault on your part, but the loss is mine. I'm tired Bessie. Tired, through and through. I tell myself I've had a good life. The best. But I don't believe myself. Not for one moment. I've been lucky never to have starved, or been maimed physically. I've lived what is known as a full life. But what is a full life? What use has any of it been to me, or anyone else?' He sighed. 'Would you like to please me, Bessie?'

'Of course, Father.'

'Then have the courage to do what you really want to in life. With courage, I believe things might make some sort of sense. Don't try to run with the pack, unless it suits you. Don't give a damn for convention, unless it suits you. Go where you want. Love where you want. Few people have the courage, but I have the feeling that if we are absolutely true to ourselves, we can fulfill ourselves. So long as it's never at the expense of other people.'

'But you said you were in love with Mummy when you married her,' said Bess, picking out the one part of the speech which she both understood and appreciated, 'so weren't you true to yourself?'

'I was certainly in love with her,' said Edward, 'and I still am.' He fell silent, looking very unhappy, then smiled and said, 'I'm pretty dreary today, aren't I darling? But I'd like you to remember me kindly.'

'Oh, but I do!' exclaimed Bess, throwing her arms round him impulsively, in a rare show of affection. 'Always! You're the nicest man I've ever met!'

Uncle Patrick was also a regular visitor to the Hill, but he never came at the same time as Kate and Edward. He was still very good-looking and the women still fell for him. Bess felt his attraction keenly; after Edward, he was her favourite older man. Patrick knew how to make the young feel at their best — Bess in particular. He encouraged her to talk, so she happily dropped into the habit of telling him all her secrets. He seemed to love listening to almost anything she had to tell him, which she found both flattering and endearing.

One day she said to him, 'I do wish you liked Mummy more. I think it makes her very unhappy that you don't.'

He stared at her amazed. 'What makes you think I don't like her?' he asked, sharply.

'Do you?' she countered.

'One doesn't always like extremely attractive women.' He laughed uneasily.

'What a horrible thing to say!' said Bess, shocked.

'Is it?' Patrick was surprised. 'Well yes, I suppose it is. I hadn't thought of it that way.'

'Was Mummy very beautiful when you were all young together?'

'Very,' sighed Patrick. 'There was never anyone to touch her.'

Bess sighed too. 'I'll never be beautiful,' she said sadly.

'You'll do,' laughed Patrick.

'I hate my face!'

'So do most of us.'

'I bet you don't hate yours!'

'Yes I do.'

'I think women have rather a bad time of it,' said Bess. 'Girls like other girls very much until they grow up, then they like men best, except for their "best friends". Men can *love* women, it seems — but they don't often like them. They like each other much better.'

'You aren't by any chance insinuating that I love your mother?' said Patrick quickly.

Again Bess was shocked. 'No, of course not!' she exclaimed. 'I don't know what's got into you today, Uncle Patrick! You're Father's best friend.'

Patrick looked away from her. 'That's right,' he agreed over-heartily. 'I'm Edward's best friend.'

'Well, aren't you?'

'Yes. Oh yes,' said Patrick. 'There's no doubt about that.' And he changed the subject.

Another time Bess said to him, 'Have you ever been in love, Uncle Patrick?'

Patrick, who had been walking quite fast, stopped dead in his tracks. Bess thought she had never seen him look so unhappy.

'Why?' he asked. 'Have you fallen for someone?'

'No. I just wanted to know about you.'

He paused for a long time, then said 'Yes, I have,' and sounded angry.

Bess was worried that she had hurt his feelings, but as she had started the conversation, she felt she had better go on. 'May I ask why you didn't marry, darling?' she asked quietly.

'Because she was married already,' he said.

'I'm so sorry.'

'I was a fool anyway. I didn't value her enough, you see. She was too generous in her love, and you don't always value the things you get too easily.'

'Is she still alive?'

'Oh, yes.'

'Do you still love her?'

'Yes. But I didn't realise it until I lost her. Again, some people — the idiots like me — don't. And now it's all too late.'

He had a walking stick in his hand and suddenly whacked viciously at a jungle tree.

'How do you know it's too late? Is her husband still alive?'

'It's too late! I only discovered it the other day. She doesn't even like me any more.' He looked past Bess into the distance and frowned.

'Are you sure?' asked Bess unhappily. She wished she had never started the conversation, but now Patrick seemed to want to talk.

'Quite sure,' he said. 'I learned it in the strangest possible way. The affair was over years ago but we continued to see each other socially; in a small community we couldn't help it. I had got into the habit of behaving rather boorishly to her — guilt I suppose. One day I telephoned her, and said one of my usual rather unforgiveable things, expecting her usual loving acceptance; but instead she said very clearly, in a cold contemptuous voice that I shall never forget, "That will do Patrick. It's over." And then she added, as though she had found out that it really was over, "How wonderful! How absolutely wonderful!" And you know, she sounded happy! Just as if a great weight had gone from her!'

'Poor Uncle Patrick!'

'My fault.'

'I wish I could say something helpful.'

'You can't, but thanks all the same.'

It was almost immediately after this visit from Patrick that Kate rang, to say that Edward was seriously ill in hospital.

'Could you possibly come down at once? I'm afraid it's cancer — and he's not responding to the treatment.'

'My God!' gasped Bess. 'I'll be right there. Give Father my love,' she added, 'and tell him I'm longing to see him, won't you?'

'Of course I will, my darling. But do hurry!' Kate's voice was shaking.

Bess put down the phone feeling weak and frightened, and ran to find Mrs McLaughlan. 'You'll have to go of course,' she agreed immediately. 'But get back as soon as you can. You know what the end of term is always like.'

There were no private cars leaving the Hill that day but Bess managed to catch a lift with one of her Chinese friends from St Mary's, who drove the fish car — a dilapidated old vehicle which twice a week brought the fish, wrapped round huge pieces of ice, from Kuala Lumpur. On its return journey it was always empty, since there were still such a powerful smell. The driver told her she'd miss the day train from KL to Singapore but that his uncle, Lim Soon, would help her. He then took her right to the door of Lim Soon's tea house, from which she was to travel in his Chinese mail car to Singapore.

The next part of the journey was noisy, but cheerful. After a short tea-drinking session, the other passengers — five Indians and three children — all clambered into the back, while Bess sat with Lim Soon in front. She was given a great stack of Chinese newspapers to hold; at various intervals in the journey, the driver gave a curious two-toned grunt and slowed down the car, which was a signal for Bess to throw out the top package, or packages, to waiting customers. At Malacca, they stopped again for tea. Mr Lim then took Bess home.

As she ran anxiously into the house, Ayah met her, looking very grave. 'Mem is at the hospital now,' she said. 'Tuan is very ill.' She spoke disapprovingly, and Bess realised that she wasn't forgiven for having run away from home.

'When will Mummy be back?' asked Bess.

'She didn't say.'

'OK.' replied Bess. 'I'll ring the hospital, right away.'

It was quite a while before the Sister came to the telephone. When she did, she told Bess that her mother would be back as soon as she could manage it.

Edward had died half an hour ago.

CHAPTER EIGHT

Although Bess had half expected bad news, she had not been prepared for Edward's death. She bitterly reproached herself for not having been with him. He had loved her so much, and she knew that he would have been looking out for her, and longing for her, to the end. She felt desolate and cheated. But when Kate returned, looking utterly broken, Bess managed to pull herself together enough to try to comfort her. She hadn't thought her mother would have taken his death so hard but Kate was inconsolable, murmuring over and over again, 'He was too good for me. He should never have married me.'

'Nonsense!' said Bess, firmly. 'He told me the last time he was up the Hill that he was still in love with you. That doesn't sound as though you should never have married him does it? And I bet there aren't many women whose husbands would say that, after such a long marriage!'

'Did he really say he was still in love with me?' Kate jerked up her head.

'Yes,' said Bess.

Kate looked as if she were going to say something more, but instead started to cry again. Presently she said, 'The funeral will be on Saturday. And if you don't mind, I shan't ask anyone else.'

'Not even Uncle Patrick?'

Kate glared at her. 'Certainly not,' she said.

'Wouldn't Father have liked some of his friends at the funeral?' asked Bess.

'Leave it, Bessie,' replied Kate. 'I was his wife, remember?'

The funeral with only the two of them attending seemed to Bess the most pathetic thing she had ever witnessed.

On the way home, Kate said uncertainly, 'Would you stay a part of your holiday with me, darling? I'm going to miss Edward so much.'

'Of course, Mummy, I'll stay with you for as long as you like. You can't possibly spend Christmas on your own, anyway.'

It was a sad but curiously peaceful time. Both women, knowing the other's feelings, were on their best behaviour. Kate was gentler than Bess had ever known her and they avoided getting on one another's nerves.

'What will you do when I return to the Hill?' asked Bess, one day. 'Will you go back to England?'

'I'll have to get some sort of job here first,' said Kate. 'Your father was still paying off enormous debts, and at my age I'll never get a job in England. When the job here is settled — if it is — I'll go and see Mother for a bit. But I don't really like the thought of retiring to England, you know. I hate the cold — really hate it — and like so many of us who have spent their lives out here I feel out of place there now. Besides, you're here and so are all my friends, and in England my painting isn't known, while here it can help quite a bit.'

'But I thought things were so good now, financially!' said Bess, surprised.

'It's all my own fault. I was terribly extravagant when we were broke and poor. Edward was always trying to make me save.... I'll manage, though. You'll see.'

'I wish I could help.'

'You've already helped by being with me now.'

'And you've helped me,' answered Bess, soberly.

Kate smiled a strangely wry smile, and put an arm round Bess's shoulders. 'Edward loved you intensely. You know that, don't you?' she said. 'He was tremendously proud of you, and I sometimes think that when the bad times came it was the thought of you that pulled him through. How oddly things work out.'

'I don't understand,' said Bess.

'I mean, how providential it was after all that you were born,' said Kate, hurriedly.

'Didn't you want children, then?' asked Bess.

'We wanted you,' replied Kate, and her eyes filled with tears.

When the spring term started, Bess went up the Hill again. Kate was still looking for a job but now all her friends were helping her. To Bess's surprise, Patrick hadn't appeared on the scene at all. He had written a sympathetic letter, which Kate showed to Bess, but that was all; and Kate seemed to think that it was all that was necessary. Bess was anxious about leaving her mother alone in Singapore, but Kate was certain that she should go back to the school. 'It would be ridiculous for both of us to be out of work,' she said. 'I'll manage. Don't worry, Bessie. It's about time I grew up, anyway.'

On her return to the Hill, Bess discovered that her friend Tim Hudson, the boy she had first met on the boat coming out to Malaya, was up on holiday. They had kept up the acquaintance — and, like so many others, he had fallen in love with her. For her part, he reminded her of Edward.

Tim was doing well in the Police. He was kind, dependable and clever. His father had died when he was young, and perhaps because he was an only child, and therefore used to female society, she found him a specially sympathetic and sensitive companion. She soon imagined herself in love with him: overjoyed, Tim proposed, and Bess accepted.

Tim's leave was due in six months' time. He suggested that they should go to England together, engaged but not married, so that he could introduce her to his mother, for her approval. 'She'll adore you,' he said confidently. Bess realised, to her dismay, that she had now committed herself to going back to England. Worse still, she was intensely looking forward to it. She was horrified that Kate might feel that she was deserting her, so when she rang her to tell her the news she said, 'But I'll be back soon, darling. We won't be away very long.'

Kate's reaction astonished her. 'You're mad, Bess!' she said. 'I can't stop you if you're really in love with this boy — but you're years and years too young! You haven't seen anything of life yet.'

'You'll like him, Mummy. You really will,' said Bess earnestly. 'He's awfully like Father.'

'Please don't rush into it, Bess!' implored Kate. 'Marriage is a trap! A trap! Women don't see it, but they need much more than marriage to fill their lives, even if they have a family! They can't and mustn't exist at second hand, living through the man's life. It's stultifying, suffocating and degrading! It is also, to put it mildly, unfulfilling.'

Bess was horrified. 'My God, Mummy!' she exclaimed. 'Were you that unhappily married?'

With an effort, Kate controlled herself. 'No, of course not,' she said more quietly. 'But I was much older than you when I got married, and I don't want you to make a terrible mistake.'

'But what about being in love?' demanded Bess. 'Isn't that important?'

'In love?' Her mother's voice was harsh. 'Being in love is a con game. Worse, it's a hideous disease which brings only pain and disillusion.'

'Weren't you in love with Father?' asked Bess in a small voice.

There was a silence on the other end of the telephone, then a laugh. 'Oh, yes, I was in love with your father,' said Kate. She sounded bitter.

'Surely he never brought you pain?' demanded Bess angrily.

There was another silence, then Kate said slowly, 'Edward is dead, darling, and that brings pain.'

CHAPTER NINE

Tim's insistence that he could only make their engagement official after Mrs Hudson had given them her blessing placed Bess in a dilemma. She had no wish for him to pay for her passage now that her own mother was so set against the wedding.

'Of course I'll give you the money!' said Tim. 'After all, it's my idea that you should come to England.'

'Supposing your mother doesn't like me?' asked Bess. 'What do we do then? I'll have taken your money for nothing.'

'I love you, and Mother only wants to do what's best for me,' said Tim.

'Supposing I don't like *her*?' demanded Bess.

'You're not marrying *her*! Anyway, I'm sure you will. She's marvellous. Besides, you and I will be spending our lives out here, and she lives in England, so we shan't be seeing much of her even if we wanted to.'

Her heart sank as he said this. She had had no idea that England was where she really wanted to live, until, by her engagement, she had forfeited her right to live there. She did, however, insist that she should find her own passage money.

'OK', said Tim. 'If that's how you prefer it. But prefer is the operative word. If you're stuck, then my offer holds. Damn it all, we can't simply not marry just because you can't pay your fare back to England! That's crazy!'

'Mummy is very against me marrying so young,' she said firmly, 'and I don't want to upset her any further.'

By a stroke of luck, a friend of Bess's named Norah Mullen came to the rescue. Norah was expecting a baby and wanted to have the birth at home; and since she already had a two-year-old son, Johnnie, whom she wanted to take with her to England, she needed someone to help her. To Tim's dismay — for it meant that she would be leaving months ahead of him — Bess got the job.

Mrs McLaughlan was very upset at the prospect of losing Bess, but since the girl who had stood in for her when Edward was dying was still available for a more permanent position, she reconciled herself and wished Bess good luck.

Bess finished the spring term at Fraser's Hill, then went to Singapore to spend one last holiday with her mother. Kate had now arranged to replace Rachel Fields, whose husband was moving job, as Librarian in Kuala Lumpur. She would start as soon as her little break with Bess was over. She was excited about the prospect of earning her own living — and even happy to be returning to KL, since Patrick would no longer be there. He had at last inherited his uncle's estate in Yorkshire and would soon be going home for good.

Perhaps now those long years of loving and unhappiness could fade into oblivion? Kate hoped — and believed — that this was so. Total disillusionment, she had found, cuts a shallower groove in the memory than rejection.

Kate had chosen for their holiday a steamer trip, up the Indrigiri River in Sumatra to a place called Rengatt. The jungle was still her idea of happiness, and she was not disappointed. All along the banks of the broad yellow river the jungle reached down to the water's edge, and there were crocodiles, parrots, monkeys and festoons of brilliant flowers among the foliage. The passage upstream took four hot, lazy days. Bess and Kate were the only European passengers; the rest were Sumatran women returning from shopping expeditions in Singapore.

The Captain was a Dutchman, who could have stepped out of — or into — the pages of Somerset Maugham. He wore dirty white silk pyjamas throughout the twenty-four hours, attaching his insignia of rank to them with a safety pin during daylight. He had vestigial traces of gallantry for Bess and Kate, and allowed Bess to help steer the steamer when the going was easy. Occasionally he took pot shots at the monkeys with an air gun, but mostly he was abstracted or drunk. Nonetheless, he managed his job, if not with panache, at least adequately.

At Rengatt they lunched with a Dutch woman, Susie Van der Elst, in a drab featureless bungalow on the edge of the river. Susie was a splendid character. Her husband and his assistant were the only other Europeans in Rengatt and were out at work most of the day; so to while away the hours, she was teaching herself languages on her gramophone. She had learned English, French, Spanish and Italian, so far: as the wife of a Dutch plantation manager who was allowed leave only once in eight years, this was optimism of a high degree. She was delighted to have a chance to practise her English, and Kate and Susie became immediate friends.

When the holiday was over, Kate and Bess went up country to Kuala Lumpur — Kate to take up her duties as Librarian and Bess to help settle her in. Bess then proceeded to Pahang for a couple of weeks in Batu Hitam, where Tim wanted to show her the house to which she would return as a bride. Mona Mavor, the wife of the District Officer with whom she was to stay, picked her up in KL where she'd been on a shopping spree and drove her there through seemingly unending jungle. The journey took two days, with an overnight stay in a Government Rest House.

The jungle had never held quite the fascination for Bess that it had for Kate. She found the journey depressing. Mona disliked her husband and told Bess repeatedly that living miles from nowhere with a man you weren't 'besotted with' was 'no joke'.

'You grow almost to hate each other,' she said fiercely, 'simply from the boredom of the same old face looking at you and the same kind of conversation day after day! I hope for your sake that you're madly in love, Bess. Don't dream of getting hitched if you aren't.'

Mona hated her bungalow and loathed Malaya. The heat and the lack of a social life were driving her out of her mind, she said. She had married Bill only to get away from the singularly unpleasant aunt who had brought her up since her mother's death. She knew she wasn't pretty, and at thirty-five had felt she was on the shelf; so Bill's proposal had seemed like a godsend. It turned out that Bill was renowned for his meanness; she swore that he had only married her because bachelors had less chance of promotion. He had picked on Mona because she was 'dirt poor' and so less likely to be extravagant.

The bungalow when they reached it was certainly without any charm. Mona was a bad housekeeper, the cooking was atrocious, and an ill-tempered tame goose was allowed to wander around at will. It took an instant dislike to Bess and hissed at her whenever it saw her, which terrified her. Bill and Mona quarrelled incessantly, which reminded Bess all too clearly of her parents in KL.

By contrast, Tim's bungalow was charming. He had all the taste which Mona lacked. But there were few European neighbours near by and Bess realised clearly how isolated she and Tim would be.

On one of the two week-ends, she was shown vividly quite how

lonely some jobs could be. They all paid a visit to the house of a
planter who lived four hours up-river from the nearest small town.
Every evening he bathed and changed for dinner. Avidly he read
the latest well-reviewed novels and all the theatre criticism. He
played classical music on his portable gramophone on records
which the heat had warped so badly that 'flit' had to be used to
keep the needle in contact with the undulating grooves. He was
twenty-six, and hoping to marry his childhood sweetheart on his
next leave — and received with enthusiasm the news that Bess
would be coming to live 'near by' as he called it. Bess was touched
by his determination to maintain an English way of life under such
difficult circumstances, but it also irritated her. 'Why on earth
keep up such state when you're completely on your own?' she
asked.

'If I didn't, I'd go completely under,' he replied.

When she asked why he hadn't made a virtue of his isolation by
studying and even writing about some of the local cultures, he
asked earnestly, 'But which culture do you suggest, Bess? Muslim,
for the Malays? Confucianism for most of the Chinese? Or one of
the Indian cultures? And if I were seen to be favouring one, what
would the others think? As an employer of all three races, it's my
duty to be impartial!'

Bess was deeply chastened by the whole experience. She wondered in panic if she should break off the engagement.

Tim had by this stage managed to get ten days' leave. First he
took her back to KL to say goodbye to Kate, then on to Singapore
to embark for England with Norah Mullen and the two children
on a small Danish cargo ship. Tim was to accompany them as far
as Penang.

It was now late summer, 1936. The circumstances were far less
luxurious than on Bess's journey out, but her cabin did at least
have a private bathroom. Norah would be leaving the care of
young Johnnie almost entirely to Bess after Tim's departure; until
then the two of them had two nights and days together, cruising
through calm waters in perfect weather, with spectacular sunsets
and bright tropical starry nights. Against Bess's better judgement,
they slept together. It was the first time for her — and she protested. But Tim allayed her anxieties: 'Even if we do have a child,
darling,' he said, 'it won't matter. We'll just have to get spliced a
bit sooner, that's all!'

By the time Tim left, Bess had reassured herself that she did indeed love him enough to marry him, even if she had to live in Batu Hitam.

The trip home took six weeks, and since it was a cargo ship, they stopped at many ports which a liner would have bypassed. At Djibuti, they heard that Mussolini — at that time engaged in his invasion of Abyssinia — was so nervous of the tales his troops would tell if they were allowed home on leave to Italy that he was sending them elsewhere! In Marseilles, Bess was given a French newspaper with the notorious headline, 'COO-EE!'. Beneath was a picture of England's King Edward VIII (so recently the adored Prince of Wales) cruising in the Mediterranean with his friend Mrs Simpson. They both looked rather skinny, and were dressed unattractively in shorts. The story read that the King found 'Wally' irresistible because she called out 'coo-ee!' instead of addressing him formally, and that on the day she called 'coo-ee, come and get married!', he would do so. There had been no hint of the King's romance in the Malayan papers, so the article came as a shock to Bess. She and the other English passengers spent the rest of the voyage discussing it.

They arrived at Tilbury in a downpour. Bess spent one night with Norah Mullen at her mother's flat in Cromwell Gardens, then on the following day went to Richmond to stay with Madge.

CHAPTER TEN

Madge had changed very little during the time that Bess had been away. There was a new and younger housekeeper now, but Effie, who had become very frail, was staying on as Madge's much-loved companion. Bentwood looked the same as ever; and he still drove a Rolls.

Madge was very moved by her reunion with her grand-daughter. Even though she still entertained on Sundays, and was also about to start rehearsing a new play, she saw fewer people these days and said that she often felt lonely. Shaw and Charlotte still visited, and Gladys Cooper, but Madge had given up her committee work. 'Dear May is dead,' she said sadly. 'She was the one who made me enjoy that sort of work. Harry would find the house more peaceful these days!'

Above all, she was starved of news of Kate. 'She's *such* a bad letter writer. Always was! How is she, darling? Does she like her new job? Did she take Edward's death badly? ... My only daughter, and so far away! How I *wish* I could see her more often! She was so talented, Bess. She had all the makings of a good actress, and you should have heard what they said about her painting at the Slade...'

'You should hear what they say of it in Malaya!' said Bess. 'It's one of the reasons she's still there. Daddy died leaving large debts, apparently. She said she was coming to see you just as soon as she can get leave from the library.'

'Oh, that will be heavenly. And now for you, darling. What about you and this young man? Surely you're much too young to marry? Are you really that much in love with him?'

'I think so, Gran.'

'*Think* so? *Think* so?' thundered Madge in mock anger. 'What does that mean? If you have any doubts at all you shouldn't dream of marrying him! Love is the only basis for marriage — I can tell you that from my own experience. And marriage isn't easy! Sex is the sugar on the pill.'

'Gran!' exclaimed Bess, laughing, 'I never thought to hear such a thing from you!'

'It's true, darling,' replied Madge seriously. 'Whatever happens later, you must have been in love to start with.' She frowned. 'Was your mother happy with Edward, Bess?'

Bess was surprised. 'I think so. Not all the time, certainly, but I'm sure she was in the end.'

'I'm glad.' Madge brooded for a moment, then gave a strange little shrug. 'Anyway, this Tim person of yours won't be here for a little while, so why not spend that time with me?'

'I'd love it Gran, but I've got no money.'

'Don't be silly, Bessie! You don't need money here!'

'It's not silly, Gran. I hate being dependent on people, even family. I'll have to get some sort of temporary job until Tim gets here, to tide me over.'

'I can't imagine what sort of a job you could get for such a short time, unless you can type!'

'No, I can't. But I can look after children.'

'All right,' said Madge, 'but do at least use this house as a base until you do.'

'Thank you, Gran. It's lovely of you to want me!'

The two of them got along splendidly. Each was as independent as the other and it was agreed that only the dining room and drawing room would be communal. Bess sent off letters to various agencies asking for work, and placed an advertisement in *The Times*. She also rang Miss Wells at Bendleford to see how she was. Miss Wells immediately asked her down for a weekend.

'I've lost touch with Gerald,' she said, 'but Deirdre is working as secretary at the Webber-Douglas dramatic school in London, where by an odd coincidence my nephew is a student. I'll ask her for the same weekend.'

'How marvellous of you to remember, out of all the children you've looked after, that we three were friends!' exclaimed Bess.

'I boast that I remember all of you,' laughed Miss Wells.

When Bess got to Bendleford she saw how much Miss Wells had aged. Her once dark brown hair was nearly white, and she wore it in a mannish bob. But she seemed delighted to see Bess again; and for Bess the intervening years seemed to vanish, leaving the old headmistress-schoolchild relationship intact.

Deirdre was now very attractive. She wasn't in the least pretty, but she still had her gift for chic; her bright brown eyes were as

merry as ever, and her laugh still refreshingly infectious. She was
loving life. She had a job which she enjoyed, and was having an
affair with a married man which she described as 'marvellous'. Her
father had remarried; her mother, now sad and embittered, lived
on the South Coast.

Miss Wells had arranged for them all to have dinner with her
brother on the Saturday night. 'It will be coals to Newcastle for
you, Deirdre, because Mark will be there. But he says you get on
well.'

'Who's Mark?' asked Bess.

'The nephew I was telling you about who's training at the
Webber-Douglas.'

'Isn't that rather an extraordinary thing for him to do?'

'Why?'

'Your brother is a clergyman!'

'The church and stage often go together,' smiled Miss Wells.

'Mark is a dish,' said Deirdre. 'Half the girls in the school have
fallen for him.'

'I'm looking forward to meeting him,' said Bess. 'It sounds
exciting, him being an actor!'

Miss Wells now smiled broadly. 'That's funny coming from
you!' she exclaimed. 'You're a Glanville!'

'I'm a schoolmistress if I'm anything,' replied Bess firmly,
'though of course I'm going to be a wife pretty soon.'

'Have you never wanted to go on the stage?' asked Miss Wells.

'No. It's odd, isn't it? But I don't think I ever have. There
doesn't seem to have been time somehow, and I've certainly had
no secret yearning.'

'You seemed to have talent as a child,' said Miss Wells. 'We
often wondered if you'd take it up.'

'Mummy and Father were always so against it,' said Bess. 'It
really hurt Mummy if I brought the subject up, and Grandma
never mentions it.'

The dinner party was a great success. Another young man had
been invited, as well as a bachelor friend for Miss Wells, and both
her brother and his wife were on their best behaviour. Mrs Wells
was a thin-faced woman, with a flat chest and a sharp tongue. Old
Mr Wells was angular too, but pink-cheeked and benignly vague.
He had a halo of white hair, and watery eyes half hidden by
powerful glasses. Mark Wells was a surprise as their son. Tall,
dark and romantic-looking, he was also, Bess thought, almost

excessively handsome, with a hint of arrogance which repelled her slightly. However, he had undeniable charm, and a pleasant smile.

Mark and Bess sat next to one another at dinner and he set himself out to amuse her. She felt an immediate physical attraction — and was sure that he felt it too. He and Deirdre told outrageous stories about the Webber-Douglas but it was obvious that he thoroughly enjoyed the school and was excited and confident about the future. 'I'm dreadfully ambitious,' he confided to Bess. 'I'm utterly determined to get to the top, no matter what it costs.' He seemed surprised and a little put out that Bess was engaged to be married, but he was very interested to hear about her life in Malaya. (This made a change from most of the other people she had met since her return, who seemed to know nothing of the country, cared even less, and thought that the name Kuala Lumpur was a joke.) Understandably, though, his chief interest was in her grandparents and their circle.

Just before the dinner was over, he said, 'Why not come and visit the Webber-Douglas one day? Deirdre can show you round, and then I could give you some lunch.'

'My, My!' exclaimed Deirdre, when they got back to Bendleford. 'You've made a hit, Bessie! It's usually the girls who do all the chasing where Mark is concerned. But do come. It'd be the greatest fun.'

Back at Richmond, Bess found a message from the Universal Aunts asking her to meet a little girl from Brighton at Victoria and see her on to the Lincoln train at King's Cross, where the guard would take charge of her. Apparently there could be many similar jobs like this from time to time, if Bess were interested. Bess was delighted, but she hoped she would seem a bit less dim and ancient than the Universal Aunts who had performed the same function in her own childhood! There was a letter from Patrick too, inviting her for Christmas in Yorkshire. 'Do come, darling,' he wrote. 'It's so lovely here, I can't tell you, and I want to show it to you.'

But Bess had to refuse. She was going to spend Christmas with Tim and Mrs Hudson.

The British newspapers were now printing news of King Edward's romance with Mrs Simpson, who had obtained her divorce by citing as co-respondent a woman named Buttercup Kennedy (though this unlikely name was not disclosed in the hearing at Ipswich). Comment on the affair wavered wildly, between claims that the King was entirely loyal to his nation and talk that his obsession was so strong that he was going to fly the country with his Wally. Madge only discussed the subject once with Bess, and that was after a dinner with friends of Winston Churchill, whom she had known ever since the May Whitty supper parties in Bedford Chambers all those years ago. Winston, she said, was very worried. The King, whom he adored, was insisting that he could make Mrs Simpson his Queen — as she was a divorcée Churchill knew the country wouldn't stand for it.

Madge and Bess listened to the abdication speech together. Bess was inclined to pity a poor man who was so in love that he would give up his throne for his loved one, but Madge was scornful. 'Silly weak little man!' she said, angrily. 'He's running away from his duty. God knows I'm in favour of royalty, but not of such namby-pamby nonsense!'

'I thought you believed in love, Gran!' teased Bess.

'Love. Not infatuation,' retorted Madge.

It was soon after this that Bess visited the Webber-Douglas and she was enchanted by it. The students, dressed in a wild mixture of unlikely clothes, seemed to be having the time of their lives — and were obviously passionately absorbed in their work. Everyone to whom Mark introduced her gave her a friendly welcome, particularly one of the staff, Ellen O'Malley, for whom Shaw had written the part of Ellie Dunn in *Heartbreak House*. She was by this time a voluminous old lady, with white hair, pale blue short-sighted eyes and a face of great intelligence. She had a warm and encouraging manner, knew Madge slightly, and seemed delighted to meet Bess.

'Does this visit mean you'll be coming to study here?' she asked warmly.

'Good heavens, no!' said Bess. 'It's just that Deirdre Baker and I were at school together for years — and Mark Wells' aunt was our headmistress — so I've been invited to have a look round.'

'You're not going on the stage, then?'

'No,' said Bess cheerfully. 'I'm engaged to a Police Officer who lives in Malaya — that's where my mother lives — and I'm getting married and going out there next year.'

'Oh, what a shame! Your grandparents were so disappointed when Kate didn't go on the stage. I thought you might be going to redress the balance!' said Ellen.

'I'm afraid not,' replied Bess.

'Well, if you change your mind you'll come here, won't you? I'm sure we'd love to have Harry Glanville's grand-daughter. And there are a couple of scholarships going for the Summer term, if you're worried about money. Who knows, you might win one!'

'I don't think that's very likely,' laughed Bess. 'I haven't done any acting at all!'

Ellen smiled her beautiful smile and patted Bess's head. 'Give your grandmother my love. I'm a great admirer,' she said.

Mark took Deirdre and Bess off to lunch with distinct enthusiasm. There was no doubt that he found her attractive. By the time Bess reached home, she felt quite sad that she wasn't going on the stage.

CHAPTER ELEVEN

Mrs Hudson shook her pretty grey curls and laughed teasingly at Tim. Her arm was around his waist and her head reached his shoulder: they looked more like lovers than mother and son. She was small and slim and surprisingly youthful, in a slightly nervous way.

They were standing on the steps of her mock-Tudor house in Sonningfield, with the porch light shining on them. Bess was still standing by the car. It was a cold clear night and stars shone brilliantly out of the winter sky.

'Darling!' exclaimed Mrs Hudson whimsically, 'You never told me she was *beautiful!*'

'Of course I did, Mum,' protested Tim. 'A million times!'

'We're going to love her, aren't we?' said Mrs Hudson.

'I've told you, I already do,' said Tim.

'Take her to her room at once, darling,' said Mrs Hudson, kissing him. 'We can't just leave her standing there in the cold, can we? Tea is ready when you are, Miss Marchmont,' she added.

'Do call her Bess, mother!'

'Bess,' Mrs Hudson corrected herself girlishly.

Embarrassed, Tim came down the steps and took the case from her. 'Which room, Mum?'

'The Pink Guest Room, of course,' said Mrs Hudson. 'I've put in some flowers. Dreadfully extravagant, but you mustn't scold me. One doesn't get introduced to one's future daughter-in-law all that often, does one?'

'I hope not!' laughed Tim, leading the way upstairs with two fat dachshunds called Maud and Bombardier barking at his heels.

'Isn't she marvellous?' he said to Bess. 'You'd never think she was old enough to be my mother, would you? I know you'll get on. By the way, I think I ought to warn you about something. She's got a guide.'

'A guide?' Bess was bewildered. 'What sort of guide?'

'A spirit guide,' said Tim earnestly. 'I know it sounds odd, but

150

it's her way of getting over father's death. He's a Red Indian called Deep Valley.'

'Deep Valley? What an extraordinary name! Does she call him Val, for short?'

'As a matter of fact she does,' said Tim, turning to her in surprise. 'How did you guess?'

Bess tried to control a sense of rising hysteria. 'What does the guide do?' she asked.

'Mother consults him about everything,' said Tim, 'and he advises her.'

'Will she have consulted him about us?'

'Oh, yes. It was his idea that you should spend Christmas with us.'

'How very hospitable of him!' said Bess drily. 'Please ask your mother to thank him.'

'That's all right,' said Tim, without a trace of humour. 'If he hadn't suggested it, I would have.'

Bess didn't reply.

'It's pretty, isn't it?' said Tim, as he showed her into the Pink Room and made a vain attempt to keep the dogs off the bed. 'Mother does all the decor herself. She's very artistic, you know. My God, it's good to be back! I'd almost forgotten how good!'

Bess looked at Tim, so eager for her approval and so happy to be home, and said untruthfully, 'It's a sweet room. I know I shall be very comfortable here.'

'When she was married, Mum spent all her time in Army Quarters, and though they were comfortable enough, once Dad had become a Major and so on, she always longed for a home of her own,' said Tim.

'Don't we all?' quipped Bess.

'So this place matters to her desperately.' Then Tim smiled. 'I'll come along to see you, tonight, shall I, when she's asleep?'

'Oh no, Tim! Your mother would be furious if she found out.'

'She won't find out. I promise. Please Bess. You do want to don't you?'

'Of course I do.'

'Well then.'

'No Tim. I couldn't relax, knowing how it would upset her!'

'It's our lives you know. Still if that's the way you feel ...'

'It is Tim. I'm here to see if she approves of me!'

'All right, darling — I certainly don't want to upset either of you.' He kissed her. 'Now,' he went on, 'Mum has arranged all sorts of things for us to do as it's Christmas, but not today. Today is for us, she says. She wants the three of us to have a lovely long chat and get to know one another, and then a simple homely meal tonight. Just us three.'

'How kind.' Despair was already settling over Bess at the prospect of spending Christmas with Mrs Hudson.

Tim looked at her lovingly. 'What a lucky chap I am!' he said heartily. 'Two such wonderful women to love and be loved by.' He kissed her, and she did her best to respond. 'Well,' he said, releasing her, 'I'll go on down, and you have a wash and brush up, and then join us in the lounge. It's to the right at the bottom of the stairs. Come on Maud, Bombardier!'

Bess looked around her room with distaste. It was a riot of bows, pink on white and white on pink. She wandered to the window and tried to look out over the garden at the back. Tim had said that the house was on the edge of a Common, so there would probably be a walk where they could go with the dogs tomorrow. She sighed.

Tim had arrived in England three days before, and had rushed straight down to Richmond to see her. Madge had inspected him warily and pronounced him a 'nice boy'.

Bess powdered her nose and went downstairs.

The lounge was as powder-blue as her bedroom was pink, and just as fussy. Both dogs were now sitting on blue pouffes, dribbling as they watched the tea being poured. There was a fire here, and Mrs Hudson looked very pretty in the lamp-light. A small Christmas tree stood on a table in the corner of the room, almost obliterated with tinsel. It had three gaily wrapped presents on it, and two at its feet. Bess was suddenly and vividly reminded of the Christmas when her grandfather died.

Mrs Hudson asked Bess searching questions.

'You see, we've never had anyone in the theatre in our family,' she said, 'so you must forgive me. I know you're a schoolmistress, yourself — so frightfully brave and hardworking, I always think — but your grandparents are stage folk, aren't they?'

'Yes.'

'Her father was a well-known lawyer,' broke in Tim, trying to make Bess sound as respectable as his mother would have wished.

'Yes, but in Kuala Lumpur,' said Mrs Hudson.

'What difference does that make?' asked Bess quietly.

'Oh, none. Just that it's so far away.'

'I hear that you have discussed me exhaustively with your spirit guide,' said Bess, hearing the barb behind Mrs Hudson's remark and trying to control her anger.

Mrs Hudson looked at her shrewdly. 'Tim told you, did he?' she asked.

'Of course.'

'Yes. Of course.' There was a short silence. 'I'll get in touch with him after tea,' said Mrs Hudson brightly.

The dogs were given a saucer of tea each, and a muffin with butter, cut up into small pieces. 'Dachshunds are such sporting little dogs,' said Mrs Hudson fondly. 'Do you know them Miss Marchmont, I mean Bess?'

'No,' said Bess.

'These ones go rabbiting, on the Common. We have a large Common at the back of the house.'

'Yes. I know. Tim told me.'

'With lots and lots of rabbits. Far too many, I'm afraid. Do you play poker?' she asked, changing the subject.

'No,' said Bess, 'and even if I did, I couldn't afford it at the moment.'

'Your father died, didn't he?'

'Yes.'

'Leaving you with no money, Tim says.'

'That's right.'

'How sad!'

'Yes.'

'And your mother works in a library.'

'Yes.'

'She must be very clever,' said Mrs Hudson, in the tones of one who disapproves of clever women.

'She is,' said Bess.

'And you are too, I expect, if you are a schoolmistress.'

'I hope so,' said Bess.

This seemed to disconcert Mrs Hudson, who flashed a glance at Tim, and said, 'Now don't get up, either of you. It doesn't take a minute to wash up. I'm only a poor little hausfrau these days, and not the teeniest bit clever, I'm afraid.' She smiled bravely. 'But I manage to get by.'

'I'm sure you do,' said Bess.

Mrs Hudson's voice hardened. 'Tim darling,' she said, 'help me carry the things out, will you?'

Tim leapt to his feet.

When he returned from the kitchen, he said enthusiastically, 'I was right! Mother adores you! She was saying how different you are from other girls, and how sad she is that she couldn't put you up for all the time I'm here because she likes you so much. She says your theatrical blood shows. So much poise.'

'Ah,' said Bess.

'Give me a kiss,' said Tim.

Bess kissed him, and at that moment Mrs Hudson opened the door. She drew back when she saw them. 'Oh, my dears, how silly of me! I should have realised you wanted to be alone! I only came back for my hankie. I think I've got the weeniest bit of a cold, Bess. Maddening, isn't it?'

'Maddening. You're sure we can't help with the tea things?'

'No thanks, though perhaps you can help me after dinner.'

'Certainly!'

'I'm so used to doing everything on my own, these days,' said Mrs Hudson, with a martyred sigh. 'It would be a treat.'

'Don't you have any help?' asked Bess.

'Only Mrs Hopgood until three o'clock.'

'Every day?'

'No! Only Monday to Friday.'

'I see.'

When she returned from the washing up, Mrs Hudson said, 'Now for Val. I hope he's in a good mood.'

'What does he do if he isn't?' asked Bess.

'Refuses to communicate,' said Mrs Hudson tartly.

She pulled out a small round table and spread a chart on it, with the letters of the alphabet arranged in a circle. Then she took up a pencil and poised it over the paper.

'He usually likes this, so we'll test him out. Val. Val, darling? Spirit guide! My only one! My true one! Talk to me. Advise me. Are you there?' Nothing happened. 'Val, darling, are you there?' Nothing happened. 'Oh dear. Perhaps he's cross, or the vibrations aren't right!' She looked accusingly at Bess. 'Val. Val, dear. It's me. Ellikins.' The pencil suddenly jerked violently in her hand, and then started to scribble angrily. 'Val. Val. Naughty! Naughty! We're waiting, Val.' The pencil set off down the paper, and spelt out 'W.E.L.L.?' 'Ah,' said Mrs Hudson, in a satisfied whisper. 'He's going to talk to us. Val, we're all here today, as you can see. Tim, me, and Tim's fiancée, Bess. We want you to tell us that you are pleased that Bess is to join the family.'

'Mother!' protested Tim, and he looked anxiously at Bess.

'Shush! said Mrs Hudson. 'Val? Are you there?'

The pencil again agitated angrily.

'We are asking your advice Val, about Bess joining the family,' said Mrs Hudson. Nothing happened. 'Val!' Nothing happened.

'Are you pleased?' The pencil began moving towards the letters again, and very slowly and deliberately it wrote out: 'W. I. D. E O. F. T. H. E. M. A. R. K.'

Bess was startled. She felt her mouth go dry. *Wide of the mark!* Could the thing possibly mean Mark Wells? But she'd hardly met him — though there was no denying he was very attractive! It was certainly a strange coincidence. Neither Mrs Hudson nor Tim knew anything about Mark. Was there something in this business after all?

'What does that mean?' asked Tim.

'I have no idea,' said Mrs Hudson, astonished. 'Let's ask him. What do you mean Val?' There was a pause. Then, 'A. S. K. B. E. S. S.'

'What does he mean, Bess?' asked Mrs Hudson.

'How should I know?' Bess shrugged her shoulders and tried to look innocent.

Mrs Hudson stared at her. 'Val is usually right,' she said. 'If he says you ought to know, then I'm sure you do.'

'Well, I don't,' said Bess.

'It wasn't a very kind question, anyway,' said Tim.

Mrs Hudson turned to him sharply. 'I don't know what you're talking about, Tim,' she said. 'I wouldn't dream of being unkind to anyone, least of all Bess.'

Tim looked unconvinced, which Mrs Hudson noticed. She pressed her lips together.

'Try some other subject,' he said.

'Very well,' replied Mrs Hudson, forcing herself to smile sweetly. 'What other subject?'

'What do you want advice about?' asked Tim.

'Only on how I can best make my boy happy,' said Mrs Hudson. She looked at him archly.

'I'm happy already,' said Tim. 'It's marvellous just to be in England.'

The pencil began writing on its own. 'B. E. C. A. R. E. F. U. L.' it said. 'Y. O. U. W. O. N. T. F. O. O. L. H. E. R.'

'Who won't fool who?' asked Tim.

The pencil began to scribble in circles, then wrote, 'G.O.N.E.', and stopped.

'Oh dear!' wailed Mrs Hudson. 'That *was* a short session! He won't utter a word after he's said "Gone". I wonder what has upset him so much?'

'Let's think of something else to do,' said Tim.

'Such as what?' asked Mrs Hudson.

'Let's talk,' said Tim. 'I love talking round a fire.'

'What shall we talk about?' asked Mrs Hudson. She looked at her watch. 'It's six o'clock already!' she exclaimed. 'And we eat at eight. Don't change into anything too elaborate, Bess dear. I usually wear a house coat. Now I think I'll have to leave you again because I have the meal to see to, and one or two people to ring up about Christmas. I do want you both to have a good time.' She looked at them meaningfully.

As soon as she had left the room Tim said, 'I'm sorry about that spirit session thing, but mother is fixated on it all.'

'That's all right.'

'You didn't mind?'

'Of course not. What's worrying me now is if I've got enough clothes to wear. I didn't bring all that many. I haven't even got that many, if it comes to that. And I had no idea we were going to have such a round of gaiety.'

'It's my leave,' said Tim, 'and Christmas. So you can't blame her. She wants to show me off. And you, too, darling.'

'Yes, of course,' said Bess affectionately.

The rest of the evening limped by, as did the whole visit, though Tim seemed to enjoy himself. Bess felt uncomfortable all the time and she was certain that Mrs Hudson disliked her intensely. She did her best to please but knew that she was failing. Maud got herself down a rabbit hole and had to be dug out; all subsequent sessions with Val were as disastrous as the first; Bess liked none of the parties they went to, and few of the neighbours, most of whom patronised her when they heard she had been a teacher.

When the ten days were over, she was glad to be leaving, and thankful to have avoided any sort of scene with Mrs Hudson.

On the last morning, however, while she was packing, Tim came into the room, and threw himself down on her bed. 'Come here, darling,' he said. 'It's been awful not being able to sleep with you, and I can't bear to let you go again. I know it's only for a short while, but I've been so lonely for you in Malaya. I can't tell you how lonely! Say you've been lonely for me, too.'

'Yes, Tim, I've missed you.'

'Then come here, by me,' said Tim.

Reluctantly she went to the bed, and Tim pulled her towards him. Suddenly he began tearing at her dress. He was speaking words of love with a desperate muffled urgency. Bess tried to escape, but they were still struggling when the door flew open and Mrs Hudson stood looking down at them, blazing with anger. 'Forgive me,' she said. 'It never came into my head that I should find the two of you behaving like animals.'

'We're engaged,' said Bess, sitting up humiliated and trying to re-fasten her dress.

'But not married,' said Mrs Hudson icily.

'Get out,' shouted Tim, furiously. 'How dare you creep about the house like this? What we do with our lives is our own affair.'

'Affair seems to be the *mot juste*,' said Mrs Hudson, and she swept out of the room and slammed the door.

CHAPTER TWELVE

Bess was utterly shattered by her visit. She also knew now that she had no wish to marry Tim. She had been thoroughly upset by her stay in Batu Hitam earlier in the year, but was reconciled by their lovemaking on board ship. This time she wanted to break off the engagement at once. She understood that Tim had been at fault on neither occasion. On the other hand, a life of extreme isolation in a land where she no longer wished to live, with a man for whom she now recognised she had had little more than a strong maternal feeling, was unthinkable. His mother's behaviour had saved her from an appalling mistake.

She was, however, in something of a dilemma as to when to tell him, because he too had been outraged by his mother. In the car, driving her back to Richmond, he was angry and apologetic. 'I can't understand it!' he said. 'She's been in floods of tears ever since but that doesn't excuse her! She's had one of her terrible migraines, and they pull her down I know — and I'm afraid she was awfully upset that I'd asked you to stay so soon after I'd come back to her from such a long separation. But all the same, it's unforgivable! I'm sorry, Bess. I can't tell you how sorry I am!'

Bess made soothing noises, but was unappeased. Yet she knew that if she broke off the engagement immediately, she would divide him fatally from his mother and send him back to his lonely job in a dangerously unhappy frame of mind. She decided she must wait.

She did however telephone the Webber-Douglas, telling Deirdre about her conversation with Ellen O'Malley and asking to be allowed to audition for one of the scholarships. Deirdre explained that she would have to prepare two set pieces, one Shakespeare and one modern, and that one must be comic and the other tragic. Bess then told Madge.

The old woman was ecstatic. 'I simply couldn't be more delighted, darling! I'll help all I can. Tim's a nice boy, but we're a *theatre* family — and you've found your way home.'

The audition was to be held in March. In the weeks before, Bess was kept busy studying and rehearsing for it as well as working in various small jobs for the Universal Aunts. She felt guilty for not telling Tim about the audition, and had still not managed to break off the engagement. I'll do it after the audition, she said to herself. Tim was desperately trying to patch up a situation which he knew was going wrong. Bess saw him as little as possible, but he was a persistent and determined young man and had no thought of giving up. His determination only increased Bess's stage fright, so that the audition when it came was something of a relief.

She did the 'sight-unseen' reading in a light semi-basement room (which unnerved her because she could see the expressions on her examiners' faces so clearly), then delivered her two prepared pieces on stage in the little theatre, in stage lighting. And on stage, indeed, as her grandmother had said she would, she felt at home. She also felt that she had done her best, and Deirdre told her that she would hear the result at the end of the following week.

To her intense surprise, Bess won one of the scholarships. Deirdre told her that being a Glanville had helped a great deal: the school was having a struggle to keep going at this time, and the publicity they would get from teaching Harry and Madge's granddaughter had swung things in her favour. Bess didn't approve, but she wasn't prepared to argue.

Now at last she broke it to Tim that she wasn't going to marry him. He refused to take the decision as final. 'You simply can't do such a thing to me!' he said. 'You aren't that kind of girl.'

'But I am, Tim, and I have,' she said. 'I know through and through that I don't want to spend the rest of my life in Malaya. I simply can't, darling. It's a wonderful country, but the life is so empty for a European woman.'

'How can it be empty, if you're married? What about children?'

'Don't you see, Tim, I've been earning my own living for some years now? I can't go back to doing nothing!'

'You needn't have all those servants,' said Tim, reasonably. 'Then there would be plenty of work.'

'That would be worse,' said Bess. 'I'm not domesticated. Besides I know now that I want to be an actress.'

'You've never wanted to be one before!'

'I know, but I do now.'

'Is there another man?' asked Tim.

Bess hesitated. She would have liked to say there was one, so that Tim could keep self-respect; but there wasn't, and it seemed stupid to make someone up. 'No,' she said reluctantly. 'There's no-one else.'

'I don't believe you,' said Tim flatly.

Madge was as proud of Bess's scholarship as if she had won it herself. 'I shall come and see every one of your end-of-term shows, darling,' she said. 'It's the best news I've heard for years!'

The summer term at the Webber-Douglas began in May. By then Bess had found a tiny fully furnished room for a guinea a week in Earl's Court within walking distance of the school. Under these circumstances, Madge didn't mind losing her.

Tim still refused to take no for an answer. Mark, although he seemed pleased to see her at the school, took no special interest.

The final break with Tim came when he and Bess were watching the Coronation procession of King George the Sixth and Queen Elizabeth. He had managed, by pulling strings at the Colonial Office, to get two of the seats reserved for Colonials on the tiered stands to the right of Buckingham Palace, and had persuaded Bess to join him. It was a dark and gloomy day, but better than the days preceding it. They had both got up at dawn, and had already been in their seats for some while before the first of the cars left the Palace. They were more united than they had been for some time, as they shared their happiness and loyalty to the Crown. The English in Malaya thought of England as 'home', and to most of them the Royal Family was the focal point of their emotion. Being a colonial was something to be proud of: London was the centre of the universe, and the Empire was the bringer of peace to the world, and of justice and security to the people it ruled. 'An Englishman's home was his castle' ... 'his word was as good as his bond' ... 'London policemen were the friendliest and best on earth.'

The whole length of the Mall was decorated with flags and the flowerbeds blazed with scarlet geraniums. The build-up of excitement began at eight-fifteen, with the first cars carrying junior members of the Royal Family and representatives of foreign powers. An hour later the first group of carriages passed, carrying prime ministers, representatives from India and Burma, the Malay sultans in all their finery, and other colonial rulers. Then to great applause came the King's only sister the Princess Royal, and with her in a glass coach Princess Elizabeth, aged fourteen, and Princess Margaret Rose, aged nine. At thirteen minutes past ten a burst of cheering further along the road signalled that Queen

Mary's carriage procession was leaving Marlborough House. Tim squeezed Bess's hand. 'This is pretty good, isn't it?' he said, eyes shining.

'Marvellous!' agreed Bess.

'Don't keep me waiting too long when I get back,' said Tim. 'I'll be so lonely without you.'

Bess sighed in exasperation. 'Please, Tim!' she said. 'We've been over this so many times. Don't spoil everything now.'

'You said you'd marry me,' he said obstinately. 'I won't take no for an answer.'

'When I said I'd marry you I was too young to know my own mind. I've told you, I don't want to live in Malaya, and I'm determined to be an actress.'

'Then I'll throw up my job, and find something here,' said Tim.

'No, Tim! No! We've discussed it all a thousand times!'

'I won't go back without you.'

'You'll have to.'

The weather, which had been improving steadily, suddenly cleared at that moment. The clouds rolled away and the sun shone out — just as, to a tumult of cheering, the King and Queen left the palace in their golden State Coach, drawn by eight Windsor greys. The Queen was bareheaded, her dark hair worn short with a small curled fringe, and she was dressed in an ivory satin gown with lace at the sleeves and gold embroidery. Over this was a purple velvet robe lined and bordered in ermine. King George wore a crimson velvet robe with an ermine collar and a red velvet cap with an ermine headband. To their great satisfaction, Tim and Bess had a perfect view; but the moment the procession was out of sight, Tim resumed the argument.

'Suppose you fail as an actress?' he asked. 'What happens then?'

'I won't fail.'

'You are still wearing my ring.'

Bess took it off and handed it to him. It suddenly seemed a symbolic gesture — a farewell to the life she had known. She gave it to Tim, who put it into his pocket without a word.

They picnicked on the sandwiches and jam tarts that Mrs Hudson had provided, and drank wine from paper cups, but the day was ruined for them both; even though the splendid return procession, with the King and Queen now crowned and the Queen smiling her own special radiant smile, held their attention for the duration of its passing.

Torrential rain fell, then, and continued to fall until twenty past four, when once again the clouds parted and the Royal Family came out on to the balcony of Buckingham Palace to wave to the people. Again and again they appeared, and Bess and Tim waved in reply and, like the others in the crowd, cheered themselves hoarse. The moment the last appearance was over, however, their resentment and anger with one another returned and they left their seats at once to make for home.

'You can find your own way, I'm sure,' said Tim coldly. 'You'll be having to do so in future, anyway.'

'Yes, of course.'

'So goodbye.' He held out a hand stiffly.

'Shan't I see you again?' asked Bess, suddenly desolate.

'No.'

'Surely we can part as friends?'

'My God! You're not even going to spare me that old bromide!' exclaimed Tim.

'Give my love to your mother,' murmured Bess unhappily.

'You know as well as I do that you don't like her,' said Tim.

'She doesn't like me,' Bess defended herself.

'You needn't try to blame my mother for this break-up,' warned Tim. 'You must have known for some time that you had no intention of marrying me. She thinks so, anyway.' He stared at her searchingly, waiting for an answer.

Bess guiltily acknowledged the truth of this to herself, but said aloud, 'I really did think I could go through with it, Tim. I never had any idea that I would want to be an actress. Now I don't want anything else. You're well rid of me, you know. I'm not cut out to be a housewife. But I've been selfish and cowardly not to tell you before what was happening, and I'm truly sorry that I've hurt you. Please try to forgive me.'

Tim didn't reply, but turned on his heel and left her where she stood. She started to run after him, then stopped, following him with her eyes until he walked out of sight round a corner. He didn't once look back.

CHAPTER THIRTEEN

Bess threw herself into her work at the Webber-Douglas. She found to her astonishment not only that she enjoyed it more than anything she had ever done in her life, but that she had real talent. Learning lines came easily to her, and she was good at both comedy and tragedy. Singing and fencing were her worst subjects but the rest was inbred in her.

Several of the girls were debutantes who were using the 'Webber-D', as they called it, as a kind of finishing school. Hardly any of them had serious thoughts of a theatrical career, but for the most part they were friendly and decorative. Bess had utterly refused to allow Madge to subsidise her, so she had very little money. The debs were shocked that anyone should be so poor, but they became adept at divining when her funds were particularly low and invited her to their homes for nourishing meals. Most of the other girls, however, were as broke as she was and with one of these she usually ate at an ABC eating house, where the two of them shared a single portion of anything that either could afford. There were times when she actually starved and fainted from hunger.

Mark Wells was one of only fifteen male students among seventy-five girls. Being exceptionally good-looking, he was very much the centre of attraction and relished it. His manner to Bess became more and more patronising, and out of school hours she practically never saw him. Since she now never saw Tim, either, life away from the school was often lonely. Not to be continuously the object of male attention was something new to Bess after the years in Malaya; and, although she loved the stimulus of London and of her work, sometimes she experienced the colonial's sense of not quite 'belonging', which Kate had described so vividly. Bess very much regretted her behaviour towards Tim; but even in her loneliest moments she realised that to ring him would only be to treat him even more unkindly.

As the end of her first term came in sight, she began to worry about how she could earn enough money during the long summer holidays to keep herself going. She could go to Madge for a time of course — she belonged there all right — but she was determined not to sponge on her. At this point she had another letter from Uncle Patrick from Yorkshire inviting her to stay for two weeks, and she thankfully accepted.

Bess was completely unprepared for Patrick's surroundings. He had inherited a stately home, not far from Leeds, and the house and grounds were magnificent. She had never been anywhere like it before. The house — built by Robert Adam — and the grounds — laid out by Capability Brown — were open to the public on six Sundays a year. Her bedroom, with a magnificent four-poster which even dwarfed her grandfather's bed in Richmond, was exquisite; and she had her own sitting room and bathroom.

Patrick seemed to come into his own here, and the attraction he had always held for Bess now became more pronounced. She even believed herself to be a little in love with him. Although she realised he was at least old enough to be her father, Patrick now seemed to her the most handsome and charming man she had ever met. In her privileged position as his god-daughter, she made no secret of her feelings; but to her surprise, and indeed dismay, he discouraged her brusquely. On the other hand, he urged her (as he always had) to talk about herself and never seemed to tire of listening to what she had to say, or of being in her company. She found the combination bewildering. He was sympathetic about her dismissal of Tim; indeed, he seemed glad.

Patrick's attitude to her theatrical ambitions was more equivocal: 'Better than being a school-marm for the rest of your life, anyway,' he said. 'And Mr Right will come along one day and put you straight, you'll see!' He grinned fondly.

'How Mummy would love this place!' exclaimed Bess inconsequentially.

Patrick looked at her sharply, then frowned. 'Yes, indeed,' he said sombrely. 'Poor Kate. She's had a wasted life for one so talented!'

'But Daddy was a darling!' protested Bess defensively.

'Yes, my dear. One of the best.'

'And Mummy seems to like being a librarian.'

'Certainly. And she's making a great success of it, I hear. She never lacked courage, your mother.'

'I wish I'd known her when she was so young and beautiful! Did everyone fall in love with her?'

'Everyone,' replied Patrick shortly. 'She was, however, married to your father, if you remember.'

'I wish they'd been happier together,' said Bess. 'They weren't, you know, until right at the very end.'

Patrick took a long time to answer. When he did so, he spoke so quietly that she could hardly hear him. '*I* wish she'd been happy, too,' he said. 'I've wished it for almost as long as I remember.' But when next she brought up the subject, he made it plain that he didn't want to discuss it further, so Bess left it alone.

Once, not knowing what she was saying, Bess touched on the subject of the woman he had loved. 'You remember we discussed her,' she said. 'Haven't you got over her enough to marry someone?'

'I'm quite happy as I am,' he replied curtly, and again she let the subject rest.

The fortnight passed far too quickly — 'glorious', she called it, to his amusement — and they were both extremely happy until the very last night. They went riding every day in the beautiful countryside, where the sun seemed to shine almost as brightly as in Malaya. They walked miles with Patrick's two labradors, had lunch and tea in the garden whenever it was warm enough, and paid visits to Patrick's neighbours, to whom he introduced Bess with touching (and surprising) pride. He often complimented her on her looks, and told her how much he enjoyed her company; and, as he had done when she was a child, he bought her lovely clothes. It seemed strange to her that she wasn't allowed to indulge in even the mildest flirtation.

On their last evening they dined alone — and had their first and last serious quarrel. Bess hated the thought of leaving such a paradise and dreaded the return to her grim little room in Earl's Court. She hadn't yet arranged a job for herself for the rest of the holiday and she knew she would miss Uncle Patrick very much. She had drunk a little too much wine, which had made her both slightly aggressive and self-pitying. She knew she was looking her best in one of the prettiest of the evening dresses he had given her, and it piqued her pride that he should show no sign of physical attraction towards her whatever. She decided to make one last effort.

She smiled at him lovingly. 'You've been so wonderful to me, darling,' she said. 'I'll never forget it.'

'You're welcome here whenever you want to come,' he said earnestly.

'Really?'

'Of course.'

'Only one thing hasn't been absolutely perfect, darling,' she said, 'in this whole magical two weeks.'

'What's that?' asked Patrick.

'That you don't find me attractive.'

'But I do.'

'What's wrong with me?'

'Nothing is wrong. You're a lovely girl, and a very sweet one, thank God.'

'But I don't have sex appeal!'

'Plenty.'

'Not for you.'

'No.'

Bess felt her temper rising. She got up from the table, went deliberately over to him, and kissed him on the mouth.

Patrick jerked his head away and rose angrily to his feet. 'What the hell do you think you're doing?' he demanded furiously. 'You're behaving like a tart!'

'I'm not a tart. I love you,' said Bess.

'I love you, too, but as a daughter, and that's how you ought to love me,' said Patrick. He was white with rage.

'I'm not your daughter. I'm your god-daughter. What's more, I'm grown up, and my feelings for you are adult!'

'Don't be a fool!'

'They *are!*'

'Behave yourself for God's sake! You ought to be ashamed. We're friends, not lovers!'

'I don't want to be a friend! I want to be attractive!' replied Bess resentfully.

'You *are* attractive and you know it.'

'Then why aren't you attracted?' she demanded.

Patrick stalked towards the door. When he turned to her again, his blue eyes were blazing. 'Coffee will be in the drawing room as normal, if and when you've pulled yourself together,' he said. 'Until then I advise you to go to your room.'

Bess began to cry. 'You're horrible,' she sobbed childishly. 'I hate you.'

'That will do,' he said, icily. 'And please never behave with me again like this, or we'll have to stop seeing one another.'

'That suits me,' flared Bess. Her old enemy, her unreasoningly violent temper, was beginning to take over.

Patrick stared at her incredulously, then said contemptuously, 'I thought you were a sweet girl. It seems I've been mistaken. So much for a life-long friendship!'

'So much for it!' shouted Bess, uncontrollably.

Patrick went out and slammed the door.

Bess remained where she was for some little time, then went upstairs to her room and stared at herself in the mirror. She could see without conceit that she was more than ordinarily pretty, and her resentment against Patrick grew. She was not used to being rejected by men. However, as a guest who had been more than generously entertained, she realised that good manners required her at least to join him in the drawing room for coffee. Calming herself with extreme difficulty, she went to him, and the rest of the evening was spent in polite and perfunctory conversation.

When he saw her off at the station, Patrick made no offer to kiss her; and in the train back to London, Bess burst into tears.

CHAPTER FOURTEEN

Bess found herself a temporary job for the rest of the holidays at a language school in Bayswater, and returned to the Webber-Douglas with relief. Mark behaved as distantly as ever towards her.

At the end of term, she asked Madge to come and see her act. She had a good part as Bunty, in *The Vortex* by Noel Coward, and wanted a yardstick by which to judge her talent. Madge was delighted.

Madge was currently in a very successful Lonsdale play at the Regency Theatre, so her arrival at the school created great excitement. As the ancient but still gleaming Rolls drew up, with Bentwood at the wheel, students were watching her arrival from every available vantage point. Ellen O'Malley was at the door to meet her, and the two old women greeted each other warmly. Madge was then escorted to her seat in the front row of the school's tiny theatre in considerable state. Bess, watching through a slit in the stage curtain, was almost sick with nerves. Bunty was her first chance to show what she might do — the rewarding but difficult part of a brittle and sophisticated young woman — and she knew she wasn't really up to it yet. However, her grandmother's presence set her adrenalin working, and inspired her to a performance well beyond her usual standard. The director, Alison Leggatt (one of the school staff) was herself acting in London with Coward at this time. Bess felt that even if she didn't yet know what acting was all about, Alison did, and this gave her the confidence to relax in her efforts to reproduce exactly what had been rehearsed. The result was obviously a success.

Alison appeared in the tiny communal dressing room almost as soon as the curtain fell, full of generous praise for Bess's performance, and she was closely followed by Mark, who seemed equally impressed although his praise came from a fairly lofty plane. They lingered, evidently waiting for Madge, who, with Ellen O'Malley still firmly in attendance, sailed in soon after.

'Harry would have been proud of you, my dear!' she exclaimed, her deep contralto voice full of emotion. 'Not bad. Not bad at all, for a beginner! We'll have to improve on that make-up a little, I think, don't you, Ellen? And there are one or two little tricks to be eliminated. Tricks are short-cuts in a performance, dear, and never truthful, and truth is what we're all aiming for, isn't it? But on the whole you were sincere, you carried yourself well, and above all you looked at home on the stage. And why not, for heaven's sake? As I told you, the stage is your home, just as it is mine and was Harry's, and our parents' before us.'

Alison beamed. Mark looked solemn. Madge congratulated Alison warmly on her production, and told her how much she admired her as an actress. She then had a word for everyone else in the room, and one and all they fell under her spell. When she was introduced to Mark, however, she looked at him shrewdly. 'Ah, I think I have heard about you, Mr Wells. Perhaps you would like to come to lunch one Sunday? Bess will arrange it.'

After Bess was dressed, Madge insisted on taking her back with her to see her own play; and to have supper with her afterwards at the Ivy, where to Bess's amazement and joy she was introduced to Noel Coward himself, and a host of other stars, as 'my granddaughter, you know, who is going to be an actress herself. I saw her this afternoon in *The Vortex*, Noel.'

'So Alison was telling me,' said Coward. 'She was very impressed.' He turned to Bess. 'Good luck, my dear. It's time we had another Glanville in the business.' His finger wagged. 'And you listen to every word your grandmother says. She's a very, very wise woman.' And he kissed them both.

At supper Madge talked excitedly about Bess's future. 'Who knows, darling? Perhaps we may work together one day, and what fun that would be! How I wish Harry had been alive to see you. How happy he would have been! He never really got over the shock of your mother's defection, you know. He was deeply, deeply hurt. Oh, darling, I miss him so much! There'll never be anyone like him.'

Bess looked at her surprised. Had she already forgotten about Violet Tremayne and all his other women? Had death made him somehow inviolate, and hers for the rest of eternity? Or had the marriage, even at its most unhappy, been worth all that she had had to suffer in the name of love?

Madge nodded as though Bess had spoken aloud, and went on,

'Yes, my darling. A wonderful man, and a great actor. There'll never be another like him.'

Madge's visit to the Webber-Douglas had two side-effects, both very happy ones for Bess. The first was that Mark, always on the make, reassessed his relationship with Bess and decided that she could be a great asset. Once again he set out to charm her, but this time in earnest. Bess was ecstatic, Madge less so. The second, and perhaps the more surprising, was that Kate seemed pleased that Bess wanted to become an actress. 'It gives me great joy, I find, darling, that the two people I love most in the world are now on the stage,' she wrote. 'I don't think I have missed not being an actress, but it is, after all, our family vocation, and it seems to give me a focal point in life to know that you are together. I plan to come to England in four months' time, and oh, how I long to see you!'

CHAPTER FIFTEEN

The following term was Mark's last at the school. He faced his
coming separation from Bess with some anxiety. He was fully
aware that Madge, unlike most of the older women he met, didn't
like him, but his all too rare visits to Richmond had shown him the
extent and influence of the large theatrical circle which still
surrounded her. With the Glanville name behind him, he was sure
he'd have put one foot on the ladder to success.

He proposed to Bess, but to his astonishment she turned him
down, although he was certain that she was even more attracted
than he was.

'I don't want marriage, yet, Mark,' she said. 'You and I are only
just beginning our lives. It's silly to get tied up. I escaped Tim
Hudson...'

'And you want to escape me?' he interrupted.

'Not you. Marriage.'

'Don't you love me, Bess?'

'That's just the worst of it, I do.'

And he really believed she did. It was driving him mad! He was
also afraid that once he was out of sight, in the job he fully expected
to get immediately, he might lose some of his influence over her.
He had guessed that her feelings for him were almost entirely
physical. Unfortunately, however much she might want him, she
steadfastly refused to sleep with him. She had no wish for a baby
before she started on her new career, she said; and she didn't
believe that the precautions which he kept assuring her would be
safe would, in fact, be effective. She had been frightened of having
a baby once before — once again, it seemed the wretched Tim
Hudson had taught her a lesson!

It was all hideously frustrating to a young man in a hurry.
What's more, Mark hadn't yet met Kate — and since Bess was
under twenty-one, Kate would have to give her approval even if
Bess relented and accepted him. Perhaps Kate wouldn't like him
any more than Madge did. If he could somehow make certain of

Kate's consent, all would be well. There was only one way of
achieving this ... a baby.

Bess, however, had another reason for not wanting an affair: she
didn't want to upset her grandmother — or indeed Kate, who was
coming back so soon and in such a happy frame of mind. She and
Mark had already known each other for a year without sleeping
with one another. They were not engaged, so why have an affair
now? The strength of Madge's dislike for Mark had had its effect,
too. For all his attraction, Bess had always had doubts about
Mark's personality, and now that he was pressing her so hard she
was not too sorry to make her mother's return a further excuse for
delaying all decisions — although she certainly had no wish to
lose him.

At this point, Bess had an unusual stroke of luck in her career.
There were so many more women than men studying at the
Webber-Douglas that it was not unknown for one male, playing
Romeo, say, to perform with six different Juliets in one pro-
duction. Bess was astonished, therefore, to discover that she alone
had been chosen to play opposite Mark in a new production of
Noel Coward's *Still Life*. The play (later to be filmed as the famous
Brief Encounter) concerns a short and poignant love affair between a
man and a married woman, who meet by chance at a railway
station: Mark's strength and virility would sharpen a character
written to be dull, and Bess was already good in emotional parts.
To their joy, Alison Leggatt was again to direct. It was an excellent
show-case for both of them, since agents and casting directors
would be coming in force to see Mark, who was considered the
school's best pupil. It was also a great honour for Bess, since usually
a final-term student would have been chosen to play opposite him.

Working with Mark in such a large part was a mixture of bliss
and anxiety for her. He was extremely talented but he was a selfish
actor, and made no effort to conceal it. 'You're bloody lucky to be
in the play when you're not a senior pupil,' he told her. 'They're all
as jealous as hell, and rightly so. Not that I'm averse to it, mind.
You're better than the rest of them put together. But the plays I'm
in this term are *my* bid for a place in the profession, not yours. You
have another year to go here, unless you marry me, so the direction
of the play has got to favour me. Not you. Understand?' And both
she and Alison Leggatt understood.

They worked extremely hard, and Mark took the opportunity
to insist that he and Bess should also rehearse out of working hours.

Bess's room in Earl's Court was extremely cramped, but he usually suggested going back to her place rather than to his much larger one, which was also nearer the Webber-Douglas. In Bess's room, the bed took up nearly the whole room — and bed, of course, was uppermost in his mind. His excuse was that he preferred to know that she was already safely home by the time he left her late in the evening. He was by now blindly determined to marry Bess: to be fair to him, this was not only because of her stage connections, but because her continuing rejection had persuaded him that he was genuinely in love. He had no doubt that he would one day succeed in seducing her, but he was not by nature patient and he was unused to waiting so long for his girl friends to give in. To smooth the way, he brought whisky and wine to the flat to drink after rehearsal; but after her unfortunate experience with Uncle Patrick Bess was exceedingly careful not to let it go to her head. Then one evening he staged the performance of his life. He proposed again and, when she refused, burst into tears. Alarmed, unhappy and goaded by his arguments that she had been leading him on, Bess allowed him to stay the night. Within a few weeks she knew that she was pregnant.

Bess broke the news to her grandmother, who was heartbroken but surprisingly understanding. Madge refused to speak to Mark from that moment on, and she wrote to Kate, who was due to set sail for England shortly. The marriage was arranged for the week after her return, as soon as *Still Life* was behind them.

Bess met Kate off the boat train at Waterloo and hardly recognised her. Her skin was brown, her hair quite grey, and she looked tiny and lost. It was pelting with rain and she was peering vaguely about her through large horn-rimmed glasses. When she saw Bess she waved wildly, and Bess ran towards her with tears pouring down her cheeks. They hugged and kissed each other for a long moment.

'Where's your luggage, darling?' asked Bess finally.

'A lovely porter saw me through the carriage window. He's collecting it from the luggage van. It's all labelled. Ah, here he is!' Kate smiled radiantly at the porter and Bess was touched to see that she still had her extraordinary attraction.

In the taxi going to Richmond, Kate could contain herself no longer. 'Well, darling? Tell me all about him! I can't wait another minute!'

'I want to know about you!' retorted Bess.

'Afterwards! There's plenty of time for that, thank goodness! And for talking to darling Mother. But you, Bess. You and this boy. Are you being foolish, my darling? Don't you remember what I felt about you and Tim?'

'Yes, Mummy. But this time there's a baby on the way, so it's different.'

'Couldn't you stop that?'

'I wouldn't dream of it.'

Back in Richmond with Madge, who was also overjoyed to see her daughter again, the three of them talked and talked until the early hours of the morning.

Kate liked Mark no better than Madge did. She was extremely worried, but tried to keep her dislike to herself in case she made things worse for Bess. She also realised that she might simply be prejudiced against him because she was so sad to see Bess marrying so young. *Still Life*, however, was a resounding success. Kate was tremendously excited by Bess's obvious talent — and Mark, as he had predicted, found a job immediately, in repertory in Eastbourne.

Bess and Mark were married quietly at Petersham, and the service took place in almost unrelieved gloom. Deirdre, who had been as worried as Madge and Kate about the whole business, came staunchly with various friends from the Webber-Douglas. Miss Wells and Mark's parents were also there. Uncle Patrick was not invited (although he sent a generous cheque) but the third of the Bendleford trio, Gerald Masters, appeared out of the blue just in time for the reception, and he and Deirdre and Bess had an excitable and hilarious reunion. Mark disliked him on sight.

'He's a poofter,' he said contemptuously.

'He's my best friend,' retorted Bess.

'Not any more, he isn't,' replied Mark flatly.

Bess had had to leave the Webber-Douglas and, as Mark had only been allowed off rehearsals for the wedding, they had no time for a honeymoon but went straight to his digs in Eastbourne after the ceremony.

Alone in the carriage going down, they took stock of one another. Mark was on the whole well pleased with what he had done and leaned forward suddenly sentimental. He took Bess's hand.

'Happy, Bess?'

'Very,' she replied, untruthfully.

CHAPTER SIXTEEN

The digs at Eastbourne were shabby but comfortable. They were also, unfortunately, dirty. The landlady, Mrs Freeman, was kind, but she was a slut and Bess, who had never been domesticated, was forced to do a considerable amount of cleaning in the two rooms they had rented. However, she soon bought a few cushions and ornaments to cheer the place up, and Mrs Freeman turned out to be a good cook — for which Bess grew more and more thankful as she was the victim of violent morning sickness. In fact she didn't feel well the entire time she was pregnant; it was only because she wasn't working that the situation was bearable.

Mark was upset for her but had little time to help. As an actor in weekly rep, he rehearsed all day, acted in the evening and had dress rehearsals on Sundays. An ambitious young actor in his first job, he was already doing well. Once again he was the most attractive man around and since most of the girls in the company were half in love with him, he was enjoying himself. He was also already playing large parts, which needed study; so apart from feeling unwell, Bess was very lonely. She put a good face on things, however, and wrote glowing letters to Madge and Kate.

When Kate came down to see her, she was shocked by what she found.

'Darling, this is no life at all,' she said anxiously. 'I can't bear it for you!'

'There's nothing to be done,' said Bess cheerfully. 'And it's not for the rest of my life. Everyone has to do rep these days when they're starting, and the baby will be here soon. Stop worrying, for heaven's sake. Mark is doing his best!'

To Bess's delight, Kate discovered a small inexpensive hotel in the area and stayed in Eastbourne for several weeks. They visited Madge from time to time, and by the time Kate's leave was up she and her mother were completely reconciled at last. Madge tried in vain to persuade Kate to stay in England. 'I hate parting from you and Bess,' said Kate gently, 'but I've got a contract, which I can't break. It's only for a further four years. Then I'll be home for good, if you can put up with me!'

Kate had made no effort to see Patrick during her stay and showed little interest in news of him. She seemed surprised by Bess's description of his grand surroundings, and almost pleased to hear that he and Bess were now not on good terms. To Bess's great relief, she never asked why.

Back in Richmond, on the night before Kate's departure for Malaya, in August 1938, Bess dreamed that she was drowning. The nightmare was so vivid that she went to her mother's room for comfort: they talked the night through. Just before they finally went back to bed, Kate took her hand. 'Bess, this is important. Whatever happens to either of us in the future, I want you to know that the fact that I had you has been the most rewarding thing in my life.' Bess never forgot those words.

After Kate had gone, Bess returned to Eastbourne, where life seemed bleaker than ever. Waiting for the baby bored her, the news from Europe frightened her and she saw even less of Mark than usual. Very occasionally, if he had a week off, they went to his parents' house at Shillington; but these visits depressed her even further. Mrs Wells, although excited at the prospect of a grand-child, despised Bess for having slept with her son before her marriage and was disappointed that he had married so early in his career. Miss Wells, by contrast, was her usual unfailingly sympathetic self, and Pa Wells, Mark's father, was a good and loving friend.

Fortunately for Bess, Gerald Masters turned up in Eastbourne, as unexpectedly as he had appeared at the wedding. Undeterred by Mark's dislike and sarcasm, he stayed for two weeks, even obtaining another room in the same lodgings. The years between had made no difference to his friendship with Bess, who came to life in his company. Mark noticed this and it did nothing to predispose him in his favour. He was, in fact, very jealous, which to Bess's relief had the effect of bringing him home as often as he could possibly manage it.

Gerald was doing well in his grandfather's bookshop but his real ambition was to become a writer. 'One day, I'm going to write plays,' he said. 'I shall write good ones, Bessie, and when there's a worthwhile part for you, I'll send for you. Won't that be fun?'

'Marvellous!'

Bess didn't believe that such a thing would ever happen, but she loved his generosity and was very impressed by the short stories he had written. The time for his departure came all too soon, and as she had when her mother had left, Bess became twice as lonely after he had gone.

At last July came, and with it the baby.

Laura was born two weeks late, and with the maximum trouble and pain. Mark was disappointed that the baby was a girl, but brought armfuls of red roses to the hospital where all the nurses swooned with excitement not only at his looks, but because he had already become something of a local celebrity. He looked at Laura with some distaste when he was alone with Bess. 'Oh, well,' he said. 'Next time, please God, it'll be a boy,' which Bess found very discouraging.

Madge was wildly excited about her first great-grandchild and insisted that Bess and the baby should come and stay. She sent Bentwood to collect them. Mark made no objection, for Laura was a sickly, querulous child who allowed her parents very little sleep; since Mark was working extremely hard, this was a serious deprivation. Besides, he was genuinely fond of 'his Bessie', as he called her, and realised how lonely her life in Eastbourne must be.

In recent months, the threat to world peace from Nazi Germany had become apparent even to the least politically minded. Madge now began making arrangements for Bess to stay with relatives of the Glanvilles in Cornwall, where it was hoped she and the baby would be comparatively safe if war broke out. Mark thought this a good idea but Mrs Wells was very angry. She announced that it was both her right and her duty to have them to stay at Shillington.

The political crisis deepened: Hitler was now blatantly threatening Czechoslovakia. The hastily convened Munich conference between Britain and France and the German and Italian dictators had solved nothing. In desperation, Neville Chamberlain embarked on a series of flights to talk to Hitler face to face, and at last returned with the historic piece of paper proclaiming, 'PEACE IN OUR TIME'. The joy and relief amongst ordinary men and women was enormous; only a tiny minority, from all political parties, were wise before the event — seeing it, in Churchill's phrase, as an 'unmitigated defeat'.

Bess and Laura returned to Eastbourne. The Munich scare had brought Bess and Mark closer together, but she was horrified to discover a few months later that she was pregnant once again. This time however, she felt well throughout the pregnancy. By August 1939, she was the delighted mother of a little boy whom they named Peter. And this time Mark, too, was overjoyed.

On 3 September 1939, in a high voice shaking with emotion, Neville Chamberlain addressed the British people on the radio: war had been declared. Mark went off to enlist immediately. To his consternation, he was told to return to his job until he was called up; he went back to the repertory company feeling deflated. Six months later, in February 1940, he joined the Oxfordshire and Buckinghamshire Light Infantry, in Oxford. Since this was so near Shillington, Bess went to stay with her in-laws.

It was not easy for her. Shillington Rectory was a grey Victorian house with solid rooms and solid furniture. It was permanently cold, even in summer, and Mrs Wells was a grim, very consciously respectable woman, who had difficulty in coming to terms with Bess. She had never wanted Mark to become an actor and was even less pleased that he had chosen to marry an actress. She and her husband loved the children, though, as indeed did the rest of the household, which consisted of a cook and two dailies; so Bess had an unexpected amount of freedom. Immediately, she found her thoughts turning towards the acting career for which she still longed.

After ten weeks, Mark was sent to an Officer Selection Board in Oxford, which recommended that he should go to the OCTU at Bulford, near Salisbury, to train for a commission. Bess and the children found digs on Salisbury Plain so as to be near him, but Mark was not a patient father; Laura's constant whining, which often led to tantrums, got on his nerves. He 'passed out' as a Second Lieutenant in three months, which made Bess very proud; but instead of rejoining his regiment he was commissioned into the Intelligence Corps, on the strength of an interview at Bulford in which his French and German were tested, and interest shown in his theatrical career. After a spell at the Intelligence Corps depot in Oxford — which took Bess and the children back to Shillington — he was posted to Northern Ireland.

To Bess's relief, Mark had no particular wish for his family to join him there. He adored Peter, but simply couldn't get around to feeling any affection for his daughter. Bess, too, found Laura hard to love, and had a pronounced feeling of guilt about it. It was decided that the children should stay at Shillington with their grandmother, and that Bess would go over to Ulster whenever possible.

It was at this point that Bess received a letter from Gerald:

Dear Bess,

You'll never believe it, but I've had a play accepted. It's to be done at the Manningham Rep, not far from Middlesborough. Manningham is a dreary spot, but the Rep is good and I've managed to get a part for you. They weren't too keen at first, as you've no experience — but once again, I'm afraid, the Glanville name has worked its magic. I wrote the part for you, as I said I would, and I couldn't bear it if you refused. After all, it's my first big chance. Make it yours.

Love,
Gerald

PS   I haven't been called up yet, as I have flat feet and a bad heart, but I do A R P work.

Almost unable to believe her good luck, Bess discussed the problem with her mother-in-law, who was very disapproving.

'What is supposed to happen to the children while you are away gallivanting?' she asked coldly. 'Are you going to take them with you?'

'Would you rather?' asked Bess anxiously.

'You haven't thought how inconvenient it might be for me and my husband if they stayed here without you, I suppose?' demanded Mrs Wells.

'Of course I have,' lied Bess, 'but they were going to be on their own with you whenever I went to join Mark. And don't you see how good it might be for Mark if I take this job? If I can get going it means that he will still have some links with the theatre when he comes out of the army.'

'What does Mark think about it?' demanded Mrs Wells.

'I haven't talked to him yet. I wanted to know how you felt.'

Mrs Wells looked gratified. 'Very well then. If Mark agrees.'

Mark was less easy to manage, but Bess assured him that his mother thought the whole idea excellent, and used the same argument about how much better it would be for him if she kept his place in the theatre open. He capitulated, and on his capitulation Mrs Wells grumblingly gave in.

Oddly, although he was only a baby, Peter seemed the more upset of the two by Bess's departure. Laura was jealous of Peter and already instinctively felt that her mother's departure, however alarming, removed one source of competition.

Manningham was every bit as dreary as Gerald had suggested; but being with Gerald had its usual tonic effect on Bess, and John Pugh, the director, though elderly and embittered and altogether unattractive, certainly knew his job. The other women in the company were all young except for John's wife, Millicent Evers, who was a fierce, spinsterish little creature with dyed red hair, a waspish tongue and a jealous disposition. The men — most young ones having been called up — were middle-aged and given to wearing toupets. Millicent's jealousy was aggravated by the fact that, although John Pugh had a chip on his shoulder, disliked Bess for being a Glanville by inheritance and detested even more her colonial background, he was immediately and violently attracted. He had an office on the landing at the turn of the stairs which led to the dressing rooms back stage, and he had a habit of sneaking out when he heard Bess's footsteps on the stone steps and pinching her behind. Bess bore it stoically, as she had no wish to lose her job.

The play had an instant local success, and so did Bess, who was offered a six-month contract which she unhesitatingly accepted. Gerald too was offered a job — but sadly for them both, in Glasgow, as resident playwright in a small experimental theatre which was far ahead of its time. He recklessly threw up his safe job in the family bookshop, and went.

Bess fast became a local celebrity, as Mark had done, and also the darling of the local critics. Neither her colleagues nor John Pugh liked such swift success, even though it was good for business. Although Bess didn't realise it, the same forces were at work which had made Kate an outsider in Malaya. The Glanville name removed her from repertory-actor level, and in a provincial atmosphere both gave her a cachet which she didn't seek and made her a target for envy — intensified, as in her mother's case, by her exceptional good looks.

John Pugh well knew that Bess found him unattractive. His revenge was to make constant cracks about mem-sahibs and pukka sahibs and Poonah, until Bess felt like screaming. But he never stopped trying to pinch her behind or force a kiss from her, and Millicent, fully aware of his proclivities, hatched a little plot to spoil the fun. She had been in the habit of criticising Bess's clothes and making disparaging remarks about her personal appearance. Now she decided that, since she herself was a redhead (even if only a dyed one) and the other juvenile was dark, Bess must become a blonde: she ordered her husband to fix it.

Bess was summoned to John's room after morning rehearsal. Millicent was there to watch over the proceedings and John launched into the attack the moment Bess walked through the door.

'It's not always a good idea in rep to be so distinctive,' he said, in his clipped nasal voice. 'It means that the public can always recognise you no matter what kind of part you're playing. I realise of course that you probably like the thought of that — I expect it massages your ego — but as we already have a redhead in Millicent, we have decided that you should dye your hair blonde.'

Bess was startled at the shifty malice in his voice.

'I see,' she said quietly.

'So get it dyed on Monday.'

'Isn't blonde just as distinctive as red?' asked Bess.

'Just do what you're told and like it,' said John.

'I'd rather not.'

'It's an order,' said Millicent sharply.

'One I'm not prepared to obey.' Bess's quick temper was getting the better of her.

'Then she must go, John.'

'Please, Millie, leave this to me,' said John in growing exasperation. He turned to Bess. 'You are being a little foolish, aren't you, right at the start of your career, and with two children to look after?'

'My husband, who is in the army,' said Bess evenly, 'likes my hair the way it is.'

'Would you wear a wig?' asked John.

'Of course. If it was suitable for the part.'

'That's settled then. You can go.'

And as Bess closed the door, she heard Millicent say, 'You bloody fool, John! You've let the little bitch get away with it!' followed by John's mumbled response, and the beginnings of a monumental row.

The wig when it arrived was a mass of bubble curls, and so much too large that Bess could only anchor it to her head by stuffing it with stockings. She tried it on at the coffee break, and the effect reduced the company to helpless hysteria. Only John and Millicent were straight-faced.

'*Much* better dear,' they said in unison.

'You mean I'm to wear it?' Bess was incredulous.

'Certainly,' said John.

'For *this* play?' they were rehearsing Lonsdale's *On Approval* and Bess was playing a soignée young heiress from Mayfair.

'For every play,' said Millicent.

'Then you can take a fortnight's notice!' exclaimed Bess heatedly.

'With pleasure,' said John, 'but I do so wonder if you're wise.'

'I'll make out. You'll see,' said Bess, her eyes smarting.

A fortnight later, she left Manningham for good.

CHAPTER SEVENTEEN

Not long after Bess returned to Shillington, Mark came home on leave. He was in two minds about her debut as an actress — jealous that she was able to appear on stage when he couldn't, but alive to the possible advantage for him in the long term if she retained links with the theatre — and he was as angry as she was at the way she had been sacked. They spent the last two days of his leave in London, where in spite of heavy air-raids they had a happy time. London looked dreary and depressed. Nearly everyone was in uniform and there were sandbags everywhere. Army vehicles threaded their way in and out of the sparse traffic, while above them great silver balloons swung to and fro, turning slowly on their thick cables and gleaming when the sun shone. Many theatres were shut, but they saw Edith Evans and Dorothy Dickson in *Diversion* at Wyndham's and imagined themselves acting there together after the war was over.

Back again at Shillington without Mark, Bess worried about her volatile temperament: she must learn not to rise so quickly to the irritations of people like John and Millicent. Staving off his attentions and her jealousy was just a routine part of the job. She must watch that temper of hers or she could jeopardise her career completely. She was already longing to act again. Her children needed her, she knew, and she struggled to give them proper attention; but even though Peter, at nine months, was a source of loving fascination to her, Laura was exhaustingly possessive and demanding. Bess realised that she was just as low on maternal instinct as her mother had always been.

It was at this point that Gerald unexpectedly contacted her again. His letter brought the news she had been waiting for:

... Windsor is going to do my play. There's a very good chap who has taken over the rep there, called John Counsell. He's gone into the army but he still keeps an eye on things, and his very pretty wife, Mary, rather wanted to do your part herself.

But they both believe in the play, and when I said I had written it for you specially, Mary generously gave way. They say you can do it there again, if you want to. Isn't that stupendous? I told them what a good actress you are, and you know how much I want you to do it, Bessie. You're wonderful in it, and you can really help me, by doing it so near town. So come on, darling. The stage is what you were made for, and we both know it in our bones.

Bess wrote immediately to Mark, who with great excitement told her to go ahead; but once again there were endless discussions with Mrs Wells.

'The children are too young for you to go dashing about all over the country, like this,' she said. 'They miss you, and these are important years for them.'

'I know, Mother, and I agree, but the stage is tremendously competitive, and we have to think of Mark. In any case I'll get back from Windsor every weekend. Chances don't come all that often, you know, and this is a wonderful one.'

'Who is this Gerald person?' demanded Mrs Wells sceptically. 'And why should he want a complete beginner like you?'

'I've told you, we've been friends ever since Bendleford. He wants me, because he thinks I'm right for his play.'

'Is he keen on you?'

'No, of course not.'

'There's no "of course" about it!'

'There is if you meet him, Mother. He's not keen on women in that sense at all.'

'What does that mean?' demanded Mrs Wells. Bess realised with surprise that, like many women of her age and generation, Mrs Wells was totally ignorant about homosexuality.

'He's one of nature's bachelors,' said Bess, 'but you'd like him if you saw him, Mother, and you'd understand. Couldn't he come and meet you?'

Gerald duly came down for the day and Mrs Wells took to him at once; but she still didn't understand about his 'bachelorhood' at all.

'He's a dear young man,' she agreed, approvingly. 'But what a waste that he doesn't want to get married, Bess! Are you quite sure he doesn't?'

'Quite.'

With his fair colouring, Gerald was someone who blushed easily. He had long eyelashes over immense blue eyes, and was thin and stooping. He had a habit of running his hands distractedly through his curly hair, and gazing at people earnestly while talking. In his effeminate way, he was very attractive. He liked older women, too, and treated Mrs Wells with exaggerated respect, even taking the trouble to charm Mr Wells, for good measure.

'What do you think, Arthur?' asked Mrs Wells. 'Do you think Bessie should help this young man out with his new play at Windsor?'

Mr Wells looked bemused. 'If you think it wise, my dear, and if Bess wants to, I don't see why not,' he said vaguely.

So it was settled.

In fact, Gerald *was* in love with a woman at this stage — but for the only time in his life. The girl he had fallen for, Greta, was neurotic enough to be almost a mental case. She was misleadingly Amazonian to look at, with dark skin and a deep masculine voice, and was learning to drive so that she could join the FANY's. She used Gerald as a psychiatrist's couch — 'my confessor,' she called him. Daughter of a peer, with a huge stately home in the Dukeries, she fell passionately in love with herself falling in love with Gerald and her long sessions talking to him about herself kept her absorbed and delighted for several months; the affair thus lasted far longer than it would have done under different circumstances. She was doing her training in London and living with her sister at the family's London home. Although she was pursued by several men from her own background she relished the fact that Gerald was a writer, and was thrilled that he seemed to be making some headway. 'An intellectual, my dear,' she told her society friends. 'Too exciting, and he's going to be a great writer. You'll see!'

Gerald fell head over heels in love with her. Since he had never quite resigned himself to being homosexual the experience was of great importance to him, even though it was doomed from the start. They were an impossible match. Greta was a sexy young woman, who although quite maternal as well, needed more physical excitement than Gerald could ever provide; Gerald, who was sensitive and clever, needed a dream girl who had a good brain and was much less egocentric. The break-up when it came was as traumatic for him as the affair itself, and he never quite got over the shock.

Madge had closed her house in Richmond and joined Harry's niece, Joyce Glanville, in Windsor. Effie had died, leaving her inconsolable. Joyce was a competent actress, who in spite of the Glanville name had never made much of a success; but she was a nice woman, and had a house that was too big for her, with a self-contained flat which she put at Madge's disposal. The two women had always enjoyed one another's company and, as Bess and Madge had been, were both fiercely independent; so things worked out very well. Bess was invited to stay with them while she was at Windsor; but, remembering the jealousies that the Glanville name had engendered in Manningham, she thought it best to live in digs in the town instead. In the event, she could have stayed with them happily. The company was an exceptionally friendly one this time. However, though she adored her grandmother, she was just as happy not to be a guest while she was working so hard.

The play seemed as good in Windsor as it had in Manningham, and Bess, having played her part before, felt less of a beginner than she really was. As always, she loved being with Gerald and they both realised how lucky they were to be working, when so many theatres were still shut. The conditions at Windsor were ideal: the director was first class — and, to Bess's relief, had no wife, nor a chip on his shoulder. Sets and costumes too were of a high standard.

Madge and Joyce were there on the first night, and the audience applauded their entrance into the auditorium. Madge looked wonderful. At eighty she still held herself superbly. Her white hair, immaculately coiffed, was piled up on top of her head, and her enormous eyes in the clever humorous face still sparkled with interest and vitality. She still acted from time to time and her fame was undimmed. Joyce was well known in Windsor, and well liked. Bess knew that their presence in the audience would help with the local critics, and she was right. The play itself was not particularly well received, but her performance was given rave notices. Joyce, who had been offered a part in another play with rehearsals starting in a few months' time in London, insisted that her director should come to Windsor to see Bess. The director was impressed and told Bess to get in touch with him when she wanted a job; Bess excitedly accepted. He told her to get herself an agent, and suggested Dolly Baker of Screen and Stage Limited. Dolly put Bess under contract and Bess felt that her career had really begun.

At the end of the run, Madge gave her a photograph of herself as a young woman. On the back of it she wrote, 'Congratulations, darling Bess, on living up to the Glanvilles. I am happy that Kate had a daughter. Madge.'

CHAPTER EIGHTEEN

Although Britain had been at war for over two years now, life in Malaya was still relatively normal. More and more troops were coming out from the UK and Australia, and on 2 December the radio announced with some pride that two great battleships, the *Repulse* and the *Prince of Wales* had arrived in Singapore to reinforce the Royal Navy's Far Eastern fleet. There was a comfortable feeling that all was well.

In Kuala Lumpur, on the evening of Sunday, 7 December, 1941, Kate was in a party of twelve at a dinner dance at the Spotted Dog. Her hosts were Margot Callendar, an Australian, and her husband Hugo, a British planter. Margot had become a firm friend since Kate's return to KL and had dropped into the habit of visiting her at the library almost daily. She was semi-seriously trying to match-make between Kate and a rather charming elderly lawyer, who had lost his wife quite recently. Both Kate and the lawyer knew what she was doing. Neither had the least intention of remarrying, but they liked Margot and they liked each other, so they were willing to play along.

On this particular evening, however, the dancing was interrupted by the arrival of Military Police, who ordered all service personnel to report to their units immediately; after a short interval they reappeared, looking grim, and repeated their orders. The dancing abruptly came to an end. At 1.15 a.m. that same night, a Japanese fleet of twenty-seven troop transports reached Kota Bahru on the north-east coast. Disembarkation began immediately in rubber assault craft. The invasion of Malaya was underway. At 4.a.m., the first Japanese bombs fell on Singapore. Two days later, the *Repulse* and the *Prince of Wales*, entirely without air cover, were sunk off the east coast by Japanese torpedo bombers while returning to Singapore from an abortive mission against the Kota Bahru troopships.

Soon fresh landings were reported further south at Kuantan, threatening the encirclement of a whole sector of the north east.

Since the sea was now infested by the Japanese, a steady evacuation of white women and children from these areas began,
towards KL and Singapore (Singapore, in spite of the bombing,
was known to be 'impregnable'). The native population on the
mainland was urged to take to the jungle. In the ensuing weeks, the
Japanese made almost unimpeded progress down the Peninsula.
Further bombs were dropped on Singapore and there were aerial
'dog-fights' over KL.

Margot rang Kate. She sounded breathless and unhappy.
'Hugo says I'm to go home to Australia,' she announced. 'We've
had terrible rows about it — I don't want to leave him. He insists
because of the two kids. So I'd better go. Will you come with
me?'

'Leave Malaya?' Kate was horrified. 'Whatever will the Malays
think of us if we all leave? *You* must, of course. Hugo is quite right
about the children. But people like me can't desert!'

'You evidently haven't heard what happened in Penang,' said
Margot grimly.

'No. What?'

'The whole population there — Europeans, Aussies, Malays,
Indians and Chinese — they've all been involved *together* in coping,
and coping splendidly, with the bombings — but not a single
Asiatic has been allowed to leave on any of the evacuation craft.'

'I don't believe it!'

'It's true.'

'All the more reason for me to stay here, then!' said Kate.

'Don't be a fool. Come while the going's good.'

'The radio says to keep calm,' said Kate.

'Well of course it does! Wouldn't you, if you were in authority?
Anyway, why not come with me as far as Singapore? That at least
is defended. Our aircraft here are pathetic. Well, you've seen for
yourself! Old American Brewster Buffaloes, and pretty few of
those. Nothing modern at all. The Jap Zeros are the latest thing,
Hugo says. They're built to a Messerschmitt design, and we're no
match for them at all. We're undergunned, and underpowered!'

'Hugo should be more loyal!' exclaimed Kate indignantly.
'We'll win through! They'll send more planes from home. They
won't let us down. You'll see!'

'Please, Kate! What use are you here? You aren't a nurse. You
aren't even particularly young. If the war reaches KL you can't do
anything as an amateur, and your job will be gone anyway. I'll

hate going without you! Please! You owe it to your family in
England to try and get away.'

'Not yet,' said Kate. 'I can't leave yet. Not until the situation is
hopeless and we're ordered to leave.'

Margot said sadly, 'I'm packing now, and we're going tonight.
Can I come to the library to say goodbye?'

'Of course you can,' said Kate warmly. 'Oh dear, how I shall
miss you!'

'Me too! Hugo can't come with us to Singapore to see us off.
He's been ordered north with the Volunteers. Anyway, see you
soon, dear!' and Margot put down the receiver.

Kate felt a sudden blaze of anger. The Malays had depended on
Britain for their defence! They had trusted the 'Mother Country'
implicitly, and now — at least up-country — Britain was apparently powerless!

The telephone rang again. This time it was her boss, Cranford,
in Singapore. 'We're going to have to close down the library in
K L, Kate. I want the whole job done in two days' time, and you're
to come down here.'

'I can't possibly,' gasped Kate appalled. 'It'll take far longer
than that. Besides what about my home, and Ayah?'

'Those are your orders, Kate,' said Cranford. 'Disobey them
and you're fired.' His voice softened. 'Singapore is safe, and my
assistant Mrs Ensor has gone back Home, so we're short-handed.
Don't argue, my dear. Just do as you're told, there's a good girl.'

Later that day, Margot and the children came to the library to
say goodbye, but when she heard that Kate herself would be
leaving in two days Margot offered to defer her journey. Kate
wouldn't hear of it, and their parting was emotional and
exhausting.

Kate returned home in a daze. She and her staff at the library
had spent hours packing the books and carrying them down to the
cellars. She was dead tired and the work wasn't even half done.
She called for Ayah and the old woman came running at once.
Kate was in tears, and Ayah's astonishment at this was so extreme
that Kate even managed a shaken laugh.

'Mem! Mem!' exclaimed the old woman, horrified. 'What
matter, Mem?'

Wearily Kate explained. 'So we'll have to go back to Singapore,' she said. 'I'm so sorry, Ayah. I don't want to, I promise.'

Ayah looked stricken. For a long time she remained silent, then she said quietly, 'I send Ali Besar, Mem.' Ali Besar was her husband, who had been to Mecca and had returned as a Hadji or holy man to Kate's service as Head Boy. To differentiate between him and the second Boy, who had the same name, he was called Ali Besar, or 'Big' Ali — a family joke, since he was very small.

He came softly into the room, followed at a discreet distance by Ayah.

'Tabek, Mem,' he greeted her. 'Ayah tell me news, Mem. We very sorry, Mem.'

'Oh, yes, Ali,' exclaimed Kate. 'And so am I! We've all been so happy here, and now we have to move again!'

'Mem,' said Ali with great dignity, 'Ayah and me very old, Mem. We no can go to Singapore any more, Mem. We stay with you, Mem, because we be with you all our lives, and Mem been good to us. Now we tired. If Mem go, we no can go with Mem.'

Kate was aghast. 'But what will you do?' she asked. 'Where will you go? I can take you to England if the war gets too bad. I have always looked after you, and I must do so still.'

'We try to look after you too, Mem,' said Ali gravely. 'We no go to Singapore. We no go England. We old now, and Ayah not well.'

'Not well? Why on earth didn't she tell me?' demanded Kate distractedly.

'We not want to worry Mem. Mem has much to do,' said Ali.

'Have you seen a doctor, Ayah?' asked Kate.

'Yes, Mem.'

'Oh my God! exclaimed Kate. 'What are we to do?'

Ayah ran forward to comfort her, as she had so often in all their years together, and Ali gently withdrew. The two women rocked in each other's arms, crying unrestrainedly.

'There, there, Mem,' crooned Ayah, over and over again. 'It is the will of Allah. You must go, Mem, and we must stay. Don't cry, Mem. All will be well, Mem. You see!'

After Ayah had left her, Kate felt utterly bewildered. The world had turned completely upside down: everything she had believed in about the British Empire seemed suddenly a sham. And that it should have been the Japanese who had revealed this to her only added to her dismay. Kate had loved the Japanese people ever since her first holiday with Edward, all those years ago; it seemed lunatic that they should now be enemies. The Chinese were different: in Kate's eyes, they were born subversives. Over and over again, Chinese schoolmasters were deported as Communists;

but they always managed to sneak back by hiring little sampans and landing on remote parts of the coast. Since they were virtually indistinguishable to most Europeans they were seldom found out, until they began spreading Communism again. The Japs hadn't been like that at all. They had kept themselves to themselves — usually setting up as dentists or hairdressers or masseurs, and above all as photographers. They were wonderful photographers — and this had aroused absolutely no suspicion at all! How idiotic the authorities had been! Photographs helpful to Japan in wartime would have been child's play to take alongside the portraits by which they ostensibly made their money...

But how foolish Kate was being, too! Britain wouldn't let down her colonies! She'd come to their rescue soon. She'd have to!

The next two days were a nightmare. Kate did all she had to do efficiently, but mechanically. Everything seemed at once horrifying and utterly unreal. She saw to it that all the books in the library were stowed below in what she hoped was safety, and in good order; also the few tables and chairs, and her desk. She sadly dismissed the staff, then locked up and pocketed the key to take to Cranford. At home, she arranged for her furniture to be put in store in K L, terminated her lease on the house and paid up the rent.

Ayah saw to her personal packing, but Kate now had a presentiment that she might be asking to be evacuated to England quite soon, so she kept only two suitcases, one large and one small. Everything else, including most of her jewellery, she despatched home ahead of her, to Richmond. After all, if all went well here she could buy new stuff; if not, better that it should await her in England, to which she would try to escape.

Neither the cook nor the 'tukan ayer' waited for her departure. They had asked for an early payment and vanished without a word. Neither had been in her service long.

Kate rang the few friends she still had in K L to say her own goodbyes, and heard to her relief on the bush telegraph that the night mail to Singapore would be running on Thursday — the day she was due to leave. More often than not these days, the railway was out of action, the lines were being blown up constantly; but from time to time scores of Tamil workers managed to get them in order again, and on Thursday the train would run.

During this time she felt so remote from all emotion that despite the aerial dog-fights over K L every day she was not frightened for her own safety at all. At the back of her mind now was a persistent longing to be reunited with Madge and Bess. Yet she knew that, when the numbness faded, she would be heartbroken at having had to part from Ayah.

Kate packed the smaller of her two suitcases herself; but, before she started, she took out the little folding leather photograph frame which she always carried in her handbag, and gazed at the faces of the two men on whom she had most depended during her lifetime.

In the photographs, both were eternally young.

Here was Edward aged thirty, with a long gentle face and the smile that he had seemed to reserve only for her: a diffident, enquiring but at the same time trusting smile. In the end his trustfulness had won. It had triumphed over Kate's passionate wish to leave him, and over Patrick's devious and wilful charm. It had in the end, through sheer goodness, made Patrick ashamed of himself for bringing Kate the most ecstatic happiness she had known; and it had kept Kate by Edward's side for the rest of his life. It had also bound Bess to him, so that although she had seen Patrick almost as often as she had seen Edward, Bess loved Edward best — better than any of them, in fact, which was ironic. And at the very end, Kate too had grown to love Edward — but by then it was too late.

And here was Patrick, looking at her with the sardonic grin which was so much a part of his attraction. The photograph was faded, but it showed the clear eyes, thick hair, strong face and broad shoulders of the man she had never ceased to desire. Kate was now fifty-five: it seemed many more than nineteen years since he had come into her life and destroyed her. And yet, he had awakened her to an undreamed-of intensity of living before destroying her. Had the ecstasy been worth the pain? She doubted it. Could she have resisted his attraction? She doubted that, too.

She closed the photograph frame and stowed it back into the bag.

Thursday arrived. The house was denuded of furniture. Kate had written two letters to England, to send her news and love — one to Bess and one to Madge. All her heavy luggage had been taken away and Ali Besar and Ayah were to drive her to the station. She had given them her car.

Kuala Lumpur's fantastic turreted station with its spires and arches was under black-out. The long platform was only dimly lit and was crowded to suffocation on this hot and humid night.

There was no train waiting, and no-one knew what time to expect it; but everyone seemed to know that it was due. Troops and refugees were everywhere, but only a few of the station staff. To Kate's surprise, one or two friends had come to see her off: her doctor, two friends from the Customs and another from the Public Works Department.

The train steamed in. Kate hugged and kissed Ayah and shook hands with Ali. People scrambled aboard in silence and the train left almost as soon as it arrived. A few miles out of K L, planes were heard overhead, but nothing happened. Then, soon after sunrise, bombs fell and two Japanese planes flew backwards and forwards strafing the carriages. Windows were broken. Several people were wounded, one or two killed. Women screamed and children cried, but miraculously the train continued on its way.

When she reached Singapore the atmosphere there utterly astounded her. No-one seemed to have the slightest idea that they were in real danger. Robinsons department store (the Singapore equivalent of Harrods) had been hit, and its restaurant devastated; but a new restaurant had been established in the basement, and here refugees from all over Malaya congregated casually and cheerfully. The few people who were leaving advertised their houses as 'To Let', in the papers. There was still dancing at Raffles, the great fashionable hotel, while at the Tanglin Club refugees changed into swimming things, washed their soiled clothes and hung them out in the hot sun to dry, went for a swim, ordered drinks from the efficient and still smiling staff, and then set off to Robinsons in their clean clothes to replenish their wardrobes. The belief that Singapore could never be taken remained completely unshakeable.

January passed. Half-empty liners still sailed for Britain. Then February came.

Though there had been one or two savage air raids, morale was still high. The hospitals were overcrowded, but St Andrew's Cathedral was now being used for the overflow of the sick and wounded. Robinsons was doing better than ever and Raffles and the various clubs were full. At last Churchill warned that the bad news from the Far East was likely to get worse; although it was to be two weeks before Singapore finally fell, a full-scale evacuation began. By this time the Japanese were actually on the island and only five miles from the centre of the city.

On 13 February, the *Mata Hari*, the *Kuala*, the *Vyner Brooke* and the *Giang Bee* set sail, with a number of smaller ships in their wake. On one of these, the *Princess Pearl*, went Kate. All were going to Australia: Kate had begged to be sent to England, but the queue to leave was now so great that she had been forced to take any accommodation going. The overcrowding on board was appalling. The *Mata Hari*, equipped for nine passengers, set sail with three hundred and twenty; the *Vyner Brooke*, equipped for twelve, took two hundred and fifty; and the *Princess Pearl* (which in fact sailed earlier than the others) took one hundred and twenty instead of four.

In the hopelessly muddled way in which everything was being managed, all of them were heading for disaster. The Japanese fleet was lying across the Straits of Sumatra poised for an invasion of the Dutch East Indies which in fact started the following day.

The *Princess Pearl* picked up a drowning RAF officer, who told the Captain about the danger ahead. The Captain at once altered course for one of the smaller islands nearby, but almost immediately six Japanese bombers found the little ship and bombed her mercilessly. By rapid changes of course and speed, the Captain did all in his power to avoid destruction — and indeed eighteen bombs fell harmlessly into the sea. But the nineteenth scored a direct hit.

In seconds there was pandemonium. Lifeboats, rafts, ropes and rope ladders were lowered. Kate, who had befriended a little Javanese boy who had somehow got separated from his parents, managed to struggle into one of the lifeboats. Afterwards she couldn't remember how she had succeeded, but somehow she carried him in the crook of one arm, with her small suitcase slung over her other wrist and her handbag hung around her neck.

The little boy began whimpering. She took him on her lap. Suddenly she remembered that 13 February was Edward's birthday, and this made her remember the photographs. As the handbag was already being a nuisance, bumping about over her life-jacket, she decided to transfer her money, her make-up, her spectacles and the photos to a small waterproof satchel (a relic of sketching expeditions in the jungle) which she had strapped on the linen belt around her waist. This already contained some small bandages, lint, a pair of nail scissors and a small bottle of Listerine, so it was a struggle to make room for them. But it was as well that she did. Four of the planes had made off, but two now returned and circled the ship. They came screaming down to sea level and systematically began machine-gunning the survivors, whether on life rafts, in boats or in the water. Screams of fear and agony mingled with the gunfire and the roar of the engines. Dead, dying or unharmed, they were all soon in the sea. It was a scene of threshing, pitiable, mindless chaos, lit by a glorious sunrise. The water slowly reddened with blood.

The little boy was clinging around Kate's neck so tightly that he was almost throttling her, howling his panic into her ears. In spite of their life-jackets, he was fighting and struggling so hard that he seemed to be dragging her down with him under the sea.

'Give me that child or you'll both drown!' said an authoritative voice behind her.

The speaker was a young man, who even in these conditions looked at home in the water. Thankfully Kate swam towards him with the child but, as she was about to pass him over, the planes came in again. She saw the feathered trace of the bullets hurtling across the sea straight at them and tried to pull the little boy behind her; but he broke free in his terror, and a second later he was dead.

'Bastards!' she shouted, holding the limp body in her arms. 'Bloody bastards!'

'Yes,' said the young man. 'Let him go.' It was a command, and sadly she released her hold.

The sound of the planes receded.

'Thank God!' said the young man fervently. 'We seem to be safe for the moment. How well do you swim?'

'Very well,' said Kate. She was shivering with fright and horror.

'You'll need to,' he said grimly. 'That's Ikan Island on the skyline there, and that's where I'm heading. Banka Island is larger, and will have better amenities, but if the Jap fleet is in the Sumatra Straits, who knows? Banka may already be in their hands.'

'How far is Ikan?'

'About four miles.'

'I'll come with you.'

'OK, but strike out as fast as you can. Oil from the ship will be pouring out in a minute, and it's difficult stuff to swim in.'

'I've never tried to swim four miles — I might be a handicap to you.'

'Nuts!' he said. 'The name is Colin Franks by the way. I know yours. You're Kate Marchmont, the painter. I bought one of your pictures last year.'

In spite of the horror of their situation, Kate smiled at his formality.

Colin smiled back. 'No more talking. We're going to need all our strength.' And they began swimming, side by side.

After the heat of the ship, the water seemed pleasantly cool at first. Soon, though, the cold became so penetrating that Kate's limbs began to feel numb. She had thrown away the offending handbag, and the suitcase had vanished when the lifeboat sank, but her life-jacket was chafing her chin painfully. She said so to Colin, who replied tersely, 'It always happens,' and they fell silent again.

Behind them, the *Princess Pearl* was listing even more steeply. Suddenly her bow reared high in the air and within minutes, in a great cloud of steam, she sank. And now the black oil did indeed pour out of her, in an ever increasing, nauseating flood.

Colin turned momentarily to watch. 'Goodbye, old girl,' he said softly. 'It was nice knowing you.'

'How about sharks?' asked Kate, after a while. 'Are we likely to get them in these waters?'

'We have to take our chance,' said Colin.

'They're attracted by blood aren't they?'

'Why? You hurt?'

'No. You?'

'Hardly a scratch. We've been lucky, Mrs Marchmont.' Colin sounded grim.

A large piece of wood floated towards them and he grabbed it.

'We can rest on this,' he said, 'if we don't get too tired pushing it.'

The sun blazed down on them, and they swam on. Sometimes they rested for a moment, their heads on their arms. Sometimes they let go of the wood and floated, then caught up with it again. Sometimes they just swam.

On and on they went.

Kate's face began to hurt. Her skin was blistering and her mouth swollen. Her arms and hands were burning. The rest of her body was ice cold. The two of them seemed now to be alone in the sea. Perhaps all the others had chosen to try for Banka? The glitter of the water dazzled their eyes. Time was stretching out to eternity: there was no future, never had been a past. The universe was sun and sea, and one small island.

'How far now to Ikan?' she gasped.

'About two miles or so.'

'Oh God!'

'You're doing well.'

Hours later they were within a quarter of a mile. Kate was so tired and sore that she could hardly keep going. 'Not long now,' said Colin. 'You OK?'

Kate nodded, closing her eyes.

A vicious current suddenly dragged them to the right for several hundred yards. Neither of them were strong enough to resist it. Then, as suddenly, they were free of it.

'We'd better make up our minds what we're going to do when we get there,' said Colin when they were on course again. 'It's only my gamble that the Japs aren't on Ikan. On the other hand, there's only one inhabited village there, so I didn't think it would be high on their list. My plan is that, if we land safely, we rest up in some hideaway for a bit. Then I'll prospect and see how the land lies. If the Japs aren't there, I'm sure the Malays will help. They're a nice race. D'you speak the language?'

'Yes, and a bit of Cantonese.'

'My! My!' exclaimed Colin. 'I'm impressed.'

'I don't speak Japanese,' said Kate. Her lips were so swollen that she was finding it hard to speak.

'One last effort,' said Colin. 'If we round that long spit to the left there, there's a bay with an easy approach. Plenty of cover, too, if the Japs are here. As I said, we'll reconnoitre later. The village is called Pagga Mera.'

CHAPTER NINETEEN

They rounded the headland at last, but Pagga Mera — a group of some thirty or forty Malay houses on stilts — seemed entirely deserted. A new stronger current was forcing them past the mouth of the little bay. These currents had been present intermittently throughout their journey: some had been helpful, others obstructive. This one was so strong that again Kate could scarcely battle against it.

Colin looked up at the sky. 'It must be about two o'clock,' he said, 'from the position of the sun. Keep your head down. We mustn't be seen.'

A great striped sea serpent suddenly twisted into sight, and Kate gave a cry of fear. Another appeared, then another, until the sea seemed full of them. They shot vertically out of the deep water, then writhed with amazing speed along the surface. They seemed oblivious of Kate and Colin, however, and before long had swirled and twisted out of sight. Kate began sobbing helplessly. Her entire face was by now blistered, the skin round her eyes had puffed up and her lips were bleeding.

The last few yards were terrible for her, as the current had returned with the strength of a giant. Her lungs were bursting, her heart was pounding and her body was wracked by cramps. The sudden cool of shade from the headland was an astonishing relief, and it pulled her together enough to make the final effort.

'OK,' said Colin suddenly, standing. 'We're in our depths. And we're out of sight of the village. Take my hand, we'll go ashore together.'

Kate stood too, but almost fell at once.

'Easy now,' said Colin. 'Only a yard or two more and we can sit down.'

Grimly she steadied herself and together they reached the sand.

As they took off their life-jackets there was a delicious breeze. Sitting in the shade of a rock was an exquisite luxury, and lying down even better.

Colin squeezed her hand. 'All right?' he asked.

'Fine.'

'Good girl.' Kate tried to smile. 'What's up?'

'Girl! I'm old enough to be your mother!' She looked down at herself and for the first time realised that, with her skirt gone and her blouse in tatters, she must look nearly naked. 'My God!' she exclaimed. '*Look* at me! Or rather, don't!'

'Don't bother to dress for me!' said Colin admiringly. 'You look fine.'

Kate again tried to smile, then yawned painfully. 'Oh Lord! I'm done in. I could sleep for a week.'

'Go ahead,' he said. 'It's worth the risk. I'll keep watch.' He shook his head angrily. 'I wish to God we knew about the Japs!'

Kate shuddered, but within seconds she was asleep; and so indeed, to his later shame, was Colin. He woke with a guilty start and looked down at Kate. She was a brave woman, he thought. And in spite of her bruises, the black oil matting her hair, the numerous cuts and grazes on her face and body, he found her appealing. He had noticed her on the boat and been attracted at once — which was how he had found out who she was. Asleep, the years seemed to have fallen away from her: she looked quite young.

She woke at last, and he said, 'All well so far, and I can see coconut palms and traveller's palms nearby. I'll get us a drink from a traveller's palm first, then we'll feast on coconuts. I've got a knife, if it will still cut. I won't be long. OK?'

'OK.'

He brought back the water, carrying it carefully in large smooth leaves, but when they tried to eat the coconut flesh their mouths were so sore that they could hardly manage it.

They sat with their backs against the rock. Apart from a few sudden harsh bird calls, and an occasional slithering and splash into the sea from among the mangroves, there was silence. The sea and sky were a brilliant blue. Palm trees grew tall and straight beside them. The sand was very white, and a few little crabs darted in and out of their holes on the beach. It was lovely and untouched. Kate shook her head. 'It's mad, isn't it? One of the most beautiful places on earth, and apparently the most peaceful, and yet we're surrounded by war and the threat of death.'

'Death always threatens,' said Colin lightly.

She took the little photograph frame and her spectacle case from an inner pocket of the satchel. The glasses were stained red from the damp leather; she wiped them and put them on her nose, then gingerly inspected the photographs, which miraculously were unharmed. 'Oh, good!' she exclaimed, absurdly pleased. She was putting them away when Colin said, 'May I see?'

She showed them to him.

'Your husband and father?' he asked.

'Husband and lover.'

'Where are they?'

'My husband is dead. Patrick is in England.'

'Will you go to him when you reach home?'

'No. The affair is over. It took years to finish, and was very unhappy.'

She suddenly found herself telling him about Edward and Patrick. He was easy to talk to, and listened intently. Finally he said, 'I'm sorry. For you all. Poor Kate!'

'You needn't be sorry,' said Kate bitterly. 'Not for Patrick. He didn't suffer.'

'If he never married, you may have meant more to him than you knew.'

'No. He was too selfish to marry, that's all. He had all that a wife could give him, with none of the responsibilities.'

'Then he's missed the point of life, hasn't he?'

'Perhaps.' Kate looked at him in surprise.

They talked on for a few minutes after that. Kate told him about Harry and Madge and Bess, and Colin told her that he had been born in London's dockland, which had prompted him to join the Merchant Navy. In due course he had seen an advertisement that a new crew was needed for the *Princess Pearl*; he had joined her two years ago — eventually rising to the rank of Purser.

'How old are you?' asked Kate.

'Twenty-six.'

'You see, I *am* old enough to be your mother!' she said.

Colin rose to his feet. 'It's time to try and find out how the land lies,' he said. 'I'll have to leave you again. Stay here, and hide if you see anyone coming. I'll be back as soon as I can.'

He seemed to be gone for hours and she was growing thoroughly nervous when at last he returned, accompanied by a Malay fisherman and a small girl. He looked jubilant. 'All's well!' he called out. 'No sign of the Nips, and Yusuf here will put us up with the family. There's a stream running near the village where we can clean up — I think we're too filthy for the village communal tong — after which you and I can have a delicious dinner under the stars at the little food stalls here in the street. And *then*, Mrs Marchmont, bed! Can you believe it? Bed!'

'My name's Kate,' said Kate. And the relief was so overwhelming that she wanted to cry like a baby.

They bathed in the stream. Kate's make-up things were intact, and she was lent a Malay baju and sarong to wear by her new hostess, while her tattered clothes were taken away to be washed. They ate delicious food under the stars, as Colin had promised, and later, in the little Malay hut, both slept the sleep of the just.

For a week they enjoyed idyllic happiness, living entirely for the moment. They talked of each other and of themselves until they knew each other well. Even though the disparity in their ages was enormous, each had a strong attraction for the other, and this strange interlude between the terrors of their escape and the likely danger ahead of them engendered a friendship as intense as falling in love.

One day, Colin led Kate back to the little beach where they had rested when they first reached the island. For once he seemed ill at ease in her company; Kate was worried.

They sat side by side on the beach, while Colin abstractedly drew pictures on the sand at his feet. At last he spoke. 'Kate,' he said solemnly, 'how often do you say to yourself, "This may be the last day of my life"?'

'Quite often,' said Kate, 'though I try not to. And if they are to be our last days, I'm glad to have spent them with you.'

'I feel the same,' said Colin. 'So ... and because anything may be in store for us — a long stay here ... a struggle to get away by sea, if the Nips come ... or even the death we so constantly think of — I want to celebrate this time we've had together.' He spoke so quietly now that she could hardly hear him. 'Kate — my dear, very dear Kate — as a sort of tribute to a very special friendship ... don't be angry, Kate... I'd like to make love to you.'

She looked at him, deeply moved. 'But I'm an old woman,' she said.

'Not to me. You're beautiful.'

'Don't be silly! I'm old, I tell you!' She sounded angry.

'Please Kate.'

Kate was silent for a long time, then she said slowly, 'Edward died six years ago. I haven't made love to anyone since.'

'I'll be gentle,' he replied.

And so they made love. And as she held his young body to her afterwards, she reflected how ironic it was, that it had taken this boy ... this stranger ... in these bizarre circumstances ... to bring her the innocent peace and fulfilment she had never found with either Edward or Patrick.

CHAPTER TWENTY

The Japanese invaded the island the next day.

Colin had gone down to the beach to see the Chinese sampan they had bought. Kate, after tidying away as usual all signs of their occupation of the little house lent to them in the village, had spent the morning by the stream in the jungle, rather absurdly writing a letter to Bess.

It had been arranged with the Malay Headman of Pagga Mera that if the Japanese arrived, the villagers, to avoid reprisals, were to admit to no knowledge of Kate and Colin.

It was midday. Kate was on her way back to eat lunch at one of the little stalls — when suddenly she saw the enemy. The shock nearly took her breath away. There were about twelve soldiers with an officer, all naked except for the small white loin cloth which was their usual undergarment; their sweating yellow bodies were slung about with rifles, bayonets and knives. Their menacing appearance terrified her. The officer had an enormous curved sword which was so long that it almost tripped him as he strutted towards her, but Kate found nothing comic in this minor absurdity.

As soon as she caught sight of them she darted back into the jungle, but they had seen her at the same moment and three soldiers gave chase. She was caught within minutes, and taken straight to the officer, who spoke English in a chilling nasal voice. He was obviously astounded to see her and asked her many searching questions. While she answered he stared at her impassively, his head cocked to one side. She told him that she had escaped from the *Princess Pearl*, but that her lifeboat had been bombed. She had made for Ikan Island because it was within sight; she wasn't a strong enough swimmer to make for Banka, which otherwise she might have tried to reach.

'You are saying that you are alone?'

'As far as I know.' She prayed that Colin wouldn't choose this moment to materialise.

The officer looked unconvinced. He snarled commands at the soldiers, who once more surrounded her and, with much pushing and prodding, set off with her through the jungle. They walked so fast that she was hard pressed to keep up; but, if she faltered, they jabbed at her with their bayonets. The heat was tremendous. After a mile or so they caught up with a straggle of Chinese from the village, who like herself were under guard. (It later transpired that the Japanese had rounded up several hundred Chinese in Singapore to use as coolie labour, but that when they had arrived in Sumatra after a terrible journey, half of them were dead, one or two had gone mad and the rest were too ill to be of use. They had been battened down in the hold, packed so tightly together that they couldn't even move, and had been given neither food nor water. They were finally left to die of starvation in a pigsty. This had prompted a raid on Ikan island for replacements.)

After a two-mile walk, Kate and her fellow prisoners came in sight of the little harbour on the other side of the island, where a ship was lying at anchor. They were driven aboard. After waiting an hour or so for the return of the officer and a further two dozen or more soldiers, the ship sailed. The Chinese were herded below; Kate was tied to the ship's railing under the burning sun. By the time they at last reached Banka, she and the others had been without food or water for twenty hours. Her only consolation was that there had been no sign of Colin. She prayed with all her heart that he was safe.

They disembarked at Muntok pier in Banka. All the prisoners were housed for the night in an outhouse, where they were given a small quantity of dirty rice and some goat's milk. They had to lie on a filthy cement floor swarming with black beetles; although, with a show of consideration which was bizarre in the circumstances, Kate was put by herself in a little pen at one end of the shed. There were no sanitary arrangements except for a drain, and by morning the stench was almost unsupportable.

The next day they were transported in lorries to the centre of Muntok. The Chinese were driven away never to be seen again; Kate was taken to a disused cinema where she found hundreds of survivors from the *Princess Pearl* and the rest of the convoy. Her relief bordered on euphoria.

For many hundreds of prisoners, conditions during the next three years varied from acute hardship to sheer horror, and Kate did her

best to adjust to a life which was almost beyond her compre-
hension. As captors the Japanese were unpredictable. Mostly they
were callous and cruel, and their treatment of the Asiatics —
whom they professed they had come to 'liberate' — was often
bestial. One Malay, caught during a black-market transaction
through the barbed wire of one of the camps, was tied to a stake in
the sun and repeatedly bayonneted in places that wouldn't kill
him but would maim him for life. Any passing soldier could join in
this brutal game, and his screams were considered a good joke.
Dogs and cats were often shot for fun — preferably in front of their
owners. The secret police — the terrifying Kempei Tai — devised
tortures so vile and degrading that even the prisoners of Belsen
could hardly have fared worse. Water torture consisted of forcing
water through a prisoner's mouth and nostrils until he became
unconscious: the water was then expelled by jumping up and
down on the prisoner's distended stomach. Finger nails and toe
nails were torn out, and pointed bamboo sticks were hammered
into the quicks; joints were broken, and muscles torn. Prisoners
were forced to kneel on glass while being flogged; and hot irons,
burning cigarettes and boiling water were applied to sex organs,
eyes, breasts and ears — all these brutalities were commonplace.
Yet the Japanese were good to children and, on a few surprising
occasions, suddenly compassionate.

During those three and a half years, the women prisoners were
moved five times. In Palembang in 1942 conditions probably came
nearest to being tolerable. Palembang was the capital city of
Sumatra; not all the Dutch residents had yet been rounded up,
and during this time many of them were generous with outworn
clothing and even food. The Malay women were generous too, and
charmingly eager to help. There was also a hospital called Charit-
as (though it had far too few medical supplies), and here those
near death were allowed to go; it was staffed by dedicated nurses
(the Australians being particularly heroic) and two utterly self-
denying doctors. For some of the women, the great consolation was
that there was a male prisoner-of-war camp quite close, where
husbands and other relatives were also interned.

Christmas 1942 was probably the highlight — if anything in
such horrifying circumstances could be so described — of the
whole internment. Indomitable women trained choirs, conducted
them and got up concerts; others sewed endlessly, making some
sort of reasonable clothing for the children. And Kate, with her

theatrical background, also came into her own: writing, casting and directing plays and revues. There was also by this time a school for children, staffed by volunteers, in which Kate taught drawing and English.

But starvation was always only a step away, even at Palembang. A diet of filthy rice, rotting vegetables and portions of meat so small that they scarcely constituted a mouthful took its toll even on the strong. Malaria, a dreadful disease they called 'the Itches', ulcers, beri-beri, dysentery, and mosquito bites which went septic, were constant hazards. The monstrous overcrowding was a source of continual irritation and discomfort, but the lack of sanitation provided the greatest hardship of all. Lavatories were no more than open trenches over which the women had to squat on bamboo planks. Open drains carried the effluent of hundreds of prisoners, and it had to be man-handled away or sluiced with water brought from considerable distances in heavy buckets.

The remarkable compensation was that, gradually, an unshake-able cameraderie grew up between the prisoners, even though the ethnic groups tended to stick together.

An all-woman environment was not Kate's natural habitat but her admiration for her fellow internees grew daily. Brave, stoical and resourceful, their humour was irrepressible. They invented nicknames for the villainous Japanese soldiers with whom they had the most contact — 'Doctor Death', 'Rubber Hips', 'the Face', 'the Beard', 'the Balls', and 'the Red Indian' — and by their ability to laugh at their captors, lessened their sense of fear and despair. Somehow they wore their rags with style, cared selflessly for the children and cooked more or less edible meals in oil drums heated by fires whose wood had to be hewn with blunt knives and then dragged miles to the camp. Naturally there were some women who were less than splendid. These were the congenitally selfish, the malicious and the self-pitying. There were also the thieves, who had to be carefully watched; and the tarts or 'free women', as they were called, who obtained perks for sleeping with the Japs: a better diet, plenty of cigarettes and extra clothing.

At length the remaining Dutch too were interned; and although most of the Australians and British tended to dislike them, to Kate's great delight Susie van der Elst was with them. The two women embraced with deep feeling and from then on visited each other almost daily. Their friendship flowered in these grim surroundings. Susie, though instinctively courageous, sometimes became desperately unhappy at being parted from her husband, Jan. Unlike the longer-term prisoners, she hadn't yet had time to adjust. But she was a Catholic convert, deeply religious, and this gave her strength. Once when she and Kate were talking she explained her faith. 'One reason why I prefer Catholicism is that they understand what I call our fourth dimension.'

'Our fourth dimension?'

'Yes. All Christians believe in the Trinity — God the Father, God the Son and God the Holy Ghost — which is a masculine, paternal vision. But the Catholics have placed Mary with them. They have emphasised that Heaven is not a man's world only, and that God who is Love also understands and appreciates woman's qualities — and in particular our gift for fulfilment through love.'

Kate grinned. 'It's quite a thought, Susie,' she said cheerfully, 'though I for one am thankful to survive — all passion spent.'

Kate was, however, aware that she too was gaining a new kind of strength. All prisoners were ceaselessly busy during the day, but Kate had plenty of time to think at night, since most people went to bed at sundown. Her shaky religious beliefs, though not sustained by any strong faith in Christianity, now produced a curious kind of spiritual serenity. She realised how spoiled she had been all her life, and how out of touch with the essentials of living. Getting from one day to the next, with self respect, was enough here; and she became aware from what she saw around her every day that goodness and courage were more important — and more rewarding — than comfort or even health. Death, since it was a constant, lost its terrors, and she found that 'flexing her spiritual muscles', as she called it, awoke an absorbing inner life which she hadn't known existed. Perversely, she was happy in the camp.

Then Susie van der Elst developed beri-beri. Her stomach swelled, and she was in constant and terrible pain. She still did her share of work, and still laughed and joked and practised her English, but she was becoming noticeably weaker.

'See how useful my English has been!' she said one day to Kate, then added half jokingly, 'I must have known I was coming here, Kate. You know, I really do believe we were all destined to come here. Isn't it odd? I have no idea why but, from the moment I saw this place, I felt I knew it. Almost as if I were coming home.' She wrinkled her nose. 'What a home!' And she laughed.

She grew iller and iller. Her only worry seemed to be that, if she died, her husband wouldn't be able to manage without her.

'He's managing now,' soothed Kate. 'I'm sure he is!'

'Because he thinks that I'm alive,' insisted Susie. 'He depends on me very much, Kate. We've had a good marriage, and if something happens to me, he will be very sad. He will get lost.'

'Nothing will happen to you,' said Kate firmly. 'You are going to get better.' But even as she spoke, she knew she was lying.

'No, Kate. I shall die,' said Susie, quietly. 'For myself, I do not mind too much, since it is evidently time for me to die; but, for Jan, it will be bad. Promise me something.'

'Of course.'

'When you get out of here, try to contact Jan, and tell him I thought of him always and that I didn't suffer too much. That will help him.'

'When *we* get out of here, we will do it together,' said Kate, 'And I will tell him how brave you were, and what an inspiration you have been to us all.'

'Dear Kate,' said Susie, affectionately. 'How happy I am to have come to know you! We have had fun, haven't we?'

Fun! thought Kate, wryly. How typical of Susie to describe their present condition as fun! Yet in a way she was right. 'Yes,' she agreed. 'We've had fun, Susie, and I'd like you to know how much your friendship means to me.'

'I do,' replied Susie. 'I sometimes wonder, in spite of being a convert, whether our only immortality may not be through the memories of those who have loved us. So don't forget me, Kate.'

'How can I, when you're going to get better?' retorted Kate.

But Susie didn't get better. One morning early she died in Kate's arms.

1943 was a bad year. The women were moved twice again, and each time conditions deteriorated. The Japanese seemed to have become harsher in their treatment of the prisoners, who weren't sure whether it was because the Allies were doing well or badly. No news of the war ever filtered through to them. Only one lot of Red Cross parcels got through (and that only after it had been rifled by the Japanese first) and almost no mail. Clothes were becoming an even more serious problem.

1944 was even worse, and they were moved back to Muntok. Here the tempo of the death rate quickened. Nearly half the women Kate had first come to know in 1942 were gone. The rest hung on grimly, laughing when they could, talking endlessly of families and Home and above all of food. They lived in squalor and filth and rags, yet they still bravely survived as personalities.

The very last camp to which they were taken was called Belalau. Although fruit grew in abundance nearby, the prisoners were never allowed to eat it. And now Kate herself got beri-beri. The death roll was mounting even more rapidly. Years of privation, heavy manual labour and exhaustion were taking their inevitable toll. Optimism about surviving until they reached Home was at low ebb. They resorted to the game of 'what-we'll-remember-when-its-all-over' — the total lack of privacy from the Japanese as well as from their own companions, even when bathing or using the lavatories; the sudden vicious face-slapping by the Japanese guards; and above all 'TENKO', the daily roll call which kept the prisoners standing in the sun or torrential rains for hours longer than necessary because the guards never seemed to get their sums right. They would remember all of these things: but the friendships, and the courage, too.

Kate was in constant pain. She, too, had a certainty that she would die. She had become appallingly thin; but, although her beauty had gone, her elegance never quite left her. Her closest friend, now that Susie was no longer with her, was a Scotswoman called Mrs Donald, who had spent most of her life in Singapore and was longing to go back to Ayrshire. She was tall, gaunt, stoical and grimly amusing, and reminded Kate of Mrs McLaughlan from Fraser's Hill. Once Kate said to her, 'Don't be sad about me, my dear. This war has brought me what I had spent a lifetime looking for: emotional fulfilment, and my own self-fulfilment too. So I've been lucky, haven't I?' She gave Mrs Donald Madge's address. 'My mother and Bess get on well,' she said, 'so you'll find out where Bess is from there. Tell them I thought of them often, won't you?'

'Of course I will.'

'Oh, and try to contact Susie's husband, Jan van der Elst ... and, if Madge and Bess ever come across a young man called Colin Franks, tell them he saved my life, will you?'

'I will, my dear. Is there anyone else?'

'No — Edward, my husband, is dead.'

So Mrs Donald was surprised to hear, when Kate lay dying, her last passionate whisper:

'Yes, Patrick, I do regret it. I've tried not to, but I do.'

Kate died in 1945, three weeks before the rest of the prisoners were freed.

The returning Australian prisoners of war received a rapturous welcome in their country. Presents, flowers and kindness were showered on them in overwhelming profusion.

In Britain, the Home Office asked friends and relatives not to meet the ships when they docked. There was no formal press coverage, no celebration, but some of the prisoners received a facsimile of a letter written by King George VI to welcome them.

CHAPTER TWENTY-ONE

Back in England, in 1942, Madge and Bess had watched with horror the short resistance of Malaya to the Japanese. They had read in the papers about the sinking of the *Princess Pearl*, although at that time they had no idea that Kate had been aboard. A little later, Madge had a letter from the clerk in Government House at Singapore who had seen to Kate's passage; he told Madge that he himself had escaped and was now in Australia, and that he had heard rumours that Kate was a prisoner at Palembang. Madge and Bess were devastated.

Later still, Bess had a letter from Colin, now serving in the Royal Australian Navy, who described his swim with Kate from the ship to Ikan Island. He said how marvellously brave Kate had been. This letter was followed by an old-fashioned leather hat-box, containing Kate's jewels and two letters: one for Bess and one for Madge.

The letter to Bess read:

Darling Bess,

By the time you get this, you will know the outcome of the war in Malaya. I have been forced to try and escape, much against my will — although, of course, I *long* to see you both — and may even reach you before this hat-box arrives. I feel very bitter that Britain has let Malaya down so badly. We can never hope to be held in the same respect here after the war. I shall try to get to England, to you and Mother, but whatever happens don't worry about me. I have a feeling I shall be all right. I have been so worried about you. You have all been in danger for so long over there, and it will be good to be back so that I can share the difficulties with you. I miss you and Mother all the time I am away from you. I long, too, to see my grandchildren. Give them my love. If I don't ever reach you, the jewellery is for you, as Mother has plenty and won't need mine. I think of you and

Mother every day, and pray for your happiness and safety. With all my love, darling,

Mother

Madge had a letter on much the same lines, and she sounded so distressed when she spoke to Bess on the telephone that Bess took the two children with her to Windsor for the weekend. This seemed to cheer Madge a little; but, the moment they were alone on the Friday night, she said anxiously, 'The Japs are terrible to their prisoners, I understand, Bess.'

'I know,' replied Bess, equally distressed. 'It's awful, isn't it? And so ironic that she's been worrying so much about us. She was so sure, wasn't she, that she would be safe? Oh, I can hardly bear to think of what she might be going through ...' Madge nodded speechlessly.

'The Red Cross are being helpful, aren't they?' said Bess wistfully. 'Do you think our stuff is getting through?'

'God knows! I hope so. I truly hope so,' and Bess saw the tears in her grandmother's eyes.

Just before she left Windsor, Joyce cornered Bess in the hall. 'How do you think Aunt Madge is looking?' she asked.

'Marvellous, considering,' answered Bess. 'Why? Don't you?'

'The doctors are worried about her heart. And I am worried about her state of mind. She's always been a great family woman, you know, Bess. She loved that old rogue, Uncle Harry, and she loves Kate too. This business is nearly killing her. She's putting up a good show for you, because she's a brave old girl; but with me on my own, she can't keep it up. I notice that she's aged about ten years since she's heard about Kate being a prisoner.'

Bess returned to Shillington to deposit the children before going on to Northern Ireland, to be with Mark. She heard no further word about her mother; but while she was in Ireland, she had a postcard from her agent. The director who had enthused over her performance in Windsor was holding auditions in London for a new play, which would have a short tour in the provinces and then move to London, to the Piccadilly Theatre. He wanted her to read the part of the leading girl.

Mark was sincerely delighted for Bess's sake, and impressed that she was making such a rapid start in her career; but his own longing for the theatre was stronger than ever, and it was re-inforced by the seeming irrelevance of his army 'career'. Northern

Ireland was at no risk. It was a military backwater. He wanted either to fight or to get back to his own job. Generously, however, he said, 'It's wonderful, Bessie! You go and have a try! It brings the day nearer when you and I will both be acting together in the West End, starring in a play with a marvellous part in it for me!'

Bess laughed. She understood his feelings well. They would have been her own in his place, and she was touched by his encouragement.

Frightened, but excited, she presented herself at the audition. She read well — and got the part.

Rehearsals would start in six weeks' time, they said, so she looked for a flat in London, and found a tiny bedsitter with a kitchen and bathroom in Dolphin Square in Pimlico. The blitz was still on, so there was no question of bringing the children to London. This made her feel guilty again; but, when she wrote to Mark, telling him what she felt, he reminded her that if she had been doing war work of any kind, especially in the services, she'd probably have seen even less of them. 'Good luck, darling,' he added. 'Remember, when you're acting in this play you'll be acting for both of us.'

The play opened to excellent notices, Bess herself gathering a few; and she felt at last that she was a real professional. Madge and Joyce travelled to London for the first night in spite of the blitz, and Madge was so delighted by Bess's handling of her part that she cried happily all through the dinner that followed. Afterwards they talked almost exclusively of Kate.

'I had a nightmare just before she left England, that I was drowning in the sea,' said Bess, shuddering. 'It's been haunting me lately.'

'If only we could have one letter, just one,' sighed Madge. 'She's always been a bad letter writer, but I know this time she'd have written if she could. She was the most beautiful little girl I've ever seen, Bessie. Oh dear, I do so want to see her again!'

'I wish I'd known her better!' exclaimed Bess. 'I've wished it so often just lately. When she gets back I'll ask her all the things I've ever wanted to know!'

In 1943, Mark was to be sent overseas. His embarkation leave was spent at Shillington — where Laura greeted him with howls of rage, and Peter with transports of delight. He embarked from the Clyde. Naturally Bess had no idea of this until later, any more than either of them knew that his destination was to be Maadi, south of Cairo.

During the time they had been married, they had come to know each other well. Bess had seen the selfish side of him sometimes, but knew herself to be selfish too, and she had seen his kindness and generosity far more often. She had never been in love with him (or he with her) but otherwise they were well suited, and they'd become good friends. She hated the thought of his going, and was terrified for his safety. This made him laugh. He reminded her that she had already been in danger far more frequently than he had during the London bombing, and she had never worried for herself.

When he had gone, however, she found the daily strain of coping with the air raids, food rationing, clothes rationing and the general drabness everywhere far harder to stand. Her nerves were already frayed by her anxieties over Kate. Now there was Mark to worry about as well. She had to will herself to count two exceptional blessings — that her theatrical career was clearly in the ascendant, and that so far no bomb had landed anywhere near Shillington.

Soon after Mark left, Joyce telephoned her with sad news of Madge. The old woman had gone to bed in no pain, and only a little more tired, perhaps, than usual; in the morning, when she didn't come down at eleven for morning coffee, Joyce had gone up to her room, and found her dead in bed.

This hit Bess badly. Among all her fears and worries, the thought that Madge might die had never actively occurred to her. She had always been in Bess's life — more influentially even than Kate and Edward, except during the brief Malaya interlude — and her unchanging standards of dress and behaviour, and her indomitable courage, had endowed her with a kind of immortality in Bess's eyes.

Bess collapsed. The management, who knew about Mark and Kate, were understanding and allowed her a week off. She was deeply ashamed of her weakness, and said ruefully to Joyce, 'How angry darling Gran would be that a Glanville hasn't been strong enough to keep the curtain up!'

In due course the run of the play ended. Bess's agent sent her to Gainsborough Pictures at Shepherd's Bush for a test, which resulted in a small but good part in a film with Phyllis Calvert. And when this, too, finished, she was cast in another picture for Gainsborough, which starred a new young heart-throb called Christopher Rankin.

Bess had one very good scene opposite him, and they got on splendidly from the start. Christopher was twenty-eight — tall, fair and athletic and already a war hero. Unlike a lot of actors who had either had to be dragged screaming into the war, or developed an ulcer within months of joining the forces and so were invalided out, Christopher had volunteered early, like Mark, and had found himself in due course a paratrooper. He had been sent on an extremely difficult and very dangerous raid on which he had won the MC; but it had left him with a heart condition, and so he was now back in civilian life. He hated being out of the army, but was naturally delighted to be a working actor again; and as young men were scarce, and he was very talented, he had rocketed to the top very quickly.

The powers that be at the studio were impressed by Bess's performance in their scene together and tested her for a contract, which she was duly given. The contract was for seven years, and started at £600 a year; if the studio took up all the options, her salary would rise to £7000 a year.

This was enormous money for Bess, and even Mrs Wells began to treat her with respect. Bess and Mark wrote regularly to one another, and Mark was full of gratitude and praise.

Gainsborough, with its parent distributing company, Gaumont British, was at that time one of the most powerful film companies in Britain. British films were still financially viable, and were extremely popular with the British public. The contract stars included Margaret Lockwood, James Mason, Stewart Granger, Phyllis Calvert, Jean Kent and Patricia Roc, and they made women-orientated pictures — romantic and luscious, and very often 'period'. Their two newcomers, Bess Glanville and Christopher Rankin, were therefore well in the public eye.

Gainsborough was run by Ted Black, with the active participation of five Ostrer brothers, who were Polish by birth. The passage to their offices was known irreverently to the actors as the 'Polish Corridor'. 'Maggie' Lockwood was very much the 'First Lady', and her kindness and very basic sense of humour did much to make life amusing for those who were working with her. Since they were the newest contract artists, Bess and Christopher found themselves very much thrown together; and, after a second successful joint appearance, the studio decided to build them up as a team with all the trappings of shared personal appearances, press interviews and photographic sittings.

It was a curious life, getting up soon after five in winter, in the pitch dark of blacked-out London, and returning in the dark after a daytime spent behind soundproof doors, immunised from the outside world. There were still air raids most nights; on Bess's morning journeys to the studios, the air was heavy with the smell of last night's fires, and the bus would often have to make detours to avoid the rubble of bombed houses. Yet in the brightly lit world of make-believe in the studios all this was forgotten by the actors and technicians, who were intent on the absorbing and often exhausting demands of filming. With such long hours, the night raids were a great strain; but, fortunately for Bess, she was a fatalist, so she never went down to the shelters but remained in her bed, and usually slept.

Her long hours also meant that she had little inclination to socialise. Just occasionally, when she had a day off and a late call the next morning, Bess would go out to an austerity lunch at a restaurant, or treat herself to the wild luxury of a pair of silk stockings. She would look sadly at the latest gaps in London's skyline and imagine the tragedies each one represented; she would listen for the distinctive sound of the buzz-bombs and dive for cover with her fellow Londoners when the motor cut out and the bomb plunged to earth. She noticed that American uniforms now seemed as numerous as British; and saw with emotion the proud notice 'Business as Usual' on boarded-up shops and banks and offices. How tired everyone had begun to look, as they battled with shortages and the ever-increasing problems of getting to work, getting home, or getting down to the shelters in the Underground before dark! And yet there was community singing in the shelters, and any wag with authentic cockney humour was assured of a delighted response; while, up above, the theatres were packed — and, although the public was informed when an air raid was imminent, the performances continued and audiences stayed put, to the accompaniment of the whistle of falling bombs and various other 'noises off'.

Gerald suddenly came back into her life. He rang her one evening to say that he had come to London, as he had written a revue which was going to be performed at the Regency. He also said that he had managed to find himself a flat in Dolphin Square, not far from Bess's own! Bess was as delighted as ever to see him, and once again he fitted into her life as smoothly as though he had never been away. He told her that Deirdre was to be married to a

Battle-of-Britain pilot in a week's time and, as it was on one of her rare days off, Bess went with him to the wedding.

Christopher was by now showing signs of becoming attracted to Bess, but she refused to encourage him. She felt that the least she could do, with Mark away on active service and Christopher at home pursuing the profession Mark loved, was to remain faithful to her husband.

Christopher respected her for this. His own girl friend had left him when he'd gone overseas, and he'd felt badly betrayed. He liked other things about Bess too, besides her beauty. She worked hard and had a truly versatile talent. She was capable and independent, friendly and funny. Her clowning charmed him, and her conversation interested him. He believed that he attracted her too, and this added a piquancy to their love scenes. He missed her on the days she wasn't called to the studio, and treasured the few occasions on which she allowed him to date her. He knew he was falling in love, and didn't want to.

In early December 1944, Mark wrote to Bess from Greece:

There seems a good chance that I'll see a bit of fighting here. I've missed everything so far, and I can't say I'm sorry — except that to be in the forces in wartime for four years without coming under fire is a bit ludicrous, isn't it? And yet they've already given me two medals for it! I can't tell you how I long to get back to the theatre, Bess. What a good thing it is that you are doing so well. As you said — so long ago that it seems a lifetime — I'll have a head start when I get out, thanks to you. Bless you. I know I'll be able to take the opportunity when it comes. I've always known I could be a really big star. My current 'engagement', though it may well prove the longest run of my career, isn't one that I enjoy. God knows, I've been lucky, but it isn't exactly what I had set my heart on doing! Would you believe it — nearly all the other chaps seem uncertain what they want to do when they get out. Not me! I'm certain all right. I want to get back to you and to the theatre. Merry Christmas, darling. Let's hope it's our last apart. Love, as always to you all,

Mark

The letter reached her on Christmas Eve. In January Mark was killed, in street fighting with the Greek Communist guerrillas in central Athens.

CHAPTER TWENTY-TWO

Bess was stunned by the news, so soon after the bright confidence of Mark's last letter. His death was at first literally incredible to her. The pain of it would come later, but at first her instinct was to cling to the familiar routine of her life, as a protection. So she kept on working, rushing down to Shillington on Friday evenings in crowded trains to see the children, and returning on Sunday afternoon to be ready for her early start at the studios. Obscurely she felt that she was still doing it for Mark as well: 'acting for both of them', as he had urged her.

Mrs Wells, by contrast, saw it as a betrayal of Mark's memory, and one Sunday her wrath boiled over. 'I thought you were working as an actress when everyone else was doing their bit for the war, because you wanted to help Mark!' she raged. 'Now I see that you were doing it for yourself!'

'Actually, I really am still doing it for Mark in a way,' said Bess, and she tried to explain her feelings.

Mrs Wells was scornful. 'Rubbish!' she exclaimed. 'You've used us here like a hotel, and neglected your children, and only because you are selfish! We miss Mark, even if you don't. Your children miss him too — especially Laura, who is quite distraught — and your place is with them! Suppose I tell you that they can't stay here any more? What will you do then?'

'I'll find a way,' said Bess. 'I'm sorry you feel as you do, Mother. And it's quite wrong to say I don't miss Mark. I miss him as my husband, and for the wonderful career which he deserved and longed for. However, if you don't want his children here, you don't. As for me, please remember that now that Mark is dead, Peter and Laura need the money I am lucky enough to be earning even more than they did before. But I'll see that they are taken away next week.'

Mrs Wells pursed her lips, and left the room. Later, Mr Wells asked Bess if she would let the children stay. 'My wife is sorry that she lost her temper,' he said. 'She disapproves of career women, so

I'm afraid she was a little impulsive. I know you understand.'

'Yes, I understand,' replied Bess. 'Though how she thinks we could afford to live if I don't earn some money, I don't know.'

Mr Wells looked anxious. 'I rather think she would prefer you to get war work,' he said, rubbing his head nervously.

'I have signed a film contract,' said Bess. 'I can't break it.'

'I know, I know,' he sighed. 'She takes Mark's death very hard, I'm afraid.' He smiled ruefully. 'And so do I. He was, after all, our only child.'

'I take it hard too,' said Bess, gently but firmly. 'He was, after all, my husband.'

In 1944, Bess had been cast opposite Christopher twice, in good starring parts; in the spring of 1945, they were offered a play together in the West End, for which they had to get permission from their Studio. The Studio was quite thankful to give it, as their contracts would be suspended for the run of the play.

Gainsborough had seemed all-powerful when Bess and Christopher were first put under contract, but its fortunes declined rapidly; by 1945 it had sacked all but six of the contract artists, and within two years the studios were completely taken over by J. Arthur Rank, who put Sydney Box in charge. The fate of Gainsborough was something about which Bess and Christopher knew nothing; but they did become involved in a campaign backed by Equity to protect British Film production by raising the quota of home-produced films (which by law each cinema had to show) and by amending the conditions which qualified a film as British. The basic qualification was that seventy-five per cent of the labour costs should be British: this percentage was easily achieved by adding studio and technical costs to the salaries of supporting players, so that for instance that wonderful film *African Queen*, with Americans Katherine Hepburn and Humphrey Bogart as its memorable stars, qualified as British. What Bess and Christopher hoped to achieve by their campaign was that in every British quota film there should be at least one British star, thus ensuring a wide public for British actors when these films were distributed in America.

It was a good idea, and there were even sympathetic noises about it coming from the American camp; but it failed because the majority of British film workers were shortsightedly content with the status quo, and the public only missed British films when they were no longer there.

The press, too, were utterly unhelpful. Most British film stars were envied for the money they were supposed to be earning (absurdly little by Hollywood standards), derided for the middle-brow content of the films in which most of them were involved, and despised for being national rather than international stars. For years after Bess and Christopher had been British film stars, they could be sure of a hostile reception from many critics whenever they appeared in the theatre. To the public, however, they were firm favourites.

As soon as the war was over, Bess found a large Edwardian flat in London near Baker Street, to which she took the children.

And now at last she heard of the death of her mother, in a letter from the Colonial Office. She also had a letter full of praise for Kate from Mrs Donald. In her heart she had long believed her mother to be dead: the confirmation was another body blow. She suddenly remembered Patrick saying that Kate had had a wasted life, and this reminded her of him. Reluctantly she wrote to him — and rang Joyce — the only two people left who might be interested. Joyce was comforting and sympathetic. Patrick wrote a stilted letter of condolence which irritated Bess and did nothing to heal the rift between them.

How few people were left from her childhood, she thought, in desolation and despair. Mark, her parents, her grandparents, and nearly everyone with whom she had played so happily in Kuala Lumpur, Singapore and Fraser's Hill, had died or had been killed! She was only in her early thirties but already she felt older than her years.

CHAPTER TWENTY-THREE

In the summer of 1948, Patrick learned that he had an inoperable cancer. He wrote to Bess to tell her so:

> ... I'm certainly not asking for your pity, but your family and I have been friends for so long ... if you can spare the time, I should like you to stay here for a few days, so that we can talk over old times and I can say goodbye. You needn't feel in the least sorry for me. I am quite happy to die, even though I haven't yet reached old age. And although I am not a believer, perhaps after all there is some sort of a life beyond the confines of the earth, and, who knows, I might see Kate and Edward again? Anyway, dear Bess, come if you would like to, to gladden my eyes; but stay away if you would rather. I shall not only understand, but I should prefer it that way, unless you actually want to see me.
>
> Mallerby is just the same — perhaps even more beautiful than you will remember. And, at this time of year, the gardens are magnificent. My nephew Giles runs the place these days, and runs it very well, I am thankful to say, so I have no fears for the future on that score ...

Bess was between pictures, so she telephoned to say that she would be coming up that weekend. Giles answered the telephone. 'I'll tell Uncle Patrick right away. He'll be thrilled, and so will we. He's talked about you a great deal recently. Till Friday then. I'll meet the two-fifty at Leeds.'

'He's amazingly serene,' said Giles as they headed out of Leeds in his car. 'I think his main regret is leaving Mallerby. As you know, it's a magical place and probably the only real love of his life; though he sometimes speaks of your mother with great affection, and indeed of you.'

'He was wonderful to me when I was a child,' said Bess, 'and I feel rotten that I have neglected him for so long.'

'I'm sure he has understood,' said Giles.

A companionable silence fell between them until they turned into the gates and saw Mallerby half a mile away across the park.

'Until his illness started,' said Giles, 'he spent all his days divided between the library and the garden, but he has a fantastic knowledge of pictures and furniture, too, and has done marvels for the house. He likes my wife, which is a blessing, and we moved in with him three years ago. Don't be shocked when you see him. He is desperately thin, and looks every bit as ill as he is; but, as he told you, he is in hardly any pain. He rests at this time of day, but I'll take you to him at tea-time.'

'Thank you.' Bess was impressed and comforted by his obvious fondness for his uncle.

'Now come and meet Sylvia.'

Both Giles and Sylvia were in their forties. Giles looked not unlike Patrick, with the same red hair and blue eyes. Sylvia had mousy hair and a loud country voice and thick legs. She laughed a lot, though Bess guessed that she had little sense of humour, and she had a kind face and a sweet smile. Their children, three boys all in their teens, seemed friendly enough.

Sylvia showed Bess to her room, which was the one she had occupied all those years ago. Bess saw it again with delight. She knew more now about pictures and antiques and could appreciate the great Chippendale four-poster bed with its blue-and-white hangings, the buff-and-rose eighteenth-century Aubusson carpet, the glowing furniture and the crisp seventeenth-century Dutch flower pictures. The man in the eighteenth-century portrait which hung over the mantelpiece looked exactly like Patrick as she had seen him last.

'I hope you'll be comfortable here,' said Sylvia. 'Uncle wanted you to have this room.'

'How sweet of him! I stayed here last time,' said Bess. She wandered over to the window, and gazed out across the lawns towards the park, which extended as far as the eye could see. 'How beautiful it all is!' she exclaimed. 'How lucky you are!'

'Yes. We're very lucky to live here,' agreed Sylvia. 'It's a marvellous house.'

At four o'clock, Giles came to fetch her. 'You and Uncle will be having tea alone,' he said. 'It's too much for him if we all crowd in.'

Patrick was lying against the pillows of a smaller four-poster and

Bess's mind at once sped back to her grandfather's death — only this room was light and joyous, where the other had been dark and cluttered. His hair had turned white, and he looked worn and weak; but his face lit up when he saw Bess, and he stretched out his arms to her, lovingly. 'Come and kiss me, Bess darling,' he said. 'I've missed you so much!'

A lump came into her throat. 'I've missed you, too' she replied. 'I've been an idiot, and it's wonderful to see you, darling darling Uncle Patrick.'

Patrick smiled. 'Pour out the tea, will you, darling, then sit facing the light so that I can see you properly? What a famous little person you are now, and how proud I am of you! To think that my little girl should have done so well!'

Bess returned the smile affectionately, not understanding the implication of his words. 'Don't let's talk about me,' she said. 'Tell me about you!'

'There's not much to tell,' said Patrick. 'They've given me three months to live. It's cancer of the stomach, but I'm not in much pain. All is well with Mallerby, and all is well with my family, including you, so I don't mind too much.'

'I'm glad you think of me as family,' murmured Bess. 'I don't deserve it, after the way I behaved.'

'Poppycock!' exclaimed Patrick. 'It was my fault, but I didn't quite know how to handle the situation.'

'Of course you didn't,' replied Bess, 'and it wasn't your fault! It was mine!'

'Not at all. You see you didn't know why I couldn't possibly allow you to become attracted to me,' said Patrick, 'even though you were my heart's darling.'

'What a lovely expression!' said Bess.

'It's the literal truth, Bess.'

He was silent for a long while.

'Kate never told you, did she?' he asked.

'Told me what?'

Patrick smiled. 'Then I see she didn't. Bess, darling ... you are my daughter.'

'Your *daughter*?' Bess was utterly astounded.

'Yes,' said Patrick. 'Your mother and I were lovers.'

'Lovers? Then why didn't you marry her?' flared Bess. Then she bit her lip, and said softly, 'I'm sorry,' and looked down at her hands.

'For one thing, Kate was already married,' said Patrick, 'and a nicer fellow than Edward never walked the earth. And for another, it would never have done. It would never have done at all.'

'Did Mummy fall in love with you?'

'Yes, I'm afraid so.'

'Didn't she love Father — I mean Edward — then?'

'Very much. But ours was a different sort of love. Don't judge us too badly, Bess. We both felt very deeply, and we both cared deeply for Edward too.'

'Poor Mummy! She sometimes looked so sad,' said Bess, and suddenly found herself crying.

'I know,' said Patrick contritely. 'I wish she hadn't had to suffer, and yet when I look at you I cannot wish our affair had never happened. Besides, it was wonderful — one of the most wonderful things that ever happened to me. I hope that in the end she didn't regret it either.'

'I hope so too,' said Bess. 'If I'd only known, perhaps I could have been a better daughter to her.'

'Don't you start reproaching yourself. Leave that to me.' Then he said, with a complete change of tone. 'Did you never wonder about your red hair?'

'No, never. I just accepted it.'

'So did Edward, thank God! Kate used to get sick with worry that he would one day put two and two together. But he never did.'

'How can you be sure?'

'He would have told us. He was that sort of man.'

'My father!' murmured Bess. 'You are my father!'

'I hope you don't mind?'

'I'll have to have time to get used to the idea. I loved Edward very much, and I know he loved me.'

'He certainly did.'

'And yet you always seemed so close to me, especially when I was a child. You weren't even a real uncle, yet you seemed much more. Now I see why. My father! ... '

'Yes.'

'How amazing!' She paused and dried her eyes. 'You said you and Mummy could never have married,' she said. 'I understand that you didn't want to hurt father — oh, I'm sorry — but what do you mean, *it would never have done*, even leaving him aside? You've said you loved her.'

'Oh yes! Oh yes, I loved her. Physically, I believe I have never

stopped loving her. Certainly no-one else ever took her place. But
we were completely ill-suited, darling. Kate at that time was
headstrong and extravagant and spoilt. She had a streak of
wildness in her nature that she couldn't control. It made her a
wonderful lover, but I could never have stood for it in a wife. I'm
not criticising her, darling, just saying that our characters were
poles apart. I know I was the only man she ever loved — which
made me desperately sorry for her at times — but just as we
couldn't help falling in love, so we couldn't have changed suffic-
iently to make one another happy in marriage.'

'Poor, poor Mummy.'

'Yes, poor Kate.'

'She was so brave when she was a prisoner of war, they said.'

'Yes, I'm sure she was.'

Bess sighed. 'It's sad one doesn't get to know one's parents
better, isn't it? A waste of loving, really.'

'Yes.' He put his hand to his head wearily, and Bess was
immediately anxious. 'I'm tiring you!' she exclaimed. 'How selfish
of me!'

'You forgive me Bess? You don't mind that I am your father?'

'My mother loved you, and I love you too,' she said gently.

Patrick smiled. 'Thank you, Bessie. I'm so happy you're here.'

She smiled, too. 'Thank you, father,' she said, and he looked
delighted. 'Now I shall leave you to rest, darling, but I can stay for
a few days, so you can send for me whenever you want to see me.'

'Bessie?'

'Yes, father?'

'May I see my grandchildren before I die? I would like to, so
very much.'

'Of course.'

So Peter and Laura were sent for. Patrick was deeply moved at
meeting them, and the children loved him at once. Even Laura
had no hesitation in taking him to her wayward heart. They called
him Great Uncle, because Bess thought it best not to tell them the
truth until they had left Yorkshire. The three de Moulins boys took
them riding, and boating and swimming in the lake; they played
hide-and-seek in the garden, and had tea with Patrick every day.
Everyone seemed happy, and no-one more than Patrick.

Bess and the children stayed a fortnight and, soon after they
returned to London, Patrick died.

He left Mallerby to Giles, but he also left a considerable sum of money to Bess and her family. To Bess herself he left a faded photograph in a silver frame, of himself and Kate, taken nearly thirty years before. Kate looked radiant, and Patrick very young. Both of them were smiling, and their arms were round each other's waists. On the photograph, in ink which was also faded, Kate had written: 'To Patrick. With all my love always. Kate.'

Part Three

LAURA

CHAPTER ONE

Laura was nine years old when her mother married Christopher. They had become lovers a year or so after Mark's death, when Bess had left Shillington for her solid rather dark flat off Baker Street, in London. A pleasant girl called Susan was engaged to look after the children; Gerald moved in as a lodger; and soon Christopher moved in too. They had planned a quiet wedding at the registry office with only the household present — but somehow the news spread. As they came out into the street, they faced a barrage of cameras and a crowd of cheerful, screaming fans.

Laura liked none of it. She hated crowds. And she regarded the marriage itself as a betrayal — not only of her dead father, but of herself and Peter. She had seen very little of Mark when he was alive (and when she had their relationship had been far from successful); but, dead, he had assumed a great importance for her. Many of her school contemporaries had fathers who had been killed in the war and become heroes, retrospectively, to their families. Mark became a hero to Laura. The fact that Christopher had won the MC (which made *him* a hero) seemed to her irrelevant, and indeed almost an insult. Christopher was alive; he was the interloper. Laura had resented him from the moment he came to live with them, divining immediately the sexual bond between him and her mother; and no matter how generously and kindly he treated her, she never grew to like him.

Soon after Bess's marriage, it was decided that the family should move. The flat in Baker Street suddenly seemed too small, and Gerald had formed a passionate desire to live in one of the Nash Terraces in Regent's Park. He found a beautiful place going cheap in Connaught Terrace, with a mews flat at the back and two garages: it became home for all of them for the next fourteen years. Gerald took the ground floor for himself, Susan was housed in the mews flat, the children had their bedrooms and the nursery on the top floor, and Bess and Christopher inhabited the first and second floors. It was in all ways 'ideal', everyone said; and Gerald, who

was a brilliant interior decorator by instinct, was given his head —
so the place soon glowed and flowered.

Gerald was by now an extremely rich and successful playwright,
and also much in demand as a film scriptwriter. He spent several
months a year in Hollywood, but looked on Bess's family as his
own; and they in turn regarded him as theirs. Indeed, Bess had
grown to depend on him to such an extent that she would have
considered life intolerable without him; and the children, especially Laura, loved him dearly.

Since they were now living right in the Park, a labrador puppy
was bought for the household. Laura adored him. He was called
Outram, at her request. No-one knew what the name meant, but
Laura liked the sound; and since he returned her love unquestioningly he became her special 'family', and so of great
importance to her.

Peter was sent to prep school at Broadstairs and Laura to an
expensive private boarding school in Wokingham. She hated her
first few terms and was homesick and miserable. She was in many
ways a difficult child, oversensitive and solitary. She had a vision of
herself as ugly and unwanted — although neither was true. Like
all the women of her family, she was already almost beautiful, with
the straight nose, lovely grey eyes and determined chin of all the
Glanville women. Unfortunately, her good looks were marred by a
slightly sulky expression. She enjoyed thinking of herself as a
misfit, and overdramatised her desire for isolation.

Two early memories had influenced her strongly, and in both of
them she had come to look on herself as a martyr.

The first concerned herself and Peter. She must have been about
three at the time — sturdy and advanced for her years. But Peter
was everyone's favourite, and she was no-one's. Until his arrival
she had been the centre of attention and, young though she was,
she had relished it. Now Peter was king.

On this particular day, lunch was over and Peter had been
bedded down for his afternoon sleep. In a moment or two Laura
herself would be fetched to have her rest. For now, however, the
two of them were alone in Peter's room, and Peter lay smiling
placidly — both at his sister and, beyond her, at the whole world.
Bored, Laura stuck out her tongue at him; Peter laughed de-
lightedly. She did it a second time, and he laughed again. For some
reason this annoyed her. She tried to pull a few frightening faces,
but this too seemed to delight him. Losing her temper suddenly,

she leaned over until their faces were almost touching, pulled down the lower lids of her eyes, and spat. The baby still smiled. Laura looked round to see that no-one was watching, tip-toed to the other side of the room, then turned and advanced towards the cot making terrifying noises, waving her head from side to side and slapping her feet on the floor. She had no idea what she was pretending to be, but felt absurdly powerful and wicked. This at last had its effect on Peter, who ceased smiling and looked at her wonderingly, though without a trace of fear. She threw her arms into the air and with a fierce growl leapt towards him, put her hands round his neck and pretended to throttle him. Peter gurgled with happiness.

At this moment, Bess walked in. Horrified at what she thought she was seeing, she pulled Laura away, shaking her violently. Laura tried to explain that it was only a game, but Bess was too frightened to listen. She hauled Laura into her room, pulled down her knickers, and spanked her with a hairbrush. Laura, just as frightened, screamed her head off. She never forgot the incident, nor her burning sense of injustice. Bess never forgot it either — though she did her best. Nor did she ever quite forgive Laura.

The second memory was almost as painful. Just before her father went overseas, he had come home on embarkation leave and appeared suddenly in the nursery where Laura was playing with her dolls. He had held his arms out to her, expecting her to be pleased. Instead, she had burst into tears and asked for him to be taken away. She hadn't recognised him in uniform (Mark was now a lieutenant), and in any case was instinctively more comfortable with women than with men. When news came of his death she felt agonisingly guilty that she had behaved so badly, and, to counter-act her guilt, created a myth for herself of a beautiful and close relationship.

At school, for the first time, she really was a misfit. To hide her shyness she assumed an arrogant and off-hand manner, which the staff took to be rudeness and which did not endear her to her contemporaries either. Her academic brilliance, which to her was immensely important, only made her a 'swot' to the other children. She became increasingly introverted, and suffered cruelly until she made friends with a tough little girl called Evelyn. As far as she was able, she lived in a fantasy world. Had she known that this had been her mother's way of escaping loneliness when she was virtually parentless at her school all those years ago, she might have drawn closer to Bess. But since she didn't confide in her, the opportunity was missed; and once again she felt that she had failed her family in some obscure but important way.

Evelyn was a year younger than Laura. She had mouse-coloured hair, neat features, slim hips and broad shoulders. She was shy and retiring, and not clever at all; but, like Outram, she loved Laura unquestioningly. She was also very good at games. Evelyn exercised a fascination for Laura which Laura found impossible to resist; indeed, both children felt a love for one another and a vivid excitement in each other's company which was tinged with a clear, if childish, sense of shared guilt. This was a mystery to them; but it heightened their pleasure and bound them together even more closely. The games mistress, a Miss Crutchley, came nearest to voicing the general view when she said musingly one day, 'I sometimes think Laura and Evelyn should be renamed David and Jonathan. They really are a devoted couple.'

CHAPTER TWO

Until the early 1950s, Bess and Christopher were busy making a series of films, both together and separately. Then gradually they were offered more and more theatre work. On the whole, the fifties were a good time for Bess. The horror and sadness of the forties was over and life was easier and happier in every way, except for the period of Peter's National Service. Rationing of all kinds finished in mid-decade; prosperity seemed at last to beckon to a tired nation, and the sumptuous New Look in women's clothes, which used material so lavishly, appeared to herald a new and better era.

Peter's carefree (and apparently work-free) prep-school days were over, too; and to everyone's astonishment, including his own, he managed to pass into Eton, for which Mark had put him down during the war. This shocked both Christopher and Gerald, who disapproved of public schools — the former because he hadn't been to one, the latter because he had. Bess was delighted.

'What the hell do you want Peter to go to Eton for?' demanded Christopher. 'It costs a fortune and will do him absolutely no good as an actor!'

'Gerald went there,' said Bess, 'and that's a good enough reason for me.'

'But I hated it!' objected Gerald.

'Never mind. It gave you a wonderful education. I only wish I'd had such a splendid opportunity myself! I want my children to have the very best. Why not, when we can afford it?'

'I tell you, it won't fit him for the world he'll grow up in,' insisted Christopher.

'It was Mark's wish,' said Bess. And this finished the conversation.

So Peter went to Eton, while Laura, to her disgust, remained at her expensive boarding school. She would have been desolate at parting from Evelyn if she had been taken away, but she was determined to go to university and had a low opinion of the teaching at the school. Besides, her mother's sense of values was anathema to her. She was completely out of sympathy with the concept of being brought up to fit into a social world which already she despised; and although she enjoyed being her mother's daughter for the perks it brought, she resented being surrounded by the famous, and so being belittled in her own eyes. She wanted to make her own way in the world — and would have liked to be the first in the family to do so. The Glanville name she despised. Like her grandparents, Kate and Patrick, she was a natural rebel; but, unlike them, she was determined never to conform. Meanwhile, she was editing the school magazine and contributing many of its short stories.

Laura may have disliked herself but she nonetheless thought of herself as rather special, and Evelyn's friendship fostered this. They were a self-congratulatory pair, and self-sufficient; and this self-sufficiency satisfied a profound desire for secrecy which both of them shared. Evelyn became in many ways the dominant partner, though she constantly deferred to Laura. Laura was physically larger, but Evelyn had an unshakeable arrogance which bolstered Laura's insecurity.

Laura took Evelyn home to Regent's Park one Easter holiday, but the visit nearly ended their friendship. For one thing, Evelyn hated dogs and couldn't bear Outram to come near her. For another, Bess took an immediate dislike to her.

'I don't know what it is,' she said to Christopher, 'but she gives me the creeps.'

'I agree,' replied Christopher. 'She looks a bit butch to me.'

'My God! What a beastly thing to say!' flared Bess. All the same, the remark worried her and she decided to have a talk with Laura.

Laura immediately flew into a rage. 'You've never loved me. Never!' she sobbed angrily. 'And now, when I've found someone who does, you don't like it.'

'That isn't true,' said Bess unhappily.

'Then why criticise my friends?'

'Only Evelyn.'

'She's my best friend.'

'But is she good for you, darling?'

'What does that mean?'

Bess hesitated. 'Darling, please don't get angry. Can't we just discuss things calmly?'

'What sort of things?' demanded Laura.

Again Bess hesitated. 'Has it occurred to you that Evelyn is rather a tough little girl?' she asked anxiously.

'Tough?' echoed Laura, genuinely astonished. 'No. I can't say that it has.'

'Well, that's how she strikes me,' said Bess, 'and I'm a little afraid that knowing her might make you rather tough too.'

'How? You mean you think she's common?'

'Of course not!' exclaimed Bess, shocked.

'Then what?'

'I just find her manner rather self-assertive,' said Bess.

'Well, you won't see her again, as I certainly shan't ask her back,' retorted Laura. 'All the same, I'm pretty disappointed.'

'I'm sorry,' said Bess. 'I was trying to be helpful, that's all.'

'You don't help by disliking my only friend,' retorted Laura.

Evelyn was unmoved when Laura reported the scene. 'What does it all matter?' she asked in a bored voice. 'So my visit has been a disaster. Well, I shan't be asked again, that's all. Why make a fuss? We see each other at school.'

'What about your parents? Could I come and stay with you?'

'Not a chance,' said Evelyn. 'You wouldn't like it. My parents aren't your class.'

'Class!' scoffed Laura. 'I don't approve of class.'

'Too bad,' said Evelyn. 'It's here to stay, they tell me.'

'But if I don't mind, why should you?'

'Mind? Now who's being snobbish? Look. I live in a crummy house on a crummy trying-to-be-posh estate in a Birmingham suburb. My father has made his money from sanitary china ware — which being translated means loos — and in his own eyes he's the eighth wonder of the world. Not that I care how he made the money, as long as it's there. But you should see where my aunts live! They haven't made money, you see.'

'Money isn't everything.'

'You could fool me,' retorted Evelyn. 'You wait until you haven't got it!'

When Evelyn had gone, Bess said unhappily to Christopher, 'I really do want to help Laura, Chris, but she makes things so difficult.'

'I know, darling, but you simply can't hide the fact that you prefer Peter, can you? And Laura's a prickly young thing.'

'So you think it's my fault?'

'Don't worry. It will sort itself out,' said Christopher soothingly.

'Oh Lord!' exclaimed Bess. 'I really don't know what to do for the best.'

'Poor old darling!'

'Peter is so easy to love, and Laura's so complicated!'

Christopher gently kissed her.

Bess did her best to get closer to Laura, but their equally quick tempers and thin skins didn't help. In fact the situation deteriorated, as Laura became aware of the effort her mother was making on her behalf and deeply resented it. But when school was over and Laura's dream of going to Oxford materialised, she saw how genuinely delighted Bess was, and how proud of her. And this pleased her.

Peter enjoyed Eton as much as he had his prep school. He made a dashing seventy against Harrow at Lords and was the hero of the hour. But again he did the minimum of work, and this time the fates refused to smile. He failed to get an Oxford place; and experienced briefly, and as profoundly as his cheerful nature permitted, a taste of the jealousy and resentment towards his sister that Laura had always felt for him.

Laura went up to Lady Margaret Hall to read French and German, and felt immediately at home. For her, Oxford provided an atmosphere at once stimulating and serene: here, for the first time in her life, her good qualities seemed more important to others than her shortcomings. Riding her bicycle with the hundreds of other undergraduates in the High, the Broad and St Giles, she felt that she had already won a small niche in that great world which she would one day conquer; she had taken a first step towards a triumphant vindication of herself. Browsing among the books at Blackwells; walking through Christchurch Meadows, deep in philosophical discussion; savouring the beauty of the ancient buildings, which reflected the earthly values and soaring aspirations of their founders; shivering by an austere fire in a North Oxford lodging house; or pontificating in a punt on the Cherwell — she felt part of an élite which could build the new Jerusalem.

At first, she made no special friends. In spite of the close relationship she had formed with Evelyn, she still found other people hard to handle. But Oxford was so different from either her home or her school that at last she was able to relax. Laura had believed both previous environments hostile: here she had no such fears, and her independent attitude at once won her some sort of popularity. She was considered a 'good sort' by her peers — someone who disliked gossip and was bright and interesting to talk to. As for the staff, her excellent brain made her for a time something of a favourite.

CHAPTER THREE

Almost her first invitation came from Professor Boase, the President of Magdalen and Vice-Chancellor of the University, who was a friend of her mother's. Usually such an introduction would have alienated her; but Tom Boase had an enviable reputation throughout the University, not only for scholarship but for his effortless understanding of the young. An acknowledged authority on the history of art, he was no less knowledgeable about the theatre and had done invaluable work as a senior member of the university dramatic society (the famous OUDS), saving it more than once by his advice from the ever-present threat of bankruptcy. In its great days, the OUDS always employed professional directors and actresses (Bess had appeared for them as Beatrice in *Much Ado*), so Tom Boase had a wide circle of theatrical friends. His invitation was an honour which Laura gratefully but nervously accepted.

Even at nearly seventy Tom had the special youthfulness of the happy teacher. Fresh-complexioned, trim and elegant, with a wall eye which actually enhanced the vitality of his features, he welcomed Laura with irresistible friendliness. Leading her upstairs to his long, panelled drawing room with its lovely mullioned window overlooking the cloisters, he introduced her to his other guests who were talking together in a cluster by the fire.

Laura was almost paralysed with shyness when she saw who they were.

'Peggy Ashcroft, Laura Wells,' said Tom, waving his long white hands vaguely in the air and adding proudly, 'Peggy did her first Juliet for the OUDS twenty-four years ago.'

Laura shook hands with her theatrical idol.

'Michael Redgrave — and his wife Rachel Kempson,' he continued, and once again Laura came face to face with actors whose work she wholeheartedly admired.

'Frank Hauser,' ended Tom, with a flourish.

'How do you do,' murmured Laura, this time not knowing Frank even by reputation.

To involve Laura in their interrupted conversation, Redgrave said politely, 'We were discussing the Scolt Lapps, Miss Wells. Have you any views?'

Laura had never heard of Scolt Lapps, let along had views on them. 'No, I'm afraid not,' she said, and blushed scarlet.

Redgrave's own shyness prevented him continuing, but she was rescued by Frank. Dark and animated, dressed in a baggy tweed suit which had a large patch in the seat of it, he was currently the director of the Oxford repertory theatre. His skill, and the affection he inspired in the acting profession, had combined to put the Playhouse on the national map and many of his productions had transferred successfully to the West End. He talked very fast and very knowledgeably, and however serious he was his voice seemed always on the edge of laughter. 'They're fascinating, the Scolt Lapps,' he said, 'they live widely scattered, in a bleak featureless snow-covered land, and communicate huge distances by telepathy. They can suggest a rendezvous to meet at an exact spot some forty or fifty miles away!'

Laura found the three famous stars intimidating. Her mother seldom entertained at home and, when she did, Laura made it a point to be out. Like Kate, she had deliberately turned away from the theatre; it was novels, not plays, that she planned to write. Kate's defection was a protest at her father's infidelities, Laura's a protest at her mother's fame. Laura wanted to make a separate way to the top, and eventually to earn her mother's love and respect by achieving success in another field. It was also a protest against Christopher for usurping her father's place in the theatre.

After a short conversation about the Scolt Lapps, a second silence fell, and her fellow guests looked at her impassively. Laura had often noticed this trait among theatre folk: they seemed to prefer their own kind and to look on outsiders as an alien species. Unlike the literary establishment, their exclusiveness was not because of an intellectual superiority complex, but because they felt both safer and more entertained among themselves.

Into this second silence Tom said, 'Laura is Bess Marchmont's daughter.'

At once the tension relaxed, until Laura replied a little too emphatically, 'I'm not going on the stage myself. I'm going to be a writer.'

Frank said cheerfully, 'That's a pity. You're very pretty,' and everyone smiled.

Laura sat next to Frank at lunch. He invited her to his theatre to meet the actors and attend one of the weekly talks he gave; and, to her own surprise, she agreed. She not only agreed but, during the following weeks, went frequently to the Playhouse, and came to know his predominantly young company well. She enjoyed her time with them, and perhaps her life would have taken a different turn, but for a visit by Evelyn for the weekend.

Evelyn had changed in the intervening time, and so, Laura supposed, had Laura. Evelyn was now more openly masculine, and Laura could see what her mother had been talking about. She was also far more demonstrative in her affection, and this was half an embarrassment, half a delight to Laura. She walked round Oxford with her arm possessively around Laura's shoulder, and stroked her cheeks and kissed her when they were alone.

'You're growing monstrously pretty,' she said on the evening of the first day. 'Has anyone told you?'

'Only Frank Hauser, at the Playhouse,' said Laura, feeling slightly uncomfortable.

'Frank Hauser? What's he like?'

'I think he thinks I ought to be an actress,' said Laura.

'Oh? And will you take up your mother's trade after all?' Evelyn sounded edgy.

'No. All my life I have wanted to write as you perfectly well know,' replied Laura.

'And you're still going to?' asked Evelyn.

'Certainly.'

'Have you met Stevie yet?' asked Evelyn casually.

'Stevie?'

'Sylvia Williams. She calls herself Stevie, because she's not as lucky as I am — she doesn't have a man's name of her own! My parents wanted me to be a boy. Did I tell you?'

'Of course. Often.'

'Yes. Of course. Stevie is quite something. She's far cleverer than most men, and she's going to revolutionise society.'

'In what way?'

'She's asked me to her rooms at St. Hugh's, tonight. I'll take you along,' replied Evelyn, smiling.

Stevie was indeed 'quite something'. To begin with, she was beautiful. She was tall and Jewish, with large dark eyes and naturally pink cheeks. She had long wavy black hair, a cheerful grin and a low and husky voice. She also had a voluptuous figure.

She and Evelyn greeted each other as old friends; then she looked at Laura. Her eyes widened in surprise, and she stared at her for so long that Laura flushed. Stevie smiled.

There was a crowd of women in the room, but Stevie was closely flanked by two girls who clearly idolised her — one pale and puffy-cheeked with curly hair, and the other big and clumsy with a prominent nose and small eyes.

After Evelyn had introduced her (inevitably, as Bess's daughter), Stevie said pleasantly, 'We were discussing last year's production of *Twelfth Night* at Stratford. Did you see it?'

'No,' said Laura.

Again Stevie looked surprised, but she said pleasantly, 'We were discussing the homosexual implications. It's an interesting play from that point of view. So's *As You Like It*.'

'In what way?' asked Laura.

'Well, surely it's obvious? Boys playing women dressed as boys... Shakespeare wasn't just making it easier for his boy actors by letting them exchange their skirts for doublet and hose. He was actually revelling in the extra transvestite twist the boys gave to his plots — something we lose today when women play Rosalind and Viola. Orsino's feelings for the 'boy' Viola, which are overtly homosexual, become even more so when Viola actually is a boy. And what about boy Rosalind and boy Celia? Just good friends? Or something more?'

'I'd never thought about it,' said Laura smiling.

'And what about *Cymbeline*?' demanded Stevie.

'I've never read it,' answered Laura.

'You should,' said Stevie. 'You really should,' and she looked deep into Laura's eyes.

Laura was instantly and powerfully attracted; and, as though she divined this, Stevie stroked her cheek gently with the tip of one finger. 'We must see a great deal more of each other, mustn't we?' she said softly. Then she turned her back on her.

Evelyn was angry. On their way home from the party, she said waspishly, and with obvious jealousy, 'I see you did think our Stevie was extra special.'

'Yes. I've never met anyone quite like her before,' replied Laura, bemused.

'I'm glad,' answered Evelyn grimly. 'That comforts me a lot.' She had had her arm through Laura's. Now she withdrew it.

'Don't be angry,' pleaded Laura, distressed. 'Stevie is no threat to our friendship, is she, so what are you fussed about?'

'Isn't she?' Evelyn was intense.

'Of course not.'

Evelyn didn't say anything for a while, then suddenly she asked with some passion, 'What do I mean to you, Laura?'

'Mean?' asked Laura, surprised. 'Well for a start you're my best friend. In fact, if you want to know, you're pretty well my only friend.'

'But now that we've grown up?' insisted Evelyn.

'Nothing's changed,' said Laura. 'How could it? We're best friends.'

'You don't feel anything more?'

'What should I feel?'

'I mean, after this Oxford stint of yours, you wouldn't feel like setting up house with me? I'm a lavatory-bowl heiress, if you remember, so we could be entirely financially independent, and you could write to your heart's content while I breed horses.'

'Is that what you want to do?'

'Yes. I'm starting quite soon. I've got my eye on a marvellous place near Newbury.'

'I thought you didn't like animals,' said Laura, remembering Evelyn's encounter with Outram.

'I like most animals,' retorted Evelyn pugnaciously.

'It's awfully sweet of you,' said Laura, hesitantly, 'but I really don't think I'd like that. You see, I want to be a success in the great wide world.'

'Through your writing?'

'Of course.'

'Then why should living with me stop you?'

'I think I want to be a journalist, as well as write books,' said Laura, 'so I'll have to live in a city.'

'It isn't Stevie, then?' asked Evelyn.

Laura was astonished. 'Stevie? No! Certainly not!' she said vehemently.

'Thank God for that!' exclaimed Evelyn. 'Then there's still hope for me?'

'I don't understand.'

Evelyn looked angry. 'Don't be a fool,' she said, shortly. 'No-one could be that naive.'

The rest of the weekend passed in argument and bad temper,

and when Evelyn left she said, 'So much, then, for a beautiful friendship.'

'I don't understand what I'm supposed to have done wrong,' replied Laura, uneasily.

This was a lie. She certainly understood what Evelyn had meant — and knew she wanted to reject it. She knew now that they had come to a parting of the ways and this made her very sad. She was only thankful that her rejection of Evelyn's proposal hadn't had to be overt.

Evelyn had been right, though, about Stevie's attraction for Laura, and this soon began to obsess her; not least because she felt an enormous sense of guilt. Stevie had started to pursue her, and she found her difficult to avoid. She was ashamed at herself for being attracted for a second time to a woman — and yet, as a natural feminist, felt almost a traitor to be recoiling from an openly lesbian relationship.

She had no idea whom to talk to about her problem, and so turned to reading the sexologists.

She read Krafft-Ebing first, and became even more depressed. His belief that lesbianism was 'congenital, due to cerebral anomalies ... [a] sign of an inherited diseased condition of the central nervous system', while it relieved her of responsibility for her condition, suggested that she was stuck with it for life. Havelock Ellis was even worse. His category of the 'true invert' seemed to apply to her; and, since he differentiated it from innocent childish homosexual behaviour, or 'faute-de-mieux homosexuality', it even deprived her of an excuse. In his view, as in Krafft-Ebing's, love between women was freakish and morbid, leading to insanity and sometimes murder or suicide; both men referred to the condition as 'tainted'.

Thoroughly frightened, Laura turned to Freud. Freud dismissed the claim that the condition was congenital, maintaining that childhood trauma was primarily responsible and that the condition could be cured by psychoanalysis. But even to him it was a disease.

John Addington Symonds was the only one to give her a ray of hope when he stated that there was probably no-one alive who had inherited no neuropathic strain whatever.

At this point Laura wrote to Gerald, choosing him as her confidant for obvious reasons. She had always regarded him with a special affection, and he in turn loved her. In their ensuing

correspondence, he was a great comfort to her: he couldn't help
her sort out the chaos of her emotions (he was the last person, he
wrote, to give advice on this particular subject), but he promised,
with no hint of patronage, to listen to what she had to say and to do
his best to understand her point of view:

> Don't think for one moment, darling, that your distress is one
> that sets you apart from the rest of us. Nearly all of us have great
> difficulty in adjusting to our emotions; and, when one is
> unhappy and ill-adjusted, isolation — even imagined — can
> become a kind of agony, as I well know. Yet, when I tell you that
> you are not alone, don't think I wish to deny that you are unique
> as a person. At the risk of blinding you with the obvious, every
> single one of us is.
> Have you tried a head shrinker? I'm afraid Bess would have
> little instinctive sympathy for the idea, but then Bess is remark-
> ably strong. But if she knew it would help you, she'd rally round
> at once. She's a generous-hearted creature. And at the moment,
> for all her strength, she's almost out of her mind about Peter's
> National Service posting to Malaya. That he should be drafted
> into danger, in a country which, although she loves it, has
> already claimed her mother, her father and most of her child-
> hood friends, seems, I must say, unreasonably cruel. Do write
> her a nice sympathetic letter about it. It would mean a lot to her.

Laura wrote back:

> Darling Gerald,
>
> Thank you for your letter. I've written to Mummy and had a
> lovely letter back. How understanding you are. I don't know
> what we've all done to deserve you! Thank you too for the
> suggestion about a head shrinker. I've already been to one, but
> he wasn't right for me, and he couldn't have cured me even if I
> hadn't already read my Freud. He painted a clear, thoroughly
> jargon-laden picture of me as I am, in his eyes, but didn't begin
> to show me how to *cure* how I am.
> Naturally he was delighted when I told him I'd tried to
> throttle Peter. He suggested gently that, once I'd failed to *remove*
> Peter, I then tried to *supplant* him, by 'becoming' the boy my
> mother wanted me to be. My first real trauma was Peter's birth,
> he says: that and Daddy's death have scarred my psyche.

When I quite reasonably suggested that even heterosexual children were often jealous of each other, he looked cross. And when he heard that I'd read Westphal (the Daddy of all the anti-lesbian psychologists) in the original German, he really hated me. I threw in Obici and Marchesini for good measure (and for swank), and that was that.

I'm glad! I felt absurd sitting there in the half-dark talking to this uncongenial stranger about myself. Anyway, I think he's nuttier than I am, and his obsessions are the driving force behind his choice of profession. He did say some quite interesting — and I hope fairly irrelevant — things about psychopathy, though, and talked about 'emotional walls' and all sorts of other like-minded things which interested me considerably more . . .

Gerald replied suggesting that she take the bull by the horns and talk to Stevie herself: 'If you "do nothing but think of her" (your own phrase), then there are only two things to do: see no more of her, which you say is impossible, or see enough of her to get to know her. Unattainable love is not to be recommended for romantics like you and me. It becomes too important.'

Stevie was pleased that Laura had returned to her. 'I knew you'd be back,' she said calmly. 'What's been wrong?'

Laura replied truthfully, 'I have no wish to become a lesbian.'

'Why not?' asked Stevie cheerfully.

'I've been reading Krafft-Ebing and Havelock Ellis,' answered Laura simply.

Stevie laughed. 'Well, before you get too muddled, read about the romantic friendships between women in the eighteenth century; and about Boston marriages and sentimental friends in the nineteenth,' she said briskly. 'Did you know that in the published correspondence of nearly every nineteenth-century woman there's evidence of a passionate commitment to another woman — and not because women were taught to fear premarital heterosexual love either — and society condoned it? Did you know that love between women in the eighteenth century was considered noble and virtuous in every way?'

'No, I didn't.'

'Well, since you've taken so much trouble already, take some more. Women must be free to live life at first hand, not as appendages to men. A commitment to another woman allows this.

What's more, it encourages the other woman to fulfil herself as a human being. Brains in a woman are welcomed by lesbians. Freedom is a recognised necessity. Work — paid for on level terms with men — is one of our goals. Seen in this light, feminism is fair and logical, and the only unwholesome thing about it is that women in this century have been conned into believing anything different.'

'Why should that have been?' asked Laura, astonished. 'Who benefited from it?'

'Men, of course. Even in the centuries when society was lenient towards the love of women, they persecuted those who demanded masculine privileges. The usurpation of male prerogative by women who behave like men has always been feared and suppressed. Why don't you work with us, Laura? You write well, they tell me, and we need someone to help us launch our magazine — why not you? We're calling it *Eve's Tree*!'

'I'd love to,' answered Laura with enthusiasm.

Working close to Stevie was exhilarating. She was capable and direct as an editor, and just and kind in her dealings with everyone. Laura was still obsessively stirred by her beauty, but she was now mentally stimulated too. Stevie's feminism was exactly tailored to Laura's own views, except for one important difference — Laura believed that one day a man would fulfil her emotional needs, because it was just possible she might want children. Stevie had found a satisfying emotional life *without* men; and she refused to become involved with Laura if Laura intended to desert her one day for a heterosexual partner.

'Marriage is slavery. No more, no less, Laura. You can't be thinking of marriage!' she exclaimed.

'I certainly don't want to rule it out at this stage of my life!' retorted Laura.

'But women attract you,' said Stevie.

'I know, but that may be an aberration,' replied Laura.

'Oh, thanks very much!' snapped Stevie angrily. 'We're faute-de-mieux are we, because you've been condemned to one-sex schools all your life, and proximity has done its deadly work!'

Stevie came, as Evelyn had done, from a very different background from Laura's. She was a Welsh miner's daughter, with a Jewish mother. 'Think of that as a mix-up!' she said. She had lived in the Valleys as a child, and they were still the yardstick by which she measured the rest of the world. She mistrusted all men everywhere — 'beginning with my father, of course,' she said grimly. She had an acid wit, a chip on her shoulder and, like Evelyn, an over-sensitivity about herself which sometimes made her an uneasy companion. But she was also enormous fun. She lived life with a zest and passion which Laura had never seen equalled, and she had high hopes that one day she would change society.

She was ardently left wing, both from her upbringing and because in her view the capitalist system was male-oriented:

'A man works to get more money than his fellows and then buys a tip-top woman to see to his needs. In return for her absolute devotion, her dependence on him and her ability to provide him with food and satisfactory free sex at home, he'll give her all he can afford in the way of material comfort and luxuries. For my money, he can stuff it! I'm cleverer than most of the men I've met, and I can provide my own house, food and clothes — and even, if I wanted it, luxury. Though with the dice loaded against me of course. It's different for you.'

'What's different?'

'Take your writing.'

'*Well?*' Laura was immediately on the defensive.

'If you wrote a book that was half-way good, they'd publish it. But not if I wrote one.'

'Of course they would if it was as good!'

'Crap,' said Stevie flatly. 'Your mother is famous. I've always had to stand squarely on my own two feet. You don't know you're born, Laura. None of your kind do. Your grandparents were famous too, and it was easy for them because your kind inherit the earth without a struggle. My kind don't. They have to be twice as good as you to get half as far.'

'That sounds like one of our essays in *Eve's Tree*,' said Laura ruefully. And they both laughed.

In spite of their constant bickering and the central difference in their outlook, Stevie and Laura were deeply in love. And in the course of time, had an affair.

'I'm going to give you sex without guilt if it's the last thing I do,' said Stevie, 'and even men can't always offer that!'

Drowned in love, Laura could only agree.

The affair lasted for just over two years. At first, the release into physical passion was a shock and a delight so extreme that nothing else mattered; but in time Laura discovered that, although Stevie had seemed so self-sufficient, in love she was demanding and dependent. To Laura their need for each other became more and more claustrophobic, and the 'emotional walls' that the psychiatrist had been talking about began to close in on her. This frightened her once again into thinking that there might be something 'wrong' with her. Fortunately, however, the obsessive quality of their love didn't interfere with their work and both girls were earnestly studious.

At last Laura began to tire of Stevie, and Stevie saw it.

The rows began and Laura was appalled. Her fastidious nature deplored the endless scenes of jealousy and suspicion, and her sense of dignity was outraged by the knowledge that they could only be assuaged by love-making.

She had long been aware of the looks of amused curiosity or embarrassed distaste which greeted her and Stevie when they were out together in 'normal society'. At the height of her passion she had gloried in brazening it out. Now she realised with dismay that she cared about what others thought about her; and, though she could barely admit it to herself — and certainly never to Stevie — she began to share their embarrassment.

The end came at an Experimental Theatre Club revue in which two undergraduates in 'drag' did scurrilous impersonations of Laura and Stevie in a sketch inevitably called 'Adam's Apple'. Stevie enjoyed it — or claimed to. Laura hated it, and fled at the interval. She wrote next morning resigning from *Eve's Tree*, and apologising for her behaviour. There was no reply.

CHAPTER FOUR

Meanwhile, Bess was once again preoccupied with Malaya, although this time at second hand.

The Emergency there lasted from 1948 until 1960. It was in reality a war; but it was never called one, for the curious reason that the London insurance market, on which the Malayan economy relied, could not have covered the losses of stocks and equipment had it been so called.

The Emergency began on 16 June 1948, shortly before eight-thirty in the morning, when three young Chinese on bicycles rode up to Arthur Walker's bungalow on the Ephil Rubber Estate in Perak, of which he was Manager, and walked into his office. The dog barked, but Arthur quietened him. One of the three greeted him in Malay, with the words, '*Tabek Tuan*' (Hail, sir), and he spoke cheerfully in reply. He was shot dead. The leader of the Chinese then led the way outside, where the terrified Indian estate clerk saw him spit on the ground. Then all three rode off.

Half an hour later, on the Sungei Siput Estate twelve miles away, twelve armed Chinese surrounded the main estate building where the fifty-five-year-old manager, John Allison, and his twenty-one-year-old Assistant, Ian Christian, were in their offices. At gun point they were taken to John Allison's bungalow, detained there for ten minutes, marched back to the offices, bound to chairs, and shot where they sat.

War had started.

The Emergency was a Chinese Communist bid to take over the country, led by the Secretary General of the local party, a Malayan-born Chinese called Chin Peng. The decision to embark on it had been taken only two weeks before the murders, although plans had been laid for years.

Chin Peng had learned the art of guerrilla war from the few British who, after the fall of Singapore, had stayed behind in the jungle under the leadership of Colonel Spencer Chapman, to harass the Japanese and prepare for British liberating forces. Chapman and other British officers — who were later landed in Malaya by parachute or submarine — formed the Malaya People's Anti-Japanese Army; and many Chinese joined them, because they hated the Japanese for their invasion of China. Chin Peng did so well that he was given the OBE. After the war, Chin Peng and his followers posed as the sole victors over an enemy against whom the white man had been powerless; and ironically it was the return of peace after the Japanese surrender which transformed the Malayan Communists from a political party into an armed resistance. Chin Peng believed that Communism could succeed in Malaya, as it had in China, because 'all the Chinese in Malaya are in sympathy'. This turned out to be untrue: the British at this time were actively planning for Malayan Independence, and a great many of the indigenous peoples were aware of this, and prepared to wait.

Late in the summer of 1957, shortly after his eighteenth birthday, to Bess's dismay Peter was called up for National Service. He was allowed five weeks at home, then sent to Oswestry in Shropshire with twenty-three other boys of his own age — one from Manchester Grammar School, and twenty-two long-haired Teddy Boys from London.

The shocks which Peter experienced in his introduction to army life were as nothing compared with those awaiting the 'Teds'. The loss of their luxuriant hairstyles brought four-letter words to their lips and tears to their eyes; and when their flick-knives were confiscated it nearly provoked a mutiny. Peter and the Manchester boy were at first cordially hated by the Teds because, having entered the army unarmed and with conventional haircuts, they had not suffered these indignities. However, with his basic friendliness and his Cadet Corps experience of arms drill, weapon training, how to arrange a bedding roll neatly for a barrack room inspection, and other martial arts, Peter became a key figure in the squad's running battle with the dreaded Company Sergeant-Major. Soon he was helping the illiterate with letters to their girl friends — thereby, incidentally, considerably extending his very limited knowledge of the opposite sex. Class barriers and backgrounds were forgotton and a remarkable cameraderie took their place.

Soon after their basic training was complete, Peter was selected as a potential officer and sent to a WOSB (War Office Selection

Board) for intelligence and character tests, which he passed. He was next posted to an Officer Cadet Training Unit at Aldershot, where he stayed for fourteen weeks; and here, during discussion groups on a wide range of subjects, it was learned that his mother and his grandmother had lived in Malaya. Although such a connection could have no possible bearing on his performance as a temporary soldier, in the curiously circuitous way that some army decisions are made he was sent to Malaya some months later, as a Second Lieutenant.

Christopher did his best to calm a distraught Bess. 'It will do him a power of good, Bessie,' he said. 'Turn him into a man.'

'He would have turned into a man anyway,' she retorted.

'He's had a very sheltered life so far. As I said to you when you sent him to Eton, he has got to face reality some time,' Christopher replied.

'I don't understand why it's only the unpleasant things that count as "reality",' answered Bess.

'You yourself wouldn't be half the person you are now if you hadn't had such a tough time when you were young,' said Christopher.

'I don't want Peter to be killed!' She was nearly in tears. 'I love him.'

'So do I.'

'You're only his stepfather! That's why you are being so callous!'

'I'm not callous, darling. Thousands of other women are going through the same agonies and millions and millions have done so all through the ages. Be the brave girl you usually are, Bessie. Peter is young. He'll probably even enjoy himself.'

'*Laura* has sent me a *lovely* understanding letter about it!' said Bess.

'I'm glad,' replied Christopher, and he meant it.

By the time Peter reached Malaya the situation there had changed dramatically, but it was still dangerous. In the early days the Communist terrorists (known to everyone as CTs) had had the advantage of surprise, preliminary planning and an effective propaganda machine: their vicious and terrifying attacks to frighten villagers into giving them food, their shooting of lonely European planters and their familiarity with the jungle — combined with an initial failure by the Government to recognise the gravity of the situation — all enhanced their success. At last Sir

Henry Gurney (who was assassinated in an ambush in 1951) and his successor, Sir Gerald Templer, managed to turn the tide by welding the services, the police and the civilian population into a united anti-guerrilla force. 1955 probably saw the real turning point of the struggle, even though 25,000 British troops were still slogging it out in the mangrove swamps and the seemingly limitless jungle. Chin Peng had fled the country and was directing operations from Thailand.

The first Malay elections — a major step on the path to Independence — were to take place in July. In June, Chin Peng offered to negotiate a Peace Settlement: the offer was rejected. The elections went ahead, and Tunku Abdul Rahman became Malaysia's first Prime Minister. On 31 August 1957, Merdeka (Independence) was proclaimed and Malaya, under her new name of Malaysia, became a sovereign State.

Between June 1958 and the end of the Emergency in 1960, Peter saw active service in Perak in the north-west, Pahang in the east and, finally, in the most southerly state of Johore. His reaction to the jungle as a soldier bore no relation to his mother's, nor to Kate's.

All the camps were laid out to an identical pattern, designed to accommodate a battalion strength of about 700 men. The tents, holding 10 to 12 men, were erected on concrete foundations, and each company line consisted of 10 to 12 tents. The whole camp was surrounded by a barbed-wire fence. Security was very tight. Except for the violent but usually short-lived tropical storms the sun beat down on the concrete all day, and the jungle steamed in the heat. At night the jungle noises seemed particularly sinister; it was known that the CTs, who now operated chiefly at night, had learned to imitate them as a means of communication. Snakes, scorpions, mosquitoes and the pervasive humidity added to the claustrophobic tensions of being surrounded by an invisible enemy — some of whom even had day-time civilian jobs inside the camps. All roads in the area had to be systematically patrolled and, if information came in of a CT hideout, an operation would be mounted to attack it. Roads were classified as white, yellow or red: white roads were safe for stopping a vehicle; yellow roads were safe in daylight; red roads were dangerous at all times. Guerrilla activity was now only sporadic, but it was cruel and bloody all the same, and the job was difficult when a battalion was new to the conditions. The patrol which Peter was leading had to fight its way out of an ambush on more than one occasion, and by the end of his time Peter had had enough.

When his tour of duty was over, he returned to England for demobilisation — and to find a job. The army didn't appeal to him, but he was glad to have been a soldier, however briefly, and he knew at last that he had a good brain if he took the trouble to use it. He still regretted that he had failed to get into Oxford, but now resolved to be 'something in the City'. His Colonel in Johore had told him to look up his brother, who was an executive of a merchant bank, and this Peter did soon after he returned. He had several interviews before he landed the appointment, and understood that his active-service experience had told in his favour.

He was very happy to be home, and Bess's emotional welcome had touched him deeply, as had Christopher's genuine but more subdued response; but the years away had convinced him he would do better to find a flat on his own than to live with them. He discovered what he wanted, in Fulham, and settled down with pleasure to his new work.

Laura, characteristically, was finding things more difficult in her determination to be a journalist. She had written to the Declan Group of newspapers, and had been interviewed in Oxford in a general Declan Organisation recruitment exercise; but her brusque manner and intimidatingly dogmatic way of speaking had frightened her interviewer, who told her to get in touch again when she knew what sort of degree she had obtained. In fact she managed a moderate Second — 'Could have been a First, but for that damned *Eve's Tree*,' said her tutor forthrightly. She wrote again to Declan's as she had been told, but received no reply so began looking around in London. She was offered a job on a small underground feminist magazine, but this she refused as being too restricting. At last she had a reply from Declan's. She was sent up North to Clevegate to be interviewed by the Editor of the *Clevegate Messenger*. She was offered a six-month trial period in the Features Department, to start in three months' time. If she made good, she would be taken on the permanent staff.

Meanwhile she was writing her first novel. When it was finished, she sent it to Collins — who turned it down. Although she couldn't really have expected it to be accepted, the refusal was a body blow.

Bess was feeling bereft without Peter. She was also very

conscious that she was growing older, whereas Christopher seemed not to have altered at all.

During the 1960s, she made only three films and Christopher scarcely more. The British film industry had dwindled, as they had known it would, but they still had plenty of work in the theatre, often being lucky enough to be given work together. The London stage claimed most of their time, but both regularly went on tour before and sometimes after their West End runs. Unlike many of their contemporaries they actively enjoyed touring.

In the days of Bess's grandparents, all the stars had toured the provinces as a matter of course for several months of every year. Theatres in those days were much more numerous than today (for instance, seven had operated all the year round in Birmingham, as opposed to the present two; nine in Manchester, as opposed to two now; and so on) and practically every city or town in the British Isles could expect visits from the most famous stars of the time. There had been double the number of actors in Madge and Harry's day, and the theatre then — like television today — provided the only mass entertainment, so was cherished along with its stars.

When Bess and Christopher began touring in earnest, the provincial theatres were in a bad way. During and immediately after the war the public had been in such desperate need of entertainment that unscrupulous managements were happily short-changing the public. Plays were billed as 'Prior to London', when there was no hope or intention of their reaching the metropolis; or 'Full West End Cast' (implying that the production had come unaltered from London), when the closest connection of the touring cast with the West End was probably their home addresses. Not unnaturally, with the advent of television, business fell away; the provincial theatres themselves became even shabbier, and fewer and fewer stars wished to go out on the road. Once again Christopher and Bess mounted a campaign. With the help of two go-ahead young managers and a group of like-minded friends, they set up a network of tours, all of which were of a high standard and many of which had long runs in London at the end of their travels. Gradually conditions improved; and, with the building boom of the sixties, the increasing involvement of local authorities in theatre ownership and Arts Council backing for expensive or artistically prestigious tours, the provinces began to receive a more adequate slice of the theatrical cake.

Laura had left for Clevegate and the *Messenger* in a chastened frame of mind. She had expected her degree to open all doors: it hadn't. Indeed, at that time, in the life she had chosen, it even appeared to be a disadvantage. However, she liked Clevegate from the start.

The *Messenger* building had been erected a few years before she arrived. It was in the centre of the town near the huge neo-classical town hall, and built on two floors in glass and concrete. On the ground floor were the presses. The upper floor accommodated the compositors and journalists. Except for the board room (which doubled as the high-ups' dining room) and the separate offices for the managing director, editor and other senior executives, the whole area was open-plan. At one end was the Features Section (women's page, arts criticism, etc.) and at the other the Sports Desk. In the centre were the 'hard news' reporters, the sub-editors and the photographers.

Laura was put to work on the women's page, with an attractive older woman called Pauline Hurst, who was the Features Editor. The Managing Director, Peter Harrington, who was tall, good-looking and fiftyish, was amiable enough, although Laura didn't see very much of him; the Editor, Tom Foster, was a broad-faced northerner who kept himself to himself as much as he could. Some four hundred people worked on the paper, which was a daily.

Laura found a flat in a tall grey Victorian house on the outskirts of the town, and Bess gave her a small sports car as a celebration present.

CHAPTER FIVE

Laura successfully weathered her probationary six months and was given a week's holiday. She went home to Bess and found her in low spirits.

For some time now, the future of the Nash Terraces had been in doubt. The original long leases were coming to an end, and there was discussion as to whether or not the terraces should be pulled down and lucrative blocks of modern flats put up instead. In the event, the decision was made to save the terraces. This was due in part to the vigorous campaign which Vivien Leigh had waged to save the St James's Theatre — which, though unsuccessful, had made the public aware that beautiful and historic buildings were being wantonly destroyed — and in part to a report by Woodrow Wyatt in one of his popular appearances on 'Panorama'. After a year of uncertainty it was decided that the stucco facades should be preserved and Regent's Park allowed to look as beautiful as it had done for the past century and more. However, most of the houses were to be converted into flats and all the interiors gutted and reconstructed — which meant that Bess and the family were forced to leave.

It couldn't have happened at a worse moment for Bess. By chance, Christopher had been in two plays running with an up-and-coming young actress called Virginia Merry. She was petite and very pretty. She was also amusing, and ruthless, and had made a dead set at Christopher from the moment she saw him. That he was happily married didn't interest her one way or the other; but that he was rich, had a good position in the theatre and had looks and charm, interested her a great deal. Flattered, Christopher was persuaded that he was in love with her. He had even moved out of the family home and was seriously considering divorce.

Although she had never ceased to love him, Bess's lifelong capacity for hiding her emotions was interpreted by Christopher as a growing indifference. As he was not without vanity and had reached an age when he was sensitive about losing his attractions, he was in special need of reassurance: Virginia's exuberant demonstrativeness was exactly what he wanted.

'I expect it's as much my fault as his,' said Bess unhappily, defending Christopher from Laura's furious denunciation. 'It usually is in these cases.'

'What's she like?' asked Laura.

'Vivacious,' replied Bess tersely, then laughed at herself. 'I'm becoming a bitch.'

'Would you have him back if he wanted to come?'

Bess was astounded. 'Well, of course!' she exclaimed. 'Why ever not?'

'He hasn't treated you very well.'

'He's treated me marvellously!' retorted Bess firmly. 'He's been quite wonderful! Monogamy is very difficult, that's all. We're none of us really made for it — and sometimes, if we're the faithful kind, we feel that we're losing out on life. I expect that's what's happened to Christopher. The trouble is, though, since trust is the basis of a happy relationship, polygamy would be even more difficult.'

'Well I think he's a disgrace!'

'Nonsense! Some people say it's the male menopause that makes men tire of their first marriage. I don't know how medically correct that is. Personally speaking, I think women are more inclined to wander in their forties, when they think their looks are going, and men in their fifties for the same reason.'

As a reaction, and much to Laura's disapproval, Bess — who was always surrounded by a collection of admirers, old and new — now began to see a great deal of an actor of whom she had always been particularly fond since they had done a revue together, many years before. 'He was tremendously good to me,' she said. 'I couldn't really sing, and was completely untrained as a dancer, but Neil took hours of trouble over me and I got by.' Neil had hung around virtually unnoticed ever since and was surprised and delighted when Bess began to encourage him.

Laura returned to Clevegate angry with her mother, whose perennial attraction for the opposite sex had always made her jealous. Bess, however, was in passionate need of Neil's support. He helped her enthusiastically in her search for a new home: he loved houses and architecture and, like Gerald, had a real flair for interior decoration. Although the children had left, Bess still wanted a home with room for them when they felt inclined to come; Susan was still in her service, and Gerald still used their house as his headquarters; so she needed a lot of space. She also wanted somewhere which Christopher could still regard as home: she knew that he loved Regent's Park, but the house prices there were now astronomical. She and Neil combed London unsuccessfully from Hampstead to Chelsea; they were at their wits' end when they suddenly heard of a Nash house at a reasonable figure not fifty yards from Connaught Terrace. It had already been modernised, and the owner wanted a quick sale as he had just been appointed an overseas director of his firm. Gratefully Bess took it. Neil helped in the move and, thanks to him and Susan, Bess settled in surprisingly quickly. She wrote to Laura to reassure her that her new home would soon be ready to welcome her.

To Bess's delight, when Christopher reluctantly came to see the house, he fell for it. He was charmed with the new drawing room, which was even larger than their previous one, and with 'his' new dressing room, which had an enormous amount of cupboard space. Susan, on the other hand, who had been happy in her mews cottage, disliked having to live in with the family; in the years she had spent in the Rankins' service, she had not only made herself indispensable but grown bossy and a trifle sour. Peter, Laura and Gerald sent loving letters, Peter adding that he had found a girl he wanted to marry and would be bringing her to meet the family as soon as he could.

This news threw Bess into a frenzy. She had always idolised Peter, and she felt that he was far too young to marry. She tried to talk it over with Christopher, but he was obsessed with Virginia Merry and his own worries and so hardly cared one way or another. Neil sensibly suggested that Bess should keep calm until she had seen the girl, since it was quite possible that she would like her very much.

'But he's so young!' exclaimed Bess. 'Even if I do like her, the idea of their marrying is absurd!'

'From what you've told me about Peter, he sounds a sensible chap,' said Neil.

'He's scarcely started to earn his living yet! He doesn't want a wife and children!' protested Bess.

'He evidently does,' said Neil firmly.

When she finally met Jane, however, Bess was enchanted. Jane at nineteen was exactly the kind of girl she would have wished for a daughter-in-law — attractive, affectionate and with excellent manners. Christopher was bowled over by her, and for the first time seemed a little embarrassed by his affair with Virginia. 'Jane's almost too good to be true,' he said. 'Peter is a very lucky young man.' He took great pains to dress well when he was going to meet her, and tried to regain his place as the head of the family. Bess saw what was going on and was extremely thankful.

'What did I say!' laughed Neil, when Bess told him how delighted she was by Peter's choice.

'Nothing alters the fact that they are still much too young,' replied Bess emphatically. 'She's adorable, but nothing can alter that fact.'

When Laura met Jane, her old enemy jealousy was once again aroused. With the one exception of his failure to get into Oxford, Peter seemed to sail through life with such consummate ease. Here he was, marrying this beautiful, extremely rich girl — a girl obviously excellently suited to him, and who equally obviously adored him! He seemed born for happiness. And I'm not, she thought self-pityingly.

As Bess and Christopher were both acting in the West End, the wedding took place at St James's, Piccadilly, and the reception was at Claridges. Christopher still hadn't finished with Virginia, but he clearly didn't want to break with his family altogether. Bess did her best to be patient and understanding but she absolutely refused to invite Virginia to the wedding.

'It's a family affair,' she said energetically. 'We don't want outsiders.'

'Oh, come now, Bess!' protested Christopher. 'These things happen, you know.'

'Yes, I do know! But Virginia at the wedding is something that's not going to happen.'

She did, however, invite Neil — and Christopher objected.

'It's unfair!'

'Why?' asked Bess. 'He's a friend, and *we're* not having an affair.'

Gerald had flown in from Hollywood for the wedding, and Laura came down again from the North, but she detested such a high-powered function. Ill at ease, and in a most unbecoming outfit, she glowered bad-temperedly throughout.

When it was all over, Christopher said to Bess, 'That wretched

Neil of yours behaved like a member of the family. If you must have boyfriends, at least see that they're discreet!'

'Look who's talking!' returned Bess. 'I've had two years of you and Virginia being coupled together in the press, not to mention having to take the sympathy of all our friends! Besides, if Neil behaved like one of the family, it's only because he will be if you go off with Virginia.'

'You mean you'd marry him?'

'Certainly.'

'Has he asked you?'

'Of course. Many times.'

'Then I don't know why I'm hesitating about marrying Virginia,' said Christopher. 'I thought I would be leaving you on your own!'

'No,' said Bess calmly. 'So please go ahead if you want to.'

After a honeymoon in the Caribbean, Peter and Jane moved into a small Georgian village house in Hertfordshire (a wedding present from Jane's parents), from which Peter commuted to the office. The fact that her brother didn't have to buy his house struck Laura as unfair, and yet another proof that he was always the lucky one. She conveniently forgot that, while she had been enjoying Oxford, he had been risking his life in the Malayan jungle.

In the end, the move which had upset Bess so much was responsible for Christopher's return to her. He approved of the new place to such an extent that he began to come home more often. This led to rows with Virginia. Bess sensibly made no comment — simply making him welcome and seeing to his every comfort. In time, he and Bess lived together again as man and wife, and Neil reverted to being the devoted hanger on: a relationship which in actual fact, he realised ruefully, he preferred.

Gerald returned from America for a long stay and was enchanted with his new quarters. During the time he had lived with Bess, he had had several lovers; but he had now fallen for an American writer ten years younger than himself, whom he brought back to England with him. His name was Walter Pfeiffer; and, although Bess and Christopher disliked the idea of yet another lodger, he settled into the family with little friction and Gerald, at last, seemed happy.

At the end of the year, Peter rang to say that Jane was pregnant. In due course, Bess's first grandchild, Belinda Ann, was born.

CHAPTER SIX

Laura was still enjoying herself on the *Messenger*. She found it ironical that she was used extensively on women's features when her views were radically different from the paper's; but, to do them justice, Pauline and Tom Foster usually let her copy through.

She was writing her second novel, and found her flat a good place to work in. She was undomesticated, so did little to brighten it up, but at least she kept it fanatically clean and tidy. There was a small garden at the back which gave her much pleasure; though no gardener, she kept the lawn and flowerbeds trim. The landlady, who lived above, was a happy creature, untidy and unworldly; the other two lodgers were pleasant, if not remotely interesting. This suited Laura, who was still instinctively a loner. She liked living in the North of England, preferring its people's blunter ways to those of the South; and in the car her mother had given her she went out often for solitary picnics on the moors.

At work she kept her political convictions to herself, since the paper was conservative, and tried hard to keep her temper and her sharp tongue under control. In this she was not always successful; but she was respected for her efficiency, and accepted as something of a card.

Even though Pauline was her immediate boss, Laura had to hand in a carbon each day to Tom Foster of the copy she had submitted. She found him a little frightening. Although a big man, he walked lightly; and he smoked a pipe, which he sucked when it was unlit, turning the bowl upside down. He had a resonant voice, and on rare occasions an unexpectedly charming smile. The other women in the office found him attractive, and to her surprise Laura shared their feelings. She tried to analyse why. He was clever, certainly; but not outstandingly so. He was, in a sardonic way, good looking; but no more so than hundreds of other men. He had, however, a powerful animal magnetism — which they all felt — which seemed to promise an almost paternal security to anyone fortunate and resolute enough to penetrate his defences. All in all, though, it was only too clear that his attraction was primarily physical.

Unfortunately, Tom seemed not to notice Laura at all. This surprised and irritated her, and for some time she tried to suppress her feelings. He often drank at the pub which most of them frequented, and sometimes lunched there; but he kept himself very much to himself, even though he seemed to listen to everything that went on around him. The first thing he ever said to Laura outside the office disconcerted her. She was sitting on a stool at the bar which happened to be next to his, and as she ordered a drink he turned to her and said quietly, but vehemently, 'I hate seeing women sitting up at the bar.'

Astonished, she replied, 'But you are doing it!'

'That's different,' he replied.

'Why?' she flashed. 'What's the difference? I can't see it.'

He stared at her steadily, without answering — and, to her horror, she blushed. She was aware that his fair hair had red lights in it, and that he had hair on the back of his beautifully manicured hands ... She left the bar stool hurriedly and went and sat at a table with some colleagues.

During the next few months she waited for him to speak to her again at the pub, but he ignored her; gradually this concentrated her attention on him. She found herself thinking of him nearly all the time, especially in the evenings at home, when she would shut her eyes and try to see his face in her mind's eye — the small well-shaped mouth, the steady grey eyes, the way he flicked his fingers when he was deep in thought, and the way he rubbed the side of his nose with his forefinger before giving a difficult judgement about an item for the paper. She imagined him smiling at her, and perhaps even complimenting her on her looks; dining with her at a candle-lit restaurant, deep in happy discussion; or driving with her to her beloved moors in his smart white sports car, and picnicking in the sunshine. She knew she was behaving like a lovesick schoolgirl, and was fully aware that her fantasies accorded ill with her militantly feminist views; but she allowed herself to indulge in them for the pleasure they gave her — not least because they were heterosexual.

He seemed to take as little notice of the other girls as he did of her; so, cautiously, she tried to find out a little more about him.

'Is he married?' she asked Pauline.

'Yes. Didn't you know?' Pauline was surprised.

'No. What's she like?'

'I've no idea. None of us has seen her.'

'Does he ever talk about her?'

'Not if he can help it.'

'Or ask anyone to their house?'

'Not that I know of.'

'How old is he?'

'Just about old enough to be your father,' answered Pauline brusquely.

This gave Laura a shock, but did nothing to lessen the attraction — the reverse, in fact, since she could now combine fantasies of him with fantasies of her dead father as well.

'Has he got children?' she asked Pauline another time.

'Two, I think.'

'Boys or girls?'

'Girls.'

She tried to find out more, but Pauline laughed, and said, 'Why do you want to know? You fancy him?'

Laura was flustered. 'Of course not!'

Pauline laughed again, but this time sarcastically.

Now that she knew he was married with a family, Laura tried to picture his home life. She wondered what was his wife like — blonde and beautiful? small and dark? a redhead? sophisticated? domesticated? clever? silly? And the daughters — how old were they? Were they a happy family?

As the months went by and he still took no notice of her except to discuss her work when she handed in her copy, Laura became almost desperate for his attention. She tried lingering sociably after the discussion was over; but he would have none of it. He made it quite plain that, though he admired her work, appreciated her good brain and found talking with her about the paper enjoyable, as a *woman* — or indeed even as a human being — he was totally uninterested in her.

She tried shock tactics.

'Sometimes I lose my nerve about doing the Women's Page,' she said. 'After all, as you may have noticed, I'm not a very feminine sort of person, am I?'

'Aren't you?'

'Did you think I was?' she asked him defiantly.

'I'm afraid I didn't think about it at all,' he replied, smiling.

She altered her hair style, started wearing a little make-up, took more care how she dressed; which didn't go unnoticed by Pauline, but appeared to escape Tom's attention altogether. In the hopes of getting some reaction she struck up a mild flirtation with young Fred Rayner, the *Messenger*'s arts critic — but this back-fired as he became very fond of her, and she realised that she was capable of hurting him. Tom still remained oblivious.

One lunchtime, she decided to take the bull by the horns. She went over to him when he was alone at a table and sat beside him.

'I hope you don't mind,' she said, 'but I felt it was time we got to know each other better. I've been here nine months now, and we've hardly said a word to each other outside the office.'

'That's right,' he replied laconically.

'I thought it might interest you to know that I edited a paper at Oxford. It was quite a success. It was called *Eve's Tree* — and it was very feminist!' She persisted in flaunting her feminism, to give her an alibi in case he rejected her.

'Oh?' he said, uninvitingly.

'... Didn't they tell you when I came?' she faltered.

'Who?'

'Anyone?' She was losing her nerve.

'No. Why should they?'

'Didn't *I* tell you?'

He grinned. 'Certainly not!'

'Pauline seemed interested at my interview with her. I assumed that's what clinched my job here.'

'Could be.' He shrugged his shoulders. 'It's what you do on the *Messenger* that interests me.'

Another day she stopped him in the corridor. 'I hear your dog has died,' she said awkwardly.

'Yes.'

'How awful for you.'

'Yes.'

'Were you very fond of it?'

'Yes.'

'What kind was it?'

'A mongrel — terrier and collie, I should think.'

'I've heard of a puppy that needs a home. Would you like it?'

'No thanks.'

And that was all.

She began to lose weight, and her work suffered. She decided to ask Bess for help; but her mother was just finishing a tour with Christopher, so Laura could only reach her by telephone and this inhibited her from discussing her problem. She telephoned nearly every night after the show, however, and this was so unlike her that Bess was worried.

'Are you all right, darling?' she asked anxiously.

'Fine,' lied Laura. 'Just suddenly homesick, that's all.'

'Could you get away for a day or two, and join us?'

'Not a hope,' said Laura, who, though she was bewildered and unhappy, had no intention of missing a single opportunity of seeing Tom.

'Not even for a weekend? We always try to get home on the Sunday.'

'Well, I might do that,' said Laura, immediately comforted. 'It would be lovely.'

'It certainly would,' agreed Bess enthusiastically. 'You're *sure* you're OK?'

'Certain.'

'You eating enough?'

Laura laughed. 'Yes, plenty.'

'And still enjoying your work?'

'Very much.'

'Well remember we want to see you any time, as always.'

'Thanks, Mum.'

In spite of the telephone calls, though, Laura became more and more miserable. She ceased to care about her nearly finished novel, and was in two minds about changing her job. She had no idea what to do next, and was under the additional handicap that she knew very little about men, since she had had so little to do with them.

One day she burst into tears in Tom's office. She searched for a handkerchief and couldn't find one.

'Here, take this,' he said kindly, offering her is own.

'Thank you. I'm terribly sorry.'

'Think nothing of it.'

'I don't know what's the matter.'

He looked at her thoughtfully, then said slowly, 'Come and have a drink with me after we've finished this morning.'

She could hardly believe her ears, and the shock of pleasure was so great that it made her cry again. He patted her gently. 'Tell me about it later,' he said. 'Mop up now.'

'I'm sorry,' she repeated, helplessly.

'Yes. Well, run along. And keep the hankie.'

'Thank you.'

She went out of the room as fast as she could, with her heart beating so hard with happiness that she felt that everyone must be conscious of it. She locked herself in the bathroom, washed her face and looked at herself in the mirror: as usual, she disliked what she saw. She went back to her office and tried to work until lunchtime but found it impossible. She didn't know where she was meant to meet him; so, when the time came, she went to his office, but he had already left. Anxiously she ran to the pub, and found him standing with a gang of male colleagues. He waved to her when he saw her and asked her what she wanted to drink.

'A beer, please,' she said, and thought she saw him frown. He said nothing, however, but gave her order, then piloted her to a table in the corner, watched with amusement by Pauline.

'Cheers,' he said, when he sat down.

'Cheers,' she answered faintly.

'Feeling better?'

'Yes, thank you. I've got your hankie, but wondered if you'd rather I had it washed first.'

He laughed. 'Don't bother.'

'It was silly of me not to bring one.'

'Perhaps you didn't know you'd need it,' he said, mocking her gently.

She looked at him sharply. 'No,' she replied.

He grinned. 'Well? D'you want to tell me what's the matter?'

She hesitated. 'I was just being silly.'

'We're all silly sometimes,' he said, and his voice was surprisingly kind.

'I suppose so.'

'Well?'

She started to speak, thought better of it, and stopped. 'It was nothing. Really. Something private. Nothing important at all.'

'I hate seeing people cry.'

'That's kind.'

She longed to tell him what was on her mind, but knew it to be impossible. So they talked banalities. Finally he said, 'Where do you live?'

She told him. 'Where do you?' she asked.

'Quite a way out.' He changed the subject. 'Do you really enjoy drinking beer?'

'Yes, I do.'

'It's not just a demonstration?'

'Of what?'

'That you can drink a beer as well as any man?'

'Well, can't I?'

'Yes.' He looked at her thoughtfully.

She flushed. 'I just hate this inequality between the sexes. It's unfair, and stupid and degrading for women.'

'Yes,' he said. He lit his pipe, with maddening deliberation.

'Don't you agree that women get a raw deal as compared with men?' asked Laura.

'In some ways. In some ways they get a better deal. Anyway, nothing can change the fact that men and women are different physically, so I can't see the use of moaning about it. And I can't say I'm sorry, either. I like women to be women, not half-baked imitations of men, and since a great many of them have to cope with child-bearing — and, more important still to my mind, bringing up the children — I can't see that they can hope to compete with men on equal terms. Few career women I have met are good at keeping their families happy too.'

'My mother is,' said Laura, and she was immediately surprised at herself for acknowledging Bess so generously.

'Ah yes,' said Tom. 'Your famous mother!' He sounded mocking again. 'I thought she might have been your problem.'

'What problem?'

'Skip it.'

'When you say few career women are good at keeping their families happy, I presume you mean just the men?'

'Not necessarily,' said Tom. 'But in my view more women depend on men for their happiness than the other way round, so by keeping men happy they are really contributing to their own happiness.' He puffed the pipe. His views were disappointingly conventional and unimaginative.

'Do you know you are talking like a male chauvinist pig?' she asked, trying to keep her voice light.

He grinned again lazily. 'Ever been to bed with one?' he asked.

She went scarlet, and he laughed again. 'You're not so hot on the subject of sex, are you?' he said. 'But your politics I agree with.'

'You don't know anything about my politics!' returned Laura, surprised. 'I never discuss them.'

'Be your age. People's politics are the kind of people they are, like their clothes,' he retorted. 'Now drink up, or we won't have time for lunch. I wish we could lunch together, but today is a busy day and I've brought sandwiches to eat in the office.'

She was dismayed, but did her best not to show it. When he had left, she ordered herself a salad and thought over her conversation with him — with mixed feelings. He had noticed her, and he had asked her for a drink; but he seemed to have divined that she was homosexual (or at least bisexual). So where did that leave her?

Nowhere it seemed, since once again he ignored her existence.

Several weeks later there was a ring at the front-door bell one Sunday morning — and there he was.

Laura was in her dressing gown and nightdress, and totally astounded to see him. 'Good heavens! It's you!' she exclaimed in confusion.

'It is I,' he replied, cheerfully.

'I'm so sorry. I'm not dressed!'

'So I see.'

'Did you want something?'

'May I come in?'

'Of course.' Again she was confused.

She led the way into her living room, and he looked around him with some curiosity. 'These your things?' he asked.

'No. They came with the flat.'

'I'm glad. They're pretty ghastly, aren't they?'

'I told you I wasn't domesticated. Can I make you some coffee?'

'Why not?'

'Have you had breakfast?'

'Certainly. It's ten o'clock.'

'I was lying in, I'm afraid.'

'So I gather.'

'Is anything wrong at the office?'

'Not that I know of.'

'You didn't come to see me about work?'

'No.'

'Then may I ask why you're here?'

'It's a lovely day.'

'Yes. Spring.'

'Yes. Spring.'

'So?'

'So I wondered if you'd spend the day with me.'

Laura's mouth went dry with excitement, and she found it hard to speak. 'I'd love to,' she stammered.

'Good.'

'I'll get that coffee, then get dressed.'

'But do,' he said, with a flourish.

She flushed. 'Won't your wife mind?' she asked.

'I've no idea.'

'You mean she doesn't know you're here?'

'No.'

'Oh.'

'Are you glad I came?'

'Oh, yes.'

'Oh, yes!' he mimicked. 'Remember what I asked you the other day?'

'The other day?' she echoed.

'I asked you if you had ever been to bed with a male chauvinist pig. I don't remember your answer.'

'I don't think I gave one.'

'I want one now.'

She hung her head. 'No,' she said quietly. 'I haven't.'

'Or kissed one?'

'No.'

'I thought as much.' He looked at her reflectively. 'Come here,' he said.

She moved towards him anxiously.

'Kiss me.'

She drew back nervously.

'Come on,' he said impatiently.

She shut her eyes, and turned her face up to his.

He put an arm round her and kissed her hard. She struggled wildly, then went limp. He went on kissing her and soon she started kissing him in return; tentatively at first, then passionately. He released her.

He nodded. 'I thought so,' he said. 'Take those things off.'

'What things?'

'Your clothes.'

'Now?'

'Now.'

'I'll go next door,' she said self-consciously.

'Don't be a fool!' he answered curtly. 'Take them off.'

'I thought you wanted us to go on a picnic,' she said feebly.

'Take them off,' he replied. 'Hurry up!'

Almost paralysed with shame, she started fumbling with the cord of her dressing gown, while he watched her impassively. She slipped the gown off her shoulders, and stood there in her night-dress.

'Christ!' he exclaimed. 'I thought that kind of garment went out with Queen Victoria!'

She looked at him, nervously. 'What are you waiting for?' he asked. 'Don't you want to? I thought you were making a play for me, for God's sake!'

'No,' she said unhappily. 'I like you, that's all.'

'I see,' he said. He smiled. 'Well, get that coffee, and get dressed. It will take about an hour to reach the place we're going, on the moors.'

Laura put on her dressing gown again, and hurried into the kitchen. Tom wandered around the room, examining everything in detail; then he heard her go into the bedroom and followed her. He watched her dress in silence, drank the coffee she provided, led her outside and tucked her into the car.

He hardly spoke on the journey, and she scarcely noticed. Wildly happy to be with him one moment, the next she was plunged into uncertainty and desolation. She had wanted him for months. Now it seemed he wanted her — and she had said 'No!' Had she missed her only chance with him? To be nearly twenty-four and so gauche was ridiculous. And she had always prided herself on her brains! At least he hadn't slammed out of the house when she refused. That must be on the credit side. And so too was this wonderful, wonderful day as they climbed towards the moors.

He drove well, and as they passed through the twisting lanes in the valleys she noticed that the hedges were turning green. Spring was certainly in the air, and several times Tom hummed little snatches of tune. Once, he grinned as though remembering a private joke. When they reached the chosen spot, he politely helped her out of the car then, taking her arm in his, strode out for a walk. She could hardly keep up with him, but was too muddled with emotion to protest. At length he headed back for the car, opened the boot and took out the lunch.

They picnicked as she had dreamed they would, but the reality was very different. Instead of the profound and interesting conversation she had imagined, he ate in his usual silence. Once, trying to get a conversation going, she said, 'I love it here! What a wonderful view!' And he replied, 'Oh Christ! Don't exclaim about views! I loathe it!'

'I have as much right to talk, as you have to remain silent!' she replied with some spirit.

'Certainly,' he said, 'if you don't mind boring me.'

'How do you know you don't bore *me* with your eternal silences?' demanded Laura.

'I don't,' said Tom, 'but I don't care.'

'Do you think I do?'

'I know it.'

'You like your own way, don't you?'

'Yes, I do.'

'Do you always get it?'

'If I don't, I don't hang around,' he said simply. There was a long pause, then he went on, 'Have you ever thought of leaving the *Messenger*?'

She was startled. 'Why?' she asked.

'Your stuff is good. You should move on.'

'Thank you.' She felt depressed.

'Don't you want to?'

'Not just now.'

'Why?'

'I like it here.'

'Because of me?'

'Yes.'

He dropped a kiss lightly on her nose. 'You surprise me!' he teased. 'Where has all that ambition of yours gone to?'

'Ambition isn't everything.'

'Indeed it isn't.'

'I love you, Tom.'

'Gratified, I'm sure,' he said.

'Don't make fun of me. I mean it.' He didn't reply. She found herself blushing again, but forced herself to speak. 'Tom, will I do?'

'For what?'

'For you.'

'Oh God,' he said, 'deliver me from feminists! Come on, let's go.'

'Where to?'

'Your place,' he answered. But when they reached it, he refused to come in.

And, once again, at work he took no notice of her.

CHAPTER SEVEN

Laura went home. This time her depression was so great that she felt on the edge of a breakdown. Gerald had helped her before, when she had been in trouble at Oxford: perhaps he would help her again? Unfortunately, Walter took an instant dislike to her, and she to him; and this naturally affected Gerald, who therefore had no wish to indulge in confidences. She tried to tell him about Tom, but his replies were flippant and unconstructive; and, after only the briefest of discussions, he said, 'Don't bother with him, dear. He's not worth it.'

'But I love him.'

'We all love the wrong people sometimes. That's life,' he said.

Frustrated, she asked her mother for advice.

Bess was flattered and touched, but she was also cautious. She longed to be of use but respected Laura's passionate wish for independence. 'No-one really wants advice,' she said carefully. 'They only want their own views approved of.'

'I want advice.'

'I'll try to help,' said Bess. But when she heard what Laura had to say, she looked doubtful. 'He sounds the very last man on earth you should choose to fall in love with darling.'

'You don't choose whom you fall in love with, Mother!'

'But he's married with two daughters!' protested Bess. 'You don't want to break up someone's marriage, do you?'

'I'm hardly likely to do that, since most of the time I've known him he doesn't seem to realise I exist!' said Laura.

'He's noticed you enough to give you a drink at the pub, and to take you picnicking all day,' replied Bess — instinctively taking the side of Tom's wife, after her experience with Virginia Merry. 'But he's far too old for you to marry.'

'I'm not asking your advice as to whether to marry him or not,' said Laura. 'I want to know what to do about my feelings for him.'

'Get out, darling! Get another job!'

'I'm doing very well in this one, and I enjoy it.'

'Your feelings for him don't seem to make you very happy,' said Bess calmly. 'You said you cry a lot. And I have a theory, in which I firmly believe, that, if one feels unhappy when one first falls in love, then the relationship which follows is always disastrous.'

'You don't seem to understand me, Mother!'

'Yes, I do,' replied Bess, firmly. 'Perfectly. You're in love with a married man who is old enough to be your father, and you're desperately unhappy because he doesn't fall for you.'

This was so indisputably true that Laura could think of no reply.

That evening, Bess repeated the conversation to Christopher. 'At least she's fallen for a man at last,' she said, 'though he's obviously most unsuitable.

'Don't worry too much, old girl,' answered Christopher comfortably. 'At the very worst he's restored her to some sort of normality.'

'He's too old — and he's married.'

'I don't see that . . . ' Christopher stopped.

'Yes?' prompted Bess, dangerously.

After only the slightest hesitation, Christopher continued smoothly, 'I think I was going to say that Laura will go her own way in the end, whatever we say, and this particular experience may do her good.'

'What about his wife?' demanded Bess. 'Poor thing! Laura has youth, and that wins all along the line!'

'Not all along, Bess,' said Christopher, gently.

'I wish she wasn't so extreme in her emotions,' sighed Bess.

'She's silly to tangle with him,' said Christopher. 'But proximity makes one do a lot of silly things, as you know, my darling.' He came over and kissed her, and Bess nodded understandingly.

Laura went back to her job, and Tom seemed delighted.

'Hey!' he exclaimed when he saw her. 'I've missed you! Where have you been?'

'Home,' she said.

'You all right? Not ill, or anything?'

'Fine.'

'Doing anything on Sunday?'

'Nothing.'

'Care to spend the day with me?'

'I'd love it. Shall I get the food ready this time?'

'Yes. We won't go out. We'll spend the day at your place, shall we? You can cook, I take it?'

'Yes.'

'You any good?'

'Surprisingly, yes.'

'Why surprisingly? You're a very clever girl.'

Absurdly gratified by his praise, and ecstatically happy at the thought of Sunday, she only murmured, 'It's only that, as I told you, I'm not domesticated.'

'Not to worry,' he said. 'You will be when I've finished with you.'

'Finished with me? What does that mean?'

'Wait and see,' he answered firmly.

Sunday when it came was the usual mixture of surprises, joy and anxiety. Tom had said he would be with her at midday, but he turned up at ten. 'I didn't want to waste so much time,' he said. 'D'you mind?'

'Of course not.'

'What's for lunch?'

'Roast beef, Yorkshire pudding and treacle tart.'

'My favourite meal,' he said. 'Now for bed!'

'For bed?' she asked astonished.

'Yes. You've got to face it some time.' He grinned.

'But I'm in the middle of cooking!'

'Is anything likely to spoil for a while?'

'I suppose not.'

'Then come along.'

'But...'

'But what?'

'I don't know.'

'Quite right,' said Tom softly. 'Look, love, let's get this straight. In all relationships we are only given just so much time — sometimes an hour, sometimes a year, sometimes a lifetime — and we've got to use that time to the best advantage. You and I have got a physical thing going for us . Either we have an affair, or we don't. Which is it to be?'

'Do you love me?'

'Enough to have an affair with you. I dislike argument, I won't tolerate rows or scenes, I despise jealousy and I like comfort. I like you, and for some reason you attract me. But I'm not in love with you, and all I want is a good time and my creature comforts. You try any tricks and we're through at once. Understand?'

'Yes I do,' she said, remembering her feeling about Stevie.

He looked surprised. 'Good!' he said. 'Then what is it to be?'

'An affair,' she said, anxiously.

'You might get hurt,' he said kindly.

'So might you,' she replied.

He grinned again. 'Get to bed and wait for me,' he said.

She waited a long time, and when he came he was looking pleased with himself. 'I've been into the kitchen,' he said, 'and everything is OK.'

He took off his clothes and she saw that he had a beautiful body. He was the first man she had seen naked, and she felt shy. She drew the bedclothes up around her, and he pulled them away.

'Relax, my dear,' he said gently. 'Relax.'

CHAPTER EIGHT

Three months later, Tom moved in to live with her. He drove her back from work one evening and, when they reached her door, humped a suitcase out of the car. All he said was 'I hope you've got enough food for two.' He was looking unhappy, but she knew better than to ask questions.

'I've left home.'

'For good?'

He ignored this. 'And after dinner you can unpack for me.'

'You're staying with me then?'

'What does it look like?' he asked.

'What about your wife?'

'What about her?'

'Nothing,' she answered hastily.

'You said you loved me, Laura?'

'You know I do.'

'Yes, well go and get that dinner. I'm starving.'

Utterly astounded, but extrèmely happy, Laura went into the kitchen to cook.

She had no idea how her landlady would react to Tom's move, but Tom talked to her the next morning and, surprisingly, she was amenable. In fact, he had charmed her to such an extent that she said, with uncharacteristic emotion, 'Yon's a gradely man, Laura. Thee be a lucky lass. I could fancy 'im mesel.'

Over the next few weeks Laura found out a lot more about him. To her surprise he claimed to have been a demonstrative little boy who craved affection; but he'd been the youngest of six children in a very poor family, with a mother who was too overworked and harassed, and too broken in spirit, to be able to give him the love he needed. His father never kept down a job because he drank, and their home was an ill-lit slum with damp walls, rotting floor-boards and an outside lavatory. Eventually it had become a habit with him, as well as a self-protection, to hide his feelings. His wife was a sexual slut, and had left him some years before for another

279

man, taking the children. He hated talking about her, and had
trusted no woman since. She now lived with yet another man, and
he never saw her; though his children, when they were growing up,
had been allowed to see him once a month. He adored them both,
and they were only a few years younger than Laura. One of them
was now engaged to be married; the other was a nurse in London,
at St Thomas's Hospital. Tom had served as a sergeant in the
Middle East, but he seldom talked about the war, and seemed to
have no wish to see the two friends he had made in the army. 'We
had things in common then. We'd have nothing in common now,'
he said.

He was a wonderful lover, passionate and expert; and physically she was totally obsessed. He wasn't an easy man to live with,
being selfish and often silent, but Laura could see a softer side to
him now, and he could be surprisingly considerate if she was
unwell. Although he would never wash up, he seemed happy to
share the cooking, at which he excelled; he was also extremely
tidy, and fastidious about his clothes. His most dangerous attribute
was a temper far more ungovernable than Laura's own, its
outbursts usually preceded by days of moody silence. The moods
seemed to come on for no reason; but if Laura herself was
responsible his rages were terrifying, and more than once he had
given her a black eye. She never learnt if his temper had driven
away his wife; in fact she found it wisest to keep her mouth shut
about anything to do with his life before they had met, unless he
himself raised the subject.

Any sign of jealousy on her part he found intolerable. 'I won't be
made a captive,' he said violently. 'I must have freedom. If I don't,
I'll get claustrophobia, and I'll be off.' This was so like her usual
self that she understood it well.

But understanding was one thing. Controlling her possessive-
ness another. Inevitably she was oversensitive to his criticism, too,
and this always drew his fire. 'Self-pity is out,' he would say, 'so
don't try that sort of blackmail with me.' Often, when she was by
herself she would find herself in tears, and would remember her
mother's dictum that unhappy love affairs signalled themselves in
advance. But she knew that she could never leave him. She knew
that, for her — physically — he was everything she needed.

He never told her he loved her, and if she asked him he became
restive. Persistence could lead to one of the moody silences she had
learned to dread. He refused to take her fully into his confidence,

and would sometimes leave the flat for days without telling her where he was going — or if he would return. She knew that, although he never looked at other women at the office, he wasn't faithful to her; but whether the women to whom he went were pick-ups, or whether he still saw a partially discarded mistress, she had no idea.

He seldom discussed work at home, though once he said, 'I shan't leave the *Messenger* ever, unless I'm sacked. I have no further ambitions. I like being a big frog in a little pond. That doesn't mean, though, that you have to stay.'

'But you're worthy of so much more!' she expostulated.

This made him laugh, and became a sort of catchword with him.

Several times Laura returned to the subject, hoping to get him to change his mind. She hated the idea that she would have to stay in the same place, in the same job, for the rest of her life if she remained with him.

'The *Messenger* is a Conservative paper!' she said. 'You're a Socialist. What price your politics?'

'A Conservative paper is just the place for a Socialist journalist. Look at Michael Foot and Beaverbrook.'

'It seems almost dishonest!'

'But quite effective — like the Trojan horse. Anyway, you're doing exactly the same.'

'My job isn't as important as yours. Besides I'm only staying because of you.'

'You're neglecting your talent you know — not that I'm complaining — but it makes your dishonesty worse than mine. I've changed my beliefs. You've ratted on all yours, and as long as I'm around you'll go on doing so!'

In spite of their bickering they got along fairly satisfactorily until one day, to her horror, Laura found that she was pregnant.

'Oh, my God!' she exclaimed. 'I don't want a baby! Not like this! Besides I'm not good with children! What shall I do?'

'Get an abortion,' said Tom abruptly.

Laura was shocked and angry. 'What a thing to say!' she sobbed.

'Isn't that what you wanted me to say?'

'Don't you care about your child?' she demanded.

'I can't say that I do,' replied Tom. 'Certainly not yet. I

already have two daughters, remember, so I have already obtained that particular form of immortality.'

'How *can* you talk of it like that — and anyway, what about *me*?'

'I've told you,' answered Tom. 'If you don't want the little bastard, get rid of it while there's time.'

'Talking of little bastards...' returned Laura hotly.

'Ah,' replied Tom. 'I was wondering when that was coming.'

'If I keep him, will you marry me?'

'Certainly not.'

'But you could get a divorce!'

'I don't choose to.'

'Then, as I said, what about me?'

'You knew what you were letting yourself in for.'

'And what about the baby?'

'I'm not marrying you, Laura, and that's flat.'

'It's not fair on him.'

'Who says it will be a boy?'

'Don't you mind that your own child will be a bastard?'

'Not at all. Lots of babies are bastards.'

'You may give him a terrible psychological hang-up.'

'You weren't a bastard, and look what happened to you.'

'Oh you're impossible! Anyway, he might grow up hating us for it.'

'He or she, surely,' he corrected her cheerfully. 'You can't insure against hate, but if we're sensible we might well escape it. Spoilt children nearly always hate the parents who spoil them — and we certainly shan't spoil our brat. Children of the famous get hang-ups — look at you — but neither you nor I are going to be famous. My belief is that if the child has the right sort of nature, nothing warps it. If it's egotistical, anything will. It must take its chance like the rest of us. We have our lives to live, too.'

Laura decided not to argue further. At this point she had no maternal instinct, and the idea of childbirth frightened her since she was a coward about pain. She also disliked the idea of giving up her job, which she knew she would have to do, if only for a time. But she didn't want an abortion. She wrote and told Bess, who, since she was between jobs, at once suggested coming North to see her.

She arrived the following week, and met Tom for the first time. Both immediately felt antagonistic. Tom disliked Bess for being famous, middle-class and forceful. He also quite genuinely believed that she hadn't done her best for Laura. He objected to her habit of calling everybody darling, her frivolity about serious matters and her too evident aversion to him. She found him boorish, selfish and uneducated.

Quite apart from the question of the baby, she wished with all her heart that Laura had found someone more suited to her — someone kinder, more responsive and more warm-hearted. Her visit was an unmitigated disaster, and her attempt to make Tom shoulder his responsibilities about the child and marry Laura (since that was what Laura wanted), was a total failure. She became angry, which made matters worse, and neither deferred to him as a man nor attempted to meet him half way. She started straight in with what she had to say, and Tom puffed his pipe at her throughout the conversation. He knew what he wanted and had no intention of being deflected.

'Laura tells me that there is no bar to your divorce and that you and she could be married quite easily, and yet you refuse!' said Bess.

'I don't want to marry Laura, or anyone else,' replied Tom.

'You don't mind your child being illegitimate?'

'I've already had all this out with Laura. No, I don't mind it being illegitimate.'

'You realise that you may be ruining its life?'

'I doubt it.'

'Illegitimate children are always looking for security, they tell me.'

'Aren't we all?'

'And you don't care about Laura?'

'Strangely enough I do.'

'But not enough to make her happy in this respect?'

'That's right.'

'Can you give me one good reason?' asked Bess.

'I have already given you the excellent reason that I don't want to. Marriage doesn't suit me. I know. I've tried.'

Bess shook her head in exasperation. 'I'm afraid I don't understand you, at all, Tom.'

'Nor I, you, Bess.'

She was annoyed by the use of her Christian name, and he saw it and enjoyed it. She persevered gamely. 'What I meant was, that if your first marriage goes wrong, your second needn't necessarily fail.'

'Oh, I think so. Given my temperament.'

She tried another tack. 'Perhaps it hasn't occurred to you to consider my feelings in the matter?'

'No, it hasn't.'

'I naturally want my grandchild to have every advantage possible.'

'I'm touched,' said Tom. 'I had no idea that you would consider me such a suitable candidate for your only daughter's hand in marriage.'

She knew he was mocking her, but she went on. 'I think it's more than natural that I should wish my grandchild to bear his father's name, don't you?'

'He or she will have yours,' replied Tom. 'Surely that is enough?'

'Do you intend to stick by Laura and the child?' demanded Bess.

'Stick by them?'

'If for instance, you find the child troublesome, you wouldn't think of leaving Laura to cope on her own?'

'I feel quite free to do what I like. Quite free.'

'Then the child would be fatherless as well as illegitimate.'

'Good gracious me, so he would!'

'Not much fun for him.'

'Surely you must have read somewhere that life is not all fun, Bess?' Tom suddenly sounded grim. 'It is interesting sometimes, boring sometimes, hilarious sometimes and tragic sometimes. It is too hard for some, and too easy for others — but *fun?*' Here he looked Bess full in the face. 'Oh, Bess! Fun?'

'You're an exceptionally silly man,' said Bess contemptuously. 'No wonder your marriage failed! But in one respect you're right. Laura is far better off not being married to you, and the child is lucky that it will bear our name and not yours!' Angrily she wished him at the other end of the universe. She hoped with all her strength that she could persuade Laura to leave him.

Tom was taken aback by the strength of her attack but, typically, he admired her for it. 'Now, now!' he said. 'Take it easy, old girl! I have as much right to live my life the way I want to as you or Laura have. Until I shacked up with her, Laura went on and on about independence until she sounded like a progressive politician from an emergent nation. How was I to know she'd change so completely when she fell in love? A false prospectus, I call it! And I liked the other Laura better. I admire a bit of spirit.

She's a clever kid, and a beauty in her way — but *boy* she's a clinger, and I prefer them cool!'

'I shall be leaving here tomorrow,' said Bess furiously. 'What my daughter sees in you, I don't know, but then she has never grown up and perhaps she never will!'

She stormed out of the room, and went to find Laura. 'He's impossible!' she exclaimed. 'I warned you about him.'

'He's the man I love.'

'*Love*!'

'Yes, love. And love is very important to me. I haven't had very much of it so far.'

'Don't whine!' said Bess. 'Self-pity is a bore.'

Laura looked hurt. 'Was I whining?' she asked. 'I'm sorry.'

'You're so full of reproaches, Laura! You're always blaming me for not loving you enough, but you never ask yourself if you've been possible to love — oh dear, I didn't mean that!'

'Does one have to *deserve* one's own mother's love?'

'A mother's love is pretty powerful darling, but we can do with a bit of help,' replied Bess strongly. 'After some of the things you've done, it's a miracle I've loved you as much as I have.

'What does that mean?' flashed Laura.

'When you were little, I actually found you trying to strangle your brother!' answered Bess, tight-lipped. 'You were so jealous of him that you were actually trying to kill him! Imagine it!'

'Had I no cause to be jealous?'

'What does that mean?' demanded Bess, but she felt guilty at once.

'You've always loved Peter so much better than me,' said Laura. 'Besides I was only a child.'

'So you remember?'

'Yes. And I've always been deeply ashamed.'

'Then perhaps, instead of eternally blaming me, you can see that you yourself should share some of the responsibility?' Bess spoke less gently than she would have wished, in self-defence.

'I never thought of it like that,' said Laura miserably.

'Then start,' said Bess.

'Do you love me, Mother?' asked Laura quietly.

'Yes, I do. I love you very much. But I don't find you easy to cope with, and this man of yours is quite detestable. He is as self-pitying as you in his own way. Perhaps that is what you have in common! For heaven's sake, darling, I want you to be happy. And with Tom you will never be — or not for long. Leave him, darling! The baby will be better off in a happy home. Come back with me, and we'll look after it. Anyway, Tom says he's not going to marry you, neither for your sake nor for the child's. Certainly not for mine. And now that I've come to know him, I'm heartily glad to hear it, and I've told him so.'

'Oh, Mother, you haven't!'

'He could do with a little straight talking about himself,' said Bess angrily.

'You've only seen his worst side, Mother. He's rather marvellous in some ways. Really. I promise.'

'You're the one who's living with him, not me,' said Bess. 'If you can find some good in him, I'm glad.'

'Oh dear!' said Laura. 'He's going to be very angry.' She changed the subject. 'Mother?'

'Yes?'

'Are you sure I was really trying to strangle Peter?'

'Yes, you were.'

'You see, I don't really believe I was. I've been over and over the scene in my mind's eye, all my life, and sometimes I frighten myself silly with it. But there's a part of me that totally repudiates it. I believe I was *acting* it. I swear it! Acting it, as I quite often did — but this time you came in, and your reaction and my own guilt did the rest.'

Bess looked unconvinced.

'I think I'm telling you the truth, Mother. I really do!' said Laura passionately.

'I'm sorry I brought it up,' replied Bess. 'It's all a long long time ago.'

'Please try and believe me, Mother.'

'All right, darling, I will,' said Bess, looking at her daughter very seriously. 'I will, I promise.'

'Thank you, Mother.' Laura was enormously relieved. 'How are Peter and Jane?' she asked, brightening.

'Very happy indeed,' replied Bess. 'Jane is a darling. I couldn't have found a sweeter daughter-in-law, and Belinda Ann is an angel. Peter is getting on so well, Laura. I'm very proud of him.'

'I'm glad,' said Laura, trying to smile. 'Peter always does the right thing.'

Bess looked at her sharply, but said lightly. 'Not always, darling. He didn't get into Oxford, and you did; and he shows no sign of

being a successful novelist, and you do. How's the new one going
by the way?'

'I don't seem to have much time for it just now. What with Tom
and the *Messenger* and the house, and now the baby, my hands
seem to be full.'

'I'm not surprised.' Bess smiled sympathetically. 'But it may be
no bad thing in the end. You may need to do a bit more living
before you write the novel you really want to. Don't worry, I'm
sure you'll do it, one day.'

'Are you?'

'Absolutely.'

'Then will you be proud of me?'

'Of course!' said Bess, and though she felt a slight impatience,
she didn't show it.

Laura hesitated. 'Mother,' she asked tentatively, 'why in
particular don't you like Tom?'

'For one thing, he doesn't like me or my kind. He doesn't seem to
have learnt that if you like someone, they're often more disposed to
like you in return.'

'Well, he has had rather a difficult life.'

'Oh? I gather he thinks mine has been too easy. Though I doubt
if in fact he has ever been hungry, as I have — or had to earn his
living any earlier.'

'His family was very poor.'

'I'm talking about Tom.'

'He did a paper round while he was still at school.'

'He was quite lucky to have his family around him. Or were they
unhappy?'

'All right, I think.'

'And did he help them, when he got on?'

'I have no idea,' said Laura.

'Ask him,' said Bess. 'I'd like to know. If he did, I'll think more of
him, but my guess is that he's one of the great tribe of the
professionally deprived.'

'What on earth is that?'

'A lot of us have been emotionally deprived, darling, and still
more of us have been financially deprived and risen above it; but
people like you and Tom have a vested interest in deprivation,
because without it you couldn't sustain your little vendettas. You
use it to fan the flames of your resentment against the "privileged",
as you call your various enemies. Try and alter your outlook,

darling. It's never too late. And, for Heaven's sake, count your blessings — because, God knows, you've had more than many people! Enjoy life a bit more! I'm all for crusades, but if you're going to help people, do it because it helps *them*, not you.'

Laura sighed. 'Things aren't so slick and easy and on the surface as you make out,' she said.

'Indeed things aren't slick and easy and on the surface!' retorted Bess. 'But Tom seems to think life shouldn't be fun. I disagree. I think fun is as important as everything else.'

'Do you think life through, in depth, Mother?' asked Laura intensely.

'Oh, God!' exclaimed Bess. 'Just listen to yourself! If you want to know if I'm a profound sort of person, ask me just that, and judge my answers! I feel deeply. I try to live my life usefully and fully. But I also keep a great deal of my life as private as I can, because too much of it has been too public for my taste. Most of us have the capacity for a secret life on a much deeper level than we show to the rest of the world. Granville Barker wrote a fascinating play about it called *The Secret Life*, which has never been performed (although Christopher and I had plans to do it once, but it came to nothing). Barker felt, and I feel, that it's the most important part of us and that we're right to keep it secret, because the soul needs space and solitude. You and Tom don't believe in souls, because you reject the unknown. You don't believe in God, because to you He represents the threat of authority. You miss a great deal; and so, to compensate, you wear your good works on your sleeves like so many girl-guide badges. It's juvenile.'

'Juvenile! Perhaps that's what we're missing — happy childhoods!'

'To quote your charming Tom, "don't make me puke,"' said Bess, suddenly angry. 'You and Tom and your trendy friends have to fill the vacuum you live in by making a religion of politics, referring to The Poor and The Starving, The Middle Class and The Privileged in capitals, as though that in itself proved you to be caring people. I don't happen to think it does. I probably do just as much in my own way to help those in need. I say this factually: I do, and willingly, a great deal of charity work. But I can't see the necessity to hate people who don't need my compassion, nor to proclaim the fact that I am providing help.'

Laura looked at her in amazement. 'You have had a very fortunate life, Mother,' she said defensively.

'I have, and I know it, but so have you, and you don't. Besides it hasn't just been good fortune that has brought me where I am. I'm a congenitally hard worker — and, though it may sound boastful to say so, I'm quite a talented actress.'

'Tom is a talented editor.'

'Good! His trouble is that he dislikes himself, yet has a great deal of self-love. It's an unfortunate mixture.'

Laura glanced at her mother sharply. She knew this to be true in her own case as well, and felt guilty. 'How do you know?' she demanded. 'You hardly know him.'

'He isn't very unlike a great many others of his kind,' said Bess. 'So insecure within himself that he fears that he might disintegrate completely if he doesn't pretend to be strong — especially where women are concerned.'

'We shall never agree on things, shall we, Mother?'

'Does it matter? Do you and I have to agree before we can love? Can't we accept each other as we are? And what about this *flat*?'

Laura was bewildered by the change of subject, but replied quickly, 'What about it?'

'Do you like it?'

'It suits us, and it's our home. What's wrong with it?'

'It looks unlived in — tidy, but uncared for.'

'It'll look lived in enough when Junior arrives.' Laura sighed.

'I'm sorry the thought of the child worries you so, darling. It's natural for women to have children.'

'He's bound to change our way of living so much!'

'Have you settled on a son? You always seem to refer to it as *he*.'

'No. I just find myself thinking and wanting it to be one.'

'And you a feminist!' laughed Bess.

Laura flushed. 'I know,' she said. 'So many things have altered. I still think women have a rotten time compared with men, though.'

'They live longer,' said Bess cheerfully.

'I can't think why!' They both laughed.

'I came up here to help, not to lecture you,' said Bess, 'but there's nothing I can really do to help just yet, is there, darling? So I'm going home tomorrow, but I'll come back the moment you need me, unless I'm working. We both have telephones, so you only have to call if you're in trouble.'

'I wish you didn't have to go so soon!'

'Tom doesn't.'

'You might like each other better if you knew each other better,' said Laura. Bess made no reply. 'Give my love to Gerald and Christopher and Susan, won't you? And thank you for coming, Mother. I really do appreciate it.'

Bess was moved. 'Thank you, darling,' she answered quickly. 'Your saying that means quite a lot to me. I just wish you were happier, that's all.'

'I'm OK with Tom.'

Bess nodded. 'That's the main thing,' she said.

The baby was born six months later. They named him Harry. He weighed eight pounds at birth and gave Laura an easy time. He was a contented child; and to her amazement Laura became a doting parent. The maternal instinct that she thought she had lacked emerged from the moment she held him in her arms, and Tom, too, seemed delighted with his son. He was helpful and tender, and spent hours playing with him.

One day he said with passion, 'Laura, if I ever lose my bloody temper with that child, do me a favour and leave me at once, will you? I wouldn't want to hurt him for the world.'

Bess was angry that they had chosen to call the child Harry. 'How dare they choose my grandfather's name, when Tom refuses to give him his own?' she stormed.

'Your grandfather isn't the only male to have been christened Harry,' replied Christopher pacifically.

'Exactly,' said Bess. 'But this child isn't going to be christened at all, poor little thing! And yet they have the nerve to call him Harry! Harry! Not even Henry!'

Peter rang to say that Jane was pregnant again. In time they too, had a son: and they called him Mark.

CHAPTER NINE

Even though Harry changed Laura's life in many ways, he didn't lessen the difficulties she experienced in her affair with Tom, except in the crucial respect that Tom loved his son and, true to his word, never lost his temper with him.

Laura seldom went to the office now — although most of the pieces she wrote for the paper from home were accepted — so her working relationship with Tom nearly ceased. This made their lack of communication on anything but the occasional domestic matter even harder for her. When he came home, he expected his drink to be mixed at once and dinner to follow at a suitable interval. He almost never talked while he was having his drink and, after the meal buried himself in the *Times* crossword or watched television. He expected the flat to be as neat as before, when there had been no child in the place, and Harry to be in bed; and meals to be appetising. If they weren't he complained, though he seldom praised her if they were. As she was temperamentally uninterested in household chores, she found this relentless insistence on domesticity tiresome; and, as Tom hated entertaining, the solitary days and largely silent evenings got on her nerves.

She told him at last, and he said, calmly, 'OK. Say when you want me to move out, and I'll go.'

'I don't want you to go!' exclaimed Laura, astounded and dismayed. 'I only want you to consider me a little more!'

'I clearly stated my terms at the beginning of our affair, which is more than most men do,' replied Tom. 'When they become unacceptable to you, I'll leave.'

'But I'm a person!' retorted Laura angrily. 'Not a cipher!'

'You're my mistress,' he answered.

She still loved him physically; and he certainly responded, though not to the same extent. But there were times when she wondered how long she could stand such a boring and subsidiary role. The other women she met, at the equally boring coffee-mornings she sometimes attended or when out shopping at the supermarket, seemed equally dissatisfied with their men; but with the added frustration, it seemed (if they talked at all intimately), that most of them weren't in love and never had been.

Sometimes, in her desperation, she tried to make out what had attracted Tom to her in the first place. She came to the conclusion that he had guessed that she was highly sexed but without hetero-sexual experience, which had given him the novel and flattering titillation of playing Pygmalion to a virgin Galatea. On the other hand, he also seemed to indicate that he had looked for strength in her and failed to find it. Bess had surprised her by remarking that Tom was a weak man: Laura had mistaken his taciturnity for strength. Had he perhaps mistaken her feminism for strength? If so, both were disillusioned, and this disillusion might one day become extremely important.

At the moment, however, she had no wish to leave him, only to change him, and this — though she tried endlessly, with tact, then entreaty, then anger — she couldn't do. But he was a good and helpful father, and she knew she would be unhappy without him, even if she wasn't particularly happy with him.

She started on her second novel again in earnest, and found that her theme — that of two ill-suited lovers trying to come to terms with themselves and each other — now had new force. The one who loves more is not only more vulnerable, but, by demanding more, becomes also immediately less attractive. With Stevie, it was she who had been strong. With Tom, it was Tom. Her dependence on Tom was partly triggered by a terror of rejection. Perhaps Stevie had suffered the same?

Meanwhile, Harry was a good baby, and, as he developed, an amusing little boy. He was bright and good-tempered and knew exactly how to make his parents laugh; also to get his own way. With him, at least, Laura was totally happy. Bess had told her to count her blessings: Harry was a blessing.

The mood of the sixties, too, appealed to her, as indeed it did to Tom. They approved of the greater sexual freedom. They enjoyed protest and demonstrations. Laura applauded the burning of bras, Tom the discarding of neckties, and both enjoyed the cult of the four-letter word. Bess felt very differently. She thought paper dresses ridiculous, disposable goods 'a wicked waste', the exag-gerated respect for the young unhealthy and absurd, and shoddy workmanship deplorable. Greed and envy and dirt seemed sud-dently to surround her, and drug abuse appalled her. If it were true that Britain was leading the swinging world, then she despised her country for it. When one day she saw three Labour politicians on television gleefully greeting what they called 'the End of the Empire', she believed quite simply that they were traitors.

The grandchildren, however, gave Bess great joy, especially Harry. 'Where he got his brown eyes and sunny nature from I shall never know!' she said wonderingly to Christopher.

'You're sure the dreaded Tom is the only man in Laura's life?' asked Christopher, laughing.

'Sure,' laughed Bess in return.

Oddly enough, despite her feeling that the times were out of joint, towards the end of the decade Bess's career blossomed again, and she was seldom out of work. Christopher too was kept busy. He worked mostly in television; she in the theatre. However, although they retained the loyalty of their public, the theatrical revolution initiated by John Osborne's acclaimed *Look Back in Anger* had made them critically unfashionable — largely because they weren't offered parts in the flood of so-called 'kitchen-sink' plays which followed. The erroneous assumption was made that, as their reputations had been made in a different sort of theatre, they wouldn't — or couldn't — adapt. Ironically, both were excited by the new kind of theatre; they welcomed any new ideas which might revitalise their profession, and had always regretted the drift away from the theatre, in the post-war years, of the young and the less affluent.

Christopher was at this time elected to the Council of Equity; he was to serve on it for many years. His brief, in his eyes, was to keep the union free of politics: he believed that constant political warfare between extremists was a dangerous irrelevance to Equity, whose purpose — simple to describe if difficult to achieve — was to improve the working conditions of its members and not to support or fight the government of the day unless its actions directly affected those conditions. Still less, he believed, had the union the right to espouse political causes. The work was absorbing, frustrating, exhausting and time-consuming, and as Bess now devoted more and more of her time to charitable work as well as spending many months 'on the road', they saw less and less of each other.

Bess was confident that Christopher was now faithful to her, but she disliked being away from him so much; so when she was offered a big starring part in a play in Australia, her instinct was to turn it down. Christopher, however, insisted that she accept. He himself loved travel, and felt that a toe-hold in Australia might come in useful some day: they both still had their gaze firmly fixed on their professional futures. So Bess accepted her Australian engagement after all. Her play was to be performed only in Melbourne and Sydney, but it ran successfully for a year. Although this delighted her, she was worried about such a long absence from home.

The Australian theatre at this time was just beginning to free itself from its dependence on Britain and America and to give long overdue opportunities to indigenous actors and directors (Bess was in fact lucky to have been allowed in by Australian Equity). The many fine old theatres were getting a face-lift and, in the small neighbourhood playhouses, the uneasy blend of amateur and professional was giving way to a purely professional outlook. Bess found the atmosphere invigorating, and a welcome antidote to her frequent attacks of homesickness.

Christopher wrote regularly, as did she to him, but his letters told her very little beyond the fact that 'everyone was all right though they missed her'. Once or twice he wrote more personally. Harry was going to the village school at present, but then to a Comprehensive. He was said to be extremely clever, and Christopher had offered to send him to a prep school at his own expense (Bess smiled at this, remembering how horrified he had been when she had suggested sending Peter to Eton!) but Laura and Tom had refused his help. Peter and Jane were having a third child and Bess would be home in time for its arrival. Belinda Ann was becoming extremely pretty, though she hadn't any brains. Susan was being a damned nuisance, and Walter had had his first play performed on television: it had had very bad notices, but Gerald thought him a genius. Gerald was to go to Italy to work on an epic about the Roman Empire. He dreaded the thought, as he despised that kind of film, but he loved Rome and was to be paid an astronomical sum. Christopher himself had just been offered another television serial, with an exceptionally interesting part. Believe it or not, Virginia Merry was to be in the same series — but Bess was not to worry, as he had met her at the read-through and she had lost her looks and become fat. She was to play Christopher's sister.

The letters were affectionate, but Bess sensed that he was keeping something from her. She longed for the time she could rejoin him.

Christopher wasn't at the airport to meet her, but Peter and

Jane came (Jane looking very pregnant), bringing Belinda Ann and Mark. Belinda Ann was indeed a lovely child, and little Mark, who was as fair as his parents, was no longer a baby. Peter explained Christopher's absence as due to an 'extra rehearsal', but Bess thought he looked ill at ease when making the excuse, and Jane actually blushed.

In the car going back to Regent's Park, Bess questioned them both carefully. She couldn't talk freely as the children were with them, but she did ask obliquely if she had any worries ahead of her. Peter and Jane looked at one another, then Jane said, 'Yes, darling, I'm afraid you might have.'

'What sort?' she asked sharply.

'Margaret has more or less moved in,' said Jane.

'Who?' asked Bess astonished.

'Margaret Bannister. Christopher met her at a party some-where. He's been lonely without you, and she's a good cook. Susan doesn't cook in the evenings.'

'I like Auntie Margaret,' interrupted Belinda Ann in a satisfied voice. 'She is always giving me presents. She gave me a lovely sleeping dolly, and she gave Grand-dad a beautiful clock and a silver cigarette case.'

'Very kind,' murmured Bess, her heart sinking.

Margaret was at the house to greet her. 'How lovely to meet you!' she exclaimed effusively, kissing Bess warmly. 'Christopher has had to go to your agent, so I said I'd be here to see you in. I've got the lunch ready for us all and Christopher says he'll be back by half-past one.'

'Good,' replied Bess impassively.

She looked at Margaret closely. She was about ten years younger than Bess and pretty, in a well-bred horsey way. She wore her clothes well and had beautiful legs. She also had cold eyes and a small, well-lipsticked mouth.

She had arranged flowers everywhere, and the table in the dining room was elaborately set.

'You must be exhausted!' she exclaimed almost as soon as Bess reached the drawing room. 'Why don't you take your things off upstairs, and I'll have a drink ready for you down here?'

Bess resented being treated as a guest in her own home, but replied mildly, 'Thanks. I'll have a dry sherry. On ice.'

'I'm afraid there isn't any on ice,' said Margaret, slightly put out.

'Never mind. I'll have it warm,' said Bess, and she went upstairs. She heard Christopher returning and waited for him to come to her. Then she heard Margaret say, 'She looks dreadfully tired, darling. I should leave her for a moment. I've got her a drink.'

'You're a miracle, Meg!' said Christopher. 'I can't think what we should do without you!'

Bess brushed her hair thoughtfully, repaired her make-up, and walked slowly down the stairs. Christopher was in the hall. Bess thought he looked ill and drawn. He kissed Bess lovingly, and almost, she thought, guiltily; then, with his arm round her, they went into the dining room.

'My, it's good to be back!' said Bess. 'I have missed my family so much, I can't tell you! Travel is all very well, but home is best.'

'I was telling Bess how pleased we all were to see her back,' said Margaret, smiling sweetly at Christopher.

'Yes, indeed!' agreed Jane fervently. She was frowning anxiously, and Peter was looking embarrassed.

Bess carefully praised everything she ate, but, although everyone tried their best to keep the conversation going, there were long silences, and awkward pauses.

After the meal was over, Jane said, 'We've got to go back to Hertfordshire, Mother, darling, but I'll telephone this evening,' and hurriedly collected the children, and departed.

Margaret said winningly, 'I'll do the washing up, Bess. I'm not a bit tired — cooking comes naturally to me — and I'm sure you two have lots to say to one another.'

'Thank you,' said Bess calmly. 'I certainly don't feel like washing up at the moment, and it would be nice to talk to Chris on my own. Please don't stay for our sakes, will you? I'm sure you want to get home. Where is Susan, by the way?'

Margaret laughed, and exchanged an intimate look with Christopher. 'For some reason or other, Susan and I don't get along too well together,' she said, 'and when I told her I'd prepare your homecoming lunch, she took herself off. She says she'll be seeing you at tea time.'

'How very unlike Susan to be rude to a guest!' said Bess innocently.

Christopher flashed a look at Margaret.

'I'll pop into the kitchen,' said Margaret hastily. 'I'd really like to.'

When the door had shut behind her, Christopher said, 'She

really has been a marvel, Bess. She has cooked for me nearly every evening.'

'How sweet!'

'And she has stopped me getting too lonely.'

'Very thoughtful.'

Christopher shifted uncomfortably in his chair. 'Don't start thinking things, will you Bess? There's no need, I assure you.'

'What sort of things?' asked Bess.

'Well for instance that I have been seeing too much of her.'

'Have you?'

Again he looked uncomfortable. 'I tell you, she has been a bloody marvel.'

'Apart from cooking, what precisely has she done?' asked Bess, quietly.

'She's been around,' answered Christopher, simply.

Bess understood. 'Fine,' she said. 'And now let's drop this exquisitely boring subject and talk about more important things. Tell me about your new TV series, and how Harry is and why you aren't looking at all well.'

'I'm fine.'

'You've lost a lot of weight.'

'Have I?'

'Have you seen a doctor?'

'Certainly not. I'm perfectly fit.' He looked cross.

Bess realised that she must go carefully. She had after all been away for a year. She said gently, 'Are you worried about anything, darling?'

'Of course not.'

'You would tell me if you were, wouldn't you?'

'Of course.'

At teatime, Bess had a talk with Susan in the kitchen which really upset her.

'Christopher wants me to leave here,' said Susan tearfully.

'What rubbish, Susan!' exclaimed Bess, astonished. 'That isn't possible after all this time!'

'He calls it retirement, but where should I go?'

'You're not going anywhere,' replied Bess forcefully.

'She's got him by the short hairs,' answered Susan. 'What she says is law around here. You shouldn't ever have left us.'

'Christopher persuaded me to.'

'Men are such fools! Even the nicest of them. Give them dose

after dose of flattery, and not only do they lap it up — and believe
it — but they can't seem to do without the flatterer.'

'Christopher says Margaret has been most helpful,' said
Bess.

'Helpful my foot! She hasn't got a husband of her own. She has
far too much time and money on her hands, she's theatre-mad and
is nothing to do with it, and she's got her eye on this house. You
take care!' Susan wiped her eyes angrily and blew her nose.

'Well she's not going to get me out of here, Susan,' said Bess, 'nor
you either, so mop up and cheer up.'

'This family has been my life!'

'Naturally, since you are one of the family.'

Susan dried her eyes again and smiled. 'It's lovely to see you,'
she said shakily. 'I've missed you so much.'

The following morning Bess went to see Gerald. 'Just how
serious is this situation?' she asked, without preamble.

'You know Christopher,' replied Gerald. 'He's a good-looking
man. The women have always been after him, and they probably
always will be. But basically he's a family man, and a good chap.
He's loyal too, so take heart, Bess. He's not the sort to throw away
so many years of his life, or yours, if he sees a way out.'

'Sees a way out?'

'You've been away a year. Margaret has been here for several
months. She has made Christopher extremely comfortable. She
hasn't a career like you, and she cooks like a first-class chef; and
Christopher has always loved his food. What's more, she is really
after him. He's probably her last chance. If you want my advice,
play it calm. Get a boy friend. How's Neil?'

'Neil?'

'Your old admirer.'

'I hurt him before,' said Bess. 'I couldn't do it again.'

'Right. Then invent one.'

'Invent a boy friend?'

'Why not?'

'It's dishonest!' said Bess.

'You sound like Laura at her worst!' exclaimed Gerald, exasperated. 'Show Christopher you care about him. Besides
their vanity, men are extraordinarily insecure, and they need
constant demonstrations of affection. So do something! Go to a
cordon bleu school of cookery! Have a face lift! Buy some new
clothes!'

Bess smiled. 'OK,' she said. 'I'll try to think of something dynamic.'

'That's my girl.'

Bess looked at Gerald fondly. 'Thank you, darling,' she said. 'You're a doll.'

'Think nothing of it,' he replied.

'How is Walter?' asked Bess.

'He's having a script conference at this very moment. He's had another of his weird plays accepted and he's feeling great.'

'Darling Gerald! I do love you so dearly!'

'And I you,' said Gerald seriously. 'You're the light of my life, Bess, to coin a phrase, and I don't know what I've done to deserve you.'

Bess left him feeling considerably better.

CHAPTER TEN

In the end it was little Harry who saw Margaret off.

Bess had bought herself new clothes, as Gerald had suggested — and changed her hair style, and dieted. She knew she looked good; and they were having a very social time, since Bess's friends were all determined to show her how pleased they were to have her back. None of their invitations included Margaret, and this helped the situation. Spending so much time in each other's company again, and seeing only their own (usually theatrical) friends, none of whom had any interest in Margaret, she and Christopher were inevitably drawn closer together.

Christopher's feelings about Bess and Margaret seemed to see-saw all summer: his habitual affection for Bess was reasserting itself, but Margaret's hold on him was remarkably secure. Then Laura wrote and said that she and Tom needed a holiday without Harry, and could he come to stay in London.

Harry arrived and at once settled himself in as the centre of attention. Margaret immediately recognised him as a threat to her position, and it turned out one evening that she was right.

Harry was having 'grown-up' dinner with them all. He was eating his pudding contentedly, watched fondly by Bess and Christopher and warily by Margaret, when he asked suddenly, 'Is a shack the same thing as a tent?'

'Yes, I suppose so,' said Bess.

'Then where is it?' asked Harry, turning to Margaret.

'Where is what?' she asked.

'Your tent?'

'I haven't got one.'

'Oh, what a pity! I wanted to see it.'

'I don't know what you mean,' said Margaret.

'Daddy says you have shacked up with Grandfather,' said Harry. 'How can you if you haven't got a tent?'

Margaret looked angry, Christopher looked astonished and Bess laughed.

'I don't think your Daddy meant that kind of tent,' said Bess at last.

'You said a shack was the same thing,' replied Harry reasonably, 'and I thought I could come too. I enjoy camping. I wouldn't be a nuisance and I have a smashing penknife.'

'Did you know that you have a pronounced North Country accent?' asked Margaret unpleasantly.

'No, I didn't,' replied Harry cheerfully. 'What is a North Country accent?'

'Can't you hear the difference between the way you speak and the way we all speak?'

'Daddy speaks like me, and so do all the children at my school.'

'What do you want to be when you grow up?' asked Margaret.

'An actor, like Christopher,' said Harry, unhesitatingly.

Christopher looked delighted, and Margaret said contemptuously, 'If you go on talking like that you won't get very far.'

'Why not?' asked Harry.

'You'll have to learn to speak properly,' said Margaret.

'Doesn't Daddy speak properly then?' asked Harry, surprised.

'I suppose as a journalist it doesn't matter,' said Margaret. 'If he wanted to be an actor, it would.'

'Have you told Mummy you want to be an actor?' asked Bess, breaking in hurriedly.

'No.'

'Why not?'

'Because I've only just thought of it,' said Harry placidly.

'You'll probably change your mind,' said Margaret. 'Lots of children think they want to go on the stage but never make it.'

'Why is that?' asked Harry curiously.

'Eat up your pudding,' said Margaret impatiently.

'It's very good,' said Harry. 'If I eat this up, may I have some more?'

'Of course,' said Bess.

'Where do you shack up with Grandfather?' asked Harry returning to the subject enthusiastically.

'Nowhere,' snapped Margaret. 'Your Daddy is talking nonsense.'

Christopher was now looking embarrassed, but Bess was still smiling broadly. Harry frowned. 'I don't think Daddy would like to hear you say that,' he said disapprovingly. 'It's rather rude.'

'Your Daddy has evidently been very rude about me,' returned Margaret.

'Has he?' asked Harry, astonished. 'Is it rude to shack up?'

'Let's get this clear,' said Margaret, really angry now. 'I have not shacked up with your Grandfather.'

'Then someone has been telling a fib,' said Harry.

'If you don't stop this ridiculous conversation, I'll leave the table!' Margaret was red-faced with fury.

'Have you had Grannie's permission?' asked Harry earnestly. 'Or have you bought the place? Mummy says you've taken over.'

'That's enough!' said Margaret. She turned with blazing eyes to Christopher. 'He's an ill-mannered little brat and if he were mine he'd be given a good spanking!' She got up and left the room, slamming the door behind her, and after a moment Christopher followed her. There were sounds of altercation in the hall, then the front door also banged.

Christopher came back to the table. 'You'll have to apologise to Margaret when you next see her,' he said grimly to Harry. 'You seem to have forgotten how to behave! I'm going to see her home, Bess. Don't wait up for me.'

'Now you've done it!' said Bess ruefully, after they'd left.

'Done what?' asked Harry, bewildered. 'What have I done? And why is shacking up rude? I only wanted to see her tent.'

When Christopher returned, very late, he came upstairs to talk to Bess, who was already in bed. 'I'm sorry, Bess, I don't think I quite realised what I've put you through. Margaret had every right to be angry with Harry — although he had no idea what he was saying — but I haven't behaved very well myself, and Harry has brought it home to me. Will you forgive me?'

'Of course.'

'Margaret and I have had the father and mother of all rows.'

'Is it over with her, then?'

'Yes.'

'Poor Christopher! It must have been a horrid day.'

'She stopped me being lonely, as I told you,' said Christopher, 'and I stupidly thought she meant more to me than she did.'

'I understand,' said Bess warmly.

During the next few days, in spite of what he had said to her, she knew that he was seeing Margaret still. She knew also that Margaret was telephoning the house when she was out, because Susan, implacable in her dislike, reported it. But she said nothing.

One evening, Christopher came in looking exhausted but somehow more in tune with himself. He was carrying a tiny parcel, which he handed to Bess. She opened it, to find a diamond-and-sapphire ring.

'D'you like it?' he asked anxiously.

'It's beautiful, darling!'

'D'you remember when we got engaged you wanted one, but I'd already bought you a plain diamond ring? Well, this time you can have your own way, and I hope it's a new start.'

Harry was enchanted with it. 'It's lovely!' he enthused excitedly. 'Where's *my* present?'

'For what?' laughed Christopher.

'Are presents always for a reason?' asked Harry, surprised.

'Always,' said Bess, seriously, 'and tomorrow we're all going out shopping together, and so long as it doesn't break the bank, you can choose whatever you like.'

Christopher smiled at her contentedly.

CHAPTER ELEVEN

Laura finished her novel about the ill-suited lovers and sent it to James and Allen the publishers. She felt reasonably satisfied with it: she had handled the main characters without sentimentality, she thought, and, despite the autobiographical element, had achieved a reasonable detachment .

Having finished the book she was eager to get back to the *Messenger*. In spite of Harry, life had been lonely in the flat, and she missed the discipline of the office. Their landlady had offered herself as a temporary babysitter during the day, on the understanding that Laura would make other arrangements if her novel was accepted.

A month later she had a reply from Geoffrey James, one of the partners in the firm, asking her to meet him in London. He was enthusiastic about the book, and suggested Autumn publication if Laura would tidy up a few loose ends. She happily agreed.

She went to London in high excitement, and over lunch he discussed a contract. He was tall and thin, with thick brown hair and a shy smile. The two of them had an immediate rapport; indeed, Geoffrey was strongly attracted. She had an original mind, he thought, and though she put up a brave front, was an extremely vulnerable woman. She seemed pathetically happy to talk to him, and he immediately divined the autobiographical element in the story: this was nothing unusual for a publisher with a new author but, as the story was a sad one, he felt sorry for her.

'I'm simply starved of any sort of intellectual conversation at home!' she exclaimed; then added happily, 'And I can't tell you how wonderful it is to be having a genuine discussion.' Then, as if suddenly realising that she was being disloyal, she blushed — and Geoffrey thought it charming.

'You shouldn't shut yourself away up there, if that's how you feel,' he said. 'Come to London for a few days, and perhaps we could go to a few shows or have some dinner and meet a few friends.'

'I'd love it,' replied Laura. It was a tonic to be taken seriously after so long, and Geoffrey's obvious interest gave her much needed confidence. She didn't know how Tom would take to the idea, but she knew that she would enjoy it.

The book received rave reviews and climbed into the bestseller lists, where it stayed at number three for several weeks. Laura couldn't believe her luck and experienced a euphoria so intense that present problems and future anxieties were banished from her mind. Soon, though, she discovered that Tom didn't enjoy her success. He loathed playing second fiddle, and disliked very much being proved wrong in his prediction that fame would never come to either of them. Laura thought he was having some sort of joke with her at the beginning, but came to realise that he was in deadly earnest. She couldn't help thinking less of him for it, but her need for him was still profound.

As usual she went home for help.

Bess was appalled. 'How ridiculous!' she said. 'He should be as proud as Punch! I am.'

'He can't help it,' said Laura. 'He has to be top dog. He doesn't even like the book either, so it's doubly upsetting for me.'

'I found it remarkable,' said Bess.

'You liked it?'

'I can't say I liked it, but I found it touching and perceptive.'

'I'm glad.'

'I wish I could help you about Tom,' said Bess, 'but of course I can't. Private troubles need private solutions. You know that you and Harry have always got a home here, though, don't you?'

'Yes. Thank you, Mother. But coming home to you for good would solve nothing.'

'Do you want to leave Tom?'

'No. But I'm sick of living up North. Tom never wants to leave the *Messenger*, and I have wanted us both to leave it for years. I've been offered the post of Features Editor now — but where does that get me? Nowhere! I want to be a writer. I always have wanted to, and this success has shown me I can write. But up North I haven't got the proper stimulus. I don't know why.'

'Chris and I could scrape up the money for a small place in London,' said Bess impulsively. 'Nowhere grand, I'm afraid, as Regent's Park is getting way beyond our means, but at least we could help.'

Laura looked embarrassed. 'It's sweet of you,' she said, 'but in fact, money isn't the trouble. Believe it or not, this book has made me quite rich. I just can't make up my mind whether to risk parting from Tom or not.'

'He still doesn't want to marry you?'

'No. And I understand it. This way, if he can't cope, he can leave me with a reasonably clear conscience. If he were married, he couldn't.'

'Why have you come to me?' asked Bess gently.

'So that by thinking aloud I can get things a bit straighter in my mind,' said Laura ruefully. Bess was pleased to see that she was speaking the truth at last!

'You can talk your head off here, darling. I only wish I could think of a brilliant solution, but as long as Tom is a part of your life, all my ideas come up against a brick wall.'

But when Laura returned to the North, Tom had solved the dilemma for her. He had left her for his secretary at the *Messenger* — who met, more easily than Laura, his requirements for submission, and good housekeeping.

Laura was outraged. 'We've been together for so long!' she exclaimed miserably. 'It's unfair to penalise me because I've been a success! And what about Harry? I thought you loved him!'

'I do, but he'll be all right with you. And you know how I feel about things. I liked the way they were; not as they are.'

'Have you no sense of responsibility?'

'None,' said Tom flatly. 'You know that, too.'

So the relationship ended as abruptly as it had begun. Tom appeared to be impervious; Laura was deeply hurt.

Once more Laura travelled south, this time taking Harry, and she received a welcome from Bess that was as tactful as it was warm.

After a week or two they went flat-hunting together, and soon found what Laura wanted, in Wimbledon — the garden flat of a large Edwardian house: near the Common for Harry, and with a big, light study for her. She also acquired Patty, Bess's dresser for many years but now retired, who was not only a good cook but adored Harry. And so for the first time she had total freedom to write and to enjoy the literary lunches and press and television interviews which in Clevegate she had had to refuse. This all helped to dull the pain of separation from Tom; and so did her new appreciation of her mother. Laura was grateful to Bess for never referring to Tom unless she needed to discuss him, and became fascinated by Bess's tales of her childhood and life in Malaya, and her revelations of family history.

Tentatively she suggested writing her mother's biography, but Bess would have none of it. 'I've always liked what privacy I can get,' she said. 'But if you want to use any of the material for fiction, I'll give you what help you want. Please let me see what you are writing, though.'

Laura agreed.

From then on they had long and frequent talks together which ranged over the hopes and fears, the triumphs and disasters, of four generations of Glanville women, and their recurring connection with Malaya. Laura learnt much about her great-grandparents that she didn't know — and even about her mother. Bess's description of her institutionalised childhood, with parents half a world away, aroused a new sympathy in her daughter; and Laura's present difficulties seemed to fall more into proportion. Madge, Kate and Bess had all had the same passionate wish that she had, to fulfill themselves; and they had found it no easier than Laura. Laura saw the obvious differences but also the similarities in all of them, which surprised and comforted her. The interplay of these elements within the pattern of heredity fascinated her.

In 1970, Christopher celebrated his sixtieth birthday. He was still a handsome man, although he was losing his hair. He hated growing old. 'Do you realise that in twenty years time I shall be eighty?' he asked Bess angrily.

'Yes, darling. And with that heart-trouble of yours, you're a lucky fellow!'

'Twenty years — it's no time at all! We've done very well, Bess, but we've never hit the top of our profession. Do you mind?'

'Do you?' she countered.

'Of course, sometimes,' he said. 'I would like to have played Hamlet; done more classics, launched more new writers, made more films...'

'And become an international star?' asked Bess.

'We blew that when we turned down those Hollywood offers.' said Christopher, and he smiled.

Bess smiled in return. 'We've lost other chances, too. But the choices we made always seemed right at the time, didn't they?'

'Always,' said Christopher firmly. 'We've only ourselves to

blame. You didn't answer just now. Do *you* regret not having reached the top?'

'Not really,' said Bess. 'I've often thought about it. We've had the talent, I believe, but perhaps not the single-minded ambition. Like you, I should have loved to have done more Shakespeare, more classical stuff, more films, too. But the other parts of life, which have seemed to me equally important, would have been put at hazard: my time with you, the children and grandchildren, for instance; a perspective on things — and much happiness, which I think of as an active definable state. And for a great deal of that happiness, I have you to thank, darling.'

'And I you,' replied Christopher seriously.

Two years later they had their silver wedding, and Deirdre turned up for the celebrations. Susan was still with them, but as a pensioner now. Chronic bronchitis, not helped by a lifetime of smoking, had developed into emphysema. But nothing stopped her enjoying the day inordinately.

Deirdre had grown fat, and determinedly jolly. Bess could hardly recognise the friend she had known so long. Her face was deeply lined and her figure billowed out from under a huge bosom. She laughed a great deal and, though she was without her second husband (who had an excellent job in the Arab Emirates, and had been unable to get leave to be present), she seemed to enjoy the reunion, and clearly retained her zest for life. Her first husband had been killed in the war; it was only when he was referred to that a shadow seemed to cross her face. At first Bess was disappointed in the change, but soon she fell under her spell again, as she always had.

Gerald had come over from America with quite shattering news for Bess. Walter had left him for good, and Gerald had no wish to return to England, so would be giving up his share of the house. Since Susan was so ill and the house was so expensive, and neither Peter nor Laura any longer needed a London home, it meant that Bess and Christopher would have to move once again.

'I can't imagine life without you, Gerald!' moaned Bess, the tears pouring down her face.

'My darling, you know that you are the most important person in my life,' said Gerald, earnestly, 'and you have been ever since we first became friends. But we can't be together any more. I don't like England these days. My work lies in America. You have

Christopher and your family, and I have the sunshine and my Californian home, and so our ways must part.'

'Are you very unhappy without Walter?'

'Very, but I have a good friend called Freddie, and I've no doubt we shall settle down together fairly well.'

During the years which followed, Laura also did her best to make a new life for herself. She missed Tom constantly. She had been told that time invariably cured unhappiness: in her case, it didn't. She wrote two more novels, but the ghost of Tom loomed over both and neither achieved popularity. She did enjoy her independence, however, and very much enjoyed the literary set with whom she was now mixing. The relief she had experienced on realising that her publisher, Geoffrey James, respected her mind, was reinforced in conversation with these new acquaintances. The critical success of her first novel had put her on an equal footing with good writers and at long last she was able to make friendships which were emotionally undemanding. Added to this, her looks had improved with age; men now found her attractive, which was a welcome boost to her ego.

Harry was an excellent companion, and they had few problems with one another. Their relationship was loving and lively and stimulating. He was doing well at school, and as he grew older he grew very close to Bess. Bess took him to the theatre more often than Laura would have liked, but she also helped him to mix with a great variety of interesting people, which gave him an ease in society which Laura had never learned. She worried that he might be a little too grown up for his age; but this was an improvement on being too childish, and she was pleased that, in spite of the fact that he was an only child, he hadn't become spoilt.

She herself spent many hours with Bess researching her family history; and, apart from her writing, she took up prison visiting, which she found absorbing and rewarding.

The years passed almost as if she were marking time, waiting for a pre-ordained signal to move in some new direction. And meanwhile her new novel neared completion.

CHAPTER TWELVE

One day, in Spring 1981, Laura was due to lunch with her publisher to discuss her latest novel. She hadn't seen him for some weeks and had missed him. The book had taken her many years to write, but it was now in its final draft. Geoffrey felt that there had been too long a gap between this novel and the last and she knew that he would be driving her to meet his new deadline for publication.

She was looking forward to seeing him. They were good friends now: they discussed everything, and agreed about most things, so found great satisfaction in each other's company. Geoffrey could make her laugh, and was a good listener too. All this was in marked contrast with her relationship with Tom and she valued it accordingly. Only one thing disturbed her. She suspected that he might be falling in love with her, and she wasn't ready for love again just yet.

Although it was Patty's day off, Laura had given herself the morning in bed. She had been feeling restless and edgy lately, for no obvious reason except that Harry was away on one of his periodic visits to his father in Yorkshire. Luckily, Tom's defection didn't seem to have upset Harry too much, and he was still very fond of him; but for Laura these visits brought Tom uncomfortably close, and took Harry uncomfortably far.

Tom had retired from the *Messenger* and had found a small house on the edge of the moors, near Ilkley, where he still lived with Rosemary. Laura realised ruefully that Rosemary had been a success. She was meek and subservient in a very feminine un-Laura-like way. She cooked and kept house better (which wouldn't be difficult, thought Laura) but she also had an inner strength and resilience which Laura had lacked when Tom was with her. Harry liked her quite well, and he was always happy to be with them.

Harry, thought Laura with relief, had an enviable disposition! No-one was ever likely to envy hers! She had made a great effort to sublimate her tenacious longing for Tom in her writing; but the success of her first published novel had not been matched by her second and third, so the going was getting tougher. Much of this new book was behind her, but she was still faced with polishing and correcting the final chapters. They were largely autobiographical and therefore too close for comfort, especially as she was determined to make them as honest as possible: not only about herself but also about those who surrounded her and influenced her. Many of the memories were still painful.

As an experienced novelist she had had no hesitation about 'playing God' in the first two-thirds of the book, attributing words and actions to the fictional versions of her parents, grandparents and great-grandparents. Part Three presented special difficulties, since she herself was the heroine. Here she was dealing with the living as well as the dead. And this inevitably brought her closer to the borderline between fact and fiction.

She remembered the essay she had been set by her French tutor at Oxford, on the famous preface to one of his novels by Alfred de Musset: in which he contrasted factual truth and artistic truth (*le vrai du fait* and *la vérité de l'art*), the former having the shapelessness of life, the latter demanding the planned enhancement of life which is the contribution of art. Her problem was to reconcile these two principles, to be truthful about herself and others without losing the imaginative freedom that belongs to fiction. But whereas she was quite often unhappy when writing about herself, the story of Madge and Kate and Bess gave her great pleasure. As she came to know them better in studying them for her story, she felt a growing admiration for their courage and tenacity. For the first time she truly warmed to her family and was proud to be one of them.

She was going through a bad patch. She felt a spinster for the first time — and a sort of ghost spectator of her own life, which appeared like an unsatisfactory film in which she had a leading part but no power to control the action. Tom of course was the male lead, but he'd already ridden off into the sunset leaving her behind. Even her beloved Harry was showing signs of wanting to go on the stage and continue the family tradition — much to the delight of Bess and Christopher, but only increasing Laura's sense of isolation. To Laura, who had repudiated the theatre as firmly as her grandmother Kate had done, the idea was absurd: not because he might lack talent but because, for her, acting was not a 'proper job' for a man. Yet she had to acknowledge that these days, with

unemployment rising so rapidly in 'proper jobs', he had just as
much chance to make good in the theatre as outside it.

Well, Harry's plans were still some way in the future. Meanwhile if she didn't hurry she would be late for lunch with Geoffrey.

She dressed with some deliberation. Under Bess's influence, she
had begun to care what she wore; and when she was to see
Geoffrey (perhaps out of vanity, which she knew under the
circumstances to be a little despicable), she always dressed that bit
better than usual.

On her way out, she found a letter from Tom. His handwriting
still had the power to disturb her and today there might be news of
Harry — possibly bad news. The letter began uncharacteristically:

Laura, love,

I have news for you which I want you to understand, and
which I am writing to tell you before you hear it from someone
else. I am marrying Rosemary. I know I always told you that I
would never marry again, but I had a heart-attack in the
summer — there seemed no point in worrying you and Harry —
and if I happened to get another which either puts me out of
action or does for me, I want Rosemary to be provided for. She's
been a good lass, and has given me more happiness than I may
have led her to believe. I've told Harry, and he understands.
He's a gradely lad, is Harry. (Remember our old landlady?)

You know of course that Harry is set on going on the stage.
Don't hold him back, love. You're a generous woman, or he
wouldn't still be fond of me. So be generous again, whatever
hang-ups you may have on the subject. He goes to the theatre
any time he can manage it, he tells me; has read every book on
the subject he can lay hands on; and is so keen on the family
succession that he wants to call himself Harry Glanville.

Now the real point of this letter is this. You and I didn't
manage to make a go of it for many reasons which we both
know. But it has always bothered me that I rejected you in the
end, because a rejection is the one thing you might be incapable
of coming to terms with. I know you left me first, but then I saw
to it that you couldn't change your mind. I want you to know
that I did that for your sake as much as mine. When you left me,
I all but went to pieces, and several times nearly told you so —
but we were destroying each other. One must have freedom to
breathe, and above all be oneself, and we couldn't give it to each

other. Nor, given the kind of people we are, could we change (though it's my belief hardly anyone can). But please know, Laura, that you were, and still are, important to me.

Tom

Laura read and re-read the letter, then fumbled for her handkerchief and howled like a baby. The telephone rang, and she let it ring until it stopped. The front door bell rang, and she ignored it. She cried until all emotion seemed spent, and until a small and insidious sense of comfort joined her unhappiness. She looked at her watch, ran for the car and drove as fast as she could to the restaurant where she and Geoffrey were to meet.

Geoffrey was sitting at their usual table. He was staring down at the tablecloth, apparently lost in thought when she entered, but he looked up eagerly as she reached the table. His kind face expressed concern at once.

'What is it?' he asked.

'Tom has written to say he's getting married,' said Laura directly.

Did his eyes show a momentary gleam of pleasure? Laura wasn't certain, but he replied sympathetically, 'I'm sorry, my dear. Do you mind very much?'

'Stupidly I do,' answered Laura.

She sat down. 'I've ordered your usual aperitif,' Geoffrey said. 'Is that all right?'

'Fine.'

'Tell me about it.' And she did so.

'I wish I could be around a little to help you if you needed me,' Geoffrey said when she had finished. 'But I have to leave for Australia tomorrow, on a job.'

'*Tomorrow?*' To her surprise she felt an intense dismay.

''Fraid so. I'm also going to Singapore, and taking a trip up country to Malaysia for a holiday. Friends have recommended the East Coast and I might as well see a bit of it while I'm in the vicinity. I shall be spending a few days in Kuala Lumpur, and a couple up Fraser's Hill, again with friends . . . Fraser's Hill is where your mother taught at that school, isn't it?'

'Yes. She was also born in KL, too, and was there for quite a bit again after she left school in England.'

'You've described Malaysia so vividly in our talks together. Would you like me to write and tell you what it all looks like now, so that you can pass it on to your mother? You never know, it might even help the final draft of that book you've been so long writing! You said there was a good deal about Malaysia in it.'

'How kind.' Laura smiled at him fondly. 'That would be splendid. You're right, there are some particular places Mother would love to hear about, I know.'

'Give me a list.'

'Only if you promise that you won't go out of your way, and that it won't be a nuisance.'

'I promise,' said Geoffrey with a smile.

She wrote her list on the back of the menu. 'Thank you,' she said seriously, as she gave it to him. 'I shall miss you.'

'I'm glad.'

They went on to discuss the book, publication dates and publicity plans in some detail; then, when lunch was over, Geoffrey lightly kissed her goodbye. As they parted, Laura felt a stunned sense of loss which persisted until she went to sleep that night.

The next morning however, when two dozen red roses arrived — with a card which read 'Try not to be too unhappy about Tom. Geoffrey' — she was inordinately pleased. And at lunch with Bess that day, her mother thought she was looking happier than she had done for some time. This both pleased and puzzled her, as Laura had told her about Tom's forthcoming marriage.

When Laura had gone, she said to Christopher, 'I do believe Laura has found a new boyfriend. She seems different somehow, don't you think?'

'Let's pray that this one is better than the last!' exclaimed Christopher fervently.

'I agree,' said Bess, smiling.

Geoffrey's first letter was from Singapore:

I'm staying at the Shangri-La in great style, but have conceived a dislike for it, as it occupies the site of your grandmother's last home in Orchard Road, and most of the street where she lived. Singapore would be almost totally unfamiliar to your mother now, except for the immigration office, which is a fine old colonial building in a fine old colonial square. There are still a few old colonial houses occupied by British business men, which have great charm, with their big ceiling fans and wide verandahs and large shady gardens; but otherwise it's simply a huge, commercial, very successful and well-run city. The Malay food stalls (we ate in a street full of them last night, and had a delicious meal) are being moved off the streets into one single complex in a park, I believe, and the distinctively Chinese, Indian and Malay shopping streets are being bulldozed to make way for glass and concrete emporiums. I find it sad. I only hope that for the Singaporeans it is good.

Raffles Hotel still stands in all its glory (I was taken there to lunch yesterday) — and the Tanglin swimming pool, which has been 'the smart club to belong to' for as long as anyone remembers, is to have a face lift! ...

From Kuala Lumpur, he wrote:

Things are changing rapidly here too, though 'Progress', thank God, has been slower than in Singapore. The 'Spotted Dog' which your mother knew has been burned to the ground, but a new one stands in its place, more magnificent, apparently, and with an even greater 'wealth of exposed beams' than before. The Lake Gardens are still as beautiful as your mother described them to you ... at least I can't imagine them *more* beautiful. St Mary's Anglican church, where your mother was christened, is still there, with a plaque which honours Edward Marchmont ... your grandfather, I presume. I hired a car to take me up Fraser's Hill, and visited your mother's school, St Margaret's. It is still a school but now a Methodist Mission school. It has a green corrugated-iron roof instead of the red one you described.

Fraser's Hill, too, is on the verge of change, though thank God they can't change the entire jungle for a while. This morning, Wah-wah monkeys hooted above a thick mist which lay under the tops of the trees. They swung their way from tree to tree, the females clutching their babies in their arms — I could have cried with pleasure at their obvious happiness!

The jungle is all set for taming, though — and when they've tamed it, to judge by a small mountain holiday resort called Genting Highlands, it will look quite horrific! Your mother would hate it, and so, I'm sure, would you.

By the way, I have a feeling that the whole area is heading for trouble. Singapore is Chinese dominated. Malaysia is Malay dominated. The Malays are turning against the British, sadly, but without doing much to heal the age-old antipathy between them and the Chinese and Indian communities. Of course I could be wrong! There's nothing easier than to pronounce on a complex situation after a week in a place — especially when you're a publisher, not a politician!

From Australia, he cabled: MISSION ACCOMPLISHED. WILL SEE YOU SOON. GEOFFREY.

CHAPTER THIRTEEN

One afternoon, a week or so after she received Geoffrey's cable from Australia, Laura had a telephone call from Christopher. He sounded unhappy.

'Don't panic,' he said. 'I've panicked enough for the whole family, damn it! Bess had another of her beastly coughing fits a while ago, and I persuaded her to see a doctor. She was obstinate — you know Bess — but I made her, and to make certain that she actually got there, I went with her. Lucky I did. The tests are back... and it's cancer of the lung, I'm afraid. She's going into hospital tomorrow morning for an operation...' his voice broke.

'Where?' asked Laura, winded by the shock.

'The Westminster,' said Christopher.

'Can I come with you?' asked Laura. 'Does Mother know?'

'Oh, yes. She insisted on knowing, and she has a fifty-fifty chance the doctor says. She's being marvellous, of course, and it's being almost too much for me! Deirdre and her husband are back from the Gulf and coming to dinner, which delights her, and of course she's tickled pink that Harry has got into the Webber-Douglas. She's been talking quite a lot about her life since we've had the news... it seems to comfort her. She talks about Bendleford and Miss Wells and Gerald and Deirdre and Mark. She's also been talking about old Edward Marchmont, whom she adored as you know, and I can't tell you how chuffed she is to hear about the plaque in the church in KL! Please thank Geoffrey for letting us know.'

'I will.'

'She's been on about "beautiful Kate", as she calls her mother, too, and Patrick and Uncle Tom Cobbley and all. It's worrying me no end! I think she thinks she's going to die!'

'Of course she doesn't!' exclaimed Laura strongly. 'It's natural she should be a bit scared. Anyone would be. You are yourself, and I expect talking about the past helps her to keep it in proportion.'

'Maybe you're right. She's been on about Madge and old

317

Harry, too, not to mention all of us lot. She says she's liked being married to me, bless her.' He sounded on the verge of tears. 'And as for Harry calling himself Harry Glanville, you'd have thought he'd given her a gold-plated Rolls!'

'When is she going in?'

'Ten o'clock. The op is at three. A good surgeon, they say. An Indian. She'll like that.' He laughed shakily.

'You won't mind my coming with you?' asked Laura.

'I'd be grateful.' She heard him blow his nose.

'Shall I tell Harry?'

'That she's to have an operation? Why not?'

'Peter knows of course?'

'Of course. He's taking us all round the corner for lunch. Join us?'

'What about tonight at the theatre?'

'I've rung the management. Bess says her understudy is good, and a nice girl. "She'll keep the curtain up till I get back," she said...Oh hell!' He was openly crying now. 'I hear her coming, and I don't want her to see me blubbing! Want to talk to her?'

'Yes please!'

Bess sounded normal. 'Hullo, darling,' she said matter-of-factly. 'Heard the tiresome news?'

'Yes, Mother, and I'll be there with all of them and Harry to see you in.'

'That's sweet of you! Don't worry, darling, will you? I'm not. I read a poem once by Stevie Smith. I can't remember it properly, but it was something about a train.'

'I know the one,' said Laura.

'Well she was right, darling. At any rate, I think so. The train starts slowly, and when we're children it sort of dawdles in lovely sunlit places, or frightens us by going through dark and noisy tunnels. Later it gathers speed going quite fast through towns and suburbs and gardens and by lakes — and jungles, of course!' she laughed. 'D'you know what I mean, darling?'

'I think so.'

'And then it becomes a high-speed express, and rushes you towards a destination you don't know — even though it's the one you've been heading for ever since you started. But it's all fascinating, if you take it that way. I'm probably explaining it awfully badly and being high falutin', and not particularly original, either — but I want *you* to have an interesting time, too, darling. It's partly a matter of attitude, and it's very important. And I think I've seen signs lately that you're learning that lesson. None 1 >o soon! You're what they call a mature student, aren't , >u, darling?' She was gently teasing. 'If everything goes all right, and I'm sure it will, I'm still glad I've said all this, because I've often wanted to. We're all just bits of nature, you know. We're born, we mature (I loved the maturing bit, as I'm sure you will) and we die.'

'Don't, Mother!'

'But everyone and everything does! Some of us are lucky enough to be born in the lucky places. And others not. I have been. The good seed on good ground has the best time, as it says in the Bible. The poor seed on stony ground has a struggle. Whether it's all mapped out for us, I've no idea. Well, I've talked enough nonsense, darling. See you tomorrow. Take care of yourself!' And she put down the 'phone.

Harry came into the room, and saw Laura's face. 'What's up, Mum?' he asked anxiously.

Laura told him.

'Poor Mum!' he said. 'And poor poor Granny! She wants me to call myself Harry Glanville, did you know?'

'Yes, darling.'

'And she's thrilled to bits about the Webber-Douglas.'

'Yes, I know.'

'I hope she'll be OK, Mum?'

'So do I.'

'I'll do her proud, Mum. I will. I promise.'

'I'm sure you will.'

'I expect all that sounds selfish,' he said, sighing, 'but I don't know what else to say.' He looked out of the window. 'There's a boy coming up the drive with some flowers. Shall I answer the door?'

'Please.'

She read the note that came with them: 'We clocked in this morning. Lunch with me tomorrow. Same time, same place. Geoffrey.'

Laura telephoned his home, and Geoffrey answered. 'Mother is going into hospital tomorrow,' she said, 'so I can't lunch.' She hesitated. 'Later in the week?'

'Of course.'

'Did you enjoy your trip?'

'Marvellous!'

'Thank you for the letters. Mother was so grateful for all the trouble you took.'

'It was a pleasure, Laura.'

'You're well?'

'Very well. I'm sorry about your mother. Is it serious?'

'Fairly.'

'Anything I can do?'

'No, unless I could ring you from time to time, when I feel down.'

'Of course.'

'I'm glad you're back. Oh, heavens — and thank you for the flowers! I feel very pampered, and I'm not used to it.'

'You will be.'

'Did the job go all right?'

'Fine. Try not to worry, and remember I'm around if you need me.'

At the hospital next day the whole family was present — Christopher, Peter, Jane, Laura and all the grandchildren. Bess looked very pretty. Bouquets of flowers were brought in from the management, the theatre staff and Deirdre; the papers hadn't yet been informed. The hospital seemed delighted to have her with them, and Bess kept up a stream of conversation and jokes with the nurses and doctors. Christopher tried valiantly to appear as lighthearted as Bess, but failed. When the family was asked to leave Bess kissed them all lovingly and had a different word of comfort for each one. Then when she and Christopher were alone, she said softly, 'Merde, darling,' licked her thumb and pressed it against the arm of Christopher's suit. Christopher went through the same little ritual, with the tears pouring down his cheeks. They had done this for luck on every first night they had had together. Christopher kissed her on the lips, and went blindly to the door. He turned back and said, 'I love you, old girl, you know that, don't you?'

'Yes, darling,' said Bess. 'And I love you. See you soon.'

But she died under the anaesthetic.

In her will, among other bequests, she left Laura the photograph of Kate and Patrick, now in a silver frame. On the paper in which she had wrapped it she had written: 'Because you understand, darling.'

Yes, I do, thought Laura, though it's taken me a very long time.